Korea

Never forget!
Salt & Light
Frank Amoroso

Forgotten

Sacrifice

A Korean War Novel

Frank Amoroso

simply francis publishing company

North Carolina

For information about this title or to order books and/or electronic media, contact the publisher:

simply francis publishing company
P.O. Box 329, Wrightsville Beach, NC 28480
www.simplyfrancispublishing.com
simplyfrancispublishing@gmail.com

This historical novel is fictional in nature. For purposes of verisimilitude, an effort has been made to present the story in the context of actual events, but, they should not be considered factual. Some of the characters portrayed in this book are modeled after historical and actual persons who are used in a fictitious manner. The author has imagined and created all the situations, interactions, and dialogue by and among historical characters and. In all other respects, any resemblance to actual persons, living or dead, or actual events is purely coincidental.

Cover Photo by Cpl James Lyle, National Archives Photo (USA) 111-SC354456 A squad-sized Army patrol, led by Sgt grant J. Miller, from the 3d Infantry Division's Task Force Dog, moves up from Chinhung-ni into Funchilin Pass on 9 December. The Tank at the side of the road appears to be a Soviet-built T-34 knocked out a month earlier by the 7th Marines.

OTHER BOOKS WRITTEN BY FRANK AMOROSO

Behind Every Great Fortune®

". . . boldly imaginative historical novel that is sumptuously detailed and filled with intrigue, betrayal and plot twists that surprise and entertain the reader."

Dread the Fed

". . . a gripping story of a crime so bold, so ingenious and so perfect, that a century later, the plunder continues and the People venerate the banksters who commit it."

Behind Every Great Recipe:
From Latkes to Vodkas & Beets to Meats

". . . a charming and unique companion book containing delicious period recipes and vignettes featuring the characters from the historical novel *Behind Every Great Fortune®*."

Wopper - How Babe Ruth Lost His Father and Won The 1918 World Series Against The Cubs
Volume 1 Pigtown

". . . a fantastical Ruthian novel based on the life of Babe Ruth!"

Wopper - How Babe Ruth Lost His Father and WonThe 1918 World Series Against The Cubs
Volume 1 Pigtown YOUNG ADULT VERSION

Wopper - How Babe Ruth Lost His Father and Won The 1918 World Series Against The Cubs
Volume 2 The Show

". . . follow Babe's exhilarating journey from the sandlots of Baltimore to superstardom in Fenway Park."

Wopper - How Babe Ruth Lost His Father and Won The 1918 World Series Against The Cubs
Volume 3 The Series

". . . the explosive culmination of the trilogy as Babe learns of the death of his father and battles not only the Cubs but anti-German zealots, anarchists, and pure evil."

German-Americans and Our National Pastime

". . . study of the enduring greatness of German-Americans in baseball."

Dedication

To my dear friend S.I.B. and all the service men and women
who sacrificed so much during the conflict in Korea.

Table of Contents

List Of Images and Maps ix

Introduction xi

Chapter 1 Destinies Intertwined 1

Chapter 2 Driving While Intoxicated...11

Chapter 3 Guerrilla Raid on Unit 731 - 1940 19

Chapter 4 Parris Island - 1949 29

Chapter 5 Boot Camp - 1949 41

Chapter 6 Soviet War Crimes Show Trial 49

Chapter 7 The Crucible 55

Chapter 8 Audition for Combat Photographer................... 63

Chapter 9 Seeking Stalin...75

Chapter 10 The Shark and the Beauty 85

Chapter 11 Beijing Green Light.. 93

Chapter 12 Kingfisher to Chonjin 101

Chapter 13 Workingman Hero.. 113

Chapter 14 Russian Meddling.. 121

Chapter 15 Leica and the Master 127

Chapter 16 Junior's Bodyguard 137

Chapter 17 Survival Diet 147

Chapter 18 Sumo Wrestlers and Geisha Girls 157

Table of Contents

Chapter 19 Rock Salmusa Deadhead 169

Chapter 20 The Extractor 181

Chapter 21 Chasing Ghosts 199

Chapter 22 Flying Fish Channel 209

Chapter 23 Operation Chromite 219

Chapter 24 Machine Gun Madness 239

Chapter 25 Giocondo in Red China 249

Chapter 26 Operation Solar Eclipse - Mourning Venus.... 261

Chapter 27 Babies Crying.....................................271

Chapter 28 Project Ramona....................................285

Chapter 29 The Big Bugout...................................303

Chapter 30 Wake Island Massacre 309

Chapter 31 Kites Over Waterfalls....................................... 319

Epilogue.. 322

Timeline...329

People, Places, and Things..............................333

Military Jargon..340

Acknowledgements 341

List of Images and Maps

- Cover image, National Archives Photo (USA) 111-SC354456, Task Force Dog
- Korean Peninsula, p. x
- Anti-Japanese guerrillas, Kim Il Sung 1930, p. 10
- Kim Il Sung, 1927, p. 40
- USMC Recruit Depot, Parris Island, SC, p. 54
- ZIS limousine, p. 89
- Image of Mao Zedong and General Peng, p. 100
- U.S. Navy Vought OS2U Kingfisher, p. 120
- Ansel Easton Adams, p. 136
- Pusan Perimeter, p. 180
- General J. Lawton Collins, General Douglas MacArthur, Admiral Forrest Sherman, p. 218
- Incheon Invasion, p. 228
- Marines over the seawall at Red Beach, Incheon, p. 238
- Battle of Unsan, p. 284
- Chosin Reservoir Campaign, p. 302
- Funchilin Pass blown bridge, p. 308
- C-119 drop of bridge section, p. 308
- G-5 parachutes delivering Treadway bridge section, p. 308
- Soviet postage stamp depicting British intelligence officer Kim Philby, p. 324
- Back Cover image of Marine bugler by USMC (Public domain) via Wikimedia Commons

Map of Korean Peninsula.

Seoul on the west coast is south of the 38th and has been called the waist of Korea.

An imaginary line from P'yŏngyang to Wonsan approximates the 39th parallel and has been called the neck of Korea.

X

INTRODUCTION

The Korean War is one of the most misunderstood and ill-conceived tragedies of modern times. Despite the death toll of an estimated 2.5 million civilians and 2 million soldiers on both sides, it did not even merit the word war. President Truman called it a police action, akin to 'nothing to see here, we're just fighting crime.' The Chinese Communists referred to it as the "Korean incident." After three years of war, most of the combatants declared a stalemate and signed an armistice (South Korea refused to sign). It is not without irony that the war in Korea has been called the Forgotten War. Today, the Korean Peninsula remains divided and is the focus of international tensions stemming primarily from the dispute over the presence of nuclear weapons there.

Korea Forgotten Sacrifice is the story of a young U.S. marine named Junior who uses his skill as a photographer and sharpshooter to disrupt and frustrate the plans of Kim Il Sung, the North Korean dictator. The Cold War turns hot when Kim invades South Korea in the summer of 1950. General Douglas MacArthur is assigned to counter the aggression and unify the peninsula. The Korean War becomes a test of resolve for the United Nations and the new government of Red China under Chairman Mao. Like a master puppeteer, Soviet dictator Joseph Stalin stokes the tensions and perpetuates the bloody conflict.

For centuries Korea was a monarchy and, in 1882, President Arthur signed a treaty of friendship and amity which recognized Korean sovereignty. Less than a quarter century later, President Theodore Roosevelt negated the prior treaty when he assented to the Treaty of Portsmouth which allowed Japan to take control of Korea. This treaty ended the Russo-Japanese War and earned Roosevelt a Nobel Peace Prize. The Japanese occupied Korea from 1910 until the end of WWII in 1945.

In the last days of WWII, the U.S.S.R. joined the war against Japan and hastened to occupy Korea, particularly the city of Konan (later called Hungnam) where it was rumored that the Japanese had built the industrial capability to make an atomic bomb. What the Soviets discovered there has never been revealed. The precise nature of Japan's atom bomb research is similarly shrouded in opacity.

Pursuant to prior agreements made by the Allies during WWII, Korea was placed under a trusteeship, divided at the 38th parallel. As a writer who is not privy to the pressures that the leaders experienced at the Allied conferences in Cairo and Moscow, it is difficult to comprehend how they thought that a divided Korean peninsula made sense.

Despite efforts to hold unifying elections, the country remained divided. Kim Il Sung, leader of the north and Syngman Rhee, leader of the south, were each adamant that the country should be unified under his leadership alone. This impasse prompted Kim to seek to impose a military resolution. His Soviet-supported forces invaded South Korea in June 1950.

The Communists in North Korea and the Soviet Union were convinced that the United States would not intervene to protect the Republic of South Korea. The leadership of the United States was convinced that Communist China would not intervene to protect the Democratic People's Republic of Korea. These miscalculations were so egregious that millions of people have suffered on account of them for almost seven decades.

Death and suffering are endemic to war. One of the worst battles of the Korea War was the Chosin Reservoir Campaign. Almost 200,000 soldiers fought in sub-arctic conditions that reached minus 90° wind chill, in the mountains surrounding the Chosin Reservoir in North Korea. Tens of thousands on both sides died in inhuman conditions in the Taebaeck mountains of Korea. Along with several mysterious soldiers, Junior is ordered to the icy deathtrap of Frozen Chosin on a secret mission. The harrowing and heroic action ensues as Junior seeks to unravel the mystery in a way that will shed light on present-day impasse.

One of the enigmas of the Battle of Chosin Reservoir is that once the retreating UN forces reached the safety of the coastal port of Hungnam, they retreated 331 miles all the way back to Pusan at the southern tip of the peninsula, rather than to Wonsan, only 85 miles to the south. By withdrawing UN forces to Pusan, MacArthur relinquished all of the gains made after the success at Incheon. For the last sixty-six years and counting, the parties have rattled their sabers and glared at each other across a two-mile wide demilitarized zone along the 38th parallel. Efforts at a lasting peace and reunification are perpetually ongoing.

Korea Forgotten Sacrifice is a novel of historical fiction. For purposes of verisimilitude, the story is presented in the context of actual events. Some of the characters portrayed in this book are modeled after historical and actual persons who are used in a fictitious manner. I have imagined and created all the situations, interactions and dialogue by and among historical characters. In all other respects, any resemblance to actual persons, living or dead, or actual events is purely coincidental.

To facilitate the reader's experience, I have included various aids — list of images and maps, timeline, people, places, and things, and military jargon. In addition, I have included QR codes which will take the reader to original film footage when using the appropriate app.

Before entering the labyrinth of our protagonist's life, the reader should know that prior to writing this book I received a literary license to imagine, speculate, and create scenarios that may or may not have occurred but which are within the realm of possibility. The goal of any imagination, speculation, or conjecture in this work is to entertain, titillate, and provoke the reader.

With that said, enjoy this novel.

Frank Amoroso,
Wrightsville Beach, NC
2019

CHAPTER

1

Destinies Intertwined

"A photograph is a secret about a secret.
The more it tells you the less you know."

~ Diane Arbus

He was the last son of the last son. Which is not to say that he was born that way. He recalled images of family gatherings depicting men; some were smiling, some wore dour expressions. Some had dashing handlebar moustaches; others wore full beards. There was even one rebel who was clean-shaven. It seemed like there were men everywhere. There were young men and fewer older men. There were other pictures, too. They had a festive air filled with brightness and the vitality of youth and promise.

It seemed that as he looked at the pictures with the men wearing more modern clothes, there were fewer men. The expressions on the faces seemed grimmer. Shoulders sagged a bit, the group, his family, was thinning – not just that the people in the photos tended toward gauntness, there were also fewer men.

No matter how hard he tried, he could not figure out when that changed. It was just a fact. Almost by coincidence, the family photograph album recorded it. The black-and-white history of the family. Photos with wavy edges were fastened to the pages with mounting corners that had to be glued in place. He remembered the foul taste of the glue and how his sister teased him that if he wasn't fast enough, his tongue would be stuck to the page. After that he barely licked the corners.

Later, when anyone looked at the album, he could always tell which pictures he put in the album because they curled up when that page was opened. The corners were not glued enough and when the pressure of the pages was lifted, his failure was evident. To remedy the situation, his mother had to get the glue bottle filled with the thick amber liquid. She called it Lepage's or asked his sister to get the mucilage. He liked the feel of the glass bottle that was curved so it fit in your hand when you turned it upside down. The bottle had a pink rubber tip with a slit across the top like a mouth waiting to spread open and release the glue when you pressed it down on the paper. Mother always fussed about the crust across the slit. His sister would have to get the scissors to scrape off the yellow crust that reminded him of the snot that dried on his nostrils when he had a cold.

There were vague recollections of a wedding he had seen in a photograph. It was a grand panorama of a ballroom in some hotel in the city. The ballroom was not too big; guests sat at about a dozen tables. Most of the younger men wore military uniforms. The bride and groom sat at a dais with the rest of the wedding party. His parents appeared happy. In another photo, they stood in front of a wall of flowers gazing lovingly into each other's eyes with the hope only youth possessed.

On closer inspection, a truer reality emerged. The fit on his Dad's tuxedo was not quite right. The pants were too short revealing an inch of white socks. The jacket stretched tightly across his broad back and quite possibly would have ripped at the seams if he had not opened the buttons on the front. The shine reflecting off his dark hair was the result of a too enthusiastic application of that green, gooey pomade that guaranteed to "control unruly locks of hair." The problem was that it turned hair into something not found in nature - miniature planks, impervious even to hurricane gales. And, as in his father's case, it encouraged untreated hair to stand wildly in rebellion; exactly like the cowlick protruding at the back of his head like the spikes of a pineapple stalk. The photograph of his father captured the burly, ill-at-ease look of a steamfitter stuffed into a monkey suit, which was precisely what he was, grease-stained hands and all.

In contrast, his mother appeared angelic. Her white satin dress draped elegantly to the floor. Her face was partially in shadow, no doubt a deliberate pose to minimize her broad features that were reminiscent of the steppes of Siberia. She stood slightly angled from the camera, her posture set to conceal a gentle bump. Only years later would he compute the dates with his fingers and realize that he was in that wedding picture. Bad reasons lead to bad consequences.

With most families, once the images were inserted into the album, they remained sequestered until the next roll of film was developed and those pictures were inserted. That wasn't the case with Junior. For as long as he could remember, Junior was enamored with the idea that a person or event could be captured in a photograph. He spent countless hours studying the family album, extracting details that escaped the casual viewer. Junior's love of photography was ignited when he received a gift from his uncle on his tenth birthday.

"Hey, Junior. Happy Birthday. Here's a little something for you, kiddo."

"Thanks. What is it?" he said, shaking the gaily-wrapped box.

"Open it and see for yourself. That's how this birthday gift thing works."

One meek shrug and several rips later, he unveiled a package containing a Kodak Beau Brownie camera kit. An instant later, he held his very own camera in his pudgy hands. The rectangular box was covered with an imitation leather which protected it from the dangers a boy might encounter. The brown and tan geometric pattern decorating the face of the camera was the most beautiful thing he had ever seen.

"Let me show you how it works," said his uncle, gesturing for the camera. With the wary look of someone asked to release a treasure with no hope of return, the boy relinquished the camera.

"This envelope contains the film. They invented this great system that uses spools to unroll the film across the lens inside the camera box."

His uncle took the camera, released the latch and removed the roll holder. Then, he tore the film package and withdrew the cartridge.

"Here, grab the tab on the film and insert it into the slot in the spool. Now, unwind the film, pulling the other spool around the roll holder until you can fit the spool into the upper slot. Great."

The boy beamed with accomplishment.

"See this silver thingamabob? That's the winding knob. Turn it until the number '1' appears in the red window on the back."

The boy twisted the key until it would go no further.

"Did I break it?" he groaned.

"No, no. It means that you are ready to shoot a picture. You just slide this lever and it releases the shutter. *Voilá*, you have just taken a photograph."

The youngster fingered the lever with the same caution as if he were about to ignite a bomb.

"Wait! Two things. First, you want to look through the viewfinder here on the top to see whatever you want to take a picture of. When you see something in the viewfinder, that means that the lens is pointing toward your target. Second, each roll of film has only six pictures. So, use them sparingly because it will get expensive real quick."

It did not take long for the boy to master his camera. At this young age, he knew that photography would be an important part of his future. He spent every waking hour scheming about how to afford more film and developing. Eventually, he saved enough money from his newspaper route to acquire a used set of developing equipment. Unfortunately, his father detested the smell of the chemicals and forbade the boy from developing film in their modest apartment.

Fortunately, his hero intervened. His uncle swooped in to the rescue and helped move the equipment into a corner of his garage. The two spent many joyful hours in the garage darkroom. His uncle nurtured Junior's creativity in film and was there to help the boy grow into manhood. And then he wasn't there.

* * *

In a faraway country on the opposite end of the planet, another boy struggled with adversity. Kim's earliest childhood memories revolved around the oppression by the Japanese when they conquered his country. Idyllically known as the "Land of High Mountains and Sparkling Streams" and "The Land of the Morning Calm," Korea was surrounded by enemies. In the first decade of the twentieth century, Japan occupied Korea to exploit its resources, including coal and uranium.

Kim recalled how his parents raged at the indignities of the imperial Japanese forces which systematically sought to destroy the national identity of Korea. From cultural transformation like mandating the use of Japanese, prohibiting the teaching of Korean, and forcing the use of Japanese surnames, to more coercive measures such as jailing and murdering dissenters, Japan was a cruel, relentless, and heartless master. Kim recalled his distress when his parents uprooted the family and moved to Manchuria to escape the heel of the Japanese boot.

"I know, little man, that you don't want to leave your friends, your school – but, life will be much better for us in our new home. You will make new friends," said his mother as he stared at the only village he had ever known as it receded behind a thicket of trees. The eight-year-old was convinced that there would never be a village as wonderful. In later life when he returned to Korea, he thought it was funny that he could not recall any details of that village. What seems so important soon becomes lost in mists beyond memory.

Kim had spent the last few years before WWII in Manchukuo, alternately raiding and evading the Japanese. The Imperial Army hunted his guerrilla band relentlessly. For the better part of the last decade, he had lived on the run, enduring rain, mud, cold, snow, hunger, and fear. His band of marauders survived by scavenging off the land. He led them through forests and mountains, sometimes sleeping in caves;

more often, they slept out in the open. To avoid alerting the Japanese to their location, they rarely lit fires.

As the 1930s waned, the Japanese Imperial Army had waged a successful war of attrition against the guerrillas. Using infiltrators and bullying the peasants, the Japanese acquired information that led to the capture of many of Kim's comrades in the leadership ranks. Starting in the southern provinces, the Japanese had utilized systematic sweeps to clear the country one area at a time. This approach was so effective that guerrilla operations were reduced to a few northern provinces.

It was 1940 and a new decade of war loomed. Kim knew that one day, his legendary escape-and-evasion skills would fail him. He wondered just how much longer his band could continue. As their circumstances became more dire, he knew that he needed a victory. This prompted Kim to conceive of a daring raid on the notorious Japanese biological and chemical weapons facility.

Known as Unit 731, the Imperial Japanese Army devoted considerable resources to the development of weapons and delivery systems for infectious diseases. In addition, there were rumors of horrific human experimentation at Unit 731. The director of the program was the evil genius, Dr. Shiro Ishii. Although the program was shrouded in extreme secrecy, there were reasons to suspect that the location of a Unit 731 facility was about fifteen miles outside the city of Harbin in northeastern China. Kim knew that the facility would be heavily guarded. Yet, the objective of this mission was too enticing to forego. As Kim's mentor had taught him, high risk means high reward. Discrediting Unit 731 would be his crowning achievement.

KOREA FORGOTTEN SACRIFICE

Reliable intelligence was their first challenge. There was so much secrecy surrounding the illicit operation that some in his leadership group doubted that it existed. They considered the reports about human experimentation nothing more than a chilling tactic of intimidation by the Imperial Japanese forces who often used psychological warfare to weaken the resolve of their enemies. Whenever possible, the Japanese preferred dispiriting the opposition. It was cheaper than bullets and allowed them to preserve the locals for slave labor.

The naysayers bolstered their argument by citing the Geneva Protocol. Sure, the Japanese were monsters; but Japan had signed the international treaty which prohibited the use of "asphyxiating, poisonous or other gases, and of all analogous liquids, materials or devices" and "bacteriological methods of warfare." Emperor Pù Yi had too much dignity; he would never stoop that low, they reasoned.

"Bah, the Emperor squats to pee. He's nothing but a whore like the rest of them," Kim scoffed. He was about to pontificate about the glaring deficiencies of a document which did not prohibit the manufacture of biological weapons or their use within a country's own borders when he was interrupted.

"Sir, I'm sorry to disturb you, but we have reports of a Jap patrol a few kilometers from our position," said the leader of the scout unit.

Kim sniffled, then coughed. He glanced at the scout and saw worry in the man's face. Ever since they had discussed the secret Japanese laboratories, his men had been skittish about any symptoms of physical distress. Kim pounded the tiger design on his chest and glared at the man.

"Tell the men that we have to move out immediately. It's time to make one more raid, then we head to the border."

"Yessir," snapped the scout, eyes lowered in regret for his reaction to the leader's cough.

Once they were safely away from the Japanese patrol, Kim halted his guerrillas and took refuge in some caves which were large enough to secrete their horses. Kim turned to Chekal Danjo, his second in command and said, "Bring me the informant."

The commander had learned the hard way that to be successful as a guerrilla, one had to cultivate sources of information from various and sundry places. Over time, the Japanese pursuit had pushed him further and further from known partisans. In alien territory, he was forced to buy information from local warlords or hunhuzi as they were called.

Kim had paid this hunhuzi considerable hard currency for information. Although he had proven reliable, Kim knew in his gut that the hunhuzi was loyal only to blood and tribe. Kim's less-than-diplomatic second in command, Chekal Danjo called him a traitorous whore to his face.

Kim and Chekal spent most of the evening interrogating the hunhuzi. His information was vague and fuzzy. To lubricate his memory, the guerrilla leader doubled the spy's compensation paying the lion's share in advance. Kim squelched the protest in Chekal's eyes by signaling that the information they would capture would outweigh the expenditure of the last of their currency. As if by a miracle, the hunhuzi recalled a wealth of detail which enabled them to devise a plan of attack.

When Kim emerged from the cave the following morning, he smiled at his band of mounted guerrillas. His bravado masked his concern that the lives of many of his comrades would be sacrificed for the glory of this mission.

"Comrades, today we make history. Tomorrow we feast with the Russian Bear!"

Anti-Japanese guerrillas under Kim Il Sung. 1930

CHAPTER

2

Driving While Intoxicated

"There's a fine edge to new grief, it severs nerves,
disconnects reality--there's mercy in a sharp
blade. Only with time, as the edge wears, does the
real ache begin."

~ *Christopher Moore*

When members of the family referred to the events that led to the death of another one of their men, they called it the tragedy in Germany. When the Office of Strategic Services referred to the death of Junior's uncle, they called it collateral damage. When his uncle's wife thought of the death of her husband, she broke down crying. When Junior thought of the death of his uncle, his brain screamed.

One day while Junior was in uncle's garage developing his latest batch of film, his father interrupted him. With characteristic bluntness, his father informed him that his favorite uncle had been killed in an accident in Germany. The boy was so distraught by the news that he ran to his bedroom and cried for hours. When his composure returned, Junior heard the voices of his parents and aunt in the kitchen and sneaked down the stairs in the hopes of learning details of his uncle's death.

Junior listened in horror as his aunt recounted the report from the agency. Her husband was on a secret mission to recover art stolen by the Nazis when he discovered the door to a hidden chamber. Saying that he wanted to memorialize the moment for his nephew, his uncle posed at the door for a picture. At the moment the shutter snapped, a booby-trap exploded, killing his uncle instantly.

His aunt handed Junior's father the picture of the body being torn at the instant of explosion. From his perch on the stairs, Junior saw the outline of his uncle's body framed by a brilliant flash of light. The image was indelibly etched into his brain. He pictured himself behind the camera when the horror occurred. The pain and guilt he felt were almost too much to bear.

His mother fretted over the effect of his uncle's death on her son. She had no idea that Junior felt responsible for the tragedy. Each night, Junior screamed in his sleep, "No, oh, my God, no, oh, my God, no . . ."

She tried to comfort him, but he never woke up. In the morning, she would ask whether he had any dreams. He invariably denied having any. Junior rationalized his denials to his mother by arguing to himself that a nightmare is not a dream. In actuality, he could not erase the last moments of his uncle's life from his mind.

Over the next several years, his parents took Junior to doctor after doctor.

"Our son is experiencing nightmares, loss of appetite, random episodes of terror and insomnia," they would say.

The doctors would say, "I'm sorry, folks, there's not much we can do. The boy has suffered unimaginable emotional trauma. Usually, we see these symptoms in soldiers who suffer from what we call battle fatigue. If he were an adult, we could prescribe medicine to help him sleep; but, he's too young for that."

"I don't know how we can go on like this. Can't you recommend something, anything?" pleaded his mother.

"He's a big, strong kid. He'll outgrow it. You know the old saying, 'Time heals all wounds.' You'll see, in a few years these symptoms will lessen and then, one day, they'll be gone."

This advice proved prophetic. As the years passed the nightmares lessened in intensity and frequency, his appetite returned, and he grew and matured physically. However, with the exception of his photography Junior was listless and disinterested in his school subjects.

He gravitated toward the rough and rebellious crowd that was prone to petty criminality. It started with vandalism, broken street lamps and smashed mailboxes, and escalated to bullying younger students for their lunch money, and, ultimately ended with extortion. Junior was never the leader, but always was a dependable and willing participant. He seemed to relish physical confrontations. Eventually, he attracted the attention of the authorities at school and of law enforcement.

He took solace in his photography. He used his allowance or whatever money he could get from odd jobs or the strongarm activities of his gang on his passion. He frequented the zoo, the waterfront, and the woods along the shore searching for subjects to photograph. Junior honed his eye to observe details. He mastered the intricacies of the interplay among exposure, aperture, and shutter speed. The photographs he produced with his rudimentary darkroom equipment were remarkable and soon collected in albums. The hours he spent studying photographs were like the time a portrait artist would spend in a museum, examining for the secrets of technique and critiquing composition.

Through his teenage years, the troubled youth teetered between those two worlds. The last photograph he took was his most memorable and the most consequential. It was taken at his cousin's wedding at a catering hall on the Eastern Shore.

In the photo, his aunt was drunk and on the ground an instant after having fallen. He recalled raucous laughter and a few off-color comments. The crowd was dancing to swing music as he recalled. His aunt's laughter floated above the pounding thump of the drums and the robust, bassy tones of the brass. She had a unique, cackling way of laughing that came across as a bit too loud and even forced.

After her husband's death, she became what his mother called a good-time-Sally, but he always thought she was funny. When there was a family gathering, she would always slip him some hootch as she called it. Consequently, he was forever hovering in her orbit. He learned to drink some, but mostly he learned to swear. The death of her husband had necessitated that she take a job at a stevedore company down on the docks. There, she developed a blue vocabulary second to none.

On this occasion, she had over-indulged trying to keep up with the Mick in a drinking game. Incoherence and loss of bodily control was only a matter of time for those who challenged the Mick. After a few rounds, the Mick's opponent (and her juvenile accomplice) were reduced to an advanced stage of intoxication. It was at this point that the band played the Mick's favorite swing music. To celebrate his victory, he dragged aunt onto the dance floor. While attempting a twirling jump that seemed like a good idea, she crash-landed and collapsed in a heap.

At that moment, Junior snapped the picture. She was sitting with legs splayed indecorously, her dress bunched around her waist. Although she laughed along with the inebriated crowd, the camera captured the painful desperation in her eyes and the pathetic distortion of her face twisted in forced laughter. Seeing her so reduced, he fled.

He ran to her car. He knew where she hid the keys. Anger, shame, and sadness coursed through his alcohol-addled mind. He just wanted to get away, to put distance between him and the hall. His eyes welled up. Leave, escape, go. And so, he did, at reckless speed. Into the rainy night, he escaped. His vision was blocked while he wiped away his tears. As he careened around a corner, he saw two pedestrians in the crosswalk. By the grace of God, Junior swerved, missing them but crashing into a telephone pole. His camera smashed into the dashboard on impact.

Several hours later, his father entered the circuit court. He wore rumpled clothes and an equally rumpled expression. He had been shocked by a middle-of-the-night phone call. On the way to the court, he struggled with the news that his son was being held for driving while intoxicated without a license. The father was distraught.

When the officers brought Junior from the holding area, he had a deep bruise on the side of his face that would soon turn black. His nose was broken and his clothes were covered with dirt, blood, and vomit. As if he had just awakened from a drunken stupor, he squinted in the bright light and raised his manacled hands to shield his eyes. The officers deposited him in the queue with the other miscreants who had been corralled that night. His father worked his way to the boy.

"Junior, Junior, over here. It's your father."

With unfocused eyes, the boy lifted his head toward his father.

"Junior, just say 'Not guilty' when the judge talks to you. We'll get you help. Remember, 'Not guilty.'"

After an interminable wait, the bailiff called Junior's case. The judge shuffled some papers, read the forms in the file and glowered down at the accused. Junior stood with his shoulders slumped and head downcast. He sniffled and wiped his nose with his sleeve. Several drops of moisture trickled off his face and landed on the linoleum.

"Look at me young man," boomed the Judge. "These are very serious charges. This document charges you with driving drunk without a driver's license and wanton destruction of property."

He paused to let his outrage settle over the courtroom. Junior tried to shrink into invisibility.

"How do you plead?"

His father whispered, "'Not guilty,' Junior."

He held his breath as he watched his son process the question. A murmur of impatience built throughout the room. It appeared as if Junior was somewhere else. One of the officers beside Junior nudged him.

KOREA FORGOTTEN SACRIFICE

"Not guilty," Junior uttered inaudibly.

The stenographer held up her hands to the judge, mouthing the words 'I can't hear.'

The Judge banged his gavel. "He pleaded not guilty. Are you his father?"

"Yes, sir."

"Stand!" uttered the nearest officer in a voice tinged with disdain.

The father stood.

"That's better," said the Judge. "Now, you listen and listen good. I'm going to allow the boy to go home with you, but I want you to bring him back here in three days."

The father bowed his head and turned to move toward his son.

"And, I expect you and the boy to come prepared to decide between a sentence to a penal institution, or enlistment in the armed forces. You got me?"

The father nodded assent.

Not too far from the courthouse, they passed the Maryland Juvenile Detention Center. It was an austere brick building surrounded by a tall chain-link fence topped with barbed wire angled inward. Junior stared blankly at the bleak building. Impatient to get home, the father tugged at the boy.

"You see that barbed wire? You know why it's tilted toward the building?"

Junior shook his head.

"It's there to prevent inmates from climbing over the fence. Take a good long look at your new home, Junior."

They continued walking toward their trolley stop. When they rounded the corner near the downtown station, they stopped at a traffic light. Across the street two flags snapped in the breeze. Next to the Stars and Stripes was a scarlet red flag adorned with a golden eagle astride a globe and an anchor. The sign above the door proclaimed United States Marine Corps Recruitment Center. Following his son's gaze, the father altered direction toward the center. Standing at a folding table in front of the facility was a Marine.

"Good afternoon, sir," said a handsome man who wore a white military hat, an open-collared khaki shirt, and blue trousers. Junior brightened as he studied the sharp posture and polished appearance of the soldier. The young man handed a brochure to the father.

"Join the Marines and see the world on Uncle Sam's dime," he said, winking at Junior.

For the first time all day, Junior managed a small smile. His eyes wandered to the pictures that lined the window; pictures of Marines wading ashore a beach dotted with palm trees, Marines driving an armored vehicle into a forest. The one which he fixated on was a picture of a Marine wearing a camouflaged uniform pointing a sniper's rifle out from a tree. What captured his imagination was a detail invisible to the casual observer.

Over the next seventy-two hours, Junior's parents fretted over the situation. On the evening before the court date, they sat at the family table. The kitchen was lit solely by the waning sunlight in order to avoid Junior's sensitivity to light.

"I think that Junior should accept his punishment for his dreadful behavior and go to Juvenile Detention. I keep imagining those poor pedestrians flattened by that car . . . . At least he will be with children his age. The state will make sure he gets an education," said his mother.

His sister did not want to lose her sibling. "I think Junior should fight it. He's innocent, it was aunt's fault. She upset him and gave him drinks. He needs to fight it."

The father exhaled with an air of weariness. It was almost as if he were aging before their eyes. The discussion continued for too long.

All eyes turned toward Junior; the silence was deafening as the cliché went. There were deep purple circles around his eyes and his face was distorted by swelling. He had trouble blinking and speaking due to a thick lower lip, courtesy of impact with the steering wheel. Following the conversation as if he were following a tennis match, he turned his head with

17

difficulty. Eventually the discussion lost momentum. It was time for Junior to speak.

"I know I fucked up."

His mother gasped. Father was about to reprimand the boy when Junior continued.

"I feel terrible about what happened. I don't remember much. The dark, the rain, the horrible crunch, the pain of the crash. No matter what I do, it ends up a fucking mess. I'm sorry. Listen, I'm angry all the time. Life is a bitch. Everywhere I look I find death. There's one thing that makes me happy – that's photography. When we were at the recruitment center, I saw a picture of a sniper in a tree. Hidden behind the leaves was a camera. The sniper was a spy, taking pictures of the enemy. I think I would be good at that. Plus, I can't stay here. I see uncle everywhere. So, I'm going to enlist."

"Sweetie, you don't have to throw your life away. Go to the Juvy Center. It'll only be a couple of years. If you go into the Marines, it'll be for six years. That's a long time."

"Mom, it's my life. I have to get away from the memories. I have to make something of myself. I want to be a United States Marine!"

CHAPTER

3

Guerrilla Raid on Unit 731 - 1940

"But the basic principle of guerrilla warfare must
be the offensive, and guerrilla warfare is more
offensive in its character than regular warfare."

~Mao Zedong

With a lusty huzzah, the men followed him single file along an icy mountain pass. Chekal deployed the advance scouts and manned the rear guard himself. Kim rode with the hunhuzi to the Unit 731 installation. According to his spy, the 731 facility was a day's ride. The location had been chosen by the Japanese because it was in a sunken area protected by surrounding ridges. Anyone approaching would be silhouetted against the sky and exposed.

"We will cross the ridge, at night," decreed Kim. This was met with skepticism and fear. The ice and darkness would make the passing treacherous.

Like Hannibal crossing the Alps, Kim led his men over the ridge. By covering the horse's hoofs with treaded rubber and muzzling their snouts, his band had advanced to the perimeter of the Unit 731 laboratory undetected.

Lying concealed in a rocky crevice, Kim reconnoitered the site. At last he was able to observe the infamous bacteriological warfare facility. Unit 731 was the designation for Japan's program to produce lethal bacteria on a mass scale to be deployed as biological weapons capable of mass murder. The experiments conducted by Unit 731 included the dispersal of plague-infested fleas into enemy territory to spread epidemic. The Unit also developed germs to be delivered by ticks, caterpillars, crickets, sandflies, butterflies, and bees for sabotage of crops, water supplies, and livestock. Among the diseases studied were glanders, anthrax, cattle plague, sheep plague, and mosaic disease.

By making the operation mobile, the Imperial Army had avoided detection. During its implementation, the unit had killed thousands of civilians using weaponized disease agents. Rumors of experimentation on human subjects swirled around Unit 731. Many of the unfortunate victims of the cruel, unethical, and diabolical biological research were prisoners who had been arrested by the *Kempeitai*, Japan's secret military police.

According to the *hunhuzi* spy, Dr. Ishii's office was in the northeast corner of the main building. The plan was daring and simple. Chekal would lead the guerrillas on a surprise attack on the motor pool, stealing as many vehicles as possible. During this diversion, Kim, the spy, and three commandos would enter the office and remove as many records as they could carry. Since the raid would take place several hours before dawn after a Japanese holiday, Kim might just catch them with their guard down.

From behind a large boulder encrusted with ice, Kim and his commandos waited for the scouts to go into action. Suddenly, the sky was lit with a burst of orange-red fire from a hand grenade. This was followed by several bursts of machine gun fire on the opposite side of the compound. They could hear engines revving and saw a truck careening towards the main gate. It struck with such force that it dragged behind it the barb wire which had encircled the camp. Kim's eyes widened as the barb wire pulled down the wooden guard tower near the gate. He heard screams, more gunfire and pandemonium as the camp awoke to the attack. More vehicles streamed through the chasm created by the truck. The lead Jeep stopped to pick up the driver of the truck. When the vehicles sped into the night, leaving fire and destruction behind them, the Japanese followed in hot pursuit. Kim's team moved into action.

One commando clambered up several crates onto the roof, while the two others sprinted to the office door. Following Kim's hand signals, the commandos battered in the door and entered looking in all directions. Suddenly, a scream and burst of gunfire broke the silence in this part of the compound. Next, he heard the sharp yelp of a guard dog as the second commando slit its throat. Kim and the spy entered the office to see one commando on the floor with his throat ripped open. A large Kunming wolfdog lay dead next to the body.

"We never saw it coming. The wolfdog came out of nowhere and attacked Moon Yi. I killed the monster with my kukri," said the commando, lifting a curved, blood-soaked knife.

"We have to move fast. Someone must've heard the gunfire here," said the spy, the muscle under his left eye twitching rapidly.

With the commando standing guard at the door, Kim and the spy rifled through the office searching for anything incriminating. Kim found a worn notebook that seemed to contain diary entries. He stuffed it along with numerous folders in the leather satchel that was slung over his shoulder.

"Company is on the way, boys," said the commando on the roof.

"Okay, let's move out," screamed Kim.

The rooftop commando provided covering fire while the three men ran past the boulder and through the fence they had entered only minutes ago. Barking dogs, machine gun bursts, and frantic shouts followed them. Kim watched the commando hurl himself off the roof to a hail of gunfire. He zigzagged across the open space to the boulder and returned fire. The second commando left Kim's side and fired at the pursuers from a different angle. This allowed the first commando to escape through the fence and join Kim and the spy. Kim whistled a signal for retreat and the other commando followed them into the woods.

The group re-formed at a prearranged point and quickly set up a defensive position. The forest was filled with barking dogs and shouting men. Searchlights flickered through the trees. The search party was closing in. The guerrillas did not have much time. Kim pulled back his sleeve, looked at his watch and cursed.

He could see a group of Japanese soldiers with howling dogs straining at thick leather leashes. They were emerging from the trees onto a rough dirt path when the sound of an approaching vehicle pierced the night. Again, Kim cursed at the misfortune of having the motorized reinforcements come from the garrison. His pursuers relaxed at the sound. The soldier in charge of the pursuit waved for the vehicle to stop and unload the reinforcements.

The two commandos inventoried their ammunition in anticipation of a final firefight. Kim felt the spy next to him tense as he considered whether he might gain any advantage by surrendering. Without taking his eyes off the dirt road, Kim reached for the spy and pressed down on his shoulder. Kim held a single finger to his lips. Just then, he heard the vehicle accelerate followed by the sound of several bone-crunching thuds and animals howling in pain. Before the other soldiers in the pursuing party could react, Kim heard his second in command.

"Don't just stand there gawking. Get your asses into this truck!" yelled Chekal.

Kim and his party did not need a second invitation. They raced onto the truck as it sped into the night. The sound of bullets whistling through the canvas canopy was a reminder of how close their escape had been. When they were out of immediate danger, Kim opened the satchel that had been slung across his back. In the center of Dr. Ishii's diary, he found a bullet hole and a slug that had been intended for him. He whispered a prayer of gratitude.

There was no time to rest. The Imperial Army was chasing them with a vengeance reserved for the most hated enemies. As the vehicles stolen by the guerrillas descended the switchback roads that ribboned through the mountain, they could see the headlights of Imperial Army troop carriers wending down the mountain after them. As the sun rose, Kim felt that his head was on a swivel, looking ahead to catch a glimpse of the river and back to see if the Imperial Army was gaining on them.

"Sir, we are running low on fuel. We must stop to re-fuel."

"No," he growled. "We will use the jerry cans to fill the gas tanks on the fly."

Kim signaled his command to the other vehicles with hand signals. Kim personally released a jerry can and poured the contents into the tank. At one point, the vehicle hit a rut in the road causing precious gasoline to spill onto the commander. Fortunately, Kim's strong grip retained control of the can.

"Look, they are stopping," whooped one of the men.

"Don't get too confident," cautioned the leader. "Their bigger trucks had trouble navigating on the twisting mountain roads, but their more powerful engines will close the gap when we leave the mountains."

A fiery flash and distant report told Kim that they had other worries. The Imperial Army had stopped to do more than re-fuel; they had stopped to fire mortars. As shells whistled toward their speeding vehicles, he signaled for the other drivers to follow them off the road and into an irrigation ditch that ran parallel to the road. Not a moment too soon.

An instant after swerving off the road, a shell exploded adjacent to them. Rocks and gravel rained down on the roofs of their vehicles, but no one was injured. That is, except for a few rear ends that were sore from bouncing heavily when the vehicles left the road. The drivers adjusted to the uneven surface of the ditch by slowing down. The reduction in speed was worth it because their new route kept them below the road and not visible to the soldiers firing the mortars.

Silence followed and Kim visualized the Imperial Army commander ordering his men back onto the trucks upon realizing the futility of continuing the mortar attack. Kim signaled the drivers to return to the road. They drove all day under the pressure of the chase. It was nearly dark when they finally emerged into the lowlands leading to the river. From here it was a sprint to the finish line. They would drive flat out and hope to out-race their pursuers.

Their only hope of escape was to get across the Amur River, the mighty waterway that separated the Japanese puppet state of Manchukuo from the Soviet Far East. In Chinese, the river was called the Black Dragon on account of the color of the water. Although war between the Soviets and Japan had not been declared, it might as well have been. The countries were natural and historic enemies, most recently in the first decade of the century when Japan administered a mortifying defeat to the Tzar's Imperial forces. Many thought that the losses inflicted in the Russo-Japanese War, 1904 - 1905 marked the beginning of the end of the Romanov Dynasty and Tzar Nicholas II, and the subsequent rise of Soviet communism.

On this day, Kim had much more pressing matters to handle rather than to ponder the history of the region. His only goal was to get his band of guerillas across the river, away from the Japanese. He had to survive and bring the evil of Unit 731 to light.

He prided himself on his ability to plan for almost every contingency. However, he was unable to negate fully the Imperial Army's radio communication ability. Although he could not stop them from radioing ahead for help, he planned to do the next best thing; he would use their own communication equipment to spread false information.

He grabbed the transmitting device and manipulated the on/off button to request help in pursuing guerrillas. By clicking the operating device, he hoped to garble the transmission enough to prevent detection that it was unauthorized. At first, he thought that his gambit had worked. Then, he realized that it had not, and worse, it actually helped the enemy zero in on his location.

In his most authoritative voice, he attempted to bully the dispatcher into accepting his request.

"I'm sorry. We cannot allow your message without the password. Unless you provide the password, we will terminate and commence search and destroy measures."

Kim was about to turn the radio off when he had a flash of inspiration. He reached into the map compartment and rummaged around until he found the code scrawled on a scrap of paper. No matter how sophisticated a unit might be, it was no stronger than the laziest soldier, the one who will always take a shortcut rather than memorize a password.

He kissed the paper and spoke the password into the device. "Proceed."

"Base, this is commander Zheng from Unit 731. We are in pursuit of a contingent of guerrillas that attacked our facility. Request assistance in apprehending them. They are headed toward Korsakovo. Please intercept. Repeat intercept. Top priority."

He waited, and waited, and waited for a response. A single bead of perspiration trickled down the side of his face. No one in the cab dared breathe. Just when he was prepared to admit that no response would come, the radio crackled back to life.

"Yes, sir. Will do. Sir, the duty officer has ordered radio silence to avoid tipping off the guerrillas. Over."

"Excellent idea. I commend your superior. Over and out."

Korsakovo was a rural community south of the regional capital of Khabarovsk. The communications center would quickly realize that Korsakovo was a most improbable destination. He knew that this ploy would only buy them a short time, but even a few minutes might just mean survival.

He indicated to the drivers to speed to the Amur River Tunnel which had been built after the Japanese takeover of Manchuria in 1931. At the time the puppet government was installed by the Japanese, the Khabarovsk Bridge was the route used by the Trans-Siberian Railway to cross the Amur River. Any damage to the bridge could sever the primary link between Far East Russia and the rest of the Soviet Union. This made the bridge an obvious vulnerability.

With the growing threat of war with Japan through the 1930s, Soviet military leadership recognized the strategic importance of this crossing and decided to build the Amur River Tunnel. Construction began in 1936 and was completed in record time. When the tunnel opened in 1941, it was the only underwater railway line in the country.

Glancing out the window at the dwindling daylight, he calculated that they would have to cross the river in darkness. As their convoy descended from the mountains, the landscape morphed into the boreal or taiga, the Russian word for forest. The pleasant smell of pines, spruces, and larches entering the vehicles helped to lift their spirits. He had every confidence in his men. They were resourceful, seasoned soldiers who had survived many hardships. Before this night was over, would they have another adventure story to tell their grandchildren, or, would they be part of some unspeakable human experiment devised by Unit 731?

"There it is," he said, pointing along the railroad tracks toward a stone structure in the distance. It was the entrance to the tunnel. His heart leapt, then fell, when he stared through his binoculars. He punched his thigh in frustration.

"What is it, sir?"

"The tunnel is blocked by a massive locomotive in front of a grillwork of thick iron bars."

"Then, we blow it open," said one of his men with an air of disdain.

"Not possible. No time," replied another gesturing behind them toward their pursuers who seemed quite a bit closer than they had been an hour before.

"He is right."

A sense of dejection invaded the cab. Kim was silent. His mind raced. Then, he saw it. Off to the right, beyond a strand of trees was a small marina.

"Head there," he commanded.

A few minutes later, his men were boarding several commandeered vessels. He backed the truck across the road at the entrance gate. Any impediment would help buy time he thought.

The radio crackled to life. Kim heard the voice of the commander of the pursuit by the Japanese.

"Central command, come in! This is Commander Higasioka requesting helicopter support. . . ."

"Password?"

"What?" screamed the commander. "We must stop them from leaving the marina!"

"Password?"

Kim chuckled at the rigid adherence to protocol. He removed a *Yanji* bomb from his vest and pulled the pin from the grenade. Through the open window, he placed the armed grenade between the door and the seat.

"Hurry!" yelled one of the men who struggled to hold the boat against the flow of the river. Kim dashed across the open ground and jumped into the boat as it broke free into the current. The men rowed for the opposite shore in the darkness as if their lives depended on it. They battled against the current and their own exhaustion. The men shivered against the chill wind and spray off the river. As long as they were within range of rifles from the shore, he worried that they were sitting ducks.

Shouts from the marina directed toward them. A squad of sharpshooters was forming near the gate. As Kim anticipated, one soldier took the initiative to remove the obstacle from the entrance. When he attempted to mount the truck, the *Yanji* erupted in a fiery explosion, killing the sharpshooters. Kim's improvised booby-trap had worked, giving his team a few more minutes to escape.

He wasn't sure whether he heard it, or, saw it first. Upstream from them, a shore patrol boat was on the river searching for them. He ordered the men to be quiet and to stop rowing. Drifting with the current was a risk, but it was less of a risk than being discovered because they were making a racket. Kim could almost feel the patrol boat captain straining to hear his quarry splashing across the river. Kim wondered how long his men could battle fatigue, cold, and fear.

The patrol boat captain had good reason for continuing this contest of wills. He also knew that a passionate geisha was waiting in his comfortable, warm bed to show him the latest entertainment techniques that were all the rage in Tokyo. With each passing minute he grew more impatient. Fingering his revolver, he cursed the guerrillas under his breath. Kim could almost feel his wrath; he signaled to his men to maintain silence. The next few minutes would determine their fate.

They rounded a bend in the river and headed directly toward the lights of the city of Khabarovsk. The captain gambled on finding the guerrillas before the Soviets guarding the city saw that his boat was encroaching on Soviet territory. The Japanese captain knew that his enemies would have no compunction in blasting his vessel out of the water.

"Floodlights," he ordered. An instant later, narrow shafts of light pierced the darkness. It was only a matter of time before the location of the guerrillas would be revealed.

Kim thought he heard an alarm sound in the distance. He saw a trail of white smoke from the far shore heading skyward. After a distinctive pop, the sky illuminated. The Soviet garrison had fired a flare to light up the river. Up high on the Amur Cliff, Kim saw a most beautiful sight. Silhouetted against the night, he saw a battery of Soviet artillery. Turning to his left, he saw the patrol boat captain with his shoulders slumped in a posture of resignation. The Japanese boat turned sharply and headed back to Manchukuo.

Kim ordered the men to resume rowing toward sanctuary and exhaled a sigh of relief and triumph. After days of hardship with no sleep, his only thoughts involved celebratory shots of soju, (a vodka-like drink) hot food, and a warm bunk. Instead, his band was greeted with bayoneted rifles, roughly clapped in irons and brought to the fortress dungeon.

CHAPTER

4

Parris Island - 1949

"All hope abandon, ye who enter here."

~ Dante Alighieri

Despite the incessant entreaties of his mother and sister, Junior never wavered in his resolve to become a Marine. After his initial disappointment at his son's decision, Junior's father experienced a secret pride about his boy's sense of direction. In an odd way, his father was slightly jealous about the potential adventures that awaited his son. Had he known about the hardships Junior would endure, his father might have felt differently.

And, so it was that in the fall of 1949 Junior disembarked from a bus at the Marine Recruit Depot in Parris Island, South Carolina for boot camp. Even though it was autumn, the air was heavy and warm. The bus from the Depot to the Reception Center was crowded with other raw recruits. It smelled from sweat, urine, and fear. He was now part of a nameless, faceless herd that behaved as though it was being driven through the stockyards. Before it stopped, a large man wearing an odd hat swung onto the bus.

"Shut the FUCK up! Welcome to Parris Island. You motherfuckers have 15 seconds to get off this bus and get in formation . . . and 10 seconds are already gone!"

Alongside the bus was a paved area covered with the outlines of feet painted in yellow. The footprints were aligned in rows, four across, one row after another in troop formation. The young men scrambled off the bus and rushed to stand on the yellow feet, more or less. The drill instructors swarmed around them, poking, smacking, and grabbing the recruits endeavoring to organize the green novices. Large and small, portly and rail-thin, disheveled and bedraggled, the recruits resembled a circus troop on parade more than a formation of soldiers standing at attention.

"HURRY UP MOTHERFUCKERS."

Junior had barely stopped moving when he realized that he was enveloped by a black cloud. Something was biting him. They were in his eyes, up his nose, in his hair. Noseeums by the hundreds. He and the others would learn quickly what the DIs called them.

Smack, swat, slap! The recruits reacted instinctively to the insects.

"THESE ARE SAND FLEAS. You WILL let my sand fleas EAT. You will NOT kill my sand fleas!"

Every time someone slapped a sand flea, a DI ran up and slapped the offender on the head. It did not occur to the recruits that the DI's were wearing insect repellent. The young men were too miserable and scared to think. When the trainers prodded them toward a nearby building, they shuffled along, heads down, eyes squinting against the onslaught. There were more than a few tears flowing over the tiny red welts inflicted by the ravenous insects.

Once inside, the recruits followed the man in front of him to a row of chairs. An ominous buzzing filled the air. Junior lowered his eyes and blinked in disbelief. His feet were covered with hair, a foot deep. One by one the recruits stepped through the hair into a barber's chair and, in seconds, were shorn. It happened so fast and was so drastic that many recruits could not recognize the head staring back at them in the barber's mirror.

Standing near the exit, Junior felt a slight breeze and realized that his head was cold. Maybe that's why grandpa Josh always wore a hat. When Junior rubbed his noggin, his fingers slid over tiny spikes that could barely be called stubble. He wondered how he would feel if it never grew back. Looking at the other recruits, Junior stifled a laugh at the ridiculous sight of hundreds of bald men. Most had scalps the color of split apples, others had scalps resembling chocolate and orange Tootsie Roll pops. An atmosphere of gloom descended on them as they waited for the next eradication of their individuality.

Impressive men wearing campaign hats used their booming voices to prod the group along the path of the intake process. Also known as Baden-Powell hats, they were wood-brown, with peaked, dimpled crowns and wide, flat brims. These hats were named after the founder of the American Boy Scouts, but, were colloquially known as Smoky Bear hats. Drill instructors wore these distinctive hats as a badge of pride and authority. As the recruits would quickly learn, drill instructors, or DIs, would dominate every aspect of their lives for the next thirteen weeks.

When the herd finally arrived in the large open room, each man was holding a full set of equipment – uniforms, rucksack, duffel bag, steel pot, bucket with octagonal soap and brush, rifle and bayonet. They stood with their arms cradling a pile of shirts, pants and hats, and a folded duffel bag. A few of the more astute, stuffed their gear into the duffels. Most were too shocked at the pace of events to think of that. Junior craned his neck searching for one of the fellows he had chatted with on the bus, but he could not find him; they all looked the same.

The DIs surrounded the men. Junior caught the eye of the recruit to his left. They exchanged looks of commiseration. Each looked toward the other's cranium and, with a slight smile, rolled his eyes. Just then, the murmur of the group was broken by a command for silence and attention. The room became as quiet as the lapse between the flash of lightning and the crash of thunder.

Someone in the rear sneezed. There was a nervous titter that was squelched by the glowering DIs. A long silence followed. The fellow next to Junior fumbled the boots that were on top of his pile. The buckles on the boots thumped loudly on the floor. The nearest drill sergeant leapt into action.

"Maggot, drop and give me twenty!"

The fellow froze, not comprehending the order.

The DI grabbed him by the shoulder and pushed him down.

"I said, give me twenty pushups, you useless excuse for a maggot!"

Tentatively, the young man began doing pushups.

"I can't hear you, maggot!"

"Six . . . seven,"

"No, we start from numero one in the goddamn Marines, maggot!"

"One . . . two . . ."

"I can't hear yoooou!"

By the time the recruit reached sixteen, his arms were quivering. At twenty, his upper body was shaking as though electrical current was coursing through him. The room was filled with recruits, eyes downcast to avoid contact with DIs who patrolled the assemblage looking for any breech in decorum.

Before the recruit could catch his breath, the DI shouted, "On your feet, maggot!"

The youngster bolted upright. The instructor moved close, so close that the recruit was bombarded by the smell of stale coffee and cigarettes. The stiff brim of the DI's hat pressed into the forehead of the recruit.

"Is that how you treat your Uncle's property?" he barked.

The boy's eyes were wide with a look that was a paradoxical mixture of confusion and eagerness to comply. If only he knew how. He froze.

Junior bent over, whispering 'Your clothes.' Embracing his own pile close to his chest with one arm, Junior began picking up the other's uniforms. The fellow quickly scooped up all his issue, including the buckle boots. One of the DIs planted his boot firmly on Junior's rump and knocked him off his feet into a heap.

"Get up, you puke! Give me thirty for being a god-damn meddler."

The recruits stood rigid in fear of attracting the wrath of a drill instructor. After a long time at attention, a tension mimetic of a vibrating tuning fork enveloped the group. Their breathing became collective, shallow and suppressed, lest it offend. Oozing malevolence, the DIs circled the herd like a predatory mob.

A door opened.

"AH-Tehn-SHUN! Officer on deck!"

A tall man in a crisp uniform entered. When he approached the podium in the front, he scanned the room with the air of a rancher surveying his livestock.

"Men, I am Captain Warren Crandall, your commanding officer. I am at the top of the food chain. You are Marine recruits. You are at the bottom of the food chain. For the next thirteen weeks, you will be trained by the finest military trainers on God's green earth. When these drill instructors have worked their magic, those of you who are worthy will become part of the greatest fighting force ever assembled – the United States Marines Corps."

On cue, the DIs shouted, "Semper Fi!"

"That, gentlemen, is the Marine Corps motto. It means 'Always Faithful' – to God, country and the Constitution. The sergeant major will take over now and you will be assigned to your platoons where you will bond with your fellow Marines as if your life depends on it . . . because it does."

Crandall pivoted. Sergeant Major Swanson saluted, holding the tip of his right index finger to the brim of his hat until he received a sharp snap in return from the captain.

"They are all yours, sergeant major. Transform these men into marines and bring them back to me. Carry on."

"Yessir!" exclaimed Swanson. The sergeant major stood before them as the captain exited. Junior stared at the sergeant major. He wore utilities that were so stiffly starched that the creases might slash his skin if he were not careful, thought Junior.

Standing ramrod straight, the man appeared to tower over the assemblage. Moving crisply, the other DIs marched to the front and aligned themselves on either side of Swanson. The recruits were motionless at this display of authority. Swanson told the recruits to listen carefully because the drill instructors were about to read the names of the men assigned to his training company and they were to get their asses behind the DI when their name was called. The sergeant major stated that each of the DIs had raspy 'frog voices.' This was, according to Swanson, because the DIs spent all their time yelling at dumbass recruits. He admonished the recruits not be dumbasses.

As each DI barked the names, companies were formed. Junior was glad that he was in the group with the fellow he had helped earlier.

When the drill instructors were finished, there were about a dozen recruits remaining in the center of the room.

"Now, there you have it. These are the dumbasses," said Swanson. A chuckle mixed with "there but for the grace of God. . ." spread through the room.

"These are the dumbasses who either did not hear their names when called, or who don't know their dumbass names."

A ripple of laughter fanned across the recruits who weren't standing out for ridicule. Swanson gestured amicably, waving his arms with palms upraised, as if encouraging the laughter. Some of the recruits in the center sensing the lightening of mood also joined the laughter.

Then, like a crack of thunder, Swanson roared, "These are the dumbasses who will get you killed in battle! They will fuck up some order, or, go wandering off and some of you will die! We do not tolerate dumbasses in the Marines!"

*   *   *

The escape from Manchukuo had required every ounce of energy and resourcefulness that Kim's guerrillas possessed. When they finally made it to Kharbovsk, his men were completely spent. When they were confined in the garrison prison, they were too exhausted to care. His group slept for two straight days. However, still confined a week later, they became despondent and mutinous. Despite ample food, Kim's men suffered from diarrhea and dehydration because they could not digest the fatty Russian diet.

"We must be patient. Our Soviet comrades will embrace us once they analyze the documents we captured," Kim counselled his men.

"You place too much trust in the white devils," shouted Jang Yong-ho, a senior non-commissioned officer who had lost his left eye when tortured by Soviet secret police. The improvised eye patch he wore over the gruesome injury gave him a menacing look.

"I lived with my family in Soviet Far East until Stalin's forced relocation. We were targeted for relocation to the desolate outpost of Ushtobe where we would surely die. Several of us opposed the plan and organized a protest. I was arrested by the NKVD, the secret police, and tortured for names of my cohorts. I sacrificed my eye to protect them. In the end, my family was sent to Ushtobe to die. I was able to escape after my young wife degraded herself with a Soviet guard. We fled south and joined this group. I hate the white devils and urge that we plan to overwhelm the guards and break for freedom!"

Several men shouted approval of the grizzled veteran.

Kim shot a glance to Chekal who quietly slipped behind Jang.

"Comrades, we have shared many hardships and sacrifices together. We have shared many triumphs together. The only thing that can defeat us is if we splinter. We must stay united. Be patient a little while longer. I trust that when our comrades in Moscow evaluate our treasures from Unit 731, we will be rewarded as heroes," said Kim.

As Jang cleared his throat to respond that patience was for weaklings, he felt the sharp point of a shiv wielded by Chekal near his left kidney.

"My friends, we are safe and warm for the moment. I think we should enjoy the hospitality of our hosts until we get word from Moscow. The rest will serve us well," said Jang. Chekal clapped him on his shoulder in solidarity.

Just then, the midday meal arrived and the men filtered toward the tables where the food was being served. A few men muttered at the turn of events, but most followed their stomachs.

Later, that afternoon Kim was summoned to the office of the commandant.

"Comrade Kim, I am pleased to report that Moscow has advised us that the haul of documents you delivered about the experiments and delivery of biological weapons constitute "smoking gun" evidence against the Japanese military hierarchy. The Soviet Central Committee is most appreciative at the evidence provided by you."

The commandant continued by noting that the Soviets were especially interested in Dr. Ishii's notebook diary that had stopped a bullet intended for Kim.

At first blush the notebook was fairly nondescript. It had a leather cover and was filled with handwritten entries and numbers in the fashion of a diary or journal. To Kim's untrained eye, the characters appeared to be Japanese. Although he could not read the journal, the Soviet officer who received it from him was ecstatic when he perused it.

"Comrade Kim, you have delivered a treasure. This is the personal journal of Dr. Shiro Ishii. Our initial analysis is that it details the progress of Japanese efforts to weaponize virulent biologic agents. Our scientists are most curious about this," he said, slapping the notebook onto his desk. This initial enthusiasm proved accurate as the cache of documents yielded significant insight to the Soviet unit responsible for biologic and chemical weapons research.

Once the elation of their achievement wore off, Kim's contingent was faced with a serious dilemma. They were assigned to a Soviet unit and trained along with other Koreans at the Okeanskaya Field School near Vladivostok. Kim lobbied to maintain the operational integrity of his guerrillas as a distinct unit under his command. These efforts were fruitless. They were integrated into Soviet military to join the fight against the Japanese on the side of Russia.

Kim learned to speak Russian and made contacts in the Russian military that would serve him well in the future. Kim was commissioned as a captain in the Soviet 88th Brigade, which was made up of Korean and Chinese guerrillas. They were placed under the command of a Soviet officer. Morale among Kim and his men plummeted. After years of free-wheeling and opportunistic action, the Koreans chafed under the rigidity of Soviet command. It was all Kim could do to keep his band from deserting.

By 1945 he had achieved the rank of major. When the war against Japan ended, no one was happier than Kim and his guerrillas.

"Good morning, Major Kim," said the orderly in the officers' mess. As the major surveyed the room, he sensed an inordinate animation. The normal conversational buzz had been replaced by a boisterous energy level. One of his oldest comrades beckoned to him motioning him to a seat he had reserved.

"Have you heard the news?"

"Yes, I heard that the Americans have dropped an atomic bomb on the Jap city of Hiroshima and wiped out most of the city."

"No, no, Major, that's yesterday's news. You're not going to believe today's news. We are going home."

"What? What are you saying?"

"Today, Comrade Stalin has declared war against the Japanese Empire. Rumor has it that regional command is cutting orders for us to deploy to Wonsan, Korea!"

The major's eyes grew wide in disbelief. His forearm pressed against his billfold where he kept an old newspaper clipping from 1943. He frequently opened and unfolded that worn article which contained the declaration made by the Allies at the Cairo Conference that after the defeat of Japan "... in due course, Korea shall become free and independent." Churchill, Roosevelt, and Stalin had all committed that Kim's country would be free and independent when they won the war. What could go wrong?

No one could have ever anticipated that those words, "free and independent" would have such profoundly different meanings to so many different parties and that the country would become the focal point of a worldwide geo-political struggle resulting in millions of casualties.

As he traveled from Vladivostok to Wonsan, Korea in 1945, a new reality faced Kim Il Sung. The Allied victory in WWII had brought an end to the brutal reign of Imperial Japan over his homeland. The Japanese were vanquished and the guerrilla leader turned Soviet Army officer no longer had an enemy to fight. His entire adult life had been spent battling Japan the oppressor. That was over. In the proverbial blink of an eye, he went from a soldier with a clearly identified objective, to a former soldier returning to the land of his ancestors which had been brutalized by occupation and war for most of this century. The task before him was no less than rebuilding his country from the ashes of four decades of Japanese subjugation.

As Kim and his group gathered on the deck of the *Kalinin*, a light cruiser of the Red Fleet, they struggled for the first glimpse of their country and the port of Wonsan on the east coast. They lifted a jubilant Russian "hurray," Chinese "shango," and other cheers as land approached. There were no crowds to meet them, no bands to greet them. Their disembarkation was somewhat anticlimactic. With their duffels on their shoulders, they stood on the dock, dumbfounded, not knowing what to do.

Kim felt the despair of a man whose purpose had evaporated. With no enemy to oppose, what would he do? There's no way that I can become a rice farmer like my father, he thought darkly.

Finally, Chekal said, "I'm hungry. Let's get some bibimbap."

"I know a place nearby where the bibimbap is delicious, the kimchi is spicy and the beer is cold," said Jang.

"Here, here," said the group as they trudged off to enjoy their first meal on Korean soil in a long, long time.

Kim Il Sung 1927

CHAPTER

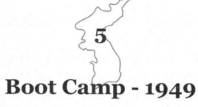

5

Boot Camp - 1949

"Boot camp was the first time I got a heavy dose of discipline. It was the best thing that ever happened to me."

~ Nelsan Ellis

Just as the Marines were considered the shock troops of the U.S. military, the DIs were the shock corps of boot camp. Through a comprehensive program of personal deconstruction, any vestige of individuality was eradicated. The elemental unit of this process was the platoon, the constituent part of the company. The drill sergeants surveyed their charges, divided into companies and got to work. Over the course of the cycle, the shocks would escalate.

After a stunned silence, the drill instructors herded their respective recruits to their barracks. Along the way, Junior fell in next to his new friend.

"Thanks back there. Y'all saved my butt."

"No problem. Call me Junior."

"Glad to make your acquaintance, Junior. I'm Arlo from Gauley Bridge, West Virginny."

"What kind of place is Girly Bridge?" snickered the recruit in the row behind them.

"You, yeah, you," shouted the DI, pointing to the recruit who had spoken last. "Yeah, I mean you. Drop and gimme twenty! If I see any of you pukes eye-balling this maggot, y'all be sorrier than a stallion on gelding day!"

Annoyed at the delay, the gunny made them double-time across an area lined with barracks. When they neared the furthest building, they heard a door slam open into the side wall of the barracks. A trainee with his shirt unbuttoned, holding his pants bunched to his waist ran toward them. His face was so contorted with fear that it looked grotesque in the dim light.

"I can't take it anymore. This place is driving me crazy. I gotta get the fuck outta here!"

Suddenly, a figure wearing a Smoky Bear hat appeared in the doorway. He lifted a rifle, aimed and fired. A flash erupted from the barrel. The fleeing man tumbled and fell into the dirt in a silent heap.

"Get rid of the fuckin' sonuvabitch! We can't abide any slackers," shouted the DI.

Four men raced from the barracks and lifted the fallen man. They carried him to the side of the building and dumped him noisily into a metal container. Then, they returned to the barracks and closed the door behind them. Barely fifteen seconds elapsed from beginning to end. Junior heard retching from two different recruits behind him, followed by a snarling command to "Drop and gimme twenty."

When they got to the barracks, the drill instructor told them to put their clothes on a bunk and be outside in thirty seconds.

"Or, all y'all will be doing pushups and bends and thrusts 'til the sun come up."

Getting into and out of the barracks, the recruits scrambled like irate hornets around a disturbed nest. The DI stood with his hat tilted down, shielding his eyes which were glued on his watch. If they could have seen his eyes, they would have seen eyes the color of coal, tinged with amusement and enjoyment at the chaos before him.

Although not tall, he was solidly built like the cliffs in El Yunque Mountain in his childhood home of Puerto Rico. Alvaro Gomax had spent his formative years in Spanish Harlem in New York City. If pressed, he would say that his best attribute was that he was a survivor. When he was sixteen, he survived a vicious knife fight with a rival gang leader. It left him with a jagged scar on the left side of his face and a criminal record for manslaughter. His sentence? A stint in the U.S. Marines.

While he was with the infantry training regiment, he survived a brawl with a redneck who mocked his wispy moustache. Gomax dispatched the good old boy with quick blows to the windpipe and sternum before a savage kick to the side. That earned Gomax an extended visit to the brig and assignment to a unit known as the tunnel rats whose job was to dislodge Japanese soldiers hiding in the caves of the Pacific islands as MacArthur's forces island-hopped toward Japan.

The second hand on his watch ticked toward the twelve. The last recruit stumbled into line with the urgency of a male Cinderella racing against the curfew. Satisfied, the DI raised his eyes.

"Mens, I'm Gunnery Sergeant Gomax. You will call me SIR. If any of you limp-dicks calls me Gunny or Drill Sergeant, you will be doing pushups 'til you puke."

He glowered at them, pacing back and forth like a panther stalking his prey. Junior was transfixed. This man exuded so much animal energy that Junior found himself memorizing the DI's mannerisms with an eye toward adopting them. Here was someone to strive to become.

"You better give you soul to Jesus, because for the next thirteen weeks, your ass is mine. I own it. Everything you need comes through me. I will be your mammy, your pappy, your confessor and your pimp. You're gonna hate me, and you're gonna love me. When boot camp is over, you will be Marines. You will be able to swim through a river of mud, storm a machine gun nest, and conquer an enemy hill, all before lunch. And you will make sure that every one of your buddies makes it with you."

Gomax surveyed the motley crew in front of him. Some were men physically like he was; there because some judge thought they'd be better off in the Marines than jail. Most were just young kids, teenagers who weren't mature enough to shave the peach fuzz on their cheeks. His job was to break them down, eliminate their bad, lazy habits and instill

43

Marines values. If that meant that some were terrified, traumatized or terrorized, then so be it.

"Tomorrow we start your trip to joining an elite fighting force. The mess is over there behind me. Breakfast is served at 0430. Then, you gotta shit, shower, and shave and be out here ready to roll at 0530. Any questions?"

Even though they had no clue about what was expected of them, no one dared raise a hand.

"Fall out!"

The recruits returned to the barracks and organized their belongings, all the while checking to see how the other guy was doing it. The barracks were two-story rectangular wooden boxes with metal double bunks arrayed on either side of a wide center aisle. Junior and Arlo paired together – Junior took the bottom bunk and the taller fellow took the top. After making their beds as best they could, they sat on their footlockers and got acquainted.

"You know, Junior, y'all are good people. I never expected to have a friend from a city."

"Me neither."

"Say, did you see where the outhouse is at?"

Junior shrugged and pointed, "It's probably out back."

Arlo ambled toward the back door.

"Gol-ly! Junior, y'all got to come over here straight away!"

Junior hustled to Arlo who was standing at a doorway, pointing into a room. When Junior reached Arlo, they both looked inside. Along one wall, there was a row of toilet bowls across from a row of sinks. At that moment, one of the recruits came around the far wall drying his hair with a white towel.

"If you want to shower you better hurry. The hot water is running low."

Arlo looked as if he had just stepped out of a time capsule.

"You know, Junior, I ain't never lived in a building that had indoor plumbing. These here barracks are great; they got toilets and showers. And to think the Gunny said we even git free breakfast. Lordy, I think I'm gonna like it here."

*   *   *

44

The challenge for the U.S.S.R. after the surrender of the Japanese to end WWII was how to implement a Soviet style government in northern Korea. Aligning his objectives with Tzarist Russia, Stalin considered the ports of Korea as valuable for the Soviet Far East not only as warm water outlets, but as a buffer from a hostile power using Korea as a springboard for invasion.

Uncle Joe directed one of his most trusted comrades to evaluate potential leadership candidates. Lavrentiy Beria, the feared chief of the NKVD secret police, flew to P'yŏngyang with this assignment. A short, slightly-built man, Beria's most distinctive facial feature was the round, rimless eyeglasses that separated his victims from his vile pig eyes. One of his victims called him vulture face. The best endorsement for Beria's unsurpassed reputation for ruthlessness and cruelty was uttered by Stalin when he introduced Beria to President Roosevelt as "our Himmler."

While en route to P'yŏngyang, Beria reviewed the list of eligible leadership candidates and contemplated the young Korean women he would ravish to satisfy his sexual appetites. As a veteran of the devastation inflicted during WWII, Beria was unfazed at the ubiquitous bomb craters, mangled railroad infrastructure, and bullet-riddled buildings. His limousine traversed the ravaged industrial district on the east side of the city. Crossing the Taedong River to the population center on the west side, Beria eyed the hotels, government buildings, and cultural attractions where he might find his nubile prey.

Over the next few days, Beria was ensconced in a suite at the P'yŏngyang Hotel, where he interviewed dozens of people. The necessity of a translator rendered the sessions boring and excruciating. During the day, Beria found his mind drifting to the evening's perversion and imagined a more extreme level of sadism to compensate him for this torture. The only break from this tedium was the interview of an energetic young man who spoke Russian.

As the process winnowed the pool, Beria found himself drawn to Kim Il Sung who regaled the NKVD thug with tales of cruelty inflicted on Japanese prisoners captured by his guerrillas. Kim clinched Beria's endorsement when he shared a rumor he had heard about a secret program of the Imperial Japanese Navy to build an atomic bomb. Kim could not have known that Beria was in charge of Stalin's quest for an atomic weapon. Yet, from Beria's keen interest as evidenced by setting aside the folder of pornographic pictures he had been perusing, Kim realized he had struck a chord. At that moment, he decided to take gamble by stretching the truth.

"Comrade Beria, when we raided Unit 731 before we escaped to Khabarovsk, I acquired the diary of Dr. Ishii. Our *hunhuzi* spy informed me that the fiend Ishii worked on the atom bomb project. I brought this journal to show you. It's in Japanese and our efforts to decode it has only revealed information on the biological weapons program. I'm convinced that there must be the key to the Jap nuclear research somewhere in this book," said Kim, producing the journal from inside his tunic.

From the arch of Beria's eyebrows, Kim knew that the fearsome head of the Soviet secret police was intrigued. Beria gestured for Kim to pass him the book. Kim felt the Soviet's mind assessing the verisimilitude of the Korean's claim.

"I'd like you to come with me to Moscow to show this book to Comrade Stalin. We will leave in the morning," said Beria, with a dismissive wave of his hand indicated that their session was over.

Stalin was impressed with the potential of the Ishii journal. Kim's lack of ties to the Korean communist party would ensure that he would be malleable. The Soviet dictator anointed Kim the leader of North Korea. Over the post-war years, Kim solidified his control of the country and molded the Korean communist party in the form dictated by Stalin. In 1948, Kim became the prime minister of the DPRK.

Kim was so busy governing his country and formulating plans for its unification that he forgot about Ishii's diary. That is, until he received orders from Stalin to appear in Kharbovsk to validate the origin of the diary in the war crimes trials scheduled for the end of December 1949.

Looking out the window as the train sped through toward the Soviet Far East, Kim considered his current situation. After so many years of hardship, deprivation, and death, he was finally on the path to success. Aboard a train heading toward the city of Khabarovsk on the Amur River in the Soviet Union, he was on orders to attend the Russian Military tribunal that was adjudicating Japanese war crimes that had been committed during World War II. He was finally in a position to exact revenge for the evil that Japan had inflicted on his countrymen in Korea and Manchuria.

The train chugged steadily toward Soviet territory. As Kim stared vacantly through the cloudy glass at the barren winter landscape, his attention was distracted by movement on the train window. Watching rain worms traverse the train window was a welcome diversion. He silently applauded the upper squiggle when it merged with another stream and raced to the edge, outpacing the lower one. Maybe the rain worms are smarter than people he mused. His life had been forever changed when, much like the upper squiggle, he used the tactic of joining forces. In his case, his band of guerrillas joined the Soviets against the Japanese. This decision had swept him to his current position as the leader of North Korea.

Kim was traveling to the Khabarovsk War Crime tribunal at the behest of his Soviet comrades to right an egregious wrong that had been committed by General MacArthur. At the conclusion of WWII, General MacArthur convened a tribunal in Tokyo to bring Japanese war criminals to justice. Although MacArthur's court convicted twenty-five of twenty-eight Japanese military and government officials of committing war crimes and crimes against humanity, the general shocked and offended the world when he granted immunity to Dr. Ishii and much of Unit 731. MacArthur justified his action by advising the Joint Chiefs of Staff that information compiled by Unit 731 would be retained in intelligence channels instead of being used in the war crimes tribunal. This data, which the U.S. could not otherwise obtain, was traded by Ishii for freedom from prosecution.

Stalin, who had no humanitarian compunction about Unit 731's activities, seized the opportunity to embarrass the United States and General MacArthur. The Soviet dictator convened his own war crimes tribunal in Khabarovsk in order to prosecute officers of Unit 731 who were in Soviet custody. Twelve Japanese physicians and military officers were charged with aggressively 'manufacturing and employing bacteriological weapons' and conducting inhumane experiments on prisoners and others. The defendants were accused of infecting their victims with typhus, anthrax, cholera and bubonic plague, subjecting POWs to vivisection, and horrific experiments involving exposure to frigid conditions.

Unit 731 callously referred to their victims as *maruta*, the Japanese word for wooden logs. There was evidence showing that over 10,000 prisoners died in horrible agony as a result of these activities. Among the other crimes alleged to have been committed by the officers of Unit 731 was the development of delivery systems for bacteriological weapons used for the dispersal of disease-infested fleas into the countryside of China and the U.S.S.R. resulting in epidemics of grave diseases.

The lead Soviet prosecutor called for Kim to testify about his acquisition of Dr. Ishii's journal. Kim would establish the provenance of the document and get it into evidence. Once it was admitted into evidence, the prosecutor would have an expert translator testify about the damning contents of the journal. Despite a nervous, sleepless night before he was scheduled to testify, Kim looked forward to bragging about his successful raid of the Unit 731 compound that yielded Dr. Ishii's journal.

CHAPTER

6

Soviet War Crimes Show Trial

"'Duty,' 'Honor,' 'Country' - those three hallowed words reverently dictate what you want to be, what you can be, what you will be. They are your rallying point to build courage when courage seems to fail, to regain faith when there seems to be little cause for faith, to create hope when the hope becomes forlorn."

~ General Douglas MacArthur

There were days during boot camp that all Junior wanted to do was to cry. He was not alone, of course, but as the weeks passed the urge to cry lessened. He was still prone to nightmares, but now they typically involved intense training episodes that often featured a nose-to-nose confrontation with Gomax.

It would never have occurred to DI Gomax that Junior, or any other recruit for that matter, should receive special treatment on account of some unique circumstance. The drill instructor's primary job was to instill discipline. As his DI had drummed into his skull, "If you all have discipline, you can depend on the Marine next to you, and you will survive!"

That was his credo when he taught military courtesy, discipline, guard duty general orders, special orders, first aid, weapons, and Marine Corps history in the classroom. And, that was his credo when he trained them in the field. They learned the importance of close order drill, fire watch, and guard duty. They spent many days at the range mastering a variety of weapons and explosives. Gomax took them on field marches to the gas chamber, the bayonet, and hand-to-hand combat pits.

*   *   *

The DI excelled at squeezing every measure of effort from his men, leaving them bruised and limp at day's end. Each day, Gomax pushed the company to within a gossamer's width of collapse. Gomax drove them relentlessly to exceed their own limitations. As boot camp progressed, Junior became stronger physically and, more important, mentally. With the realization that he was capable of performing tasks that he never imagined, Junior's confidence grew.

At the beginning of the cycle, Gomax paired up the recruits by last name. Although it was a coincidence that Junior and Arlo were buddied up, the DI was pleased. Gomax knew, like a master psychologist, that they would complement and support each other. He was right. By the end of the first week, the tough city kid from Baltimore and the black hillbilly from Appalachia had bonded and were inseparable.

Whether it was learning how to march, or, the techniques of hand-to-hand combat, or, any of myriad skills taught during boot camp, Junior and Arlo dove into the training with enthusiasm. Arlo won the distinction of top marksman, while Junior scored highest in camouflage.

One day they were assigned to garbage can duty. Arlo and Junior not only cleaned every speck of residue; they made those cans shine so much that the mess sergeant almost fell down the backstairs because he was blinded by the reflection coming off the cans. He accused them of surreptitiously buying brand new cans. Only intervention by Gomax saved them from peeling potatoes for a week.

Several weeks into the cycle, the recruits marched deep into the woods. They passed a sign that announced:

DANGER Rifle Range – Caution Live Ammo.

Gomax led them to a rudimentary amphitheater of wooden benches.

"I am Gunnery Sergeant Texas Howard. I will be your Marksmanship Instructor for the next three weeks. This is an M1 Garand rifle. It weighs 10.5 pounds with a bayonet attached," he said holding up a weapon. "Y'all have been carrying one for six weeks now, y'all have cleaned it and slept with it. Why?

"I'll tell y'all why? Because this is my rifle. There are many like it, but this is mine. It is my best friend. It is my life. Without me, this rifle is useless. Without my rifle, I am useless. No matter the job the Marines give you, every Marine is a rifleman. Always. Even if you become a cook or a clerk, y'all are a Marine rifleman!

"What does every Marine rifleman have?" he said scanning the amphitheater. "Well, every red-blooded Marine has a red, hot lover – some of y'all are virgin maggots. So, I'm gonna give y'all something to love. This here rifle! When y'all come back tomorrow. Your rifle will have a name. My rifle is Wanda. What's y'alls called?"

Junior pondered that question until late into the night, then he recalled his uncle telling him about the Valkyrie of Germany. His favorite Valkyrie was "the wild and stormy one."

The next day at the rifle range, the recruits lined up in formation and directed to "Port, ARMS." From that position, they were ordered to sound off with the name of their rifle.

When it came to Junior's turn, he shouted, "Kára, sir!"

"While y'all are on my range y'all will obey every safety rule. We don't want y'all to get shot dead, before y'all have a chance to go home and beat the shit out of Jody who has been dicking y'all's honey pie while y'all been on this island paradise."

That got through to the group. A moment of homesickness flashed through the mind of each man. DI Howard fired a blank round into the air. A few of the recruits nearly jumped out of their skins at the sound.

"Safety first! Say it. Safety first!"

After the instructor talked them through the safety rules, he made them memorize them until they could repeat them by number on cue. The trainees learned different firing positions, how to aim, compensating for the wind and how to adjust their sight's elevation.

"You will learn to field strip your rifle and re-assemble it – blindfolded – in the dark – during a shitstorm."

He let that sink in.

* * *

Kim arrived at the Soviet Army Officers' House where the trial was held and studied the dock and the balconies of the colonnaded hall. Picturing himself mesmerizing the gallery with his testimony, he smiled. His reverie was interrupted by one of the Russian prosecutors.

"Ah, Comrade Kim, you are here early. That is good. Unfortunately, the defense team has conceded to the genuineness of the journal and its chain of custody. Therefore, we no longer need your testimony to admit the journal into evidence. Thank you for your trouble," said L. Smirov, the State Prosecutor.

Just like that Kim was deprived of his shining moment. His disappointment was somewhat assuaged when the lead prosecutor gave him Dr. Ishii's journal as a souvenir of the war crimes trial. As Kim turned to leave, the prosecutor handed him a sheaf of papers.

"These are the translation. You might need them someday," said Smirov.

Kim thanked him, folded the papers and stuffed them into the journal.

The following day, a deflated Kim boarded the same train for a return trip to P'yŏngyang. He regretted missing the opportunity to witness the historic guilty verdicts that were rendered after only six trial days. The tribunal deliberated for a total of five hours. Most of those convicted were sentenced to prison terms of twenty to twenty-five years; however, pursuant to a secret deal, they were released in 1956.

During the train ride back to P'yŏngyang, Kim contemplated the course of recent events and had to admit that his circumstances had improved immeasurably. He was the Supreme Leader of the DPRK with the trust and confidence of Joseph Stalin, the most powerful man of the communist world. Kim's fortunes were ascendant.

Mindlessly, he fiddled with the journal, thinking how he might utilize it to demonstrate his central role in the war crimes trial. He was already thinking of establishing a state museum to preserve memorabilia of his achievements. Along with pictures of the Deplorable Dozen, as the newspapers called the criminals, this journal would form a nice museum display.

As he ran his fingers over the cover, he noticed that the sheaf of papers was so thick that it had caused the cover to bulge to the point of tearing. On removing the papers, Kim noticed a seam inside the lining of the journal. With his penknife, he sliced open the seam. Folded into the back cover was a piece of paper that would confound Kim for years.

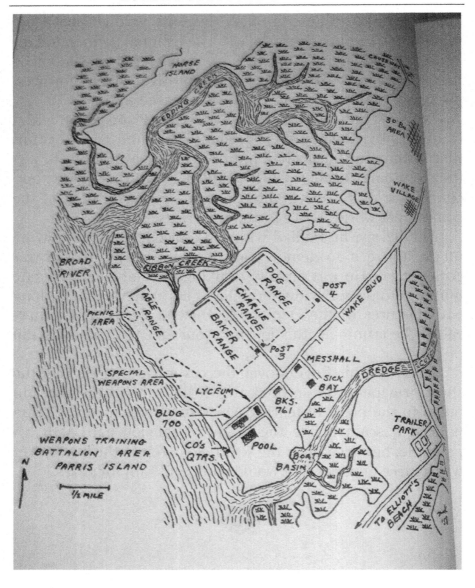

CHAPTER

7

The Crucible

*Cru·ci·ble, [ˈkroōsəb(ə)l], noun, a place or situation
in which concentrated forces interact to cause or
influence change or development.*

~ Merriam-Webster Dictionary

When Gomax's platoon marched through the training facilities at Parris Island, they had transformed into a salty platoon, experienced, confident, toughened. Each time the platoon excelled in an activity it would receive a ribbon to hang on their platoon guide-on. The recruits would take turns carrying the flag festooned with ribbons. It was a great honor. Junior recalled one afternoon when he was carrying the guide-on as they passed the Marine Recruit Depot and hearing the DI berate the new recruits.

"Don't you look at them. Don't you dare eye-ball them salty troops. You don't deserve to look at them, maggots!"

Junior's step quickened and his eyes moistened at the realization of how far his platoon had progressed. They were actually close to becoming Marines.

The weeks flew by and Gomax directed their training toward the three-day finale of boot camp. The extended ordeal was known as the crucible and was designed to test their knowledge, skill, and endurance. Failure in the crucible meant repeating boot camp, or worse.

Apprehension among the recruits grew as the time for the crucible drew nearer. Rumors, superstitions, and fantastical accounts of ancient blood rituals circulated through the company. No one knew how stories of bizarre happenings spread; but there was reason to suspect certain DIs as the propagators. It seemed odd that the rumored ogres would assume a trait particular to the nationality of one or another of the instructors. In any event, the lore associated with the crucible had the effect of setting the recruits on edge.

The crucible did not start out well for Junior and it ended worse than he could ever have anticipated. One of the early parts of the three days was a field simulation of a battle known as capture the flag. Junior was assigned to the scarlet team with the objective of capturing the gold team's flag. Naturally, the gold team was tasked with defending their flag and capturing the scarlet flag. The competition took place in a swampy area well beyond the rifle range in an area that the recruits had not entered previously.

The teams wore arm bands corresponding to the color of their flag. Each recruit was issued a rifle loaded with wax blanks. Team leaders were chosen by the team and they were given an hour to reconnoiter and formulate offensive and defensive plans.

The hour passed quickly and Junior was designated as an advance scout who would probe gold's defenses and report back. After trekking through miles of woods, Junior successfully located the gold flag. Using his talent for camouflage, he approached within twenty yards and counted the number and location of defenders. Exhilarated, he reversed his steps and headed back toward scarlet's base camp.

About halfway back, he spied a gold patrol. Improvising, he changed course to elude them and it was not long before he was lost. Since he was deep in the forest, he was unable to orient his direction using the sun. To avoid going in circles, he notched trees with his bayonet. Making his best estimate, he headed toward what he hoped was scarlet base. Above the quiet of the woods, he heard trickling water and smelled the distinctive odor of decomposition. The stench threatened to overwhelm him. He inhaled through his nostrils and exhaled slowly through his lips as Gomax had instructed them to do when sighting a target. It worked.

Junior recalled that the rudimentary map given by the drill instructors depicted a swamp not too far from where they had established their base. The base must be near he thought. He pushed aside some branches and stood before the most amazing sight he had ever encountered.

Down a slight decline, he observed what could only be described as a swamp rainbow. The unique combination of plant oil, pollen, and tannic acid created a film that acted like a prism illuminated by the fading sun. Light streaming through the forest canopy hit the water at the perfect angle, refracting into colors of such vibrancy that Junior was awestruck. The palette of hues winked at him as the water rippled ever-so-slightly in the breeze. The colors radiated morphed and sparkled in kaleidoscopic shapes. He concentrated, trying to emblazon the scene in his mind. Junior imagined focusing his camera to capture this splendor. He was so transfixed by this miracle of heaven that he drifted into another world. Why had he been chosen to experience this spectacular rainbow?

He failed to hear footsteps approaching. But then, many enemy soldiers had failed to hear this Marine approach. It was Gomax, the skilled assassin.

"Maggot! You're dead!"

Startled, Junior wheeled toward the voice. His rifle slipped from his shoulder. The butt hit the ground hard and the weapon discharged. Gomax winced, his hand rushing to his cheek. A wad of hot wax burned as it spread over his skin.

"Godammit, you fool. You could have shot my eye out," he screamed as he scraped the hardening wax off his blistered face.

"I'm sorry, it was an accident," Junior repeated over and over, until Gomax threatened to throttle him if he said it one more time.

Junior spent the rest of the day in the cemetery for recruits captured or killed during the flag exercise. Gomax said nothing of the circumstances of Junior's capture, just that he was disqualified.

For Junior, the next day and a half of the crucible were uneventful. He aced the obstacle course and was instrumental in his team's success in various problem-solving challenges. He did not realize that Gomax was biding his time.

On the final morning of the crucible, Junior and Arlo broke down their tent and carried their gear on their backs like the others in the platoon. They were excited at the prospect of completing the ordeal and being declared Marines. Gomax informed them that their cumulative scores were good enough to be in contention for cycle honors, provided they did not fuck up the final challenge. Their assignment was to navigate numerous natural and man-made obstacles as a team, cross Ribbon Creek and then double-time to a pre-determined location for further instructions. The first platoon to reach the finish line would get the max points and probably win the competition.

Confident and anxious, the men moved out, chanting to a familiar cadence.

As the platoon passed the Armory, Gomax barked, "Junya! Report ta da Armory an' secure a weapon."

"Sir, I have my trusty M1, sir. Her name is Kára, sir. She is clean and mean, sir!"

"Are you dis-obeying me, maggot?"

"No, sir. The private will go to the Armory, sir."

Junior followed Gomax to the Armory window.

"This recruit gets this," said the DI, pointing to a Browning Automatic Rifle.

"A BAR?" said the dispensing corporal, incredulously.

"Yes, plus this twelve-magazine belt and combat suspenders, with three or four extra magazines for his pockets. This is the typical accompaniment for combat."

Junior scooped up the gear and strapped it on. The M1918 Browning Automatic Rifle was a heavy automatic rifle utilized by the Marines as a portable, light machine gun. It was capable of firing between 500 – 650 rounds per minute. The BAR weighed 16.5 pounds. The ammo nearly doubled the weight.

Off to the side, Gomax touched the blistered skin on his face and smirked. This petty act of revenge would have dire consequences for both men.

"What the fuck?" said Arlo when he saw Junior emerge from the Armory. "You look like David Morgan's swamp mule, loaded for an excursion to help General Washington."

"Who?" said Junior with a slightly annoyed, dismissive tone. Then, he turned away, preferring to be alone with his thoughts. Outside the Armory, Gomax happened to come into Junior's line of sight, but he refused to make eye contact.

The final day of the crucible went without incident, until the end. The plan was a five-mile forced march to the finish line terminating near the mess hall. The route was to sweep through the wooded area, negotiate the obstacle course and cross Ribbon Creek at its narrowest point before completing the course.

The recruits climbed and crawled over and through the walls, hurtles and pits. The DIs watched with anger etched on their faces as the soldiers exhorted each other and teamed to navigate the obstacles.

The mud crawl under barbed wire while tracer bullets whizzed over their heads was especially difficult because it presented a situation where soldiers might panic. The combination of the noise, cold mud that infiltrated every part of your body, and the visual danger of the tracer rounds that blazed through the air was designed to rattle even well-rested soldiers. These recruits were exhausted, after having expended every ounce of energy over the past few months.

A trough of mud faced Arlo who slid onto his belly and entered the pit. Arlo cradled his M1 in his arms as he pushed his legs, grabbing purchase with his boots pressing into the mud. Junior was directly behind him. The rat-tat-tat of the machine guns was deafening and made more fearsome by intermittent firing. Some men flinched at the fiery tracers passing overhead, others at the firing that came in unpredictable bursts. Even though the course was outside in the open, the layer of barbed wire that criss-crossed over them, gave more than a few recruits an irrational feeling of confinement. Claustrophobia in an open field.

Junior followed Arlo, wedging one foot after another into the squishy brown ooze with dogged determination. He cursed when his foot slipped and his knee scraped against a rock. He took a deep breath and cursed the mud, the bullets, the wire. He humped up to resume his crawl. Something tugged at his back.

An expletive escaped his lips as he turned to see the problem. His magazine belt was snagged on the wire.

"Arlo, I'm stuck," he hissed when the machine fire ceased for a second. His friend froze, then wiggled back to Junior.

"What's up?"

"I secured the extra magazine belt to my backpack. Now, it's caught on the effin' wire."

"Scootch over to your right."

Junior slid sideways.

"Your other right, maggot," said Arlo with obvious levity in his voice.

"You're a regular Bob Hope," grunted Junior as he moved over.

Arlo wiggled his way next to Junior and waited for the machine guns to stop. Just as he got to his knees, the firing resumed. He dove face first into the mud.

"Fuck!" both men screamed.

At the end of the course, their platoon mates screamed encouragement. Gomax stood with arms crossed, glowering at the delay. The other platoons were progressing smoothly through the course.

Arlo made several attempts to wrench the magazine free of the thorny wire. He was unsuccessful.

"The barbs have pierced the leather strap, I can't pry it loose."

They slumped in the mud, disconsolate.

"Arlo, you go ahead. Get through so that you can graduate. I'll figure something out. Go!"

Tears were in Junior's eyes. He cursed at the prospect of failing boot camp, but he couldn't bear responsibility for his buddy failing also.

"Stop it, Junior. We make together, or not at all. You're the smarty. Now think!"

Junior shifted and felt something jab against his thigh.

"I've got it, Arlo. Here, take my toothpick and cut the damn ammo belt."

"Right, why didn't I think of that."

Over the next few minutes Arlo used the bayonet to hack through the leather, freeing Junior. The troops at the end of the mud pit cheered and whooped. Arlo emerged first, followed by a smiling Junior. His elation ended when he made eye contact with Gomax who glared at him with a malevolence reserved for Satan himself.

The platoon was energized as they headed toward the last few miles with the worst behind them, or, so they thought. A slight breeze blew toward them. It carried the aroma of a feast to come. The soon-to-be Marines salivated without realizing why. All they knew was that they were ready to celebrate completing boot camp. What they did not know was that there were rumors of a sizable wager between Gomax and another DI.

The plan was to double-time to Ribbon Creek, then cross at its narrowest point. From there it was a short march to the Mess Hall. When they got to the creek, Gomax entered the water and, rather than crossing it, turned right, marching with the creek. The platoon followed.

The ebbing tide created a swift current in Ribbon Creek. The soft marshy bottom made walking treacherous. It was as if their boots were being sucked off their feet. As Gomax walked further, he heard some grumbling in the ranks. The water rose from their thighs to waists and the armpits of some. The DI ordered them to carry their weapons above their heads to keep them dry. M1s were lifted high. In the rear Junior struggled to keep his balance with the heavy BAR above his head.

Gomax trudged along, oblivious to the splashes and muttered curses behind him. In his anger and disgust, he forged ahead without regard to the separation from his men. The recruits were more than uncomfortable, they were on the verge of hypothermia. The sun was below the tree line. They were up to their chests in chilly water that sapped their core body temperature.

Junior's teeth chattered. He had lost feeling in his feet. He stumbled, struggling to stay above the surface. He heard something snap in his shoulder. The BAR tilted and the barrel grazed the water as his arm buckled.

"Junior, are you okay?"

He slurred in reply.

"What?"

Junior stepped into a hole and sank. The BAR disappeared into the murky water. Arlo slung his rifle across his neck and waded toward Junior, splashing his arms before him to go faster.

"Help! Junior's in trouble. We gotta get him."

Several of the recruits raced to help. Arlo dove, reaching desperately below the surface. After an interminable moment, he resurfaced, gasping for air.

"I can't find him."

He threw off his pack and dove again. Swimming vigorously with the current, his hand felt something solid. He grabbed. It was the leather ammo belt. Arlo tugged and felt resistance. His heart leapt. Junior's at the other end. He followed the belt until he reached his buddy.

"I got you," he said half to himself, as he struggled to find footing. His legs pumped like pistons in a racecar. The current fought him and he started to lose traction. If his feet slipped, he would go under, too. There was a splash behind him and he felt strong arms grab him around the chest.

Seeing the dire situation, the other recruits had scrambled up the bank and formed a human chain to pull Junior and Arlo to safety. They grabbed Junior under the arms and struggled against the current toward the steep slope. After a few tense moments, they reached shore and dragged Junior on his back. His lips were blue and his skin was the color of a fish belly.

"Quick, rub his arms and legs. We've got to get him warm," shouted Donato, the kid who was an ambulance driver from Connecticut. He straddled Junior's chest and started rhythmic pounding.

"Come'on, you bastard, breathe!"

CHAPTER

8

Audition for Combat Photographer

*"Build me a son, O Lord, who will be strong
enough to know when he is weak, and brave
enough to face himself when he is afraid, one who
will be proud and unbending in honest defeat, and
humble and gentle in victory."*

~ General Douglas MacArthur

During his first voyage on a troop transport ship, he had plenty of time to reflect on the previous six months. Junior was now a private first class in the United States Marines. As he viewed the endless expanse of the Pacific Ocean, he recalled how the Marine recruiter had told him that he would "see the world on Uncle Sam's dime." That certainly had been true. So far, he had endured boot camp in Parris Island, South Carolina, and traveled cross-country by train to Camp Pendleton, California where he had been trained as a Rifleman, Military Occupational Specialty 145.

His mind drifted to the day they graduated from boot camp and the intense pride he felt for all his comrades in arms. They were Marines. They earned it!

"Hey, Junior, we made it, man!" shouted Arlo who was rushing around hugging every marine within arm's length. With his arm in a sling, Junior joined in a group hug and the men jumped in unison. When the hubbub subsided, Junior and Arlo walked over to the mess where a celebratory meal was being served.

Off to the side, a man with a surly demeanor watched the festivities. A blistered scab covered his left cheek, a scar, on his right cheek. Ordinarily, he would have been at the center of these celebrations. His wispy moustache bristled against the rim of a brown-paper-bag-encased-pint bottle that he swigged. In an effort to blend into the crowd of relatives and well-wishers, he wore civilian clothes. He could not have worn his marine uniforms if he had wanted to because they were at the tailor's shop where his gunnery sergeant stripes were being replaced by the single chevron indicative of a private first class. That was the verdict of the board of inquiry – loss of rank and suspension without pay for two months. Another swig, another muttered curse. Gomax departed before he lost control.

"Hey, Arlo, did you get your orders?"

"Yes, Junior," he responded, pulling an envelope from his shirt. "I'm going to Fort Lee, Virginia, for training as a food service specialist in the U.S. Army Quartermaster School. Can you believe it? I got the MOS I wanted. Imagine me, a cook."

"That's great, buddy. I'm happy for you," said Junior, in a voice that betrayed his disappointment.

"What'd you get? Where are you headed?"

"I'm going to California to be trained in riflery."

"I'm sorry, Junior. I know you had your heart set on becoming a photographer. Don't worry. Things will work out for you. I know it."

The next morning, his best friend in the world boarded a bus and was gone. He wondered if he would ever see him again. Even though they promised to keep in touch, in their hearts, they knew that any communications would trickle to vapor.

He would never forget DI Gomax. He recalled the DI's version of the recruiter's mantra: "Join the Marines, see the world, meet interesting people and . . . kill them!" When he said this in a sign-song way, Gomax's face lit up with childish delight. The recruits laughed and would egg him on, relishing the venom-laced respite from training.

Junior chuckled at the memory of the very first day of boot camp. A low mist surrounded the barracks. It was dark and the nervous recruits huddled in groups waiting for the unknown. When Gomax appeared, cigarettes were snuffed and conversations ended. The DI walked to the center of the open yard.

"Mens, line up alphabetically by height!"

With the perspective of a Parris Island graduate, Junior laughed at the stupidity and panic that ensued. There was always a lesson behind even Gomax' most inane orders. Obey, think, think, obey. That was the Gomax he loved.

The Gomax he hated, well that was a different story, and Junior had a near-death experience to show for it.

* * *

It was 1949. Along with his fellow soldiers who had graduated from advanced training, Junior lined up at the railing and watched as Tokyo harbor drew closer. His orders were tucked away inside his shirt. He was to report to the headquarters of the Supreme Commander of the Allied Powers. The bus pulled up to HQ in the *Dai-ichi* Life Insurance Company building in the Chiyoda ward. Across the street was a serene moat that ringed the Imperial Palace.

"Good morning, gentlemen. I am Sergeant Major Angus Morgan," said a marine with a scowl that he had groomed over the last twenty years.

"We are in charge of General Douglas MacArthur's security detail. For those of you who have your heads where the sun don't shine, the general is a five-star general, the highest ranking officer in the Army. Here, in Tokyo, he is a god. The general does not like to be disturbed. Your duty will be to protect the general at all costs. You will do this as if you are invisible avenging angels from the Bible. You are to be as still as furniture and, under no circumstances are you to be heard. Am I understood?"

Hearing nothing, the sergeant major released the contingent to Master Sergeant Jones for further orientation, quarters, and shift assignments.

Jones explained that MacArthur was one of the most distinguished officers to ever serve in the armed forces of the United States. Not only had he graduated at the top of his class from the U.S. Military Academy at West Point, his record of achievement was unprecedented and would probably never be equaled. MacArthur demonstrated his military excellence in combat during both world wars and rose to the highest rank of five-star general.

Perhaps his greatest campaign was as commander of all U.S. army forces in the Pacific where his strategy of island-hopping recaptured valuable territory and defeated the Imperial Japanese military. MacArthur orchestrated the unconditional surrender of Japan on September 2, 1945 aboard the *U.S.S. Missouri*. He made an important decision to spare Emperor Hirohito and treat him with dignity. MacArthur saw this act of mercy as important to the psyche and morale of the people.

Named the Supreme Commander of Allied Powers (SCAP), MacArthur had absolute power over Japan. In the immediate aftermath of the war, his priorities focused on demobilizing the military, purging the fanatical militarists, and releasing political prisoners. Then, he set about restoring the war-ravaged economy which suffered from food and housing shortages. In order to achieve this, he imposed a liberal constitution that completely re-structured the society. MacArthur's reforms included modernizing real property ownership by replacing the feudal system of land ownership.

The so-called MacArthur Constitution provided women's suffrage, land reform, and instituting new policies relating to public health, education, and labor. Perhaps the most revolutionary aspect of the MacArthur Constitution was the "no-war clause" pursuant to which the Japanese people renounced war and included abolition of its armed forces.

"Despite all these accomplishments. Tokyo remains a dangerous place," said Sergeant Jones. "As you might expect, there are factions who hate Americans and there are communist subversives who want to undermine the general's reforms. So, don't let the calm surface fool you into thinking that this is a bullshit assignment. Trust me, it is every bit as dangerous as a war zone. Stay sharp and be safe."

Over the next several months, that warning faded. Junior fought boredom every time he stood guard duty. Often, the most exciting part of his day was to get a glimpse of MacArthur as he barged through the hallway surrounded by sycophants seeking his attention. The newly minted PFC was relatively ignorant concerning world affairs. In fact, when he first heard the word Korea, he had no idea what or where it was.

Even though the active hostilities of World War II had ended in 1945, the world had entered a new ideological war known as the Cold War. Almost immediately after WWII, the Soviet Union moved aggressively to expand its influence and dominance, particularly in Iran, Turkey, and with respect to nuclear arms control. President Truman announced the Truman Doctrine in March 1947 when he said, "[It is] the policy of the United States to support free peoples who are resisting attempted subjugation by armed minorities or by outside pressures." This change in American foreign policy was in direct response to the forcible expansion of Soviet totalitarianism.

Tensions between the U.S. and the U.S.S.R. increased dramatically in 1948, when Stalin challenged the western powers by imposing a blockade around the city of Berlin, Germany. That city was situated within the territory of East Germany, but had been divided after the war equally among the victorious powers. Not wanting to risk an armed conflict on the ground, Truman circumvented the blockade by going over it. At the height of the Berlin Airlift an Allied plane carrying life-giving supplies arrived in West Berlin every thirty seconds. Eventually, Stalin blinked and withdrew the blockade fifteen months later, in May 1949. The situation in the East was no less perilous.

Across the Sea of Japan, the civil war that had raged in China for decades culminated in victory to the communist forces of Mao Zedong, and the defeat and exile of the nationalist forces of Chiang Kai-shek to Taiwan (previously called Formosa). In the autumn of 1949, Mao declared the birth of the People's Republic of China. Naturally, the Chinese Communist regime aligned with the Soviet Union.

There was another nation on the other side of the Sea of Japan that was primed to become the collision point of Soviet Communist expansionism, Chinese Communist fragility and the concern in the United States over the "Red Menace." That nation was Korea, which by agreement at Yalta had been divided at the 38th parallel – the Soviets controlling the north and the western powers, essentially the Americans, controlling the southern portion of the Korean peninsula. Korea was divided at the waist of the peninsula, along the 38th parallel. Soon, events would conspire to create an intolerable situation and MacArthur would face one of the most severe and challenging military crises of his career.

MacArthur commandeered the top floor of the insurance office building. It was where he and his senior officers worked to reconstruct Japan into a constitutional democracy. Due to the limited number of support personnel working on that floor certain accommodations were made. Among them was the use of the break room where personnel could go for a hot beverage. The room was shared by all personnel who worked on the top floor. There was a universal understanding that access to the coffee station was a courtesy for enlisted men and they were to steer clear of the officers and vacate when an officer entered, or was present. Occasionally, officers would converse with senior noncommissioned officers in order to expedite certain matters. Everyone, even the field-grade officers, knew that to get something done, the noncoms made things happen.

One night after midnight, when Junior entered the break room for a cup of coffee, two men were already there. They apparently did not see him. Junior lingered and he overheard an intriguing conversation that would change the course of his life. A brigadier general advised the sergeant major that another one of MacArthur's photographers was missing in action and that it was imperative that they find a replacement as soon as possible. Junior raised his eyebrows and leaned in to hear any additional details. The sergeant major saw Junior, and stiffened.

"What do you think you are doing, private?"

"Sir, I just wanted to get a cup of java . . . I can leave."

"No, no," interjected the general. "finish getting your coffee. Lord knows, guard duty requires caffeine."

Junior half-bowed in appreciation. The general had seen enough action in WWII that he had a soft spot for individual enlisted men. Besides, Junior reminded him of his grandson back in New Jersey.

"Where are you from, son?"

"Me, sir?" said Junior, surprised that the general was engaging him in conversation. The sergeant major leaned back slightly out of the general's line of sight and glared at Junior with a world-class scowl. The general nodded.

"Baltimore, sir."

"Ah, Baltimore, one of my favorite cities. My wife is from nearby Ellicott City. I remember meeting Babe Ruth in his father's bar. He was the greatest ever. It's a shame that he died so young last year."

"Sir, my father loved him also. He cried when Babe died," said Junior.

During the silence that followed, the sergeant major tapped his foot and signaled with his eyes that Junior better scram. Junior ignored him and decided to go for it.

"Sir, permission to speak freely."

"What's on your mind, son?"

The sergeant major glowered and coughed. The general raised his hand with a "have patience" gesture. The sergeant major harrumphed.

"Begging your pardon, sir, I heard you mention an opening for a combat photographer. I was wondering how one goes about applying for that job."

"Can you shoot pictures in the daytime without being seen or heard?"

"Yes, sir, I think I can be real sneaky when I have to be," said Junior.

The general chuckled and turned to the sergeant major, "I want you to get this boy an audition for the combat photographer position before the end of the week."

"Thank you, sir!" said Junior, drawing himself to his full height and snapping off his best-ever salute, before executing a flawless about-face and exiting the room.

Three days later, the officer in charge of the guards approached Junior and said, "I don't know what you did, but you are to report to the gunnery sergeant downstairs in one hour. You're going to take some pictures."

Junior hustled downstairs and waited at the curb admiring the image of the Imperial Palace in the reflection pool in front of it. Just as Junior was framing a picture in his mind, the serenity of the scene was interrupted by a jangle of metallic noises and a dirty cloud of exhaust. As the jeep rumbled up to him, Junior stared at the sudden armed presence. The vehicle gave off an ominous vibe.

A .50 caliber machine gun was mounted on a pedestal in the back. Perched on a makeshift metal bar he used as a seat, was a burly marine in full combat gear, steel pot, and flak jacket. Wearing a sleeveless shirt, the gunner's arms glistened in the midday sun. Junior envied his python-like arms that were decorated with "Mom" emblazoned over one arm and "Semper Fi" spanning the globe-and-anchor on the other. The marine pursed his lips and spit a steam of tobacco juice onto the pavement at Junior's feet.

"You, Junior?" barked the driver. "Get in!"

Junior's butt barely made contact with the seat before the jeep sped from the curb. Between shifts, the driver handed Junior a camera.

"Here's your camera. Take care of it. The last guy didn't make it."

Junior gaped at the reddish-brown streak along the viewfinder and realized that it was dried blood. An image of the last photographer sprawled over the device sent a chill down his spine. A metal container at his feet was filled with film packets.

"Listen, kid. We're going through some of the roughest streets of Tokyo. There's a lot of hostility out there. Snipers and such. Watch your ass and take your pictures. If it gets hot, we're flying out of there."

A distant rat-a-tat-tat, rat-a-tat-tat, punctuated the driver's advice. Junior concentrated his shots on alleyways and rooftops, anywhere he thought there might be a threat. The jeep turned into a shantytown of corrugated metal shelters, leaning haphazardly on each other like a bunch of drunks. Junior tried to ignore the deplorable living conditions and focused in on faces. A shot rang out and a round pinged off the shield protecting the gunner.

A deafening roar followed as the machine gun spit out hot lead with frightening speed. The hair on Junior's head spiked at the sudden tumult. His ears rang as if he were in an echo chamber. He jerked the camera when the .50 cal opened up again. Cursing himself, he steadied his breathing and pressed the camera against his chest.

The driver pointed toward a parapet and the gunner swung the weapon up, peppering the surface with bullets. During a pause to reload, another shot ricocheted off the jeep. The driver fired a burst at the sniper. Junior snapped several shots and captured the sniper reeling back as a round split his skull. Anticipating others escaping, Junior focused his lens on the windows and captured several figures retreating into the shadows. He snapped pictures of men in black outfits in the alley.

"Better skedaddle. Hold on, Bronco," shouted the driver as he accelerated the jeep away from that neighborhood.

"Hey, Gunny, don't you think it's time for lunch?" shouted Bronco, who was gripping the machine gun with one hand and holding his helmet on with the other. A maniacal laugh poured out of his mouth.

"You got it," said the gunnery sergeant, who steered the vehicle toward a shopping district where dozens of restaurants lined the streets. They were not far from the docks. A pungent, salty odor permeated the air. Junior wiped perspiration off his forehead with the back of his sleeve. The image of the shattered skull of the sniper sapped his appetite.

"Gunny, I'm not hungry. If it's okay with you, I'll just walk around the docks and shoot some more pictures."

"Suit yourself, private. Just remember that there are plenty of slant-eyes who will slit your throat if they get a chance. They will take pot shots at you, so, stay alert!"

"Yeah," Bronco said, "The world needs more lerts!"

He slapped Junior hard on the back. "Get it, kid, more lerts?"

Junior almost lost his balance, then, gaped in disbelief at Bronco. Junior gave him a wry smile and walked toward the bustling port. Where his eye wandered, his lens followed. Junior captured images of men straining to lift cargo, stacks of waiting machinery and, of course, faces of a wide array of nationalities inhabiting the scene. He used his lens to direct light onto the film where chemicals stored the image for developing in the darkroom. Junior took pictures from his knees, stomach and every angle he could manage. At one juncture, a security guard almost swatted him with his truncheon while Junior balanced on a bollard to peer into a tugboat.

When they arrived back at the HQ, Junior asked the sergeant major, "Who do I take my film to for developing?"

"You're it," he said. Chuckling at the look on Junior's mug, he pointed down the hall. "Dark room's down there."

Junior had taken several hundred images, and he spent every second of his free time in that room, developing his pictures. His eyes were blood shot from lack of sleep and the chemical by-products of the developer, the fixer, and the stop bath.

Two days later, Junior walked to a large bulletin board that had been installed outside MacArthur's office. The board was eight feet high by sixteen feet wide and was perched on a row of tables. It was there for candidates to pin their glossy black and white photographs for the general to review. The board was covered with vertical rows of pictures, two per candidate. The only space for Junior to pin his pictures was at the far right. Out of the two hundred photos he had taken, he chose the ones he liked, posted them and waited.

MacArthur's evaluation occurred a couple of days later at 0530. All the photographers were at attention at the bulletin board in front of their photos.

"AH-Tehn-SHUN! Officer on deck!"

MacArthur emerged from his office, puffing on his ubiquitous pipe.

As was his habit, he said, "Easy," to the men, rather than the more conventional "At ease."

MacArthur studied each row of photos with a magnifying glass. He questioned the photographers about various aspects of their submissions. Junior waited with his hands behind his back. His heart raced as he strained to see the general and listen to his comments. When MacArthur finished with the images of each candidate, he dismissed him with an aloof wave.

Sweat formed on Junior's forehead as he second-guessed his selection of photos. Why did he include that picture of the man pulling the rickshaw? He cursed himself for botching the developing of the first four pictures. Should he have increased the contrast on the last roll he developed? His stomach turned queasy. Was it nerves, or, the cloying pipe smoke? In his preoccupation, Junior lost track of MacArthur. Suddenly, the general loomed over him. At six feet, with impeccable posture, MacArthur cast a shadow over Junior. The young man's eyes shot upward and his Adam's apple imitated a yo-yo.

MacArthur peered through his magnifying glass at Junior's pictures. The general's face was inscrutable. Junior's right hand gripped his wrist so tightly that he lost feeling in his fingers. When he realized that he had not taken a breath in a while, he nearly panicked, not wanting to gasp in front of the general.

"You shot all these pictures yourself?"

"Yes sir," said Junior, glad for the opportunity to breathe.

"Anybody hear you?"

"I don't believe so, sir."

He looked at all of them, and he looked at Junior.

"Okay," MacArthur said and walked into his office, leaving a perplexed private and a trail of smoke in his wake.

CHAPTER

9

Seeking Stalin

To gain (the answer as to whether he would be cowardly in battle), he must have blaze, blood, and danger, even as a chemist requires this, that, and the other. So, he fretted for an opportunity.

~ Stephen Crane, *The Red Badge of Courage*

The Marines are a mobile strike force, trained to operate under extreme conditions, often without food or shelter. To prepare, marines learned to live in the field. Junior was no stranger to the field. He had to admit that he enjoyed the solitude of nature, that is, when there was no enemy trying to blow you to pieces. As he packed his photographic equipment into a small rucksack, he reflected on how he had arrived at this moment.

After overhearing by chance that the general needed a combat photographer, Junior auditioned for the position by taking images of whatever interested him in war-torn Tokyo. He had no idea how his pictures had impressed MacArthur. The pictures of several of the other candidates were suitable for postcards. Junior's were gritty and captured the least glamorous sections of the city. He had hesitated to include the shot of the sniper at the moment his head splashed open like a melon shot on the target range. Word filtered back to him that it was MacArthur's favorite.

The days after the bulletin board inspection of the photos of all the candidates were agony for the young private. In the mess, he just pushed his food around on his plate and drank coffee incessantly which caused him to toss in his bunk so much that his roommates banished him to the stairwell. Then, about a week later, while he pulled his shift, the sergeant major approached him.

"The general's office, now! And, Lord help you if you fucked up something."

Before he knew it, Junior was at attention in the office of General MacArthur who was looking out the window. Approaching seventy, MacArthur exuded power and charisma. He was tall with an imperious mien. Only traces of liver spots on his face and hands betrayed his age. His piercing, dark eyes were set in a nest of crow's feet. Blessed with prodigious intelligence, he did not suffer fools gladly. In dress and posture, he fostered an image of the rugged warrior complete with jutted jaw and fierce glare. One could not imagine him owning casual clothes, let alone actually wearing something like a cashmere sweater, or, Bermuda shorts. Rumor had it that the impeccable general slept in a starched set of utilities.

"Each month, eight to ten of our men are shot in Tokyo. We keep a lid on that information. We must maintain the appearance of peace, or chaos will surely follow," MacArthur said, in a voice bearing the slightest trace of command fatigue. He turned toward a board with Junior's pictures on it and examined several with his magnifying glass. With a sage look, the general nodded.

"The report from the gunnery sergeant who drove you when you took these pictures said that you were under fire from snipers or hostiles for most of time. I set it up that way to see how you perform under duress. In reviewing of your pictures, I cannot tell which ones were taken when they were firing at you. That's what I want. I need a photographer who can stay alive and bring back valuable intelligence, not pretty tourist pictures."

MacArthur touched Junior's elbow and, with the warmth of a grandfather counselling a grandson, said, "Are you sure you want to be one of my combat photographers?"

"Yessir, sure. Why not?"

Taking that as acceptance, the general was very explicit.

"We will have to stovepipe this. You follow?"

"No, sir, I have no idea what that means, sir."

The general's ears turned red. Then, he exhaled, catching himself from berating the soldier before him. MacArthur adopted the posture of a teacher coaxing a backward student up to the level of the rest of the class. He smiled.

"Every mission I assign you is top secret. Stovepiping means that you report only to me. You are not to tell anyone, nor talk to anyone about where you go, or what you do, you are not to say anything to anyone. Just me, no matter what, just me."

"Yes, sir. Okay, general."

"Not even your sergeant. Not even your mother. And, certainly not the enemy," MacArthur said as he handed Junior a small packet. "In case you are ever captured, bite down on this."

As man's creative mind invented new machines, systems, and technology, one of the first considerations was how could this be adapted to advance our selfish objectives. In other words, how could this new advance be used to subdue, that is, kill our enemies? Throughout the twentieth century, American military contractors had built the biggest, fastest, most powerful aircraft in the world. The result was that in the aftermath of WWII, the warbirds of the United States held overwhelming dominance over the skies.

While most aircraft companies built bigger, faster, heavier (and louder) aircraft, MacArthur saw the need for the opposite. Using funds earmarked for the reconstruction of Japan's industrial base, he authorized Project Ornithopter, named in honor of Leonardo DaVinci's fabled flying machine. The general engaged Piper Aircraft to build a plane to his specifications. He wanted a silent spy plane that could penetrate enemy airspace without detection.

When the chief engineer saw the specs, he remarked that the plans called for a plane so alien to progress that it would set aviation back decades. He assigned the project to Dominick Grainger, a brilliant young designer, who was not shackled by decades of rigid thought that had calcified military aircraft design. Grainger embraced the project and supervised the construction of an elegant hybrid between a Piper Cub and a glider.

The Ornithopter was built for silence. It was custom-fitted with mufflers and sound-proofing that made it as silent as the wind when using its engine. Depending on wind force and direction, the plane could glide indefinitely. Grainger realized that the wind was not always predictable and dependable. He solved this issue by developing an electric propulsion system for virtually silent operation at treetop altitude. The unique lightweight motor was powered by a battery charged when the aviation-fuel engine was in operation. To offset the weight, the Ornithopter was covered with a rayon skin. Other synthetic materials replaced metal parts where possible.

No detail escaped Grainger's attention. Taking his cue from the manta ray common to the Florida coast where he was raised, Grainger ordered the belly of the plane painted cumulous white so that from the ground, it would blend in with the sky. The top surface of the plane was painted in a mottled forest-green camouflage pattern to blend in with the ground when seen from above.

*   *   *

When future historians analyzed how all the parties arrived at the point of armed conflict in Korea in 1950 there were many explanations. Of course, greed, ambition, power, ideology, ignorance, misunderstanding, cultural differences, ego, and plain old evil contributed to the toxic storm that resulted in catastrophically bad consequences. From the macro conflict between communism and capitalism, the ill-conceived decisions made during WWII, the civil war in China, the end of colonialism, and the advent of nuclear weapons to the micro divisions within Korea exemplified by the diametrically opposed leaders, Kim Il Sung and Syngman Rhee, there was plenty of blame to go around.

Vice President Harry Truman ascended to the presidency when Franklin D. Roosevelt died in April 1945. Truman had been a haberdasher in Missouri before getting into politics. He was proud of saying, "I'm from Missouri. You've got to show me." He carried this pragmatism into his world view and made the difficult decision to unleash the atom bomb on Japan in order to save the lives of millions of Americans and Japanese that were projected to be lost in a ground invasion to conquer Japan.

Stalin wanted Soviet communism to dominate the world. While he firmly believed in force to achieve his goals, he preferred to engage in what became known as the Cold War, constantly pressuring the Western powers using means like the blockade of Berlin to test their resolve. One of his favorite sayings was "One should distrust words. Deeds are more important than words." Stalin viewed the withdrawal of American troops from the Republic of Korea as a deed of concession. Unfortunately, he miscalculated Truman's resolve. The Korean Peninsula would soon become a flashpoint for the clash of ideologies. The Cold War was about to turn hot, very hot.

Despite the pronouncement at the Cairo Conference that Korea would be free and independent, resolution of the Korean question would remain muddled after WWII concluded. At a December 1945 meeting of foreign ministers from the United States, the Soviet Union and Great Britain in Moscow, the then-Allies agreed that the Korean Peninsula would be divided at the 38th parallel for up to five years with the Soviets as trustees of the North and the Americans of the South. The failure to provide a definitive mechanism to achieve a free and independent Korea was a classic case of procrastination. The parties were blithely oblivious to the looming calamity.

Predictably, the United States and the Soviet Union could not reach agreement on the nature of a government for a united Korea. The issue was sent to the United Nations. In the spring of 1948, the General Assembly resolved that the UN would supervise elections for a national legislative body for both parts of Korea. South Koreans elected Syngman Rhee as president and representatives to the National Assembly which ratified a constitution for the Republic of Korea. The Soviets barred the UN Election Commission from holding elections in North Korea. Months later, separate elections were held and the Democratic People's Republic of Korea was established with Kim Il Sung as its new president.

Toward the end of 1947, President Truman made a fateful decision to reduce the size of American Armed Forces in South Korea once elections were held. The following year, 50,000 American military personnel were gradually withdrawn from the ROK. This decision to withdraw American troops in 1948 helped to alter the perception and reality of America's commitment to Korea.

Within this witches' brew of turmoil, one event stands out as perhaps the catalyst that started the death spiral to war. Junior's first mission was precipitated by a speech delivered by Secretary of State Dean Acheson to the Washington Press Club in January 1950. In it, Acheson delineated areas of importance to the United States in Asia. Conspicuous by its absence was any mention of Korea. Several world leaders took immediate notice – Stalin, Kim Il Sung, and Douglas MacArthur.

The distance between Pusan, Korea and Fukuoka, Japan was 133 miles, as the seagull flies. MacArthur knew that the speech by Acheson would be considered a signal that the United States would not intervene in an attempt by the Democratic Republic of Korea to conquer South Korea under the pretext of unification. The general knew that the problem would fall to him and he wanted as much information about the nature and size of the threat as he could get. That meant sending Junior across the 38th parallel behind enemy lines.

Sunrise was several hours away when Junior walked across the tarmac in Seoul to rendezvous with the plane that would take him on his first mission. Tiny ice crystals crackled under his boots. He could see puffs of his breath in the chill pre-dawn gloom. Although Junior had flown in small planes before, this one was unique. With a sleek body and its long wings drooping to the ground, the Ornithopter appeared to be a mythical bird in the instant before flight.

The nature of his mission was to conduct clandestine reconnaissance of enemy location and strength. The orders for this mission were simple. He would be dropped above the 38th parallel into North Korea. From there he was to proceed north until he discovered North Korean troop concentrations. He was to take pictures and bring the film back for MacArthur and his staff to analyze. He was to travel light and move fast, mostly under cover of darkness. The mission was to last three days – one day to trek in, a day of reconnaissance, and a day to trek out to the extraction point.

His rucksack contained his camera, a sighting scope, a map, red-flashlight, three-days-worth of canned meat and fruit from

C-ration packages, and a rudimentary first aid kit. He forgot to take the toilet paper, so he resorted to using leaves. His only weapons were his bayonet and .45 ACP M1911A1 pistol. These weapons were only to be used in extreme emergency. Otherwise, he knew what to do if captured.

* * *

In a wooded tract outside of Moscow, a ZIS limousine passed through a double-perimeter fence. It stopped at the guardhouse at the entrance to the winter home of the Soviet leader. The passenger strained unsuccessfully to view the dacha. His trained military eye detected several camouflaged 30-millimeter anti-aircraft guns. A thick forest of spruce trees surrounded the low, two-story dacha rendering it virtually invisible. Located in Kuntsevo, a community on the outskirts of Moscow, it was Stalin's "nearby" dacha, to distinguish it from his summer dacha in Sochi on the Black Sea. Painted forest green, the building blended into the terrain.

The Ministry of Internal Affairs (MVD) provided security for the premier of the Soviet Union. In 1946, the MVD replaced the dreaded and feared NKVD as the arm of government responsible for gathering intelligence and terrorizing political enemies of the regime. The name change was purely cosmetic. Stalin suffered from the paranoia that afflicts many dictators. A contingent of 300 special troops of the MVD guarded his dacha.

The guard saluted and waved the ZIS 110 up the hilly entrance. Kim Il Sung settled back into the plush upholstery of the limo. He smiled at the luxurious lifestyle of the ruling elite. Stalin was so enamored with the American 1942 Packard Super-Eight, that he ordered his technicians to reverse-engineer the car and build a Sovietized version. The initials ZIS stood for Zavod imeni Stalina, translated in English as 'factory named after Stalin.' The result was a fleet of limousines that were exactly like the Packard, except for the bullet-proof glass and figurine on the hood.

With a deep hum, the straight-8-cylinder engine powered the automobile up the steep drive. The limo circled the stone fountain set in a basin at the dacha's main entrance. Kim was pleased to see Colonel A.M. Ignatiev waiting for him. The colonel had helped Kim consolidate power over the party and government of North Korea by guiding him in the process of sovietization that the Soviet Communists had perfected in the post WWII era. Ignatiev knew that Stalin appreciated Kim's facility with the Russian language. Kim was a quick study who followed directions with a ruthlessness that the Soviets admired.

Ignatiev instructed the footman to bring Kim's luggage to the upstairs bedroom where Prime Minister Churchill had stayed when he visited Moscow in 1942. Kim considered the room assignment a significant upgrade from the room he had stayed in during his visit the previous year. He recalled how frustrated he was during that visit when his request for armaments and permission to proceed with his plans to invade the south were summarily denied. Over the last twelve months, the tide seemed to be moving in his favor. Based on the financial arrangements he had made before leaving P'yŏngyang, Kim was optimistic that the premier would see things Kim's way this time.

The front door opened to a wide hallway that was paneled with light, quarter-sawn oak. Along the hall there were large portraits of two comrades that Stalin admired – Vladimir Lenin, the architect of the bloody Bolshevik Revolution, and Maxim Gorky, the eloquent anti-Tzarist writer. To Stalin, the portraits were spectral reminders of the practical and aspirational aspects of the struggle. Like Lenin, Stalin never hesitated to engage in ruthless, brutal suppression of those who dissented from his edicts which were cloaked in flowery, idealistic rhetoric à la Gorky. As Ignatiev and Kim advanced toward the premier's office, the man who had adopted the Russian name for Man of Steel appeared.

"Comrade Kim, welcome to my humble abode," said Joseph Stalin. His arms were spread wide welcoming them into a large and bright room to the left of the hallway. His thick moustache, bushy eyebrows, and steely gray hair which was brushed straight back, provided artists and caricaturists with prominent features to dominate any representations of Stalin. These features drew attention away from his pockmarked skin, the residual reminder of a childhood bout with smallpox.

At 5' 6" Stalin was an inch shorter than his Korean counterpart. What nature had deprived the Soviet leader in height, it had over-compensated with a dominating presence that was punctuated by his ability to charm, or terrorize depending on the circumstances. He had dazzled and steamrolled Winston Churchill and Franklin D. Roosevelt at the 1943 Teheran Conference and again at Yalta in 1945. Being in Stalin's company was a challenge because his mercurial moods could transform a benign social event into a scene of carnage, physical or emotional. It was like having lunch with a Caspian cobra, a venomous species infamous for its bad temper.

Stalin was born Iosif Vissarionovich Djugashvili. His father was a semiliterate cobbler and his mother was a laundress. Despite his impoverished origins, he had a native intelligence that identified him as a future priest in his hometown of Gori, Georgia. While in the seminary he embraced Marxism and became an acolyte of Vladimir Lenin, leader of the Bolshevik Revolution. Throughout his career, Stalin was known for his use of violence, or as he called it "revolutionary methods" to achieve his objectives.

Kim and Ignatiev entered the dictator's office and stood before a wide table covered with military maps. A fire crackled and flared in an enclosure decorated with blue-and-white Delft tiles. Kim detected a hint of the demonic as the fire reflected in the Soviet's porcine eyes. Stalin reached for a bottle of clear liquid on an adjacent table and poured a generous amount into each of three tumblers. Passing them to his guests, he raised his glass and shouted.

"Nastrovia!"

The men gulped down the vodka and threw the glasses into the open fireplace. A butler appeared with a tray of blini and caviar and additional glasses. Another toast, and the process was repeated. As a warm feeling of conviviality spread through his core, Kim mimicked the dictator. Having spent the war years in the Soviet army, the Korean leader was familiar with their hard-drinking customs.

"Thank you, Comrade Stalin. It is indeed a great pleasure to be here again and spend time with you and my dear friend, Comrade Ignatiev. He has been invaluable in helping me consolidate communist authority in my country," said Kim.

Stalin smiled at Ignatiev.

"I can hardly believe that an entire year has passed since your last visit. I am anxious to hear how our economic and cultural alliance is faring. You know, we have committed considerable resources to assist in your economic development," said the Russian dictator.

Kim hesitated. He felt that it would be impolitic to blame failure on the Soviets who stripped the country of its industrial equipment when it withdrew in 1945. The Korean leader chided himself to remain focused. With his elbow he pressed against the packet of papers in his breast pocket. It was a list of all the arms and munitions his country needed from the Soviets. Don't get sidetracked with petty matters, he told himself. Soviet weapons will liberate the south.

"It goes well," he lied. "The initial two years have provided a solid base for future progress. I think we have reached the point where we must reunite my country," said Kim.

With a barely perceptible shake of his head, Stalin announced that dinner was served in the grand salon. Not used to being denied, Kim began to muster his arguments. Only a baleful stare from Ignatiev stopped him.

"I hear that the chef has prepared a stroganoff that will make you forget the bulgogi you eat in P'yŏngyang," said Stalin as he gestured to his guests toward the salon. Uncle Joe clamped a paternal hand on Kim's shoulder and escorted him to dinner. While walking along the corridor, Kim admired the parquet floors. Stalin replied, "I detest carpets. I prefer to hear the footsteps of those who approach. Don't you agree?"

CHAPTER

10

The Shark and the Beauty

"One should distrust words. Deeds are more important than words."

~ Joseph Stalin

After a sumptuous dinner, they retired to a veranda off the main corridor on the ground floor. Stalin walked to the banister and surveyed his domain. A rose garden, vegetable patch, and strand of fruit trees stretched out from the dacha. The air was redolent with the aroma of freshly turned soil.

"Comrade Kim, come here and smell the fertility of Mother Russia. Every spring we prepare the rich, black soil for planting, we work hard, and our Mother rewards us with the fruits of our labor in the autumn," he said, breathing in the fragrant night air.

Kim shuffled across the wooden deck. His movements sluggish as a result of consuming too much heavy Russian food. He was not used to dining so extravagantly. The deprivation of his guerrilla years had shriveled his appetite. His stomach gurgled in rebellion to the chef's generous use of *smetana*, Russia's version of sour cream. Kim forced a smile to his lips.

"Ah, yes, my comrade, the earth is the source of many blessings."

A butler lumbered toward them, brandishing a tray containing a box of cigars and a decanter of cognac. Stalin gestured to his guests to partake. Kim and Ignatiev puffed on cigars, lit by a liveried servant. Stalin followed suit.

In later years, Kim would recall this moment in vivid detail. Ignatiev toasted to the dictator as the self-declared "shining sun." That appellation stuck in Kim's craw because it was too

85

similar to the name that Kim himself had adopted during his days as a guerrilla fighting the Japanese. Kim had assumed the name Kim Il Sung, meaning "Kim become the sun." Stalin had even acknowledged that he had fashioned his title after the Korean's *nom de guerre*. Kim could only smile and mutter something about imitation being the highest form of flattery. He needed the support of the Soviet leader too much.

"This night reminds me of a similar visit one year ago where you and I agreed that it was not the right time to invade, excuse that crude word, to reunify your country. So, my Korean friend, tell me what has changed in the past year that warrants a reversal in our understanding?"

Kim drew on his cigar until the cherry glowed brightly. This was his chance, probably his only chance, to convince Stalin that his analysis was trustworthy. The Korean leader had rehearsed this moment in his mind endlessly. Now that it was here, Kim had trouble finding his voice. He fortified himself with a sip of cognac.

"We have successfully deployed thousands of guerrillas throughout South Korea. They await our signal to go into action with plans to sabotage and destroy essential infrastructure," said Kim, searching Stalin's countenance for acquiescence.

The Soviet dictator was so impassive that Kim thought that he might have fallen asleep. Only the incessant puffing of his cigar evidenced Stalin's consciousness. Kim sipped his drink and played his next card.

"The Korean Communist Party has 200,000 members who groan under the abusive government of Syngman Rhee. As soon as our forces cross the border, they will welcome us as liberators. We have a massive information program ready to launch along with our military campaign," Kim said. Recognizing that the Soviet leader was not going to engage in a dialogue, Kim forged ahead.

"With the withdrawal of American troops over the past year, the international situation has changed. Using Soviet tanks and heavy artillery, we will destroy Syngman's joke of army. We will overrun Seoul in a matter of days and conquer the peninsula in three weeks."

Kim Il Sung puffed vigorously on his cigar to reignite it. His eye caught his own reflection in a window. A thought flashed through his mind – the look of concern of his face mirrored his internal turmoil. He lifted his chin and peered at Stalin through cigar smoke. A cloud of smoke from Stalin wafted toward Kim's smoke. Ignatiev watched with amusement as his boss remained obscure. To Ignatiev's experienced eye, Kim's plea bordered on desperation.

Kim knew that his window of opportunity was rapidly closing. The U.S.S.R. was the only power capable of satisfying North Korea's military needs. He reached into his pocket and withdrew a packet of papers.

"Comrade Generalissimo, you are the Great Architect of Communism, a task that requires boundless resources. My humble country is a loyal ally and wishes to demonstrate it with these documents," said Kim. Simultaneously, he unfolded several documents, including certificates for tons of gold and silver. The Korean deftly slid the certificates under a list. With a flourish, he handed the list to Stalin.

"Comrade, this is a tally of our needs to reunite my country under the Communist banner. I won't bore you with the details – planes, tanks, ammunition, and other combat equipment . . ." he said, proffering the list.

Stalin waved it away. Ignatiev rescued Kim by taking the paper. Stalin pointed to the certificates. Kim almost hesitated to release the bearer instruments, but knew he had to comply. The Soviet leader riffled through the certificates, tabulating the amounts in his head. He smiled at the number totaling over 100 million rubles.

"Comrade Kim, this has been an instructive session. Our intelligence sources in the south confirm your analysis that the deterrent forces of the Imperialists have indeed vacated. I will present your proposal to the Politburo at our next session. Due to the changing international situation, I will support it and let you know their conclusion."

Kim had no way of knowing just how different Stalin's perspective of the world was. From Uncle Joe's perspective the most important events of 1949 were the establishment of Red China which guaranteed a communist ally in Asia, and his country's detonation of an atomic weapon. The U.S.A. no longer had a monopoly on the bomb and that dramatically changed any calculus.

Over the next several days, Kim huddled with Ignatiev and other military officials clarifying the list of needed armaments. Engineering and communications equipment were added. As far as Kim could tell, Stalin was absent from the dacha. Being away from P'yŏngyang wore on him. Finally, he could wait no longer and ordered his plane to prepare for departure.

When he arrived at the airfield the following day, Kim was surprised to see Joseph Stalin standing in the hanger.

"Comrade Stalin, it is a pleasure to see you. You have heard that events at home require my presence no doubt?"

Kim followed Stalin into a small office. The Soviet leader poured vodka.

"My friend, the Politburo has given approval for your plans to reunite your country as long as Comrade Mao agrees," said Stalin, raising his glass. Kim's grin faded as Stalin announced the condition for approval.

"Death to the puppet Syngman Rhee!" shouted Ignatiev, not wanting Kim to spoil the moment. After they drank, Stalin added, "If you should get kicked in the teeth, I shall not lift a finger. You will have to ask Mao for all the help."

As they walked toward Kim's plane, Stalin sprung one more surprise. When they approached Stalin's armored limousine the dictator reached into his pocket.

"Comrade Kim, as a token of our enduring friendship, take these keys. The leader of a united Korea deserves this beautiful example of Soviet technology."

Kim stood before the ZIS limo, his lower jaw dropped open in a lopsided grin that reminded Stalin of the traditional Russian folk clown. Kim saw himself reflected in the shiny exterior and his chest swelled. Clearly moved, Kim could only respond, "Comrade, you do me great honor. Thank you."

* * *

Standing on the tarmac in Seoul, Junior went through a mental checklist of the requirements for his first mission. A young officer in a flight suit approached Junior.

"I'm your driver this morning, sir," said the pilot. "Lieutenant Commander A.C. Hayfisch. Handle is Mako."

"Sir, this is the strangest looking bird I've ever seen. Is this thing going to fly?"

"For sure. It's based on the ideas of Leonardo DaVinci enhanced by the marvels of aerodynamic science. This baby will glide low over enemy territory as quiet as a whisper," said the pilot.

"You mean like one of those seabirds that glides just above the waves?" said Junior.

Mako nodded.

"Okay, then we'll call her the *Stormy Petrel*," replied Junior with self-satisfied grin.

"Sorry, she already has a name. This baby is the *Giocondo*," said Mako, patting the fuselage. Before Junior could pout, Mako said, "Time to mount up and put her through her paces."

A couple of hours later, the weather was clear and dry when Junior deplaned. Quickly finding cover in a strand of trees, he gave a half-wave to the *Giocondo* as it disappeared over the trees, barely louder than a whisper. He oriented himself and began his journey north, generally following the Ryesŏng River. Fueled by adrenaline and the desire to avoid disappointing the general, he covered fifteen miles and arrived at his objective just before dawn.

Junior was too jacked-up to rest. Disregarding instructions to sleep in the morning, he secreted his gear and brought his camera to the highest point in the area. There, he climbed midway up a tree and created a small foliage nest for his observation post. Using tree sap, bodily fluids, and armpit warmth, he spun his lair. When completed, it allowed light in, blended in so that it was undetectable from the outside. Junior descended from the tree and checked his work from every angle. Satisfied, he climbed back up for a much-needed rest.

As he drifted into a fitful sleep, Junior thought of his friend Arlo who by now was a full-fledged Marine cook. His last letter advised that he was being shipped out to a place that might be on the same continent as Junior. Arlo enjoyed his occupation, although he was still prone to burning his arms when handling field ovens. Junior's sleep included the smell of food cooking. He heard banter typical of soldiers waiting to eat.

"Hey, Cookie, where's the grub! We're starving."

"Calm down, go dig a latrine. It'll be ready when you come back."

He peeked out from his hideaway to see a platoon of soldiers congregating around one who was boiling a pot of whitish liquid. The aroma of rice wafted upward. Saliva filled Junior's mouth. He found himself drooling. His saliva traveled down twenty-five-feet and plopped into the pot of boiling rice. Conversation halted, eyes darted upward and a few soldiers reached for their weapons.

Junior willed himself awake at the subconscious realization that the words he heard were not English. Just in time, he intercepted the spittle in mid-flight, and wiped it on his sleeve. Now, fully alert, he froze. As the soldiers ate, Junior barely breathed. After an interval, a soldier who was much taller than the rest and who carried himself with an air of authority, barked an order in a language different from the first language. The order was echoed through the ranks and the soldiers moved out single-file.

Later, when Junior was debriefed by MacArthur in Tokyo, the young photographer learned that the initial language was Korean and the second was Russian. On this occasion, MacArthur adopted a "see, I told you so" expression to the officers assembled.

Back in the tree, Junior spent the next few minutes stifling a laugh at the image of his spit spoiling his enemy's lunch. His ribs ached. He wanted to guffaw, but knew that his life depended on silence.

He spent the rest of the day watching troops bivouac in the open meadow before him. It wasn't long before the noise of digging and shuffling of equipment was drowned out by the heavy grinding of military vehicles and artillery moving into position on a rise near the river. Junior took pictures until his thumb blistered from firing the shutter so often.

As the sun was setting, Junior packed his gear and disassembled his lair, careful to disperse the residue lest his future missions be compromised by discovery of an abandoned lair. His mantra was simple, take only pictures, leave no trace behind. He melted back into the country and headed back toward the extraction point.

Five hours later, he heard sounds that were consistent with a military group resting for the night. Restless turning, snoring, and flatulence combined to disrupt the woodland quiet. Junior could try to circumnavigate the enemy position, or rest himself until they moved out. He did not want to risk delay and jeopardizing his pick-up, so he decided to go around them. What Junior could not know was the nature of the unit that stood between him and his destination. It was a group of raw recruits fresh out of boot camp on their first venture. This factor would have significant consequences.

Junior was careful to keep the river within earshot while giving wide berth to where he thought the encampment was. The sounds of frogs and insects provided cover for his slow progress through the underbrush. The earth was soft beneath his fingers and it released a smell that reminded him of peat moss from his grandmother's garden. A scat-like odor reached his nose as his hand grazed some pellets. Deer or rabbit he thought. Just then, a water deer bolted in front of him and bounded across the field. As it passed him, Junior saw the creature's elongated tusks glinting in the dim light.

Suddenly, the night erupted with gunfire. There were flashes of light about two hundred yards off to his right. Bullets from the rifle of a jittery recruit standing guard whizzed into the shrubbery around him. He hunkered down, trying to control his breathing. Another burst of gunfire cut through the night. It was from his left. Another guard was firing at the first shooter. Junior was in the middle of a firefight.

Then, he heard the thud of a bullet hitting flesh and bone. The firing to his left stopped. Junior crawled rapidly toward the river. He wanted to get as far away from these lunatics as he could. Going hand over hand, slithering and crawling he moved as quickly as he could without making much noise. As he reached a small crest a hand grabbed his wrist. The grip was strangely clammy and it enveloped his wrist like a death vise.

Junior's heart nearly burst out of his chest. The sound of blood rushing through his veins pounded in his ears. He crept forward to see who had grabbed him. Fingernails dug into his skin. Barely visible in the scant moonlight, Junior saw the scared eyes of a teenager not much older than himself. The big difference was that the enemy soldier had a sucking chest wound as a result of a gunshot to the chest. A flash of confusion crossed the soldier's eyes as he comprehended Junior's features. Before the wounded soldier could scream for help, Junior clamped his free hand over the man's nose and mouth. He twisted and struggled to no avail.

Junior slithered away, his only concern now was to put distance between himself and the stirring camp. He heard orders shouted and hoped that the leaders would conclude that skittish guards had fired on each other. He estimated that he had a couple of hours of darkness to make his escape. Only then, would he have time to consider the intensity of his first real combat.

CHAPTER

11

Beijing Green Light

*"The death of one man is tragic,
but the death of thousands is a statistic."*

~ Joseph Stalin

During the flight from Moscow to Beijing, Kim Il Sung paced from one end of the plane to the other. Even as his aides napped, the Supreme Leader busied himself with charts and maps, scribbling lists and reminders. He had just come from the most important meeting of his life in Moscow and had achieved his objective of convincing the Soviet leader to give him the go-ahead of his invasion plans. Now, he headed to the new, most important meeting of his life with Mao Zedong. Comrade Stalin had acquiesced to Kim's plans to invade the south, provided – and it was a huge proviso – that Mao also consented. Not only was the unification of Korea at stake, but the unification of China as viewed from Mao's eyes was also at hazard.

The blood vessels in Kim's forehead pulsed as if each rush of blood carried a myriad of thoughts that crowded his mind. He had reliable intelligence that Mao was planning an invasion of Taiwan. No doubt Mao would instinctively consider any military invasion of South Korea by North Korea as a threat to the success of Mao's own campaign. Indeed, Stalin had suggested to Kim that the combined effect of his military plans and Mao's would increase the likelihood that the United States would intervene.

Kim thought that his brain might explode. He lifted a bottle of *soju* from his briefcase and took a long pull. He preferred the gentle burn of the Korean liquor to the harsh sear of the Russian vodka served by Stalin. Kim Il Sung slumped into his seat and drank until his brain shut down for rest.

When the plane finally landed, Kim was bleary-eyed and slightly disoriented. It seemed like they had been flying for days. The stops to refuel and change crews were a blur. He checked his watch and tried to calculate what day it was. No matter, he was scheduled to meet the chairman two hours after his plane touched down in the Chinese capital.

On arrival Kim went to a guest house near the Forbidden City and freshened up for his meeting with Mao. Looking out of the window, Kim studied the high walls of the perimeter of the Forbidden City and the placid water of the moat. By design, no part of the interior of the Forbidden City was viewable from outside the walls. From his vantage point, he could see the roof of the Imperial Palace. Atop the yellow-tiled roof, he focused on a statue of a dragon, the symbol of the emperor. It dominated the view and made him resolve to decorate his own palace with a grandiose statue of *Chollima*, the mythological winged horse symbolic of the heroic spirit of the Korean people. Of course, that would have to come later he told himself.

His sources told him that Mao and all the top officials of his government lived in Zhongnanha, part of the original Imperial Palace within the Forbidden City. That was definitely not a practice he would bring to his government. He could barely stomach the toadies and sycophants that populated his government now. Having them as neighbors would be a sacrifice for his country that Kim was not prepared to suffer.

As he waited for the chairman, his mind squirmed like a *huang shulang,* the yellow weasel endemic to Beijing, caught in a trap. His thoughts flitted from one detail to the next. He had to project absolute confidence and, most important, his paramount job was to assure Mao that Stalin had fully endorsed his plans to invade the south.

Kim did not mind the delay. It was a tactic that he himself used. When Mao finally arrived with his entourage, Kim plastered a deferential smile on his face. Mao's shiny black leather shoes clacked on the marble floor as he approached. His clothing was in sharp contrast to his expensive footwear. Threadbare, wrinkled, and stained, Mao's uniform, if one could call it that, was the antithesis of the crisp, starched uniform worn by Kim. Despite the chairman's shabby clothes, he carried himself with the charisma and authority befitting a military commander who had recently declared the founding of a great nation.

Kim had been forewarned that Mao dressed like a poor peasant. However, he had not prepared his nose for the onslaught of foul odors that accompanied the Chinese leader. It was all Kim could do to avoid gagging at the putrid smell that seemed to emanate from Mao. Before he could stop himself, Kim unconsciously began to identify the constituent elements of the odor. As best as he could tell, it was an amalgam of urine, sweat, and rancid meat.

"Comrade Chairman, you do me great honor to take time to meet with your humble neighbor," said Kim, bowing at the waist while trying to keep his nose from getting too close to his counterpart.

Mao nodded slightly and gestured toward the chairs surrounding a conference table, lacquered a shiny black. Kim sat at the opposite end of the table, hoping that whatever ventilation there was would be flowing toward the Chinese leader.

His face was as flat as an oval serving platter and betrayed as much emotion. He had dark eyes that darted from face to face as if searching. His guest wondered what the chairman was trying to detect. Mao had a reputation for paranoia. As the leader of a newly minted revolutionary government himself,

Kim could appreciate the Chinese leader's wariness. Kim stayed still and counted the number of armed guards bordering the room. Kim placed his palms on the edge of the table and felt himself stiffen involuntarily under the intense gaze.

Dispensing with pleasantries, the chairman said, "Tell me about your visit to Moscow."

He reached into his pocket and withdrew a pack of cigarettes. A cigarette barely reached his lips before an aide thrust a lighter under the tip. Mao puffed several times, blowing smoke toward the aide. Kim waited in vain for Mao to offer him a cigarette. Rather than light up his own cigarette, Kim contented himself with inhaling the ambient smoke.

The Korean leader outlined the crux of his dealing with Stalin, emphasizing the Soviet's firm commitment to arm the DPRK military with advanced weaponry and to provide military advisers. Kim detailed Soviet involvement with logistical aspects of the planned invasion.

"Comrade Kim, when is this reunification scheduled to happen?" said Mao in a low, raspy voice. Kim was tempted to correct the Chinese leader by substituting the word liberation for reunification, but chose to avoid antagonizing the notoriously volatile dictator.

"We don't know. There are a lot of issues that are unresolved, but we are determined to move quickly," said Kim.

Mao released a stream of smoke through his nose. A haze clouded his eyes. His skin took on a grayish hue. Without uttering a word, Mao calculated the impact of a North Korean invasion on his own timetable to invade Taiwan. The extended silence verged on rude discomfort. Mao withdrew another cigarette and chain-lit it.

Kim sipped from a glass of water, gulping more loudly than he wished. Mao inhaled and a satisfied smile crept onto his face revealing teeth discolored with a greenish tinge. Rumor had it that the leader never brushed his teeth, but instead rubbed them with green tea leaves for cleaning. The memory of months in the jungle during his days as a guerrilla fighter flashed into Kim's mind, along with his determination to brush his teeth frequently once he returned to normal life. He rubbed his tongue over his teeth, thankful for his pearly whites.

Kim's statement about moving quickly triggered Mao into a long diatribe about his decades-long struggle against the Nationalists, then the Japanese, and finally the defeat of Chiang Kai-shek barely six months earlier.

For some reason, Kim could not take his eyes off the mole on Mao's chin. It was slightly elevated and darker than the rest of his skin. A single strand of black hair sprouted from the center. As the dictator spoke, this hair swayed to the cadence of his voice. Its effect on Kim was almost hypnotic.

"What does Comrade Stalin think about the Americans? Does he believe Acheson's speech this January means that they won't intervene?" asked Mao.

"He doesn't believe in words. He believes in actions," replied Kim. "The U.S. has withdrawn its army from Korea. Without the support of American troops, we will drive the South Korean Army into the sea in a matter of weeks – before the Americans will be able to respond, it will be over. My country will be one, once again."

After a pause to inhale his cigarette, Mao opined that "the Americans would not intervene to save such a small country."

Although Kim winced inwardly at the slight, he refused to react. Rather, he saw an opening in Mao's statement and Kim decided to overstate his position, figuring that Stalin and Mao had not communicated directly.

"Shipments of tanks, planes, and other munitions are en route. Comrade Stalin asked me to advise you of our plans and to report any disagreement," said Kim, with all the confidence he could muster.

Using both hands to steady the coal, Mao paused to light another cigarette with the last one. Kim noticed that the discarded cigarette was less than half-consumed. When the Chinese ruler nodded his head, Kim smiled. At last, the ant could proceed without being crushed by elephants.

As Kim rose to exit, Mao said, "Fight no battle you are not sure of winning."

The North Korean leader was too elated to heed the warnings of Stalin and Mao.

*   *   *

MacArthur knocked the residue from his pipe. Ever-conscious of his public image, MacArthur had nurtured an everyman persona by insisting on photographs featuring him with a corncob pipe grasped firmly between his teeth. This was pure fluff. Although generally spartan in his tastes, one of MacArthur's indulgences was smoking an exquisite pipe. The pipe that MacArthur preferred was made from the outer portion of the burl called *plateau*. He pinched some of the Harkness F tobacco from a pouch and stuffed it into the bowl. A slight whistle emanated from his lips as he puffed and puffed on his briarwood pipe. A pleasant vanilla-aroma suffused the anteroom to his office.

Before focusing on the photo-filled board before him, MacArthur contemplated the superior grain of his pipe. He allowed himself the hint of a smile. As the cloud of smoke dissipated, MacArthur leaned forward with his magnifying glass to study the images for the umpteenth time.

"Where's Junior?" he barked to no one in particular.

"Sir, the sick bay just notified us that he is . . ."

Junior's head appeared at the staircase. As he reached the top steps, he came into view. His right arm was secured by a bright white sling. In mid-puff, MacArthur stared at him.

Junior approached. After an abortive attempt to use his right arm, he gave an awkward salute with his left hand.

"Easy," said MacArthur, ordering those present to stand at ease. "I understand that your hand was infected by the fragment of a tooth embedded from a bite by an enemy soldier. Nasty, vicious germs from human bites."

MacArthur turned toward the board where the images were pinned. A look of "I wish someone had told me that before I covered that guard's mouth. I would have slit his throat with my bayonet instead," went unseen by MacArthur.

"When I put these photos together, I calculate the presence of 6,000 infantrymen, two artillery units and thirty-three Soviet T-34 tanks," said MacArthur.

"Those estimates have been confirmed by our mil/intel analysts, general," said Brigadier General Willoughby, chief of MacArthur's intelligence unit.

MacArthur took a photo from the table and presented it to Junior. Yellowed slightly around the edges, the picture depicted a row of large military vehicles stacked with crates that seemed covered with foreign letters. The descriptive legend on the back of the photo read: 09 08 1945, Soviet Forces, Kangwŏndo, North Korea.

"Did you see any vehicles loaded with cargo like this?"

Junior studied the photograph for a long minute.

"No, general. No, nothing like this, sir."

"Are you sure? How far around the encampment did you go?" Willoughby asked.

"Sir, I traveled three-quarters of the way around, Sir."

"You see, general, these pictures present an incomplete account," said Willoughby. "My analysis is that the North Koreans would not have mobilized these armaments unless they had sufficient munitions to support them."

"With due deference to your analysts, I'm not so sure, general. I suppose the munitions could be on the far side, but it doesn't explain why they are staying in place like they are waiting."

Then, almost as an aside, MacArthur said, "What do you think, Junior? Could there have been multiple trucks carrying munitions that you missed?"

"No, sir."

Willoughby scoffed. "Of course, he is going to say that, sir. How can he be so sure?"

MacArthur turned to the private as if to say, well?

"Sir, I'm sure that there were no trucks like that. I would have gone completely around the facility, but there was a huge, flooded, rice paddy that stretched for miles on the far side."

在延安时，彭德怀经常这样与毛泽东一起边走边谈工作．

CHAPTER

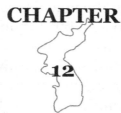

12

Kingfisher to Chonjin

"To fight an evil foe sometimes takes a willingness to go to the dark side—to use bribes and blackmail, disinformation and propaganda, even assassination."

~Evan Thomas Vanity Fair article about William "Wild Bill" Donovan

Several miles away, Kim sat in his tent reviewing maps and readiness reports by lantern light. He rubbed his bloodshot eyes. He reached for the cup of *nogcha*, green tea, that had turned cold. The tea was as bitter as his mood. His plans to reunite his country depended on his agreement with the Premier of the Soviet Union, Joseph Stalin. Kim recalled standing in Stalin's dacha toasting to the dictator as the self-declared "shining sun."

The U.S.S.R. was the only power capable of satisfying North Korea's military needs. For his part, Stalin saw it as an opportunity to pocket a significant quantity of Korean treasure in return for war materiel. Their toast sealed Stalin's agreement to sell Kim the armaments that he required to defeat that puppet, South Korean President Syngman Rhee. Kim was gratified that shipments of planes and communications equipment had arrived at Chonjin, however, he was irritated that Stalin continued to interfere with their invasion plans by indirection. At the moment, the invasion was on hold while they waited for munitions from the Soviets.

What good is a tank without 100 mm rounds for the main gun and 7.62 mm rounds for the machine guns?

"Sir, sorry to disturb you, but I thought you might want to see this report as soon as possible," said General Kang Kŏn, chief of staff of the Korean People's Army (KPA).

"I've been reading so many reports that my eyes are ready to bleed," said the Supreme Leader and Commanding General. "Just give me the gist – short and swift, I want only the bloody details."

"Yes, sir. That demon Rhee has embarked on a purification program and is arresting all known communists. One of our sources says that Syngman has spies who have infiltrated our organizations. So far, he has jailed or killed comrades in Seoul, Taegu, Pusan, and Suwon. No reports received yet from Taejon, but I think we should assume the worst."

Kim groaned.

"What about our agents in the secret police?" asked Kim.

"We are waiting for several to report, sir."

"What about Pak Hŏn-yŏng? He promised me that 200,000 communist sympathizers would join any military liberation and overthrow Syngman Rhee's puppet state."

"No one has heard from Pak. He went underground when the crackdown began," said Kang.

"Damn, the timing of our operation is so fragile and now this," said Kim, his voice rising.

"Comrade Kim, our troops are prepared to bring glory to your Supremeness as soon as you give the order to advance."

"Stop your fawning, general, it makes me think you are weak. We must reunite the south before the cold weather. No excuses. I have promised Comrade Stalin that this operation will be swift and complete. I promised that our brothers in the south would welcome us as liberators. How can they do that from prison cells?"

"There are still many who will, general. We just have to acknowledge this setback. There's not much that we can do at the moment. Our operatives have either been arrested or have gone underground to avoid detection."

The table rattled with the force of Kim's fist slamming down. Kang lunged for the tea cup, barely catching it before it spilled over Kim's maps and papers. The officer hopped awkwardly on one foot to keep his balance. Cold tea splashed onto his tunic.

Kim stalked around the tent, hurling curses at Syngman Rhee's ancestors. He pounded his fist viciously into his hand.

"I want everyone in our network to intensify their efforts to capture the Imperialist spies. All spies are to be delivered to me immediately. I will make the Japanese torture camps look like amusement centers! I will make every spy suffer."

* * *

MacArthur was never satisfied. He always wanted more images, closer images, images from a different angle or direction. And, he always wanted them yesterday. Junior thought that never being satisfied was what must make a five-star a five-star.

Junior was exhausted. The moment he returned on the Ornithopter from a mission, he rushed to the dark room where he would spend however long it took to develop the images which were promptly delivered to MacArthur. Sometimes, the fixing solution on the photographs was not completely dry and Junior had to flap the sheets like the wings of some crazed flamingo careening down the hallway to the conference room that he had heard referred to as the Command Post.

The general paced his office, stopping to examine photographs that hung from every available surface. It was a few months since his seventieth birthday, yet, he had more stamina than men decades younger. Framed on the wall behind his work area hung an adage that captured his attitude toward age. It read: "Youth is not a time of life – it is a state of mind."

MacArthur's young, novice photographer had taken extremely detailed pictures of troop movements, petrol storage facilities, and construction sites. MacArthur was especially interested in a series of sites that showed construction occurring in a line roughly parallel to the 38th parallel. A comparison of photos taken during that spring led MacArthur to a chilling conclusion.

"That brazen son-of-a-bitch is building a line of airfields within twenty miles of the border."

"Sir, is that unusual?" asked Junior.

"Most definitely," said MacArthur. "The Norks must be preparing for a summer offensive. If those airfields were purely defensive, they would be situated throughout the country and near the capital to protect strategic areas."

The images were arrayed across a conference table in MacArthur's office. A swirl of smoke rose from MacArthur's pipe. Peering into the thinning gauze of tobacco smoke, MacArthur's eyes became unfocused, as if he were consulting the layers of smoke that drifted to the ceiling. Invariably, as the smoke dissipated, clarity returned and he would pronounce a solution.

"Junior, I want you to find those planes for me."

And so it was that Junior spent several weeks photographing railroad depots adjacent to the Chinese North Korean border searching for crates that would accommodate the shipment of airplanes. When that effort proved fruitless, MacArthur scanned North Korean ports along the Sea of Japan. Bingo!

MacArthur identified the port city of Chongjin, North Korea as the most likely entry point for armament shipments from the Soviet Union. Chongjin was less than sixty miles south of the Tumen River which separated North Korea from the Soviet Union. The border between the countries was eleven-miles wide.

The general ordered Junior to report to Captain Frank Jones, commanding officer of the *USS Salisbury Sound* based at the U.S. Navy base at Yokosuka, Japan. The ship was currently deployed in the Sea of Japan. The *Sally Sound,* as the crew called her, was a *Currituck*-class seaplane tender.

"It's time," said the sailor to Junior who was sipping his coffee in the galley. He was wearing an insulated flight suit and heavy boots. Since he did not yet have his sea-legs, he carefully climbed the ladder to the deck.

In the pre-dawn morning, there was a moderate northerly breeze. Junior shuddered at the change of temperature. Adjusting to the floodlights on deck, he blinked several times. Before him was a marvel of the United States Navy, Seventh Fleet version. Perched on a rail at the ship's stern was a Kingfisher seaplane. It was officially denominated a Vought-Sikorsky XOS2U-1 monoplane.

A young officer also in a flight suit approached Junior.

"Hey, good morning, Junior. I'll be your driver this morning," said Mako.

"Nice to see you again, sir. How does this thing work?" said Junior, gesturing at the machine on deck which reminded him of pictures of medieval war machines from history books.

They both looked at the plane that was lit by floodlights beaming down from the bridge. It was a small, single-engine aircraft with pontoons hanging down from the wings. Attached to the gray underbelly of the plane was a slotted device that straddled a rail facing seaward.

"This here is the launcher," said Mako, pointing to the rail. "Basically, it's a big spring that catapults the plane off the end of the ship. Then, if we have enough lift, we go up, up, and away."

105

"If there's not enough lift, what happens?"

"Can you swim?" said the pilot, jabbing Junior playfully in the shoulder.

Hours later, they were flying over the Sea of Japan when they hit a squall. With the small aircraft tossing around, Junior was thankful that he was wedged into his seat by all his gear. He peered over the pilot's shoulder through the rain-splashed windshield. The wipers were totally ineffective. Visibility was next to zero. The vista had assumed a dull color of gunpowder as dawn approached.

"Unless our drop-off point is on the other side of this storm, we will have to abort," said Mako. Junior nodded, but resolved that he would parachute out the plane in a storm to avoid disappointing MacArthur. Time seemed to slow. The wind continued to buffet the light craft. A steady staccato of raindrops rat-tat-tatted the thin aluminum skin of the plane.

Mako tapped the fuel gauge – a nervous tic to alleviate anxiety. The Pratt & Whitney engine produced a steady, reassuring thrum. Several hours passed and Junior passed from anxious alertness to drowsy sleepiness. In a split second, he was jarred from his semi-conscious state to full alert.

"Hang on," shouted Mako, who banked the plane sharply to the left. Suddenly, the cockpit exploded with light as the plane emerged from the clouds and faced the rising sun.

"There she is," said Mako, pointing to the coast of North Korea.

Later, after Mako killed the engine and made a silent landing in the shallow water of a shielded cove, Junior exited onto a rocky beach. Securing his rucksack, he saluted Mako and watched the seaplane lift off from the cove. He removed his flight suit and adjusted his drab, quilted workingman's clothing. Taking only his camera, Junior buried the rest of his gear and sat down to wait.

106

It wasn't long before Junior rendezvoused with one of Syngman Rhee's agents in the north. Using rudimentary English and sign language, Junior and his guide trekked through the wooded forest on the outskirts of Chongjin. Before dawn, Junior entered the city and slinked from shadow to shadow until he reached the docks. He was rewarded with a photographic bonanza.

*　　*　　*

As the big American limousine turned into the alleyway, the edge of the flag on the fender brushed against the corner of the building. The vehicle stopped in front of a modest shop in Tokyo's Ginza District, bearing a plain wooden sign engraved with the words "Kabuki Sushi." The passenger was the Supreme Commander of the country. He was recognizable in every section of Tokyo. Yet, his contact insisted on a surreptitious meeting. MacArthur agreed to humor the spook, not because he often shared invaluable intelligence (which he did) but, because he promised to deliver a valuable commodity.

The bright midday sun reflected off the aviator-style sunglasses that were a trademark of the general. He unfolded his lanky frame from the rear door of the limo. MacArthur was more than a foot taller than the average Japanese under his jurisdiction. When he sauntered into the restaurant, the owner and his wife bowed low in deference to the man with absolute authority in their country. Yet, there was no resentment behind their eyes because MacArthur had shown respect to the Japanese people in the implementation of a new constitutional government incorporating meaningful land reforms and women's voting rights, among other things.

A faint, greasy smell of tempura vegetables wafted through the air. MacArthur adjusted to the dim interior and searched for his contact. A hush enveloped the room as the owner ushered the general to a private room in the rear. With heads down, the locals peeked at the eminent personage as he passed. A beaded screen parted to reveal a small room. A man wearing workingman's garb, his face shaded by a cap pulled low over his eyes sat. A wide smile creased his face.

"Douglas, it is so good to see you," said the man with the cheery, blue eyes that were framed by wire-rimmed glasses. He sprang to his feet with the agility of a far-younger man. Although William Donovan was approaching sixty and his waistline showed his penchant for thick steaks, he had boundless energy. His now-silver hair crowned his round face that was the perfect composite of a brilliant spymaster and an impish leprechaun.

During the Great War, Donovan had served under MacArthur in the legendary Rainbow Division. It was renowned for its exemplary role in every major battle on the Western Front. In 1917, then-Colonel MacArthur was the Chief-of-Staff of the 42nd Infantry Division as it prepared to join battle in Europe when the United States entered WWI. Donovan had been the Regimental Commander of the 1st battalion, 165th Regiment of the 42nd Division. The Division was composed of National Guard units from 26 states.

While training at Camp Mills in Garden City, New York, MacArthur commented that, "The 42nd Division stretches like a rainbow from one end of America to the other." That description captured the imagination of the soldiers who delighted in the special designation. They proudly wore a red-blue-and-yellow patch in the shape of a quarter arc which identified them as the Rainbow Division.

As the only American to receive the nation's four highest awards – the Medal of Honor, the Distinguished Service Cross, the Distinguished Service Medal and the National Security Medal, "Wild Bill" was a bona fide war hero. He also received several Purple Hearts and a Silver Star. For his support of Pro Deo, Catholic intelligence after Europe fell to the Nazis, Donovan was knighted by Pope Pius XII with the Grand Cross of the Order of St. Sylvester.

However, those accolades were not Donovan's greatest claim to fame. It was his founding of the Office of Strategic Services, the country's first centralized foreign intelligence service that cemented his place in history. Donovan's brainchild would later receive the name, Central Intelligence Agency. Although President Truman did not tap Donovan to run the agency in the post-WWII era, Wild Bill was still considered by many in the global intelligence community as America's chief spy. After all, Donovan recognized that effective espionage relied on personal relationships and during this interregnum, he worked hard to retain and maintain his connections. So, when he extended a lunch invitation to MacArthur, the general readily agreed.

Had MacArthur's eyes not been shielded by the sunglasses, Donovan might have seen a flicker of disdain as MacArthur considered rebuking the effrontery. Only his wife and his mother had the temerity to call MacArthur by his first name. However, in the time it took to remove his aviator glasses, the general had calculated that he would accept the familiarity of the spymaster in order to nurture an important ally in his ongoing tussles with that fool in the White House. In FDR, MacArthur had a kindred soul, someone who was as arrogant, devious, and ruthless as himself. The relationship between MacArthur and Roosevelt thrived because of the mutual respect they had for each other.

The opposite was true with President Truman – MacArthur had no respect for the little man from Missouri. Not only did MacArthur consider Truman to be seriously out of his depth, he resented Truman's meddling in areas that were matters of expertise which only MacArthur possessed.

The prime example was Truman's boneheaded-ness with regard to the new communist government in China. Truman did not want to antagonize it and he failed to understand MacArthur's support of the opposition led by Chinese Nationalist Chiang Kai-shek. Truman even had the audacity to send his special envoy, Averell Harriman, to berate MacArthur for his recent visit to Taiwan to bolster Chiang's government in exile. Imagine that, thought MacArthur, that haberdasher in Washington reprimanding the highest-ranking officer in the United States military. The cheek of the man.

"Sake, gentlemen?" asked the proprietor.

MacArthur waved dismissively and the man scurried away, not wanting to incur the wrath of the Supreme Commander. These men were too important to engage in the exchange of pleasantries. By means of their own discreet sources, each had complete knowledge of the other's daily activities.

"So, tell me, Billy, how goes Operation Paper?"

"Not nearly as well as hoped. When we set up this operation, we supported Chinese nationalist general, Li Mi's forces in Burma near the Thai border. We fully expected him to launch guerrilla attacks against the Chinese Communists in Yunnan," said Donovan.

"Yes, Li Mi was supposed to harass the Chinese and divert their resources away from Taiwan. My sources tell me that there have been only a few attacks on the Red Chinese and they were totally ineffective. Why? What happened?" asked MacArthur.

"The answer can be reduced to one word," said Donovan.

"Opium," they said simultaneously.

"Yes, they figured out that they could make more money and face less danger if they joined the opium trade," said Wild Bill.

"With the growing storm building in North Korea, do you think that Operation Paper might enable us to divert Chinese troops away from North Korea?" said MacArthur

"No, sir. It's just not realistic to expect Li Mi's ragtag mercenaries to provide meaningful assistance," said Donovan.

MacArthur steepled his fingers and rested his chin on the tips of his index fingers. He sighed in acceptance of an unappealing reality. His mind raced with the logistical challenges that would soon be his responsibility. Once open hostilities between the north and south commenced, MacArthur had no doubt that he would be thrust into the breech. He had to swallow a smile at the prospect – another chance to display his brilliance.

"What's going on in the capital? When is Truman going to fire that embarrassment of a Secretary of State?"

"Acheson? That pantywaist? The intelligence community still has not recovered from his January speech at the Press Club in Washington when he announced that the United States does not consider Taiwan or Korea to be within our defensive perimeter."

"Stalin and Mao no doubt interpreted Acheson's speech as an invitation to invade and annex both of them," said MacArthur.

"My sources tell me that Mao is preparing for an all-out invasion of Taiwan," said Donovan.

"Uncle Joe won't allow that and besides I've recommended that we move the 7th Fleet into the Straits of Taiwan. That should keep Mao from attacking Chiang's island," said MacArthur.

"Plus, it will deter Chiang from attacking the mainland," chuckled Donovan.

The two men ate in silence, each lost in thought over the fluid situation. Donovan sipped green tea from a cup that was lost in his chubby fingers.

111

"My mother always taught me never to visit without bringing a gift," said Wild Bill. He reached to the seat next to him and lifted a canvas and leather rucksack. MacArthur perked up and raised a quizzical eyebrow.

"I know that you have been reconnoitering the North Koreans and I figured that you could use the best technology available to the United States military," said Donovan. MacArthur leaned forward with an expression of curiosity.

With the elán of a medieval magician, Donovan unsnapped the top flap and pulled out a camera that exuded complexity.

"This, Douglas, is the Leica camera that was developed for the *Abwehr* (German Intelligence). It boasts the most advanced, sophisticated optics ever devised. Only five of these babies were ever made."

"It's heavier than I expected," said MacArthur, as he hefted the device into position under his chin. He fiddled with the ring on the lens that controlled the focal point. "Nice, crisp movement. The clarity is outstanding. This will improve our capabilities significantly. My current combat photographer is fearless. He's going to love being able to zoom in on his targets with this monster."

"The best thing about it is that it as quiet as a tombstone on the moon," said Donovan.

A rare smile creased the general's weathered face. MacArthur glanced into the rucksack and saw several thick binders lining the bag.

"Technical manuals," said Donovan, anticipating the general.

CHAPTER

13

Workingman Hero

"Luck favors those in motion."

~ General George Patton

Although each of Junior's missions presented unique challenges, this one to the port of Chongjin was the most difficult one yet. His previous missions were out in the country in open terrain where his camouflage skills gave him confidence that he could avoid detection. Now he was infiltrating a city, a foreign city at that. His life depended on blending in and avoiding interaction with anyone. As he entered the bustling port, he felt a vague familiarity because the frenetic activity reminded him of the port of Baltimore where he had spent parts of his wayward youth.

He heeded a wave from his guide to keep up. Junior's life was in the hands of a young North Korean working as an agent of the government of Syngman Rhee. All Junior knew about him was his name, Seung and he spoke basic English. The spritely young man was about the same age and height as Junior. Both men were dressed in dark work clothes and wore flat caps low over their foreheads. Junior carried a wooden toolbox in a canvas sling.

When Junior first saw the carrying system for his camera, he knitted his eyebrows. To the casual observer it was an oily canvas sling cradling a wooden toolbox. It was typical of tradesmen like carpenters, plumbers and mechanics who worked in and around the docks. Most workers used a shoulder strap to carry their equipment. Along the shoulder strap where the workman would hook his thumb was the shutter release. A concealed wire ran to the camera nestled in the front of the toolbox. The lens was positioned behind an ingenious slide that synchronized with the shutter when Junior snapped a picture. The viewfinder was covered with a filmlike cloth that appeared to be an ordinary rag. However, through the fabric, Junior was able to see the image in the viewfinder by glancing down into the toolbox.

Seung led Junior through the dusty alleys until they reached the piers. They merged into the throng of bodies that traversed the busy thoroughfare. Seung weaved through the crowded street, often tugging on Junior's sleeve to direct him through the mass of humanity. Here and there, street vendors hawked food that Junior could not identify. The aromas triggered his salivary glands and he chided his stomach for growling. A woman stirring something that looked like a bird in a wok seemed to hear his hunger. She called to him. Junior averted his eyes and pushed closer to Seung.

When there was a clearing in the crush, he snapped pictures of crates, uniformed soldiers and vehicles. A din of shouts, whistles, and the whir of pulleys and gears masked whatever noise the camera made. Although he did not know the Cyrillic alphabet, Junior took dozens of images of cargo bearing stenciled Cyrillic characters. Loud laughter coming from a group of soldiers in medium blue uniforms caught his attention. They were much taller than the khaki-clad soldiers facing them. The tall soldiers had Caucasian features and spoke with a clipped Slavic accent that was alien to the high-pitched sing-song that Junior identified as Asian.

Seung swiveled his head to make sure that they were not attracting attention. Junior made sure that his camera captured the shorter soldiers handing a pile of brown garments to each of the taller soldiers. Junior hoped that he was close enough to capture the wing insignias sewn on their collars.

"Junior," said Seung, tilting his head toward a policeman who was staring in their direction. The officer moved toward them. Seung grabbed Junior's elbow and hustled him toward a nearby alley.

A loud whistle pierced the air. Seung accelerated his pace, tugging Junior in his wake. The patrolman shouted for them to halt. They disappeared into a labyrinth of narrow passages. With every step, the toolbox slammed into Junior's thigh. He struggled to keep up with Seung and lost sight of him when the guide squirted around a corner. Junior could hear the policeman closing the gap, but the marine kept running. He felt a sticky liquid on his leg, no doubt from a cut caused by the sharp edge of the toolbox. As Junior labored, he contemplated stopping and confronting the policeman. Figuring that gunfire would draw even more attention, he made sure he knew where his knife was and choreographed a plan of attack.

Junior turned a corner with the officer barely a step behind him. Suddenly, a thump, a crash, and a groan pierced the air. Junior turned to see the policeman writhing on the ground and Seung standing there wielding a thick board. Junior pulled his knife and approached the downed man. Before he could slit the man's throat, Seung grabbed his arm. The Korean's eyes were wide, his lips trembled, and he shook his head. With a look that said I hope I won't regret this, Junior sheathed his weapon.

The officer groaned and his head thumped on the ground. He was out cold. The two fugitives locked eyes, turned and sprinted down the nearest alley. They didn't stop running until they reached a wooded hill on the outskirts of the port. Once they were certain that they had eluded any pursuit, they stopped to rest behind a rocky outcropping.

Seung grinned as he re-created his ambush of their pursuer. When he was able to restore his pulse to normal, Junior laughed at Seung's pantomime, especially when he flopped backwards from a blow to the ribs. Junior had to suppress his laughter at his guide's antics, lest they attract unwanted attention. Secure in their hiding place, they shared their meager rations and took turns resting. While his partner napped, Junior tended to his wounded leg and reloaded his camera.

When the sun set, the air cooled. The change in temperature roused Seung. His eyes widened when he did not see Junior. Seung pursed his lips and sang like a warbler. He listened for their pre-arranged signal. Silence. The young guide feared that his charge had wandered off and been captured. Seung crept from the safety of his hiding place toward the crest of the hill. Seeing nothing, his hopes flagged. Then, he heard a faint click carried on a slight breeze.

Inching up the hill, Seung squinted into the dusk until he discerned a supine figure near the top. It was Junior, completely concealed, taking pictures. From this vantage point overlooking the port of Chongjin, Junior had spent his time shooting pictures of the maritime traffic in the harbor. Junior waved to Seung as he slowly retreated from his perch.

It was time to contact his ride home. From his pack, Junior extricated a rectangular device shaped like a brick. He shielded it within his jacket. When activated, it lit up like a Christmas tree. Red, blue, green, and yellow lights flashed in sequence. After several minutes, the blue light shone steady. That signified to Junior that the communications plane was within range. He punched an encrypted message onto the keys. Junior chuckled to himself that this was the military's way of calling for a taxi. His ride would arrive at the pre-arranged location in exactly twelve hours.

*　　*　　*

The ZIS limousine slowed to a crawl as it navigated the streets of Chongjin. In the backseat, the Supreme Leader of North Korea braced himself with a hand-strap as the big car rocked through a series of pot-holes that would have swallowed up a lesser vehicle. With his eyebrows furrowed, Kim glanced toward his fellow passenger, the mayor of Chongjin. The mayor's eyes pleaded for understanding as he attempted a helpless shrug.

"Our roads dishonor our city."

Kim grimaced as his prized possession bottomed out in a particularly treacherous rut.

"The time is approaching when this city will be rebuilt like a Phoenix rising from the ashes," announced Kim, with an air of prophecy.

The mayor nodded. Neither man could foresee just how accurate the ashes part of Kim's statement would be as a result of the wrath of MacArthur's forces in the coming year.

When the limousine stopped, Kim's countenance brightened as he beheld rows and rows of crated Soviet weapons stacked along the docks. Kim smiled. For the first time, he had the means to achieve his dream of reunification.

"Mr. Mayor, Mr. Mayor, I have urgent news to report," said a police official. He was built like a *ssireum* wrestler, stout in a muscular way. When the mayor tried to dismiss him with a desultory wave, the officer's eyes penetrated the officious façade. The mayor shot a look at his distinguished guest, bowed and excused himself.

"What is it that is so important that you interrupt me with the Supreme Leader?"

"One of our police officers was attacked last night by an American spy."

"How can you be sure?"

"Our man said that he was wearing American boots and goes by the name Junior," said the policeman.

117

"Where is this spy?" asked the mayor.

"We don't know for sure, but believe he is on foot, heading south along the coast. We have set up checkpoints on all roads to the south," said the officer.

"Okay, then, send a search team with dogs in pursuit. Keep me posted of all developments. The Supreme Leader would be displeased if his plans were compromised."

Meanwhile, many miles to the south, Junior was preparing for his exfiltration. He and Seung had returned to where Junior had buried his stuff. He shed his workman's garb and donned his flight suit. His skin goose-bumped in the chill dawn air. Next, he packed the film cannisters in a watertight bag. He knew that his hero would be pleased with the valuable intelligence. With the film and his camera secure in his backpack, he exhaled in relief.

Seung saluted and pointed Junior toward the rendezvous point. Returning the salute, Junior mouthed a thank you to his new friend. As Junior trudged away, he wondered what the future held for Seung. Junior shrugged, he had more pressing concerns. Between the canopy and the early hour, the forest was still dark as he picked his way to the coast. When he got to where the land sloped to the beach below, a feeling of cold dread engulfed him. The inlet which had been so placid and bright when they had landed a few days ago, was immersed in an impenetrable fog.

If this rendezvous failed due to the weather, Junior would be alone in enemy territory with just his backpack. There was no way to communicate with Seung who had darted off to God-knows-where when they parted. He felt a flicker of anguish when he pictured the downed police officer that he had spared. By now, the authorities may have debriefed the police officer. A manhunt for him was probably already underway. No way, he thought. What did the man actually know?

A low drone interrupted his self-recriminations. Mako. It had to be Mako forging through the fog to extract him. Junior hustled down an embankment, disregarding the brambles and underbrush. He wanted to be on the beach when the seaplane reached the shore.

Junior was not the only one who heard the plane. A patrol of North Korean soldiers and police headed toward the sound. Their progress was hindered by the poor visibility and ignorance about the precise landing spot. As they approached the bay, the military commander ordered a sniper team to take position on the nearest high point. He calculated correctly that the fog would dissipate first from the hills. The remainder of the search party raced to the beach.

For his part, Mako aligned his approach on a large tree at the south end of the cove. It was the same tree he had used the previous time. He cut the engine. The Kingfisher swooped into the inlet like a wraith. The difficulty that the North Koreans were having as they attempted to pierce through the miasma was compounded by the abrupt silence. A long moment passed before they heard the pontoons hit the water, or was it just the sound of waves hitting the jetty at the far end of the cove.

Mako landed smoothly and coasted toward the shore where he would turn parallel to the beach and take off with his passenger. Visibility on the water was about fifteen feet. Mako slowed as much as possible to allow Junior to board.

Although the fog muffled noise, Junior heard the shouts of the patrol entering the shoreline. He stopped, reached down and pulled out a cylinder from his pack. Doubt about how far he could heave it caused him to pause. Yes, he would sling it. From another pocket in the pack, he produced a Y-shaped device, lit the flare and shot it was far as he could. A bright light arced through the fog, landing several hundred feet from him. The sudden light caused confusion to his pursuers who were drawn to it. Junior high-tailed in the opposite direction.

When Mako heard his pontoons scrape the sand, he steered the plane seaward. The engine ticked as it cooled. After a few moments, he heard splashing and saw Junior emerge from the murkiness. Junior's appearance was accompanied by the whistling of bullets. They were under fire, probably from snipers on the hill, he thought. Mako started the engine and readied for takeoff.

Just as Junior scrambled for the pontoon, Mako heard a loud thwack. Junior grunted. The pilot left his seat and pulled Junior onto the plane. Several shots thudded into the fuselage. The plane drifted toward the jetty at the end of the inlet. As Junior lay gasping on the floor, Mako launched himself back into the pilot's seat and wrestled with the controls. The Kingfisher roared to life, bounced a few times on the ripples and lifted up into the clouds.

U.S. Navy Vought OS2U Kingfisher

CHAPTER 14

Russian Meddling

*"Photography is an art of observation.
It has little to do with the things you see
and everything to do with the way you see them."*

~ Elliot Erwitt, photographer

Once the Kingfisher was safely out of the range of North Korean forces and had reached altitude, Mako leaned over to remove Junior's backpack. He heard glass and metal rattle as he tugged. Once the pack was removed, Mako saw that there was a stain of blood on the left shoulder of Junior's flight suit. The pilot stuffed a sterile gauze pad under Junior's uniform. The youngster barely reacted and was snoring before Mako buckled himself back into his seat. During the return flight, Junior mumbled about the Chongjin docks where the camera toolbox had captured images of crates stamped with funny Russian letters. His head lolled toward Mako.

"How is Seung? Was wrong. Should have slit his throat."

Junior was out of sickbay by the time the *Sally Sound* reached port. One of the bullets aimed at him had struck the camera and deflected into his deltoid muscle. The flight surgeon who removed the bullet remarked that the camera died a noble death and had absorbed most of the energy of the bullet, saving Junior from serious injury. The gash on his thigh caused by the slamming toolbox required stitches and was painful when Junior climbed ladders on the ship.

Before he could find Mako to say thanks, Junior was whisked away by an escort sent by the five-star. Now, in MacArthur's office in Tokyo, Junior recognized copies of the pictures he had taken in Chongjin.

"While you enjoyed your beauty rest on the *Salisbury Sound*, I ordered your film developed. For the most part, these pictures are remarkable," said MacArthur.

"Sir, thank you, sir," said Junior, failing to see the warning light.

"You see this writing, here?" said MacArthur, pointing to a picture of a stack of crates bearing ОКБ им. Яковлева markings.

"These crates are from the Yakolev Aircraft Manufacturing Company. They manufacture fighter planes for the Soviets. They are excellent planes, but have piston engines."

MacArthur drew his attention to another row of pictures.

"These crates bear the markings, Илью́шин Ил-10, that's Russian for the Ilyushin Il-10. These are single engine, propeller, ground-attack aircraft. The good news is that Uncle Joe Stalin has not given Kim any of his MiG jets. We will have definite air superiority in any conflict."

The five-star general scanned the photos, occasionally squinting through his magnifying glass. He tapped loudly on several pictures.

"These, these are the pictures that I find the most intriguing. Tell me about them, Junior."

"Yes, sir, general. There were several dozen officers who appeared to be white men. They wore blue uniforms, but they were handed piles of brown uniforms by a group of shorter Asian men, sir."

MacArthur raised his magnifying glass and peered at the photos.

"These pictures are fuzzy," MacArthur snapped. "I can't tell what is on the collars of these men in the darker uniforms. Do you remember, Junior? Did you get a clear view? Without detail, these pictures are rubbish."

Junior gulped. He flinched slightly at the general's criticism. You try taking pictures from a toolbox while being jostled on a busy street, he thought. The searing eyes of the patrolman entered his mind.

"Junior, where are you? I asked you a question. What's your answer?" said MacArthur as he peered down at Junior.

"Yes, sir, of course, sir. I did, sir. The men wore wings on their collars, sir!" said Junior, rising to his full height.

"My guess is that the wily Soviet aviators will wear North Korean uniforms when they fly against us," said MacArthur triumphantly.

MacArthur took out his pipe. While he was puffing it alight, he said, "By the way, I understand that while you were in Chongjin, valuable property belonging to the government of the United States that had been entrusted to you was destroyed. Is this true?"

"Begging your pardon, sir, are you referring to the camera? Sir," said Junior, his voice rising.

"Of course, I am," said MacArthur, reaching for a slip of paper. "Here, this is a bill from Uncle Sam for the cost of his camera. The paymaster will deduct an appropriate amount from your pay each month until this is repaid. Understood?"

"Yes, Sir. Whatever you say, sir," said Junior, his voice quivering. His hands clenched and unclenched at this news. He fought to keep his eyes from welling up.

"Until further notice, you are to utilize this camera for your missions," said MacArthur, lifting up a canvas-and-leather rucksack from behind his desk.

"Here, it's for you. The finest piece of photographic equipment owned by the U.S. military should be used by its best photographer," said the General.

Junior opened the rucksack and saw an elegant, sophisticated camera the likes of which he had never dreamed existed.

"General, I don't understand, Sir," said Junior.

"Son, you have performed admirably and have demonstrated skill and courage. The information you have gathered is far beyond what a normal combat photographer produces. You have provided us with intelligence of the enemy's capabilities that exceeds what we have gotten from our spies. Therefore, I am conferring on you the title of combat spytographer, first class."

Junior did not quite comprehend what this all meant, but he suspected that he was back in MacArthur's good graces. His brain was so overwhelmed that his vocal cords ceased functioning. He barely heard MacArthur droning on.

". . . and so, I have cut orders for you to take a furlough. You will leave on Wednesday," said MacArthur.

Junior looked up at the general and asked him to repeat what he just said.

"Furlough. You look puzzled," said MacArthur.

"What is that?" said Junior.

"It means that I'm going to give you 20 days-time-off. A vacation."

"Sir, begging your pardon, Sir. I can't afford to take a vacation," said Junior.

"Why not? I'm ordering it," said the general.

"General, sir, I have to pay for the camera that got shot up, sir," said Junior.

After a moment, MacArthur let out the biggest guffaw anyone could remember.

* * *

The day had been exhausting, an endless succession of meetings. The Supreme Commander of the DPRK sat alone in his headquarters staring at the ceiling. It was well after midnight. He never expected to have this problem. As he wrote in his journal, he mused about how life plays cruel jokes on men. Earlier in life he would have considered his predicament a wealth of riches. Now, it was a colossal pain in the ass. How could he reconcile the competing interests of his Soviet and Chinese comrades while maintaining his primary goal of liberation?

During his lifelong battle with Japanese Imperialism, he readily fought alongside Chinese Communists to oppose Japan's occupation of his country. So, when Mao proposed returning ethnic Koreans from the Chinese Army who had fought the Japanese, Kim had no choice but to accept enthusiastically. Where were their loyalties? Were they an enemy within? Recognizing these dangers, he concluded that Mao had outfoxed him.

As Kim wrote about the crafty Mao, he recalled advice from a friend in the diplomatic corps who recounted a meeting with Mao who stated in a moment of alcohol-induced candor, "I am shameless, impolite and sly. I play tricks, tell lies, use spies and never keep promises." If Mao admitted it, who was Kim to disagree? And what did it portend for the future?

Stalin is no better, Kim wrote. He has siphoned off much of our national treasury for armaments, but withholds ammunition until his generals are satisfied with the invasion operations plans. Kim was shocked when Soviet Major General Ilshun Postnikov tore up Kim's plans and declared that his staff would draw up the plans. When Kim protested that the Soviets did not know the terrain and local resources, the Soviet commander said, "All that has the significance of a dog fart. We will use our tanks to blitz the weak imperialists of the south. No need for you to worry."

"All I want to do is liberate my fatherland, yet I am insulted and buffeted by these bull elephants. Stalin dictates operational planning. Mao inserts spies loyal to him into our forces. Shackled by my comrades, I am supposed to defeat that Satan MacArthur and his demonic puppet, Syngman Rhee. I will tolerate all indignities to achieve liberation. Then, I will rule supreme!"

After another swig of *soju*, he glanced at a picture of his wife and son that was on his desk amid a disheveled clutter of plans, reports, and maps. He vowed that his nine-year-old son would see his country united before he reached manhood. Like many of Kim's hopes and promises, it was not meant to be.

CHAPTER

15

Leica and the Master

"Another glorious day, the air as delicious to the lungs as nectar to the tongue."

~ John Muir

The workmen had just finished extending the display board in the war room outside MacArthur's office. It now measured thirty feet in length and was covered with images of military subjects in North Korea. With his ever-present magnifying glass, MacArthur hunched over a series of pictures of the Chongjin docks. He scrutinized the faces hoping to wring the last shred of intel from the grainy enlargements. It took an effort to straighten up, but his eyes gleamed with satisfaction. His efforts had yielded enough information to formulate a plan. It would be a bold and daring plan, befitting a genius like me he thought.

MacArthur's concentration was interrupted when he sensed a presence hovering at the doorway. It was Donovan.

"Douglas, we've got a problem, the technical manuals for the Leica are written in German that is so technical that our translators can't make heads or tails out of it," said Wild Bill. "We have checked the roster of every man stationed in the Pacific theater who is fluent in German. Every one we have brought in is stumped by the technical words. We have no one who can decipher this stuff."

Smoke from his pipe swirled around MacArthur's head while he pondered. He gazed toward the ceiling.

"Well then, Bill, we'll just have to go to the source, the head of the U.S. European Command. Get a hold of General Handy in Germany for me."

While Major General Donovan trundled off to the comm center, Junior was settling into his seat on a DC2 preparing for his furlough. He was thrilled at the prospect of his trip. When General MacArthur had asked him where he wanted to go, Junior had not hesitated.

"Sir, I want to see Iwo Jima, sir."

"And why may I ask?" said MacArthur.

"General, sir, when I was in boot camp, we had a DI who was one of the Marines who planted the flag on Mount Suribachi, Sir. During one of our classes on Marine History and Tradition, another DI showed us a famous picture of six Marines straining to hoist the flag, sir. They told us that the photographer was named Joseph Rosenthal and he won a Pulitzer Prize for the picture. Our DI, sir, was one of those men. I vowed that if I ever got the chance to see it, that's where I would go, sir," said Junior.

"And, so you shall, son," said MacArthur.

Junior sat on the plane, tapping his foot, wondering what was the holdup. Just as the door was closing, a young flight officer bolted onto the plane. He handed an envelope to the pilot and then, carefully stowing his canvas and leather rucksack, he sat next to Junior who was lost in thought.

"Junior."

"Mako, how the hell are you? . . . sir."

"I'm glad to see you, again. The last time I saw you, they were wheeling you into surgery."

"Oh, yeah, I got nicked. Went right through the muscle. All healed up now, sir."

"Junior, stow that sir business while we are together on the plane," said Mako with a wink. "So, what are you up to?"

"I'm on my first farlough; going to see Iwo Jima where the marines were heroes."

Hayfisch chuckled, but let the malaprop stand. He figured that he would have plenty of time during the long flight to break the news. The plane headed northeast.

After their first of many fuel stops, Mako sidled up to Junior.

"Listen, Junior, I have good news and bad news for you. Which do you want first?"

"What?"

"Okay," said Mako after inhaling and exhaling. "Your orders have been changed. You are not going to see Iwo Jima on this trip."

Junior stared at him with a look that mixed disbelief with a hint of scanning for a punch line. This had to be a joke. The general would not let him down.

"The good news is that we are going for an adventure in the American west. That's right you and me together. You'll see. It'll be better than going to Iwo Jima; that's just a lump of unfriendly volcanic rock covered with black soot. Trust me, I've flown over it, there's nothing there to see. Your memory of that Rosenthal picture is about as good as it gets."

Junior was too weary to protest. During his time in the marines, he had learned that his personal disappointment was irrelevant. He closed his eyes and cursed silently.

After what seemed like endless stops and takeoffs, and equipment changes, they finally arrived. Junior's stomach lurched as the plane dove at a steep angle between two peaks in the Grand Tetons. The afternoon sun was beginning to wane when the plane taxied along the rutted grass runway to a makeshift camp. They unloaded and waved to the departing aircraft. A whispering silence replaced the sound of the aircraft.

In stillness, Junior stood at the edge of the camp. He had never seen a vista of such majesty. A field of wildflowers stretched before him. The angle of the sun produced an amber luminescence on the petals that exhilarated and humbled.

Across a verdant meadow in the distance was a ring of mountains standing as silent sentinels adorned with snowy sheaths. Junior breathed deep as if cleansing himself of all the impurities of a lifetime. He settled into a sitting position, Indian style.

Before the sun receded behind a peak, he heard the braying of an animal. A man wearing a floppy hat, weathered coat, and dungarees, appeared traversing a ridge that shielded the camp. His face was hidden by a bushy, black beard. At average height and solidly built, he held the reins of a reluctant pack mule. Quite suddenly, he drew a sawed-off shotgun from beneath his coat.

"What the fuck are you doing in my camp? Who the fuck are you?"

Mako with hands raised, responded in a quavering voice, "My name is A.C. Hayfisch, I'm a lieutenant in the U.S. Air Force. We were sent here by President Truman to . . ."

"I didn't give my camp to the U.S. government. Get the fuck out of here!"

"But I have an order for you from the President of the United States to teach this guy how to use this camera equipment," said Mako, nodding toward the camera which was resting on top of the rucksack. "It's from Leica."

That last word seemed to mollify the man. "Leica, you say?"

"Yes, it was commandeered by General Eisenhower when he marched into Germany. It came with technical manuals, but they are indecipherable because they are in technical German."

"Why not get a German interpreter? Why come here? I no *sprechenze* German."

"Sir, you are a world renowned photographer," said the lieutenant, watching the bearded man's chest inflate. Mako continued.

"This gentleman here has come here at great expense. His name is Jürgen Wolfgang Langwasser. He is the chief optics engineer for Leica and has flown here from Wetzlar, Germany

130

to translate the technical terms and to help us understand all the aspects of this spectacular camera."

The man narrowed his eyes and regarded the tall German whose eyes darted between Mako and the shotgun.

"Hmmmph."

The photographer turned and led his mule off to a water trough and a pile of hay. He appeared lost in thought as he unloaded and tended to the animal. While brushing the mule, the man stole an occasional glance at the camera.

Hayfisch and the others stood watching with perplexed looks. This encounter was not going according to plan. Junior was the first to move. His stomach was churning. Hunger was a great motivator. Within minutes, he stood before a roaring fire and was preparing dinner on a camp grill. Cold beers appeared and the group settled in for their first real meal after days of traveling. It wasn't long before the camp was filled with the aroma of steaks grilling, potatoes baking, and convivial chatter.

"Excuse me, gentleman. Maybe we can start over. I apologize for my gruff behavior, but you caught me by surprise. On reflection, I should be more hospitable. Visitors up here are as rare as city-folk getting to experience the magic of wildness in this century," he said, with a sweeping gesture toward the panorama before them. As the sun set, darkness advanced across the meadow to the mountains, leaving only the brilliance of the snowcaps in the golden light.

"Allow me to introduce myself. I have a funny name," he said, "Ansel Easton Adams, photographer. Welcome to my humble camp," said the man with a slight theatrical bow.

With his foot Mako nudged a camp chair in Adams' direction. Smiling, he joined them. When the meal was completed, Adams invited Langwasser into his tent. The Leica camera was the guest of honor. Together, they dissected the operation of the camera; they took it apart and put it back together. Hours later, when the sun rose, Adams and

Langwasser could still be heard inside the tent thrashing out the nuances of the Leica.

When they finally emerged around mid-day, they looked haggard. As Jürgen headed toward the latrine, Ansel followed, peppering him with questions.

"I'm still having trouble understanding how this camera can take photographs in complete darkness," said Adams.

"It's the system of mirrors that we have designed to accommodate the maximum wide aperture with revolutionary high ISO settings to achieve this capability," said the German, as he tried to do his business with a modicum of privacy.

"But if the camera does what you say it does, won't developing the images taken at night produce a green tinge?" said Adams, his eyebrows knitted in concentration.

"So?" was Jürgen's reply. "Now, can we please take a break to eat? I'm famished."

Later, Ansel, Jürgen, and Junior huddled around a table familiarizing themselves with the camera. The technical level of conversation was so beyond Mako's ken that he decided to contribute by dreaming up a nickname. As he drank his beer, he tested various names in his head. Coming up with nothing suitably clever, he waited for inspiration.

"Junior, the lens on this camera is a masterpiece. It is 1500mm and can capture the features of a person from about seven football fields away. That sort of acuity is unheard of," gushed Ansel.

"To accomplish this capability, we had to make the lens über large," said Jürgen.

"That's an understatement," scoffed Ansel. "It's forty-two inches long and weighs about thirty-five pounds. But that's no problem if you use a sturdy tripod." Adams pointed with pride to his venerable tripod crafted of top-grade hard-rock maple.

"I wish I could lug a tripod with me when I'm on a mission," said Junior. "But I don't have that luxury. However, the boys back in Tokyo have devised the perfect solution for using this camera in the field."

Ansel and Jürgen gave him skeptical looks. Both shook their heads from side-to-side. Junior held up a hand while he reached into his equipment bag. He unveiled a custom-made harness designed to strap onto his torso.

Adams snickered, "That looks like something Mae West would wear."

"Maybe so, but it works," replied Junior, as he hefted the camera into the cradle on the front of the harness. With his left hand raised behind his ear, Junior did his best showgirl strut around the campground. Raucous laughter filled the air.

"There you go," exclaimed Mako, hoisting a beer, "the nickname for the Leica from now on will be Maisey."

"Hear, hear!" they chorused.

"Okay, let's take Maisey out for a spin and see what she can do," said Ansel, donning his cap and photographer's vest.

When Jürgen stood in place, Ansel gave him an inquisitive look. The German waved his hand, saying, "You and Junior go ahead. I need a nap."

In the days that followed, Ansel and Junior were inseparable. Mako mused that the two men were as different as light from dark – age, backgrounds, training, and on and on. The common denominator was the Leica. Each morning, they carried the photographic marvel into the wilderness for daylong shooting and experimentation. When they returned to camp, Ansel and Junior would work in the developing tent late into the night, bringing into reality the images they had captured with Maisey. Over time, Ansel revealed to Junior secrets in the process of manipulation of chemicals that coaxed glorious beauty and detail out of the scenes recorded on film.

The mantra which Adams continually reinforced was that, "The negative is the equivalent of the composer's score, and the print the performance."

Usually, Mako and Jürgen spent their evenings amusing themselves by playing cards or enjoying the prints that were clipped like laundry on ropes crisscrossing the camp.

Occasionally, the photographers would emerge from the tent to ask Jürgen for clarification or elaboration of some obscure aspect of the Leica.

"Tomorrow night, Junior and I are going to put Maisey through her paces in the dark," announced Ansel.

A noticeable chill descended on the camp when the sun set. Mako and Jürgen joined the two photographers on their maiden nocturnal shoot. Before they left the camp, Ansel rubbed their clothing with his special blend of pine needles, mashed acorns, dirt, and a secret ingredient.

"Phwewy," said Mako, "That stuff is foul. What is that pungent ammonia smell?"

"Skunk urine," said Ansel, as he smeared his concoction on Jürgen's jacket.

"*So ein misthaufen!* What a pile of crap!"

They wore headlamps as they proceeded into the woods. They were treated to another world; the arboreal world of nocturnal creatures. The distinctive "who" of an owl competed with the insistent buzz of cicadas and the night was punctuated by the intermittent howls of a pack of grey wolves across the valley. Junior strained to maneuver Maisey into the best position for capturing the night forest. He stopped frequently, muttering adjustments to himself while Adams coaxed him into varying his angles.

After several hours, Ansel halted the small column with an upraised hand. By turning off his own, he gestured for them to extinguish their lamps. His beard twitched as he sniffed the air, reminding Junior of his family beagle. Adams determined the direction of the wind and walked toward it.

"We need to maintain silence for the next part of the hike because we are entering the cougar's territory," whispered Ansel, the words barely emerging from his thick beard. Junior and Mako exchanged wide-eyed glances. They had progressed another hundred yards when they saw it.

Reclining on a branch in a tree before them, was a large male cougar. He was gnawing on a small mammal, probably a baby white-tail, that he held between his paws. Junior immediately zeroed in on the magnificent creature with Maisey. Mako said a silent prayer of thanks that the claims of noiseless operation were accurate. The four men stood in the darkness transfixed. Leaves rippled in a slight swirling breeze.

The cougar raised his head and sniffed. Maisey captured the cougar's snarl as Junior triggered the shutter, his eyes peering down into the viewfinder at his chest. Suddenly, the creature sprang into the air, bounded several times and was poised to land on Junior who was pre-occupied with the shutter release. With equal alacrity, a shotgun blast shattered the air.

Mako lowered the gun. The cougar thudded to the ground with a mortal wound before the sound receded. The animal made one last lunge and landed on Junior. He grunted from the force of the blow. The only thing separating Junior from the cougar's *canines* was the length of the Leica lens. The foul hotness of its dying breath nearly singed Junior's face. A mucousy, glob of saliva from the dangling tongue dripped onto his cheek. As warm blood flowed onto his shirt, Junior rolled the cougar off him. He snapped several more pictures of the dead creature.

"Maisey is good," he said, with a sigh of relief mixed with exhilaration.

Mako shook his head in amazement at Junior's aplomb. Jürgen retched at the bloody carnage. Except for a tear on his cheek, Ansel was stone-faced. With his jaw clenched tightly, he ushered them away and they trekked back to the camp in tense silence.

Ansel Easton Adams

CHAPTER

16

Junior's Bodyguard

"Once destroyed, nature's beauty cannot be

purchased at any price."

~ Ansel Adams

After an urgent radio transmission requesting the extraction plane, they spent several hours packing, then waiting. Mako's attempts to explain to Adams his instinctive reaction to the cougar's leap fell on deaf ears. The photographer stomped around the camp, throwing their possessions out of various tents and structures into a pile on the rocky ledge by the firepit. The large vein which marked the center of his forehead pulsed with rage.

When the plane finally landed and taxied into position for loading, Mako exhaled and made one last survey of their equipment to make sure that they had everything relating to the Leica. He was under strict orders to leave nothing about the top-secret camera behind. The way he saw it, he had done his best to protect the camera and Junior.

The young marine was the last one to board. His eyes searched Adams for acknowledgement of the bond they had formed. Ansel clamped one hand on Junior's shoulder and whispered into his ear. Junior smiled. The hirsute photographer handed him an envelope and gave him a paternal nod.

As the plane took off, Junior and Jürgen waved goodbye. With his fingers together, Ansel gave them a royal wave, his forearm moving stiffly from side to side.

"What's in the envelope, Junior?" asked Mako after they were above the clouds.

"Prints from last night's shoot," said Junior, passing them to Mako and Jürgen. Both men marveled at the magnificent images of the night creatures tinged in green. Junior's favorite was the one where the cougar was suspended over him in mid-leap, its claws, whiskers, and mouth stretched wide in attack mode. The creature's head strained forward, its ears erect and its face contorted in furrows of murderous rage. The picture was taken an instant before Mako's shotgun blast ended its life. Junior shuddered in awe at the raw power captured in the image. His reaction brought to mind the words whispered to him by Adams. He treasured Ansel's encouragement.

* * *

"Junior, you know how to work this Leica now?" said MacArthur

"Yes sir," said the young marine, handing the general the photo of the cougar.

MacArthur gasped as he stared at the attacking predator.

"Stunning. This is the essence of ferocity. You took this with the Leica?"

"Yes, sir, general, I did."

"What time of day was it, Junior?"

"Close to midnight, sir. It was pitch black in the forest, sir."

"This level of detail is amazing. You can see how extended his whiskers are. Did you know, Junior, that a cougar's whiskers are so sensitive that it can detect miniscule changes in the movement of air? That helps it detect prey."

"Sir, I did not know that, sir," said Junior, thinking, so that is how the cougar knew we were nearby.

A knock on the door caught MacArthur's attention.

"Enter."

"Sir, it's time for your meeting to finalize the details for the Fourth of July celebration. General Willoughby and the Japanese Chamberlain are waiting in the Imperial Palace," said Sergeant Major Morgan.

MacArthur gave Junior a look that said I'd rather stay, but duty calls. In point of fact, MacArthur relished the planning of ceremonial events. He was a master of pomp and circumstance and never saw a camera lens that he did not like.

"Son, you are dismissed, but I want you back here at 1400 hours for a briefing on your next assignment. By the way, I think you need a bodyguard, son. I've got somebody in mind," said the general as he donned his trademark Philippine Army Field Marshal's cap. Junior screwed his eyebrows as he stared at the general's wake.

It was a hat that the publicity-conscious general had modified by adding a gold embroidered U.S. insignia instead of the standard brass insignia, plus a row of embroidered gold leaf that circled the hat and more gold leaf that sat on the visor like a serving of scrambled eggs. Although the hat violated numerous regulations, there was virtually no chance that he would be reprimanded for wearing it.

Later that day, as Junior approached MacArthur's office, he smelled an odor that he recognized but could not place. Before his mind could identify the smell, he stood at the entrance to the office and was shocked by what he saw. A grizzled soldier was standing at attention before a seated MacArthur. Damp mud covered his legs to mid-thigh where it tapered to a dried, dusty crust.

"Soldier, you stink, where did you come from?" said MacArthur.

"The swamps of South Carolina, sir."

MacArthur grunted and turned his attention to the papers on the spartan table that he used as his desk. In deference to MacArthur's prodigious memory and ability to retain details, the table had no drawers.

"Begging your pardon, sir. Twelve hours ago, I was training a bunch of maggots in the swamp and I get shanghaied on to a jet fighter and end up here. Have I done something wrong, sir?"

Annoyed at being questioned, MacArthur slapped a folder on the desk and stood. A flush of crimson rose over the general's face. He was almost a head taller than the soldier and walked slowly toward him. Junior cringed.

MacArthur's impeccable uniform, pressed to perfection was in stark contrast to the disheveled drill instructor. The only adornment MacArthur wore was five-stars arranged in a circle on each collar. Despite the absence of ornamentation, the general's demeanor was so regal that most men succumbed in his presence. Years of command, especially the most recent ones in Japan where he was the Supreme Commander in every sense of the title, had given MacArthur the aura of a demigod. At six feet with patrician features and an imperious bearing, MacArthur preferred to subdue by force of personality.

The only personality type that was not susceptible to MacArthur's powerful presence was the type exemplified by Gomax. The combat veteran who had endured so much that he no longer cared.

"I ran your file. The ledger shows a lot of bad, but some good. You've been busted a lot of times Joe. That tells me that you despise authority."

MacArthur's face was inches from the soldier's face. As MacArthur spoke, his pipe jabbed the soldier. Smoke filled the space between them and swirled into the soldier's eye. Junior gulped as the pipe illuminated the jagged scar on his left cheek. The reflection off the pale, shiny skin raised the hair on the back of Junior's neck. The general imposed his dominance on the soldier, just as the soldier himself had done to Junior on Parris Island.

"The file also shows that you've distinguished yourself in battle. You know your business. You know how to keep people alive."

The only reaction from Gomax was an ocular flicker of acknowledgement. He stood as rigid as a flagpole, but Junior could feel an air of disdain and resentment radiating from the man.

"See that little bastard over there?" said MacArthur gesturing toward Junior.

"Yes, sir," said Gomax, thinking how he would bust his ass once they were alone.

"You trained him?"

"Yes sir, I was the drill instructor for that maggot, sir," said Gomax. MacArthur smirked.

"He may be a maggot to you, but to the North Koreans he is enemy number one," said MacArthur. He swiped a flyer from his desk and displayed it inches from Gomax' face.

"In case you don't read Korean, let me translate. It says: 'Wanted for Subversion of the People's Republic — Number 1 Enemy — the Ghost Photographer — for Spying, Murder, and Sabotage. Last seen in Chonjin. Known Ties to Cowardly Dogs of Imperialist Spy Network. Reward for Death or Capture.' Then there is a sketch that could be any round-eye. I guess we all look alike to them."

The last sentence was barely audible. The general paused.

"Now, he may be a maggot to you, but to the United States military, he is a fearless and talented photographer who I consider a valuable asset to our efforts in this part of the world. Do you get my drift?" said MacArthur, his voice tinged with venom. Gomax shifted his eyes toward Junior. There was a momentary flutter of incredulity before MacArthur bellowed.

"Let me make myself perfectly clear. You are to keep him alive. I'm ordering you to keep this man alive. Use every skill you know. Don't question anything. Guard his life even if it costs you your own. If need be, you are to forfeit your life for his," said MacArthur.

"Are you ordering me, sir?" Gomax said.

"Are you deaf or stupid? You're God-damn right I'm ordering you to keep him alive. If it means that you have to transfuse your own blood into him, or rip out your own kidney to save him, or, take a bullet in the face for him, you are ordered to keep this bastard alive no matter what it takes. Are we clear?" said the general, in a voice that rattled the window panes.

"Yes, sir!"

"Now, get some clean clothes for your sorry ass and report back in one hour for a briefing on your first assignment."

Gomax did an about-face and exited the office, glowering at Junior the whole time.

Three days later, Junior and Gomax had infiltrated North Korea and were on a covert march through the mountainous terrain just north of P'yŏngyang, the capital of North Korea. They traveled at night through coniferous woods of the Siberian fir, spruce, pine, and Korean pine. To relieve some of the tedium, Junior kept Maisey ready to shoot mountain antelope, goats, tigers, and leopards indigenous to the area. Gomax led the way, occasionally hissing to Junior to pay attention.

"God-damn maggot is gonna get us wasted," muttered Gomax under his breath.

Their objective was to reach P'yŏngyang, the capital of North Korea and the oldest city on the Korean Peninsula. It was situated on a river-valley plain along the winding Taedong River. The city was approximately sixty-eight miles east of the Korea Bay on the Yellow Sea. The heavily forested mountains to the north and east that sheltered P'yŏngyang would provide perfect cover for the surveillance planned by Junior and Gomax. MacArthur wanted them to go to P'yŏngyang Air Base to document North Korea's capabilities. He emphasized the importance of photographing officers. The general hoped that the Leica would provide sufficient detail for the next phase of his plan.

Gomax raised his right hand in a halting motion. They were in a small pine grove in a rocky outcropping within binocular range of the air base. Even though it was hours before dawn, the marines could hear furious activity of men and machines. While Junior snapped pictures until the rising sun threatened to expose them, Gomax set up a camouflaged shelter. The DI was so skillful that when Junior returned from relieving himself in the forest, he could not find the shelter. Gomax tortured the young marine by not answering calls for assistance. Just when Junior was about to give up and build his own shelter, Gomax relented and gestured his location to the frustrated Junior. He was never so glad to see Gomax. Both fell into a deep sleep during the day.

* * *

Meanwhile far away, Kim Il Sung, the self-proclaimed Great Leader of the DPRK, sat at his desk staring at the operations plan for the invasion of South Korea. Across from him was his Army chief of staff, General Kang Kŏn. He had spent the last two months working with Soviet Major General Postnikov to devise a battle plan acceptable to Comrade Stalin. Postnikov was liaison with a team of Soviet military advisers assigned to the KPA. The combined military leadership worked at the National Security Department under extreme secrecy. The process had been grueling due to endless revisions, each of which necessitated translation between Korean and Russian and back. At long last, the battle plan was complete.

The group had taken great pains to make the plan appear to be a counteroffensive. This was in keeping with the self-serving narrative that the actions of the North were in response to hostilities initiated by the South. In furtherance of the propaganda charade, under the guise of field exercises, the North Koreans moved their troops into position along the 38th parallel for a three-pronged attack on the South.

"Most Exalted Leader, with the arrival of the Soviet munitions, our preparations are complete. Earlier this week, ten trucks carrying our high-ranking officers arrived in Hwach'ŏn near the border. The Command Post there is now operational and ready to proceed on your orders, sir," reported Kang.

Kim was on the cusp of achieving his dream of liberating his country. He was so confident that he would control Seoul within two or three days that he had made special preparations for his triumphant ride into the capital of South Korea.

"The package is loaded and ready to roll as soon as you give the order," said General Kang.

"Excellent, my comrade. Our entry into Seoul will indeed be glorious. Are the photographers lined up?"

"Yes, sir," replied Kang.

The Supreme Commander smiled, already envisioning himself driving up to the Gyeongmudae, the presidential residence known as the Blue House, to make his victory speech.

His expectation was that Seoul would fall within days and that President Rhee would capitulate before there could be any meaningful reaction by the United States and its Allies in the United Nations.

In the early morning hours of June 25th, commander-in-chief Kim convened a meeting of his cabinet. He announced that South Korea had attacked the DPRK. Referring to the constitutional requirement of cabinet authorization for a declaration of war, Kim ordered the war to begin and asked, "Do you all agree?"

To no one's surprise, the cabinet rubber-stamped Kim's request for a declaration of war.

One hour later, at 4:00A.M. on Sunday June 25th, 1950, Kim gave the fateful order to attack South Korea. It is doubtful that Kim Il Sung was familiar with the admonition of the Scottish poet, Robert Burns, but the Supreme Leader was soon to learn that the best-laid plans of mice and men often go awry. In the ensuing years, there would be millions of casualties and unimaginable grief as a result of this action. The ramifications would be felt well into the next century.

At the outset, the attack was successful beyond the wildest dreams of the North Koreans and their Soviet and Chinese allies. Aside from surprise, the KPA had numerous overwhelming advantages in manpower, equipment, and organization. The KPA's well-trained troops outnumbered the army of South Korea by an almost 2:1 margin. Kim's forces possessed a staggering advantage with 242 Soviet T- 34 tanks, 54 armored vehicles, and 176 self-propelled artillery pieces compared to a total of only twenty-seven armored cars possessed by the Army of the Republic of Korea.

Anxious to observe the culmination of all his years of planning, Kim raced to the front in a *bronetransporter*, a Soviet armored scout vehicle. He followed a tank brigade as it rumbled through the Ŭijŏngbu corridor toward Seoul. His exhilaration rose as his vehicle advanced deeper into South Korean territory. In centuries past, this historic route was used by the invading Mongols and Manchus to capture the Korean capital. The plan was to capture Seoul and then lead his army through Suwon, Osan, Chonan, Taejon, Kumchon, Taegu, terminating at the tip of the peninsula at Pusan.

From the crest of a hill, he observed the attack of an armored division composed of T-34 tanks, mechanized infantry in half-tracks, and self-propelled artillery. Through his field binoculars, he watched as rockets fired by the anti-tank bazookas ricocheted off the T-34s, like robins bouncing off a plate glass window. Given the sloped armor construction of these tanks, the 2.36-inch rocket projectiles used by South Korean forces simply deflected or deformed on contact, inflicting no damage. Kim laughed gleefully as the tanks overran the ROK position. Satisfied that the "counterattack" was proceeding as planned, the Supreme Leader withdrew to the communications center.

On June 25th at 9:30 A.M. Kim announced to his countrymen that the South Korean puppet clique had not only rejected his overtures for peaceful reunification, but had had the audacity to initiate an armed invasion of the Haeju district, north of the 38th parallel. He assured the people that this blatant violation of their sovereignty would not be tolerated and that the responsible South Korean authorities would pay for their crimes against the fatherland. A counterattack to repel the invaders was underway and Kim vowed to take decisive measures for smashing the enemy.

His voice rising to a fever pitch, Kim shouted into the microphone, "The war which we are forced to wage is a just war for the unification and independence of the fatherland and for freedom and democracy."

Kim concluded with the slogan, "Everything for victory in the war!"

By this time, the Republic of Korea was appealing to the United States and the United Nations to intervene and effectuate a ceasefire to stop the hostilities.

* * *

Back at P'yŏngyang Air Base, from his perch overlooking the facility, Gomax was uneasy.

"Hey, maggot, I got a funny feeling something ain't right."

"What do you mean?" said Junior.

"You notice how few officers been by in the last day or so? It ain't natural. Use that thingamagig that you got to call for a pick-up," said Gomax.

Junior hesitated, giving Gomax a questioning look that said you know that we are not scheduled to leave for two more days. With a stony stare like an icicle to the heart, Gomax unclipped the flap over his service pistol.

"Now, are you gonna make that call, or will I have to do it over your corpse?"

Junior fumbled through his pack for the device that would signal for their extraction. The red, blue, green, and yellow lights flashed in sequence. Despite repeated attempts, the blue light failed to shine steady. He shrugged to Gomax who glared in response. As the hours passed, Junior grew despondent at the failure to raise the communications plane.

Dawn approached and Gomax jerked awake.

"You hear that?" he said to no one.

Junior strained to hear.

After another ten minutes, Gomax jumped up and hissed, "We gotta bug-out. We gotta get our asses far away from this airfield. Those are bombers and they are headed this way."

They packed their gear, dismantled their shelter and ran north through the rugged terrain. No sooner had they crossed the adjacent ridge, than the ground shook. As they ran for safety, they heard a secondary explosion triggered by the ignition of aviation fuel tanks. Looking back, they saw a searing mass of flame arching toward the sky. The fiery explosions that rocked the airfield were so intense that the heat penetrated their field jackets and almost blistered their skin.

CHAPTER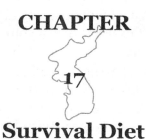
17

Survival Diet

*"Great responsibilities have been placed upon us
by the swift movement of events."*

~ Harry S. Truman

The battle order for the People's Army commanded by Kim called for a coordinated offensive across the 150-mile-long border between North and South Korea. It included amphibious landings on South Korea's west coast and aerial attacks on strategic targets by Russian-supplied YAK planes. Their battle plan relied on surprise and speed with the objective of destroying South Korea's military before the United States and other western powers could mount a defense. By their estimates, the so-called Fatherland Liberation War would be over in weeks.

Employing infantry, artillery, and armored cavalry units along six invasion routes stretching from the Sea of Japan to the Yellow Sea, the North Koreans planned to overwhelm the puppet government of Syngman Rhee and his Imperialist masters. With the withdrawal of American troops in 1949, South Korea was outnumbered and outgunned and had no weapons to thwart the advance of the Russian T-34 tanks that Kim deployed across the front.

The operational plan that his Soviet advisers had devised called for the North to control the capital city of Seoul within four days. The specific day of the invasion was left to Kim. At 0400 on Sunday, June 25, 1950, North Korea initiated the Fatherland Liberation War by attacking South Korea at the

Ongjin Peninsula on the western portion of the 38th parallel. Kim smiled at his own cleverness on attacking on a Sunday emulating Hitler's Operation Barbarossa, the offensive against the Soviet Union in 1941 which was also launched on a Sunday in June. When the Soviet command staff learned that Kim chose a Sunday to copy Hitler, they were incensed.

"Comrade Kim, we have received word that the counter-offensive on South Korea was initiated on a Sunday to honor Hitler's Operation Barbarossa when the Nazis invaded Russia. I stood in defense of Mother Russia to repel the Hun onslaught. We take exception to your adopting Hitler's tactic," said Ilshun Potnikov, Soviet liaison to the DPRK.

Knowing that his campaign had the imprimatur of Stalin, Kim apologized in desultory fashion and emphasized his adherence to the Soviet Deep Battle approach to warfare by simultaneously implementing multiple tactical, operational, and strategic operations against South Korea. He knew that the Soviet hierarchy was fully committed to supporting his push for fatherland unification and would not be deterred by some perceived insensitivity of his part. He made a mental note to avoid repeating such a mistake in the future. Continuation of the steady stream of Soviet ammunition, planes, and pilots was his main concern.

In one of the greatest attempts at political lies in modern times, Kim and Stalin peddled a narrative that it was South Korea that had started the war by sending its forces above the 38th parallel into North Korea prior to June 25th. Both dictators ascribed to the Big Lie propaganda technique espoused in *Mein Kampf* by Adolph Hitler. All planning documents and the final battle order were cast in language of a counter-offensive. History and certain undisputable facts have recognized the deceitfulness of the Communists. Several weeks prior to the fateful day, the government of North Korea had evacuated all residents living near the 38th parallel. The North's invasion plans were extremely detailed and had been repeatedly rehearsed before the war began.

Recognizing North Korea's actions in the early morning hours of June 25th as a full-scale invasion, Syngman Rhee notified the United Nations Commission on Korea and the U.S. Embassy and requested urgent support. He immediately made preparations to move the seat of his government out of Seoul, away from Kim's lightning advance.

News of the North Korean invasion reached President Harry Truman on Saturday night while he was en route to his home in Independence, Missouri. The President took a Sunday afternoon flight back to Washington and immediately engaged his National Security team in strategic discussions. The consensus was that the Soviets were behind the invasion and that the invasion was a direct challenge to the Truman Doctrine. The analysis by the Department of State was articulated by Undersecretary James Webb who presented the possibility that the Communists viewed the action by North Korea as similar to the civil war in China.

Truman scoffed at this notion admonishing Webb, "Now don't you go putting boogers in the sugar bowl. There is a world of difference between a civil war and one country crossing borders and invading another."

"The only thing that the Russians understand is force," said Louis Johnson, the Secretary of Defense.

"By God, I'm going to let them have it!" exclaimed Truman. He hadn't felt this agitated and determined since he faced down Stalin during the blockade of Berlin. It was barely one year earlier, in May 1949, that Truman had broken Stalin's attempt to starve West Berlin into submission by airlifting necessities to the beleaguered capital. Truman knew that if he failed to defend South Korea, Taiwan would be the next country to fall to the totalitarian forces of Communism.

From the moment that President Harry Truman realized the nature and extent of Communist perfidy, he knew that his best, and perhaps only option, was to unleash American military power under the leadership of General Douglas MacArthur. The inevitability of MacArthur's selection was

149

based on three factors: Experience - in MacArthur, Truman had a leader with experience of conducting military operations in the Pacific theater; Proximity - MacArthur and his command structure was in Japan just across the Sea of Japan and the Korea Strait; Speed – MacArthur was an operational genius when it came to the logistics of moving men and materiel.

The irony of this situation was not lost on the President. The two men could not have been more different. MacArthur was tall, arrogant, and accomplished. If there was anything akin to a military aristocracy in the United States, Douglas MacArthur would have qualified by virtue of a stellar pedigree. His father, Arthur MacArthur, Jr., was a West Point graduate who rose to the rank of Lieutenant General, received the Congressional Medal of Honor, and served as Governor-General of the U.S.-occupied Philippines in 1900.

Douglas also attended West Point where he graduated at the top of his class achieving the highest grades since Robert E. Lee. Douglas MacArthur had a legendary career that led to his promotion to five-star general. When MacArthur received the Congressional Medal of Honor, he and his father became the first such pair to receive the nation's highest award. In WWI alone, MacArthur received five Silver Stars for personal and conspicuous bravery. MacArthur affected a patrician air and he delighted in showing his disdain for President Truman at every opportunity from refusing to return to Washington when summoned, to making the President wait for his arrival on ceremonial occasions. MacArthur even launched an unsuccessful campaign for the Republican Presidential nomination to oppose Truman in the 1948 election.

In contrast, Truman was short of stature, almost half a foot shorter than his nemesis. Harry S. Truman's father was a livestock dealer in Missouri. Harry attended college for only one year and joined the Missouri Army National Guard as an enlisted man. By the time the United States entered World War I, Truman had risen to the rank of lieutenant. He served valiantly and when the war ended, he was discharged from the Army as a major. He held a series of clerical jobs and for a time owned a haberdasher's shop before entering politics. He rose to the U.S. Senate and then was tapped for the vice presidency by Franklin Delano Roosevelt in 1944. He became President in April 1945 when FDR died.

The plain-speaking Truman disliked the pompous MacArthur who returned the sentiment with icy contempt for "the little haberdasher" as he called the President. Yet, in June 1950, history had thrust them together as the two major impediments to the success of Kim's plan to "liberate" South Korea and unify the peninsula.

Truman acted quickly and decisively. He ordered the U.S. 7th Fleet into the Straits of Taiwan to deter any plans by Mao to attack. The nascent Red Chinese regime lacked the naval and air power to contest American might. Next, Truman took advantage of a Soviet mistake in United Nations.

After World War II, when the United Nations was established in 1945, five nations were given permanent seats on the powerful Security Council – the United States, Great Britain, France, the Soviet Union and the Republic of China. Each of these nations was given veto power over resolutions of the Council, including the most important power to authorize the use of military force for peace-keeping.

One of the first major disputes that came before the Security Council was precipitated by the victory of the Chinese Communists over the Nationalist forces in the Chinese civil war. On October 1, 1949, Mao declared the establishment of the People's Republic of China. In January 1950, the Chinese Communists and the Soviets demanded that the Nationalist Chinese government be removed from the Security Council and replaced by Mao Zedong's government. This demand was rejected and the Soviets walked out, boycotting further participation in the Security Council.

Unimpeded by a Soviet veto, the Security Council passed resolutions that North Korea was the aggressor in the dispute and that the United Nations would form a military command led by an American general. MacArthur's mandate from the United Nations originally charged him to "unify Korea." He had explicit instructions from Truman to drive the enemy out of Korea. In one of the greatest miscalculations of his storied career, the general boasted, "I can handle it with one arm tied behind my back."

General Douglas MacArthur, aware of the military and strategic importance in the situation of Korea raved, "By occupying all of Korea we could cut into pieces the one and only supply line connecting Siberia and the South..., control the whole area between Vladivostok and Singapore...nothing would then be beyond the reach of our power."

Like a frisky war horse chomping at the bit, MacArthur surged into action. Within days, MacArthur boarded his plane, *The Bataan*, at Haneda Airport on his way to Korea to inspect the defense perimeter along the Han River. It was the primary waterway of the capital city of Seoul and was a strategic link between the Yellow Sea and the central western regions of South Korea. The general arrived a day after one of the early tragedies of the war.

On June 28th, with North Korean occupation of Seoul imminent, there was a mass evacuation of the city via the Han River Highway Bridge. While the bridge was occupied with hundreds of civilians including women and children, South Korean engineers blew it up. Although the Chief Engineer was executed for ordering the detonation that resulted in hundreds of deaths, he was subsequently exonerated of blame. Nonetheless, MacArthur was present in the immediate aftermath of the Han River bridge to witness the carnage of desperate refugees. He informed President Truman that deployment of American ground forces was imperative.

If MacArthur gave any thought to the fate of Junior and Gomax during this crisis, it was at best fleeting. He was pre-occupied with saving the Korean Peninsula from being overrun before viable countermeasures could be implemented. MacArthur's immediate reaction was typical of the American military in the 20th century. "Let's bomb the snot out of the bastards."

Among the first targets was the P'yŏngyang Air Base where Junior and Gomax were conducting surveillance. Thanks to Gomax's hearing and survival instincts, the two marines had bugged out in time to avoid being incinerated.

* * *

"I'm sick of eating this crap," said Junior, as he tossed the metal can to the ground. "It's been weeks since . . ."

"For Christ sakes, maggot, quit your bellyaching. Unless you got some hidden up your butt, that's the last can we got," said Gomax, in a matter-of-fact tone.

He reached for the pack Junior used to carry his camera equipment.

"What are you doing?" asked Junior.

"I'm checking your pack for food. Hey, what's this?" said Gomax, pulling several brick-shaped items from the pack.

"Be careful," yelped Junior. "That's plastic explosive."

"What's it for?"

"If it looks like we are going to be captured, I'm under orders to destroy this camera equipment," said Junior.

Gomax shrugged and said, "We are out of vittles, maggot."

"What! Tell me you're not serious," said Junior, his eyes wide. "Now what?"

"Don't get your panties in a wad. Now, the fun begins," said Gomax. "On your feet. We gotta keep moving north."

They stopped only once to refill their canteens. Gomax carefully dispensed the water purification pills, admonishing Junior to avoid untreated water at all costs.

"There's all sorts of parasites and animal shit in the water that can take you out as fast as a bullet."

In the beginning, Junior checked the communication device frequently, hoping to get a signal through for their extraction. After a while, he checked it out of habit more than any expectation that the blue light would hold steady. Gradually, Junior checked it every other day and only when they were at an elevated position. The flashing lights became dimmer as the battery waned. The young marine marveled at the ability of Gomax to forge ahead in silence without the slightest trace of discouragement.

Day after day, Junior trudged his way behind Gomax in the darkness. He welcomed the lightening sky for it meant a chance to rest.

"Hey, Junya, you ready for some breakfast?" said Gomax, with a little too much delight. He took out his bayonet and hacked at the bark of a tree until he uncovered a mass of wriggling larvae the color of pus. Gomax popped several into his mouth and pantomimed rubbing his tummy in satisfaction.

"Your turn," he said offering one to Junior in an upturned palm. Junior grimaced and shook his head.

"If you don't eat this, you're gonna starve. The general ordered me to keep you alive and I will, even if I got to force feed you like a baby," said Gomax in a menacing tone.

Junior searched the surrounding woods for an escape. Before he could react, Gomax sprang and pinned him to the ground, knees on arms. The older man pinched Junior's nose until he gasped for air. He roughly shoved a handful of larvae into Junior's mouth and forced it shut.

"Now, eat your breakfast, Junya," Gomax cooed, mimicking a doting mother.

Junior squirmed and gagged, but eventually relented and swallowed. This process continued until the cache was empty.

"There you go. Wash it down with some water, and get you some shuteye."

Again, no steady blue light and another night on the move, only now they headed east rather than north. When the morning light appeared, they stopped. Junior watched as Gomax tore a small branch from a sapling and fashioned a Y-shaped handle. He tied a piece of mesh to it for a net and used it to capture flying insects.

"These buggers are tasty if you rip off the wings first," he said, offering one to Junior. When Junior hesitated, Gomax glared as if to say don't make me feed you like a baby. Junior popped one into his mouth and closed his eyes to steel himself. The crunch of the exoskeleton, followed by a faintly nutty ooze was not too repulsive.

"You are on your own now, Junya. This here is an official United States Marine Corps aerial insect net, BYO," said Gomax as he handed his companion an improvised net.

"What does BYO mean?" asked Junior.

"Build your own. Now, get some winks."

After a fitful sleep where he dreamed that he was being carried away by locusts that resembled the flying monkeys of *The Wizard of Oz*, Junior woke to the sound of Gomax cursing and hacking at some creature with his machete.

"There, I got your ass," said Gomax standing over a decapitated snake. "Now, we are gonna chow down."

Junior cringed as Gomax lifted the snake to drain its blood and bile into his canteen cup. Next, he tugged his bayonet down the length of the snake, stopping only to extract the heart which he popped into his mouth plucking the organ from the blood vessels as if he were removing a cherry from a stem. Ignoring the retching noises coming from Junior, Gomax washed down the still-beating heart with the snake blood cocktail.

"Junya, get some water from the creek."

When Junior returned with his steel pot filled with water, Gomax had a fire blazing.

"Put a water pill in there and we are gonna boil this bastard real good," said Gomax proudly displaying lengths of butchered snake. Careful to avoid contaminated water, Junior dropped a halazone tablet into the cooking water.

"What is that?" asked Junior, pointing at a single burner cooking device.

155

"What's this?" said Gomax. "It's my handy-dandy pocket stove."

"Where did it come from?" asked Junior, his face crinkled in disbelief.

"It's an official government issue Model 520 Coleman Military Burner, pressurized liquid fuel type. Weighs only three pounds and burns anything especially piss after you drink some good old moonshine," said Gomax, emitting a maniacal laugh. "I call it the roarer on account of the sound she makes when I crank her up."

Junior had to admit that Gomax was an endless source of amazement. The youngster began to salivate as the smell of the boiling snake cooking in the helmet permeated the area. After endless days of ingesting larvae, wood lice, and all manner of worms (earth worms were the most repulsive), the thought of chewing on meat led to a feeling of gustatory anticipation that Junior had never experienced before. He remembered his mother's adage that hunger is the best seasoning and appreciated its profound wisdom.

Gomax emerged from the woods clutching a handful of leafy vegetation that resembled lettuce. He sprinkled it into the pot and stirred it with his bayonet.

"I found these here roots under a rock by the creek. This'll add nice flavor to our feast."

Despite the sinewy texture of the serpent flesh, Junior savored each morsel. Eating it like corn on the cob, he was not deterred by the multitude of tiny bones; it felt good to eat a vertebrate. After the snake sections had been consumed, the two men shared the broth. Reinvigorated, Junior withdrew the commo device and switched it on. The blue light shone strong and steady. Their ordeal was nearing an end.

CHAPTER

18

Sumo Wrestlers and Geisha Girls

"The soldier above all others prays for peace, for it is the soldier who must suffer and bear the deepest wounds and scars of war."

~ General Douglas MacArthur

When Junior and Gomax returned from their reconnaissance mission in *P'yŏngyang,* MacArthur's headquarters was a hive of amplified activity as the U.S. military planned and organized its response to the Communist invasion of the Republic of South Korea. Field grade officers flittered around the legendary general like so many worker bees spilling out of a beehive that had been knocked to the ground by a honey bear. MacArthur was at the center surrounded by the buzzing surge of vibration filling the room as plans, logistics, and contingencies were hatched and delivered, most dying before taking flight. On seeing Junior and Gomax enter, MacArthur pointed to his watch and raised four fingers signifying an appointment later that afternoon.

With bullets flying and bombs dropping, the U.S. military establishment ramped up, spoiling for a fight. They ignored the assessment of the State Department about the situation on the ground in South Korea. The State Department expressed the prospect of a military disaster in which UN forces would "either be driven to the sea or bottled into rugged mountain passes and soggy rice fields for annihilation." Time would demonstrate just how prophetic these words were.

Gomax and Junior hurried to their barracks and performed the three S's of military life – shit, shower, and shave. After a couple of turns through the chow line, they racked-out until it was time to meet the general. At 3:45 P.M. they were ushered into a secure interior conference room waiting for their boss. Along one wall was a circular array of headshot images of military personnel. Based on the uniform collars or hats, there were close-up photographs of North Korean, Russian, and Chinese officers. Junior recognized them as pictures that he had taken from his perch outside the air base at *P'yŏngyang on his last mission.*

"Gentlemen," said MacArthur. "Easy. Be seated."

Before their fannies hit the metal chairs, MacArthur launched into a detailed summary of the North Korean invasion, the conquest of Seoul, and the six prongs that were advancing through South Korea like shit through a goose. He told them that the Commie bastards were trying to vanquish South Korea before the western powers could get men and equipment on the ground to thwart their takeover.

Using a map of the Korean Peninsula and a pointer, MacArthur explained that the South Korean Army had collapsed and Syngman Rhee's government was temporarily reconstituting in Taegu with plans to relocate to Pusan the southernmost city on the peninsula as soon as U.S. forces could establish a defensible perimeter around the city of Pusan. The pointer thwacked on the map at the location of Taegu, and again at Pusan. MacArthur warned that if the Pusan perimeter did not hold until the U.S. could respond with sufficient force on the ground, the South Koreans would be driven off the peninsula into the Korea Strait. He vowed that the United States would not allow that to happen and that they were part of his secret solution.

The door opened and a stocky man wearing nondescript utilities entered. MacArthur gestured for the men to remain seated. Even though the silver-haired man carried himself like an officer, he wore no rank. Aside from his name appearing on his uniform shirt above his heart, the only identifying emblems were patches depicting a spear tip on each wing of his collar. Junior's face wore a befuddled look; while Gomax slouched back in his chair as if awaiting a bravura performance. He would not be disappointed.

"Gentlemen, this is 'Wild Bill' Donovan the originator of America's spy organization. We fought together in the Great War and, in WWII, Bill established the Office of Strategic Services, now the Central Intelligence Agency. He will brief you on your next mission," said General MacArthur.

Donovan adjusted his wire-rimmed glasses. Wielding the pointer like a rapier, Donovan described a plan to assassinate as many enemy leaders as possible. He moved from the map to the wall of portraits.

"Good afternoon, men," said Donovan. "Welcome back. Congratulations! Your last mission was so successful that it provided us with the capacity to cripple the enemy and buy time for Douglas to move enough men and materiel into Korea to win this damn war."

Junior blinked in disbelief. He had never heard anyone call the general by his first name. Gomax smirked, knowing that he himself had called MacArthur many names, most of them profane.

"Welcome to Operation Solar Eclipse. This wall contains the constellation of Kim's leadership cadre. We are going to eradicate each of these scumbags, one-by-one, until there is no one left to lead the invading troops. Cut off the head and the slimy snake dies. And, you are the tip of our spear. You will have three days leave, then we will drop you behind the enemy's forward wall and you will systematically assassinate these men. We have designated the priority according to our solar system – 10, Pluto; 9, *Neptune;* 8, *Uranus;* 7, *Saturn;* 6, *Jupiter;* 5, *Mars;* 4, *Earth;* 3, *Venus;* 2, *Mercury* and numero uno, Kim as the sun, in the center."

The pointer slammed on each photo as Donovan counted down.

"How do you want us to do this?" drawled Gomax.

"You, sir, are the best sniper in the United States Marine Corps. You can blow a man's head off from 5 football fields away. Junior will be your spotter. We expect you to take them down safely at long range . . . . However, if your best approach in any circumstance is to slit their throats, then you do it. The U.S. military does not care if you shoot, stab, strangle, or poison them, as long as you kill the bastards. You have one hundred percent operational discretion to complete the mission."

Gomax smiled.

"There are only two rules of this engagement. First, under no circumstances are you to kill Russian or Chinese officers unless your own lives are in extreme danger. We do not want to give them any excuse to expand this conflict. Kill no Russian or Chinese officers, understood?"

"Yessir," both replied.

"The second rule is also simple. You are non-existent entities. You will be going in sterile. No military insignias, rank, or identification."

Gomax nodded. Junior raised a questioning hand.

"That means that as far as the military is concerned, you do not exist. If you are killed or captured, the United States will disavow you. There is a price on Junior's head. Kim will do anything to eliminate the "Ghost Photographer." Consider yourselves a special attack corps," said Donovan.

"Y'all mean a kamikaze mission, right?" spat out Gomax.

"Expendable," reiterated Donovan. "The target zone is crawling with hostiles. The enemy is moving more quickly than we expected. You will have to be mobile and flexible. Remember, your country may be asking for the ultimate sacrifice, but the current situation is desperate."

Junior looked to MacArthur who gave him a solemn nod like a grandfather sending his beloved gelding to the glue factory. Junior shrank away as if hit by an arctic wind. As they left the briefing, he saw MacArthur pull Gomax aside and pass him an envelope.

"Junya, prepare your ass for some serious carousing. The old man just told me to show you the time of your life. We are gonna have some kickass fun tonight!"

After changing into civvies, they boarded a train on the Yamanote Line and got off at Harajuku Station. They walked across the Shrine Bridge, a wide pedestrian walkway made of reinforced concrete. It was a pleasant balmy summer night and the bridge was jampacked with people. The atmosphere was festive. Junior's eyes almost swiveled out of his head as he took in the scene. There were gaily-dressed musicians mingling with jugglers and other street performers. He smiled as Gomax tugged at him to get him through the maze of people. The only tense moment came when a one-legged Japanese war veteran spat at them while screaming loud curses and shaking a scrawny fist.

"That sonuvabitch looks like one of the Jap pricks I nailed when we took Iwo Jima. Fuck him!" said Gomax, who launched a glob of spit toward the heckler. The yellow mucous ball missed and hung precariously on a concrete bridge support before turning into an elongated blob which slowly descended to the road surface.

The Americans crossed the bridge and joined the queue to secure tickets for the sumo wrestling bouts on the grounds of the Meiji Shrine. Wishing that he had brought a camera, Junior admired the Shrine. Built in the traditional *nagare-zukuri* architectural style to honor the reign of Emperor Meiji and Empress Shōken, the building had an asymmetrical gabled roof distinctive to Shinto temples. It provided a solemn backdrop to the sporting event that was infused with religious rituals.

With tickets in hand, Gomax hustled Junior toward the entrance. He stopped to purchase several skewers of yakitori, grilled chicken, which he handed to Junior. Next, Gomax bought over-sized beer bottles and boxes of senbei crackers and salted peanuts. They made their way through the crowd to reserved seats near the sumo ring, called the dohyo. Gomax removed his shoes, gesturing for Junior to do the same, and sat cross-legged on red floor cushions.

They were situated a few rows from the ring. Unlike an American boxing ring, there were no posts or ropes to define its perimeter. The *dohyo* was constructed of straw bales covered with a thick layer of clay that was topped with sand. It was about eighteen feet square and contained a fifteen-foot circle. Over the

161

buzz of the crowd, Gomax explained that the wrestler won when he pushed his opponent out of the circle. Once any part of his body went beyond the circle, he lost.

Junior's gaze was drawn to the structure suspended over the ring. It was an inverted V-shaped roof, festooned at the corners with thick silk tassels – orange, green, black, and white, representing the four seasons. This roof was constructed of thick square timbers and there was a series of pitch-black logs attached perpendicular to the spine. The main body of the structure was stained light tan, with dark mahogany accenting the horizontal members. Ornate brass plates and navy-blue banners with white lettering completed the decoration. Support for this impressive canopy was indiscernible, lending it a magical aura like a floating guardian angel.

Gomax guzzled a beer and consumed the chicken by swallowing each piece, and withdrawing the skewer from his mouth without dripping any sauce. The uncharacteristic delicacy of Gomax's method of eating amused Junior. The veteran tipped his bottle toward Junior in a toast to their good fortune. Junior noticed a slight, weary sadness in his companion's eyes. The moment was interrupted by the rhythmic beating of drums which hushed the crowd.

In the distance, Junior saw a formation of bare-chested men waiting to enter the arena. His eyes bulged in disbelief as they approached. They were huge – broad, squat blocks of humanity wearing only leather loincloths from which hung ceremonial strips of fabric. The skin of each sumo glistened with sweat and his black hair was pulled back into a top knot, perched on his head. Marching slowly to the cadence of the drum, each wore an expression of extreme solemnity as the sacred space of the dohyo was approached.

With his eyes glued on the spectacle, Gomax uncapped a bottle of sake that he had taken from his jacket. He raised it to his lips, but was interrupted by a strong hand on his wrist. With an admonitory wave, a robed attendant gripped the older marine. Feeling Gomax coil preparing to fight, Junior knew that all hell was about to break loose.

162

Suddenly, the man smiled and produced two ceramic cups, indicating that they were for drinking the sake.

"Well, I'll be damned," uttered Gomax, adding with a phony smile. "Arry-git-o, thanks, (*sotto voce*) you yellow bastard."

Once the wrestlers, also called *rikishi*, had entered the arena and taken their places around the circle, another group moved into the spotlight. Leading the way was a diminutive man dressed in a colorful, ankle-length silk kimono. Arrayed on his kimono were tassels and embroidered rosettes to signify his rank among referees, or *gyōji*. He wore a black lacquered headdress known as an *eboshi*. The *gyōji* carried a wooden war fan, *or gunbai,* patterned after the solid wood fans used by Japanese military commanders to signal orders to their troops. He was followed by five judges who wore black formal kimonos and assumed their places around the ring. The *rikishi* also stepped down and took their places.

Taking in the cavalcade with rapt attention, Junior felt a surge of pride in his own military training. He identified with these *rikishi* who were the product of discipline and tradition. The first two combatants stepped onto the *dohyo* and simultaneously stamped one leg, then the other to squash bad spirits. Junior distinguished them by the more reddish shade of one's leather belt. After facing each other and staring into each other's eyes to detect any doubt or fear, they returned to their corners. There, they grabbed a handful of salt and tossed it high in the air to purify the ring and protect them from injury. Junior later learned that the salt purification ritual was called *shiomaki*. A sip of water prepared the *rikishi* for combat.

The wrestlers moved to the center of the ring and toed their marks, squatting with arms outstretched to demonstrate that they bore no weapons. The *gyōji* shrieked the names of the combatants in a high-pitched voice calling them to battle. The sumo warriors faced each other in a crouched, ready position and sprang into action at the flick of the war fan. The thunderous collision that ensued startled Junior with its sound and fury. The men crashed and grunted into one another until red belt grasped the other's belt, lifted and drove his traction-less opponent out of the circle. This feat of brute strength was met with ecstatic applause. The sumo faced each other across the circle and bowed toward each other with respect.

The bouts continued in this fashion, none lasting longer than thirty seconds. All the while Gomax downed shots of sake and became louder and more demonstrative in his actions. He complained about the *gyōji* to the judges to no avail. Noting that they were drawing hostile attention of some locals, Junior tried to quell his companion. Gomax would have none of it. He screamed and gesticulated wildly at the umpire. Between bouts, the *gyōji* whispered to one of the bouncers and nodded toward the Americans.

When three large goons approached Gomax, he cursed them, gathered his shoes and shouted, "We were just leaving this pigsty anyways. That worm of a referee is crooked. I don't care how much I drunk, I knows a rigged game when I see one. C'mon Junior, let's get some poontang."

The cool night air did nothing to sober his companion. Junior led them back over the bridge.

"Over there," said Gomax pointing to a side street that was lined with small shops and restaurants. They walked along the road toward the Shibuya River until they reached the façade of a teahouse with three large planters, containing red, white, and blue hydrangea bushes. A small brass plate on the red lacquered door identified it as the Teahouse of the Auspicious Blessing.

"This is it. The old man made reservations for us here," said Gomax, steering Junior toward an ebony door.

"Come in, gentlemen. Welcome to our *ochaya*. This teahouse is your home for the rest of the evening," said a pleasant woman in impeccable English. "My name is Miyumi and I am here to see that you are well taken care of. The general has taken care of everything. Please, your *tatami* is this way."

Their *tatami* was a dining/entertainment room that was down a long hall decorated with sensuous watercolor paintings of geisha girls. Miyumi wore a red kimono emblazoned with gold and silver dragons. Her arms were tucked into her sleeves. She bowed, turned and padded down the hallway, her straw sandals barely scuffing the black tile floor. As they followed her, Junior stared quizzically at her back where the material bunched in a rectangular shape above her waist. He thought to himself, why is she wearing a parachute?

As if she had read his mind, their hostess said, "In case you are wondering, I am wearing the traditional formal kimono. It is essentially a large, rectangular fabric that wraps and folds around the body. Ornate patterns provide beauty and a sash known as an *obi* is tied at the waist to keep the kimono from shifting and opening. Over time, the sashes became wider and more decorative. The pack-like feature at the small of the back is actually the knot securing the sash; it is called the *otaiko*. In more modern forms to enhance the beauty of the pattern in the fabric, some women insert a stiff pillow in the *otaiko*. I do not. My *otaiko* is a skillful knot."

She led them to a private room which featured a low square table, silk cushions, and a few tables lining the far wall. A soft, warm light from several wood-and-translucent paper fixtures lit the room. To the right and left of the *tatami* were private areas that were separated by *shōji*, or room dividers. The *shōji* were attractive wooden frames that held a lattice of bamboo above decorated paper backlit to emphasize the Edenic floral designs painted on its surface. A faint aroma of lavender suffused the *tatami*, giving the room a heavenly aura.

"Please remove your shoes and make yourselves comfortable. Tonight, you will be served by Akiko and Nami, two of our most delightful geishas. They will entertain you by performing ancient dance, song, and other feminine arts. They will be assisted by an apprentice, or *maiko*, named Sachie. Your banquet, we call it *ozashiki*, will be served momentarily. We have promised the General that we will make this night most memorable."

When Gomax and Junior were seated cross-legged at the table, Miyumi clapped ever-so-lightly. The men heard the approaching sound of a flute playing a serene melody. With a theatrical flourish, Miyumi opened the *tatami* door.

Akiko entered first. Her face was a mask of pure white highlighted by wings of turquoise shadow that ran along her

165

nose and continued over her eyes. The color was bounded by delicate raven eyebrows that floated like expressive crescents separating the ocean from the clouds. A shiny crimson heart punctuated the center of her mouth. Her otherwise white lips were parted in song – an eerie high-pitched song of welcome. She wore a traditional kimono the same vibrant turquoise as her eye shadow and was speckled with scenes of the countryside. The tantalizing aroma of delicacies wafted from covered dishes on a bamboo tray that Akiko placed on the table.

Before Gomax and Junior could absorb the celestial vision of Akiko, Nami entered. She wore a silk kimono of shimmering gold, embellished with green flying fish that seemed to leap from one curve to the next. Her face was coated with a patina the color of meringue. Emerald shadow graced the arc of her eyelids, fading to the white of her forehead separated only by two angled black lines that gave her face a somewhat startled look. With full lips painted fire-engine red, Nami sang in pleasing harmony with Akiko. Nami carried a tray filled with plates of chilled food in a colorful palette of sashimi, sushi, and assorted roe. She arranged the plates with rainbow precision.

The last and youngest attendant to enter was Sachie, the apprentice, or *maiko,* whose status was delineated by a strip of red around the collar of her garment. Her colloquial title was *o-shaku,* meaning "one who pours alcohol." Since form follows function, Sachie bore a tray covered with bottles of sake, beer, and bourbon. A strap around her neck supported the tray which cantilevered from her waist. This freed her hands to play a *shakuhachi,* a bamboo flute-like instrument. Sachie played the melody with such élan that Junior's attention was riveted on her. Had it not been for the white make-up, her blushing would have revealed a depth of feeling that was both exhilarating and confusing. Her pure white kimono was decorated with cherry blossoms, delicately shaded in pinks, mauves, and fuchsias. Her eyelids fluttered as she passed Junior on her way to the far table where she set up the bar.

Seeing his friend's infatuation with Sachie, Gomax remarked that, "She's prettier than a blue-nosed mule."

The impact that Sachie made on Junior was unforgettable; something in his stomach lifted in much the way it felt when he parachuted. Even when Akiko sat next to him, served him gourmet cuisine and told humorous tales designed to titillate and arouse, Junior could not take his gaze from Sachie. She was a vision of perfection.

"*Kanpai!* Cheers! Bottoms up!"

They raised their cups of sake and toasted. This procedure was repeated frequently as the geishas served the sumptuous meal explaining the history, significance, and gustatory secrets of each course. As the party ate their way through the culinary progression of the magnificent feast, Akiko and Nami regaled them with stories, riddles, and dances which reenacted legends.

Sachie made sure that their cups were replenished and even led a few *kanpai's* as they graduated from sake to beer to bourbon. All the while they played drinking games. Whether by design or bad luck, Akiko frequently lost and chugged down another drink to the shouts of "*Kanpai!*" from her companions. By the end of the meal she passed out on the tabletop, snoring genteelly.

Gomax and Nami rose and shuffled off toward a side chamber that slid open with a flick of the *shoji*. Junior spied a futon before the ornate divider slid closed. What followed was the rustle of fabric, curses at the ancestry of the varmint who invented ceremonial knots, and cries of triumph at joys revealed.

Sachie insisted on clearing the plates while singing the sweetest songs Junior had ever heard. When all was in order, she embraced Junior and shared the first kiss each had ever experienced. Their knees weakened as their passion grew and they sank to the floor clinging to each other praying that this feeling would never end. And so, Junior experienced his first *ozashiki* banquet and much more.

* * *

While Junior and Gomax were enjoying a night of all nights, Kim Il Sung was celebrating the swift progress of his army into Seoul, the capital of his enemy. North Korea's Army ushered

Kim Il Sung into Seoul. He drove the ZIS 110 limousine given to him by Stalin himself. Looking remarkably like a 1942 Packard, the black limo sparkled in the summer sun.

His destination was Gyeongmudae, site of the executive offices and residence of the President of the Republic of Korea. It was known as the Blue House in deference to the signature blue roof which is covered with individually-kilned clay tiles. The Blue House featured a smooth, curved roof in traditional Korean style. It was part of an elegant complex of buildings set in the scenic backdrop of Bugak Mountain.

Like many conquering leaders enjoying the spoils of their victory throughout history, Kim and his general staff celebrated in the Blue House. His chef had prepared a feast. Kim rose and raised his glass of *soju*. Kim had customized his uniform by adding an azure collar accented with a red stripe to honor his service in the Soviet Army during WWII. He surveyed the group and smiled broadly, his prominent slightly buck teeth shining in the brightly lit hall.

"*Geonbae!* Cheers to the victorious!"

In the days that followed, the North Korean Army consolidated their gains, but failed to press their advantage. In what would prove to be a significant blunder, Kim and his staff spent the next week preparing for the next phase. The North Koreans had fully expected the government of South Korea to collapse and surrender. Instead, Syngman Rhee's government fled to Taegu and was clinging to the hope that they could survive until the Imperialist dog MacArthur could save them. Kim's delay gave MacArthur the chance to mobilize.

At the conclusion of one of their planning sessions, Kim boasted to his general staff, "I will personally lead the assault on Taegu and crush Syngman Rhee and his puppet clique forever and all time!"

Little did Kim know that this attack would put him on a collision course with Junior, the Ghost Photographer, and Operation Solar Eclipse.

CHAPTER

19

Rock Salmusa Deadhead

"He had a way of touching your elbow or shoulder, upping his chin with a slight jerk and crowding into his eyes such a warm blessing; for him for the way he made you feel you'd contributed a boon to the whole human race."

~ Major William Ganoe

Those fortunate enough to fall head over heels in love can identify with Junior's state of mind on the day after the *ozashiki* banquet at the Teahouse of the Auspicious Blessing. In contrast to Gomax who was in a deep sleep, sounding like a cyclone in a closet, Junior awoke euphoric. The feelings of loneliness, guilt, and insecurity were driven to the inner recesses of his mind and were replaced by more tender feelings. Sachie's face, smile, and demure eyes totally consumed him. He checked his watch frequently, hoping that his next meeting with her would come sooner. Before leaving the teahouse, Junior and Sachie arranged to meet again the following afternoon. Time slowed, sagging like a Dali watch.

He distracted himself by cleaning the equipment he would need for Operation Solar Eclipse. They would be in extreme jeopardy while they tried to assassinate the military leaders of the North. Grit and moisture were two of the most devastating elements for cameras and firearms. During their last mission around P'yŏngyang, he and Gomax had been stranded without communications for an extended time. Their equipment had been exposed to extreme conditions and required significant elbow grease to restore to optimum functionality. He spent most of the morning with cleaning tools, solvents, and cloths working on his gear.

As noon approached, his stomach yearned for a reprise of the balanced culinary masterpiece they had eaten the previous evening. Thinking of the upcoming foray behind enemy lines, he was reminded of their survival on insects and snakes, day after day until they were exfiltrated. He would use the memory of last night's banquet to sustain him on the next mission.

Trying not to look conspicuous while standing on the train platform, Junior glanced up and down searching for Sachie. Even though he was of average height for an American, he towered over many of the Japanese. Looking down at the bouquet of colorful summer flowers that he held for Sachie, Junior regretted that decision. Was he a lovesick fool who was embarrassing himself by violating social norms? Surrounded by hundreds of Japanese, he could not even begin to guess. Was he imagining the condemnatory glances of passersby? Would some anti-American zealot harass Sachie for fraternizing with a *gaijin,* a stranger?

He slouched and chided himself for not wearing his flat cap for anonymity. He decided to go bareheaded so that Sachie would have a better chance of recognizing him. Trying to be inconspicuous, he gave a prolonged glance to each passing young female. A rush of anxiety flooded his mind as he realized that he might not be able to recognize her. Despite his fantasizing about spending his life with this angel, it dawned on him that she would not be wearing the elaborate whiteface makeup of a geisha girl. What do a geisha's eyebrows look like when she is off-duty?

Feeling a tug on his sleeve, he turned to see Sachie smiling up at him. His doubts evaporated only to be replaced by an awkward grin. Her flawless complexion was just as radiant as the previous evening. Junior had no trouble identifying her. He realized that her natural beauty had been obscured by the whiteface. He thrust the flowers in her direction without uttering a word. She squealed with delight.

"Junior, you should not have bothered. You are such a gentleman," she said while leaning toward him with a slight bow.

"*Arrigato*, thanks" she whispered, her ivory teeth glistening.

In contrast to the dazzling kimono she had worn at the teahouse, Sachie wore a brown suit jacket and ankle length skirt. She was shorter than Junior remembered, but that was no doubt due to her lack of the bouffant geisha wig that she had worn while performing as a geisha. Her almond-shaped eyes twinkled in the sunlight.

"Come, this way. Our train is ready to depart," said Sachie.

They spent the trip learning about each other. Sachie shared that she grew up in Nagasaki. She learned English at the Roman Catholic missionary school that was located in the outskirts of the city. During WWII, her father worked in the naval shipyard and her mother worked at a munition's factory. Sachie teared up when she recounted how her parents were killed by the A-bomb attack.

Junior could say nothing; he placed his arm around her shoulders and gave her a reassuring hug. She dabbed her eyes with a handkerchief that was crumpled in her hand. They rode in silence until they had to change trains. When they were resettled, Junior told Sachie about the decimation of the males in his family and how most had lost their lives in the world wars. Without mentioning the obvious, each wondered whether Junior would be added to the toll.

When at last they reached their destination, the majestic sight of Mt. Fuji served to dissipate the tension. The sight of Mt. Fuji dominated all perception. Junior gaped at the snow-capped mountain which rose over 12,000 feet. Perfectly proportioned, it projected power, strength, and harmony. He thought of his teacher and wondered how Ansel Adams would capture the mountain on film.

"Fuji-san," said Sachie, pointing proudly toward the mountain. "It is the tallest peak in Japan. Many consider it sacred."

"I can see why," said Junior. "It is magnificent."

"Would you like to climb to the summit?" asked Sachie, with a hopeful tone.

"Yes, I would, very much."

"Good, let's catch that bus to the Fifth Station where we can get the Yoshida Trail to the summit."

For Junior, the two-day leave with Sachie was the one of the best times of his life. They stayed at a *ryokan*, a traditional lodge, relaxed in the *onsens*, thermal springs, and dined on Japanese fare. Over the course of the weekend, the pair reveled in each other's company. Had Junior been more educated he might have recognized that he was playing Romeo to Sachie's Juliet. Of course, he was not, and his infatuation blossomed to produce a yearning ache in his heart.

As the proverb teaches, all good things must come to an end. Their idyllic time came to an end on the train platform where their holiday began. Junior studied her upturned face and felt a rush of emotion. Sachie responded by hugging him with a strength that belied her slight frame. In the silence unbroken by inadequate words, she reached into her pocket and produced an article on a leather string.

"This is a *magatama*, a Japanese token of affection. I wish for you to have it and wear it close to your heart. It will protect you from evil," Sachie said as she lifted it over his head.

Junior blushed and fingered the polished granite amulet that hung from his neck. A deep olive-green, it reminded him of the color of his marine utilities. Curved and rounded at the top, it tapered to a point much like a claw or tusk. Junior's heart swelled as he leaned toward her and whispered, "*Arrigato*. Thank you. I will treasure this always."

* * *

By the time he returned to the base and met with Gomax, Junior was totally rejuvenated. Converse to his usual trudge, his gait was light, almost spritely. He hummed the melody of a Japanese song that Sachie had played for him on her *shakuhachi*, bamboo flute, when they had reached the summit of Mt. Fuji. It was the sweetest sound he had ever heard.

"Welcome back, lover boy," snarked Gomax when he saw Junior. "I'm sure you got no shuteye, but that's not my problem. We are leaving at zero-dark thirty. Dropping behind enemy lines north of the Sobaek range. The brass figures that Kim's gonna hit Taejon, so we gotta get there ahead of him."

Until his mind kicked into gear, Junior just gaped at Gomax. One minute he was basking in the afterglow of the best few days of his life, and the next he was preparing for his most dangerous mission ever. Trying to disguise a feeling of resentment, Junior switched to combat mode. He double-checked his camera equipment, making sure that he packed enough film and plastic explosives in case he found himself in a Little Bighorn situation. Next, weapons and ammo were packed. Then, he stuffed extra clothing and some personal items into his rucksack.

As Junior walked to the area known as the pantry to secure rations for the mission, Gomax bellowed, "Get your ass out of there, Junya. With what we gotta carry to complete our mission there's no room for vittles. We'll eat bugs and snakes just like last time."

Junior blanched at the thought of eating grubs and worms again. He was still digesting the delightful Japanese food that Sachie had introduced him to and the thought of bony snake stew was repulsive. His stomach roiled. He never thought that he would pine for C rations.

The following day, Junior followed Gomax through the woods of the Sobaek Mountains which formed a spine through the center of South Korea. Their destination was the junction of the Kum River and the Seoul-Pusan railroad, approximately eight miles north of the city of Taejon. They were about three days' march from where they hoped to find Kim's command post for his assault on Taejon.

After the North's invasion and the inevitable fall of Seoul, President Syngman Rhee moved his government from the capital eighty-seven miles south to Taejon. The city was located at the southwestern foothills of the Sobaek Mountains. The Kum River, a natural defensive boundary, flowed a dozen miles north and west of Taejon. Situated on a coastal plain between Seoul to the north and Pusan to the south, Taejon was the locus of numerous road and rail lines, making it a strategic hub for whomever controlled it.

In recognition of its importance, MacArthur sent the 24th Infantry Division under the command of General William Frishe Dean to defend Taejon and slow the rapid advance of the North Korean army. This would prove to be an ill-fated mission for the U.S. military and Dean personally.

During their planning session, Donovan and Gomax had identified a railroad tunnel near the junction of the river and railway which they believed would be a natural place for Kim to locate his headquarters. The two marines located a perch in the mountains with a good sightline of the junction. They erected an ingenious sniper's hide with a 270° view of the junction. It was virtually invisible from a distance of more than five feet. Sheltered by a rock ledge, it was impervious to the elements and detection by the enemy. It was large enough to secrete them for days if necessary. They secured their gear deep within the crevice.

After days of eating forest grubs and worms, Junior was despondent. His stomach growled and his head pounded. His pity party was interrupted by a shout.

"Hey, Junya, get some water from that there stream and fire up the pocket stove. We are gonna feast tonight!" said Gomax.

His partner emerged from the underbrush holding a long, writhing snake behind its head. Gomax chortled as he prepared to dispatch the creature and drink its fluids. Junior grimaced as his stomach churned at the coming spectacle.

Junior busied himself following orders as he watched Gomax decapitate the rock salmusa. The snake was reddish-brown, overlaid with irregular lighter blotches with black borders. The rock salmusa was indigenous to the Sobaek Mountains and typically found near streams. Part of the viper family, it bore an inverted V marked the top of its head. The one captured by Gomax had a plump body that was close to three feet long. The older man drained the snake and gutted it. The gunny hummed as he cleaned and chopped the snake before tossing the chunks into the water boiling in the steel pot.

The younger man used a hand-pump to pressurize the fuel, then he opened the control valve to release the fuel/air mixture for ignition. The stove fired with a roar. He had to admit that the snake feast would be a welcome addition to their diets. Two days of eating insects was two days too many. While waiting for dinner, Gomax took the snake skin and fashioned it into a bandanna for his helmet.

Then, Gomax committed a grave mistake. Absent-mindedly, he picked up the snake head. It reflexively bit him, injecting venom into the meaty web between the thumb and forefinger of his right hand. The veteran stifled a scream.

In between muttering curses in numerous languages, Gomax directed Junior to his pack where, after rummaging for an agonizing period of time, he located a glass vial labeled 'antivenom.' Gomax's skin was dove gray and his face was covered with perspiration. He slumped back against his pack, his eyes closed. Junior removed the packaging and injected the medicine into the vein at the stricken man's elbow. Gomax breathed deeply trying to avoid hyperventilating.

The young marine examined the wound, careful to keep the area bitten below the victim's heart to keep the toxin from spreading faster. He saw two marks where the fangs penetrated the skin of Gomax's hand. A bright, red swelling turned the hand into an angry, bulging mass. A persistent ooze seeped from the fang puncture marks. Gomax drifted into incoherent, semi-conscious mumbling that was punctuated by creative expletives aimed at the snake and officers who had wronged him.

Gomax remained delirious through the daylight hours. The young marine wracked his brain for any information he ever knew about poisonous snakes. The only thing he could recall was that snakes used their tongues to smell, and locate prey. No one had ever told him that the neurons in a snake remained active and could trigger a bite reflex for as long as twenty minutes after decapitation. Apparently, Gomax did not know this either.

Whenever his companion awoke, Junior tried to feed him some broth from their snake stew. Gomax sputtered, incapable of swallowing. His eyes were bloodshot and rheumy. Worst of all, his hand was so swollen that it looked to Junior like a sausage on the grill whose skin was about to burst open. The fang wounds oozed, a noxious and viscose fluid. Gingerly, he re-wrapped the hand with new gauze. Junior worried that Gomax would not survive. He prayed for Gomax.

During the night, Junior reconnoitered the area within a mile radius of their position. He saw activity by the railroad tunnel down near the river. Trucks and heavy artillery pieces were being moved into the tunnel to avoid discovery by overflying aircraft. His heart quickened when he saw the soldiers erecting large tents, then putting camouflage nets over them. Could this be the command center for the North Korean attack on Taejon, he wondered?

He hurried back to their camp, only to find Gomax retching dry heaves. The veins on his neck bulged. Junior talked to him softly in an effort to comfort the stricken man. Gomax was burning with fever. Wishing that MacArthur were there to provide advice, Junior placed a damp compress on Gomax's head and forced back tears. He debated calling for extraction, but decided against it, based on the grave condition of Gomax and the fear of disappointing the general.

*   *   *

Less than a mile from where Gomax battled for his life, another group of men raised glasses filled with *soju* toward a man at the head of the table. By virtue of his bearing and the gold on his epaulets, it was clear that he was in charge.

"Death to the American puppet, Syngman Rhee!"

"*Geonbae!* Cheers! Long life to the liberator and unifier of our fatherland!"

"May *kukhon*, our national spirit, lead us to victory over the Imperialist dogs and their mangy puppets!" shouted Kim Il Sung.

His eyes scanned the occupants of his command tent. He and his general staff were celebrating their success. They had executed their battle plan to perfection and had driven the imposters from the capital city of Seoul. Now, on the outskirts of Taejon they hoped to capture Syngman and finally end the charade government propped up by the dreaded Americans. Supreme Leader Kim praised their achievement and promised to drive the Imperialist swine off the Peninsula. He predicted an American humiliation reminiscent of the British evacuation at Dunkirk. Kim concluded by reminding them that there was still important work to be done. He called a 0600 meeting for the next day to finalize their plan to overrun Taejon and end the puppet regime.

"Sleep well tonight because tomorrow we march on Taejon to crush the 24th American Infantry and capture the puppet Rhee. By this time tomorrow, we will have a victory party in a united Korea under our leadership!"

*   *   *

Before sunrise, Junior felt a hand on his shoulder, shaking him awake. It was Gomax. The venom induced illness had broken. Gomax appeared pale but he had willed himself to alertness.

"It's time to get to work, Junya," said Gomax.

In his good hand, he held his bolt-action, Springfield M1903A4 sniper rifle. The wood stock was burnished with a well-worn patina. A Unertl 10x scope ran almost the full length of its blue-black barrel which was tipped with a camo-colored flash suppressor. This sniper's rifle was customized to fire .30-'06 rounds with lethal effect, at targets more than six football fields away. Gomax looked to his grotesquely swollen shooting hand and tried to flex it to no avail.

"You are the shooter, Junya. I'll be your spotter," said Gomax, with the tone of a professional soldier passing the baton to the next man up.

"But, . . ." protested Junior.

"No buts, soldier. Get your ass into position. We got work to do," said Gomax, in a voice that would brook no dissent. Junior squirmed into the shooter's position in the hide, followed by Gomax who wielded the spotter's scope.

Almost half-a-mile down the slope, Kim was conducting a final briefing with his staff officers. A map colored with strike arrows aimed at a central target lay on the table before him. His back was toward the Americans and several officers stood across from him.

"There, you see at the table, the two brass facing us?" said Gomax.

Junior sighted toward the group.

"Yeah, I see them," said Junior.

"Those are your targets. Judging from our pictures, they are Pluto and Jupiter," said the gunny.

"What about the guy with his back to us?"

Gomax focused the sight on the man.

"Forget him. He's a Russkie. You see his blue collar. That's a Soviet uniform. Aim for the one on the left first. Then if you have time, take out the other one," said Gomax.

"Okay. Give me a reading," said Junior, with a slight tremor in his voice. A mixture of excitement and worry raced through his mind. He wanted to complete the mission, but firing coldly at an enemy was much different than firing at paper targets. Doubt about the mechanics of operating the bolt action rifle crept into his thinking.

"Wind, 8 mph from your left. Range, 610 yards. Fire on your mark," said the spotter.

"Got it," said Junior, adjusting his aim. The rifle was propped in a natural point of aim. He looked through scope, aligning his crosshairs at the point between Jupiter's eyes. Junior reminded himself to synchronize his breathing and heart beat before slowly squeezing the trigger with the fleshy part of his index finger. Then, hours of practice took over. He aimed and fired. For a millisecond he watched the vapor trail of the bullet. He knew it was on target. Before the bullet smacked into Jupiter's forehead, Junior ripped back the bolt, chambered another round and centered his aim on Pluto.

Just as he squeezed the trigger, the man in the blue collar reacted to the bullet whistling by his left ear and ducked to his right. Junior's second shot ripped through Kim's cap before blasting into the eye socket of Pluto.

"Junya, great shooting. You nailed both them sons'abitches," said a jubilant Gomax. He slapped Junior on the back with his injured hand and yelped in pain.

"Dumbass," he said to himself. "Now, we gotta stay hidden for the next few days, 'til the heat dies down."

Down at the command tent, there was pandemonium. Soldiers ran every which way, looking for cover. From under the table, Kim stared at his fallen comrades. Both had been with him since his guerrilla days fighting the Japanese. Now, their brains were splattered over the ground. His eyes welled with angry tears.

"Find the bastards who did this!" he screamed. Searching the foothills, Kim rose and yelled, "There will be a reward and

179

promotion for anyone who kills the cowardly scum who snipered our leaders!"

Kim stood, fists clenched, with both arms raised, cursing at an unseen enemy. He did not know that the Ghost Photographer had pulled the trigger. Nor, that his blue Soviet collar was the only thing that had kept him from death and fulfilling his dream of liberating his country. As an aide ushered him out of sight, he vowed on the blood of his brothers-in-arms to make sure that their sacrifice would not be in vain.

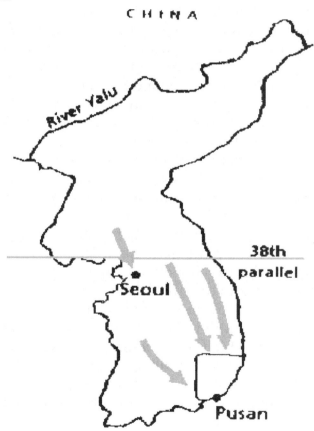

CHAPTER

20

The Extractor

"Everybody has a plan 'till they get punched in the mouth."

~ Mike Tyson

It was like they were invisible in a bubble that was shielded from the war raging below them. In the aftermath of the sniper killings, prudence dictated that they stay hidden for several days, at least until the invading army moved away. The sniper hide above the Kum River outside of Taejon was the ideal place for Gomax to rest and continue to recuperate from the salmusa venom that had almost finished him.

Idled and confined in darkness, Gomax slept so deeply that Junior had to check his breathing periodically to make sure that he was still alive. Using his flashlight sparingly to preserve the batteries, Junior cleaned and rebandaged the wound twice a day. Over time, the swelling subsided and the oozing lessened. The color of Gomax's hand changed from chili-red to purplish maroon fringed with chartreuse.

During these days, Junior dared not venture out of the hide. He listened to the sound of artillery and an occasional explosion in the distance as the opposing forces battled for control of Taejon. Once in a while he heard the distinctive thrum of airplane engines and hoped that they were American planes bombing enemy positions.

When it was quiet, he sustained himself with thoughts of Sachie. He could hardly wait to return to Tokyo and be with her. The coolness of the stone amulet around his neck was a source of comfort. Even though he was without paper, he composed letters and snippets of doggerel in his head romanticizing his vision of the remarkable woman who had captured his heart. His reverie was interrupted by the sound of voices. He figured that it must be a search patrol. The language was not English. As they grew closer, he withdrew his Colt M1911 pistol and unsheathed his Bowie knife. Junior coiled his legs beneath him to be ready in case their lair was discovered.

The conversation stopped. He heard the faint noise of water, followed by a foul urine smell. Someone was peeing directly above their position. It trickled along the rock ledge and dripped on to his back. The warmth and intensity of it made him recoil in disgust. To his horror, he noticed that some of the piss was dripping onto Gomax. Junior shifted his weight in order to shield Gomax, lest he awaken startled and give away their hideout. Drops onto his helmet caused an unnatural metallic ping. Junior removed the helmet and gritted his teeth as the urine landed on his head and trickled down his neck.

A voice rang out. The urination stopped and Junior heard the soldiers chattering excitedly. The only word Junior could discern was salmusa. He guessed that they had found the head of the snake and were arguing over its significance. Time slowed. Junior reminded himself to breathe. After what seemed like an eternity, the voices faded and he found himself listening to the rustling of leaves and other woodland noises.

Another day passed in quiet before Junior removed the comm device from his pack. The blue light held steady indicating it was safe to transmit. He sent an encrypted message advising that Pluto and Jupiter had been neutralized and requested additional instructions.

"Gomax," said Junior. "We gotta bug out. Wild Bill sent us new orders."

"Huh? Get the fuck off of me," said a groggy Gomax, swiping away Junior's hand from his shoulder.

"Suit yourself, but I'm leaving. We gotta rendezvous with a Korean operative in Seocheon in four days. It's up river about forty miles. Do you think you can hack it?"

Awake now, Gomax bristled at the last comment. He moved quickly, gathering his gear. He stood and cracked his head on the rock ledge.

"Stupid motherfucker," he admonished himself. "Junya, you dismantle this hide, while I find us some vittles."

Although his stomach churned at the suggestion of insects and grubs for dinner, Junior was happy to see Gomax revitalized.

*　　*　　*

In the *Dai-ichi* Life Insurance Company building, Tokyo, over one thousand miles away, an old man sat behind the table he used as a desk. He could not remember the last time he had felt this alone. It was well past midnight as MacArthur sat in his office surrounded by reports, maps, and plans. The situation was dire. He needed time; time to get his resources where they would stop the invaders. The North Korean Army was driving through South Korean resistance like the proverbial hot knife through butter. The South had no tanks of their own and no weapons to stop the Soviet T-34 tanks that spearheaded the thrust south. South Korean rocket projectiles just bounced off the slanted armor of the T-34s. The situation with American forces was hardly any better.

Since the closest U.S. forces to the fighting were in Japan, MacArthur sent the 24th Infantry Division under the command of General William F. Dean, into the breach with instructions to halt the communist advance. General Dean designated a group known as Task Force Smith led by Lt. Colonel Charles B. Smith to defend several major transportation arteries. The initial engagement between the task force and the North Koreans was a disaster.

Badly outnumbered and with no weapons to stop the Soviet T-34 tanks, the U.S. Army was routed at Osan, a city around twenty-two miles south of Seoul. The most distressing aspect of the reports on the Battle of Osan was the ineffectiveness of U.S. howitzer and bazooka fire on the T-34s. The tanks advanced with impunity as shells and rockets bounced off the armor as if they were merely annoying wasps. The only question for MacArthur was could his ill-equipped forces delay the advance long enough for reinforcements to arrive? He calculated that it would take at least another month before he could deploy M46 Patton tanks to counter the North Korean tanks. MacArthur focused all of his plans on slow-rolling the North Koreans.

*   *   *

After their victory at Osan, the North Koreans barreled another sixty miles south to Taejon, the next city of import. To MacArthur's dismay, the defense of the crucial city of Taejon by the 24th Infantry Division under General Dean collapsed within three days. Even worse, General Dean was missing in action and feared dead, or captured. MacArthur knew that the North Koreans were capable of persuasion and feared that the capture of a high-ranking officer like Dean might jeopardize significant strategic and operational information. MacArthur prayed for Dean's safety, but shamefully admitted to himself that the general would be better off as a corpse than as a prisoner.

The one bright ray of good news was an intelligence report that on the morning of the Battle of Taejon, snipers had killed two prominent North Korean officers. MacArthur surmised that the assassinations were the result of Operation Solar Eclipse, but he had no confirmation. He hoped that Gomax would fulfill his duty to protect Junior. The general would have been surprised and proud to learn that the opposite was the case. On this lonely night in his office, he could only speculate about their fate.

After the defeat of South Korean and American forces at Taejon, President Rhee moved his government to Pusan at the southern tip of the Korean peninsula. In a show of false bravado, Rhee changed his mind and moved back north up to Taegu. Reasoning that Kim was obsessed with capturing Rhee, MacArthur did not try to persuade the headstrong Rhee to stay in Pusan which was much safer. As MacArthur anticipated, Kim took the bait focusing his offensive on Taegu in the center of the Pusan Perimeter, rather than to attack the much more vulnerable eastern flank.

In just a few weeks, Kim's army had blitzed through ROK defenses and pushed over 300 miles deep into South Korea. The North Koreans continued south to Taegu where Kim planned to end this war of liberation. In this success lay the seeds of its downfall. In a frantic attempt to replenish critical supplies, the roads, rails, and rivers teemed with enemy activity. As Kim's army traveled from Taejon south seventy-six miles to Taegu, its supply lines were stretched to the breaking point. UN naval operations had sealed off the coast, eliminating seaborne re-supply and, on a daily basis, the airpower of the forces of the United Nations attacked Kim's greatest vulnerability and degraded his ability to re-supply his forces. The invaders were running out of supplies and time.

MacArthur appointed General Walton H. Walker of the 8th Army commander of all UN forces in Korea and instructed him to establish a defensive perimeter to protect the seaport of Pusan which was the entry point for United Nations' troops and armaments. MacArthur understood that by committing the 8th Army to Korea, Japan would be left under-protected and vulnerable to invasion by the Soviets. To provide for the defense of Japan, MacArthur took the risky step of creating a 100,000-man force of Japanese citizens.

The Pusan Perimeter was an arc covering the southeastern portion of the peninsula that roughly coincided with the Naktong River. It was 140 miles long and included numerous cities and important rail lines. MacArthur entrusted the protection of Pusan to General Walker.

Nicknamed the "Little Bulldog" on account of his lack of height and abundance of tenacity, the portly, square-jawed Texan applied the mobile defense principles he had learned from George Patton in WWII. By speedy and unpredictable movement of his outnumbered and out-gunned army, Walker kept the enemy tentative and surprised. Walker's execution was superb and his tactics kept Pusan from falling into enemy hands. Thanks to Walker's leadership, the initial momentum of the North Korean attack was blunted and MacArthur gained invaluable time to bring reinforcements to the Peninsula.

* * *

The bright midsummer sun illuminated the Sobaek Mountains. From an observation point above the lair, Junior trained his high-powered binoculars on the rail lines and saw flatbed cars carrying artillery and armored vehicles toward Taegu. Swiveling toward the roadway, Junior watched a cavalcade of military vehicles moving southward. He shifted his gaze to the river to see cargo barges laden with supplies plying the Kum River. Junior slithered on his belly like a salmusa back to the lair to report.

"Gunny, there are Norks everywhere. The roads and rails are jammed with Nork traffic heading south."

"How's the river?"

"Busy, but there are scrub-pines close to the riverbanks. On the other side of the pines is a coastal plain with open farmland. The river is probably the best way for us to travel undetected," said Junior.

"That's a Rog," said Gomax, "We leave at sundown."

It was nearly midnight when they finally reached the river. The dense underbrush and humidity made their trek arduous. Weakened by the after-effects of the snake bite, Gomax lacked his usual vigor. Although the swelling in his hand had reduced, the older man winced every time he used it to lever himself past some obstacle. During a break, Junior consulted their topography map, using his red-lens light. It showed the way ahead sloping gently downward. This meant more arable land and less cover. Their night march ended when they came upon a section of river-swamp. Ahead at a bend in the river, they saw the lights of a village.

"Junya, I'm fagged. I gotta rest," said Gomax, who sank down with his back against a tree. With his eyes closed, the marine appeared to have aged, a lot. Charcoal shadows under his eyes seemed to merge with deep lines etched into his face running down through his thick, scruff of a beard, giving him a foreboding, cadaverous appearance. Maybe, thought Junior, the Grim Reaper transforms the victim into himself before the end. When Junior bent to ask for instructions, Gomax was fast asleep. His head lolled to one side and his mouth sagged open. Drool seeped onto his neck.

Realizing that nourishment was imperative if Gomax was to survive, Junior thought that sneaking into the village might be their only hope. Yet, having just endured the passage of a conquering army, there might not be anything edible left and the inhabitants would certainly be on high alert to protect what might remain. A while back, they had passed what Junior thought was a *kaffir* field. He decided to double back to find some maize for them to eat.

Junior had no choice, food or starvation. He knew that the General would not tolerate failure, so, he went hunting for something to eat. As he crawled along the riverbank toward a farm bordering the river, Junior's hand sank into the soft mud. He stopped. His mind raced to his childhood in Baltimore along the mudflats of Bullneck Creek where his buddy, Dinky, reached into soft mud and got the surprise of his life. When Dinky withdrew his hand, there was a snapping turtle hanging from it. Despite desperate efforts to force the turtle to release the finger, the boys failed. Eventually, an animal control officer pried the snapper off Dinky and rushed the boy to the hospital where a talented surgeon re-attached the ligaments and saved the finger. Junior speculated whether a shell full of turtle soup might be worth sacrificing a pinky.

Hunger doused his fears and Junior plunged his hand into the soft burrow. Bracing himself to be stuck, stung, or pinched, he probed the hole. His fingers encountered a soft, leathery object. Exploring around it, he felt multiple similar objects. He scooped out mud from around the objects and saw a cluster of round items that brought to mind dirty ping-pong balls. Junior silently whooped in exaltation that he had discovered a nest filled with turtle eggs. They would feast tonight.

The restorative effect of the turtle egg omelet on Gomax was astounding. The color returned to his face and the crevices that had lined his face were reduced to fissures. His disposition, too, changed from morbid hostility back to its usual surliness.

When Junior commented favorably on the change, Gomax hurled a string of expletives at him that was so anatomically intricate and genealogically creative that it could only have be deciphered by a platoon of drunken sailors. In the past, Junior had taken Gomax's abuse to heart, but now Junior saw it as a welcome sign that his companion had turned the corner to recovery. Junior sent a prayer of gratitude skyward.

"After all that time holed up with your sick ass, I'm gonna get some of the stink off me," Junior announced after their meal.

"Alright, but don't you go pissing in that there river," said Gomax.

"Why the hell not?" asked Junior.

"You are one stupid motherfucker. Ain't you ever heard of the candirú?" said Gomax in an ominous drawl.

"No. I'll bite. What's a candirú?" asked Junior.

"It's a teeny fish that follows your piss stream and swims right up into your dick. It's got these barbs on it, so's once it's in there, you can't pull it out. Hurts like a sonuvabitch."

"You're joking, right," said Junior nervously.

Gomax shook his head and added, "It's also known as the pencil fish and the toothpick fish."

"What's the difference?"

"That depends on the size of your pecker," guffawed Gomax.

The remainder of their journey passed without incident thanks to the skill and instincts displayed by Gomax. It was as if he was the noncom in charge of assignments for the North Koreans. He anticipated every patrol and the location of every guard post. Junior snapped pictures of enemy positions whenever it was safe.

They arrived at the rendezvous point near the village of Seocheon just before the first rays of the sun rose above the horizon. Junior had lost track of the days and wasn't sure whether or not they were a day late. They hid in a thicket of willows amid dense undergrowth and tried to rest. Junior pulled first shift and was on guard, scanning the surrounding area while Gomax slept. As the sun rose higher in the sky, Junior's worries followed with it, becoming more intense as time passed.

Walking along the river shallows with a characteristic stiff-legged gait, a white-naped crane searched for its next meal. Junior salivated as the bird snatched a fresh-water sprat which flashed silvery as the crane swallowed it. He watched the outline of the fish as it slithered down the crane's crop. His attention was drawn to his right by a flock of mandarin ducks taking flight. A flicker of movement in the tall reeds pushed Junior to high alert. He flicked off the safety on his trusty rifle, Kára, and squinted toward the swaying plants. It might be the wind, it might be an animal, or it might be a hostile; all he knew was that it was moving in his direction. He steeled himself for a close, lethal encounter.

The sweet song of a warbler wafted in the breeze. It was a distinct, familiar sound. Junior paused. The song sparked a memory. He moved his finger off the trigger. The last time he had heard a warbler's song it came from the lips of his friend from Chonjin. Seung was his guide through the city of Chonjin where Junior captured images of Soviet arms entering the port. Junior warbled in return and watched Seung emerge, with a broad smile spread across his ochre skin.

Junior stood and waved. With his upper body bent forward, Seung high-stepped through the grass toward him. The pair hugged, an awkward combination of relief and joy. They ducked out of sight and exchanged updates. Gomax heard the whispering and propped himself on one elbow to listen.

"The People's Army passed through here last week and left only a skeleton force," said Seung. Junior smiled in relief.

"Our biggest problem is Commie guerrillas. Before Rhee lost control of the area, he eliminated scores of suspected Communists. A lot of hostiles are still out there."

"What do you mean 'eliminated'?" asked Junior.

"He croaked them," barked Gomax. "We gotta move. Save this political blather for later. Too exposed, move out!"

Signaling by hand, Seung led them to a small farmhouse on the outskirts of the village. It was a traditional rural Korean home, a *hanok*, with a thatched roof. The exterior walls were made of mismatched beige and tan panels between dark brown mullions and beams, giving the structure a vague checkerboard look. The men huddled along an irrigation ditch while Seung made sure that the coast was clear. Junior watched a rudimentary waterwheel turning under the force of water diverted from a nearby stream via a wooden halfpipe. The sound of splashing water, augmented by the sound of a grindstone crushing grain in an adjacent mill, created an idyllic moment amid the chaos of war.

A warbling drew his attention to Seung who was outlined in a doorway beckoning them. They scrambled inside and unshouldered their gear. Only a table, two chairs, and a wooden wash bin furnished the main room. The marines slumped down onto a slatted bamboo floor covering. Seung handed them robes made from ramie fabric, a natural cloth, traditionally worn by peasants.

When muffled sounds came from an adjoining room, Gomax reached for his Colt, Seung signaled that everything was okay.

"Your packages are waiting in the next room," he said. Seung explained that he was holding two people, one was a North Korean defector and the other, a prisoner captured by the ROK before they bugged out.

From an entrance at the rear, a woman carried a tray of food. The aroma of freshly cooked food convinced the men that eating would take precedence over evaluating the packages. Enthusiastic growls escaped from their deprived bellies. Junior and Gomax watched their hostess set out ceramic bowls and ladle out servings of *kkomjangeo bokkeum,* a Korean stir-fry made with inshore hagfish. Her manner of swirling the mixture reminded Junior of Sachie and his heart panged. He missed Tokyo more than he ever thought possible.

The back room was more of a storage area than living quarters. A guard, cradling a carbine at his chest, nodded a welcome.

"This is my companion Min-jun," said Seung in languages they both could understand.

"Howdy," said Gomax. "Mind if I call you Injun?"

The other nodded and grinned.

The packages sat in separate corners. The older woman wore the uniform of a North Korean officer that identified her as a colonel. Shoulders back and chin up, she sat with her hands secured to the arms of a chair. With her jet-black hair cropped close around her face, she effected an air of confidence and privilege. She glared at the newcomers.

"We got us a high-ranking sonofabitch here," said Injun, pointing the rifle toward the older woman.

"I don't care how you interrogate me, but tell this asshole not to call me a high-ranking sonofabitch," shrieked the colonel. "I am a military officer, claiming political asylum. I resent the way this low-life talks to me. I have sensitive top-secret information for General MacArthur. Unless you take me directly to him, you will rue the day you screwed with me."

Gomax sidled up to her and looked her up and down.

"Y'all think I give a flying fuck about your rank? Once you surrender, you become a prisoner. We are gonna get you to Tokyo when we can. So, be a good gal and keep you trap shut. Got that?"

She nodded in the realization that her Stanford education did not matter to these savages in this God-forsaken place.

He turned to the other prisoner who was huddled on the dirt floor. Gagged and trussed like a steer ready for branding, her eyes were frantic with fear as they flitted from the guard to Gomax. Raw, bloody bruises covered her face. Her uniform trousers were torn and splotched with mud and manure. The buttons of her tunic were ripped off and she struggled to keep her breasts covered. She whimpered and shivered as Gomax approached her.

It did not take a genius to see that the guard had raped her, probably more than once. Junior glared at the guard, daring him to see how he would fare against someone his own size. Seung touched his friend's arm, as if to say, not now, not here.

Sensing a confrontation that could turn lethal, Seung said, "We nabbed this one the other night. Caught her stealing a chicken. Claims she's a captain in Kim's militia. No ID. She might have some useful information about the immediate plans of the *Inmun Gun*, Kim's army."

"Junya, get on your comm thingamabob and get some idea what they want us to do."

Within hours, Lieutenant Commander A.C. "Mako" Hayfisch was taxiing his plane onto the runway at Pusan West Air Base. In comparison to the nose art of many American planes which typically depicted scantily clad women and sported provocative names, Mako's plane was boring. The nose of the plane was decorated with an image of the tip of a spear within a simple red circle. "John 8:32" was painted in black beneath the circle. This was a reference to the agency's unofficial motto: And ye shall know the truth, and the truth shall make you free.

His bird was a DC2 that had been specially modified to fit the specifications of Wild Bill Donovan. The base model DC2 was introduced by the Douglas Aircraft Company in the 1930s. One of the early all-metal planes, it was originally designed to replace wooden and fabric aircraft that were deemed unsafe for commercial use. With robust tapered wings, retractable landing gear, and twin engines powering variable-pitch propellers, the DC2 was revolutionary.

Since it was capable of flying low and slow, Donovan recognized the plane's potential for specialized use as a vehicle for catch-and-hoist. He ordered the modifications to produce what was designated as the DC2E. The "E" stood for Extractor. The fuselage was retrofitted with a large cargo door aft and the cabin floor was reinforced to support a powerful winch. The engines were packed with extra dense insulation and exhaust baffles which reduced the noise produced as much as possible. While these measures increased the potential for overheating and reduced top air speed, Donovan considered the trade-offs worthwhile. After all, the Extractor was built for stealth not speed. To permit self-defense, .50 caliber machine guns were mounted on either side of this DC2.

On reaching the correct coordinates, Mako's crew dropped a shipping kit to the men below. As the chute drifted to the drop zone, the flight crew activated the timing schedule for the mission. Experience had shown that once the shipping kit left the hold, there was a finite amount of time before even the least diligent enemy would react with deadly force. Even though the *Inmun Gun* had moved south, the flyers certainly respected the capability of the People's Army, especially as bolstered by local partisans. The clock was running.

Seung's men followed the parachute and retrieved the cargo. The crate contained two components. The package-delivery suits and the ground network aerial tether system, in military parlance, GNATS.

Junior and Gomax brought the suits to the *hanok*. With an abundance of screaming and tussling, they stripped the women to their bras and panties and forced them to put on the bright orange jumpsuits. The suits were designed to accommodate men weighing up to 300 pounds. On these petite Asian women, the resulting image was comical, sort of like scrawny kids wearing pumpkin costumes for Halloween.

At the highest point on the hill, the team assembled GNATS. It consisted of two poles notched like giant slingshots that they augured into place about one hundred yards apart. They stretched a thick cable much like a clothesline across the space between the uprights.

Gomax and Junior brought the women prisoners out to a large open field near the marshes. The captain's face was distorted by a look of panicked terror. She struggled, convulsing and writhing with all her might against the ironclad grip of Gomax. His face was set in a rigid mask as he controlled the much-lighter prisoner.

Junior followed, leading the colonel onto the field.

The colonel was placed about thirty yards from the poles. She was in a swale about a dozen feet lower than the clothesline. The other was placed another thirty yards ahead of her in a slight depression, lower than the first woman.

Once the correct spacing was achieved, the long rope was dragged to the first woman and looped through the ring at the back of her jumpsuit. The rope was then dragged to the second woman and tied to the ring on the back of her jumpsuit.

Using high-intensity lights flashing yellow, the men on the ground signaled that the removal system was ready. Mako throttled back the DC2 and banked in toward the field. Pilots called the tactic of flying below 1000 feet flathatting and Mako was an expert. His altimeter read 450 feet as he approached the clothesline. On cue, the co-pilot activated the rear tailgate. A whirring sound of hydraulics filled the cabin and the big door locked in the open position.

Per its original purpose, the rear opening was large enough to drive a truck through. However, Donovan conceived this alternative use while on a re-supply mission over France during

WWII. He reasoned that if cargo planes could drop materiel, they could also pick up cargo. The DC2's ability to fly "low and slow" made it the perfect fit for Donovan's extraction program.

The present catch-and-hoist system was devised to secure the aerial removal of high-value assets, without the risks of take-offs and landings. Even Wild Bill had to concede that the operation was not for "packages" who were faint of heart. Still, over the years, with the addition of padding at the hatches and springs to absorb some of the shock, the survival success rate had increased to an acceptable level.

Mako aligned his approach with the center of the clothesline. When the plane was on a direct course, the winch operator released the brake and the cable engineer threw the hook far enough to clear the rear of the plane. The winch drum spun furiously, unspooling the long cable.

"Hook's away," shouted the airman, gripping the handrail that secured his safety harness. Gloves heavy enough to handle thick metal cable covered his hands. Even though the plane had throttled back, the sound of the wind rushing by the open tail-hatch was deafening. The airman's flight suit rippled in the gale which made speech impossible. The retrieval crew, the cable engineer, the package handler, and the winch operator signaled each other by hand. Otherwise, communications with the flight deck and the wing gunners was via internal radio using helmet-mounted earphones and mikes.

The big fishhook-like device that was attached to the end of the cable plummeted toward the ground. It trailed behind the plane like the tail of a kite. Mako flew parallel to the ground to facilitate catching the hook on the clothesline cable. He had miscalculated the height of the rise and the hook bounced along the ground, spinning wildly off target. It whizzed past the clothesline without engaging.

Wanting to see the operation close-up, Junior and Gomax were like spectators, oblivious to the danger posed by the hook which bounced erratically like an off-kilter football. The hook flitted, heaved, and swung directly toward them. Without an

195

instant to spare, they scrambled for cover, diving behind a boulder just as the hook whooshed past. They barely avoided decapitation. A stark, white gash marred the rock, evidence of the hazard posed by a hook and cable traveling well in excess of 100 mph.

The winch operator engaged the brake and switched on the machine. The smell of oil approaching the burning point permeated the cabin as the cable hummed back toward the plane. By the time Mako had returned to the drop position, the crew was ready to redeploy the hook and cable. The next two passes were equally unsuccessful. Mako sensed that by now someone on the ground had alerted the enemy and the DC2 would be a sitting duck if they sent anti-aircraft units, or, even worse, YAK fighter planes. His plane lacked the speed or armaments to fend off a serious attack.

Mako decided to make one more pass before aborting the mission. Adjusting airspeed and altitude to lessen bouncing the hook, he zeroed in on the clothesline for the fourth and final time. Mako was flying cherubs five, holding steady at 500 feet. Rather than going in head-on, he altered his approach a few degrees to give himself a better angle. The yoke was leaden, slow to respond to his pressure. He drew back on the throttle-lever as much as he could without stalling.

"Bingo!" yelled the winchman, at the same instant Mako felt a slight tug aft.

Nudging the throttle forward, he pulled the yoke to orient the plane on a 30°ascent. Grappled by the hook, the clothesline followed the DC2. The winch-man activated the powerful motor and cable coursed around the drum. A second later, the first package was yanked aloft. Realizing what was happening, the second woman ran. Her legs churned, bicycling in the air as the rope lifted her. Swallowed by distance, speed, and altitude, the screams of the women went unheard.

Junior watched the two orange figures who wriggled like drunken marionettes tethered to the shrinking plane. He held his hand to eyes to shield the sun. The flaming-orange figures became silhouettes as the aircraft headed out over the Yellow Sea.

"Damn," said Gomax. "That looks like fun."

Junior's thoughts went to his transmitter. It was time to get back to Tokyo and find Sachie. He was glad that their extraction would be by more civilized means; at least, he hoped so.

* * *

The dictator entered Taejon in an armored personnel carrier. While it lacked the pomp of his entry into Seoul one month earlier when he drove triumphant in his ZIS Soviet limousine, Kim recognized that the conquest of Taejon was an important military milestone. He regretted leaving the big limo in Seoul, but he needed all available rolling stock for military vehicles. Besides, he thought, the paint job might get damaged during hostilities. Better to keep the limo pristine for his victory tour over a unified fatherland.

As a transportation hub, Taejon was indispensable to supplying his army with ammunition, fuel, and food as he hunted down that mongrel Rhee and exterminated his government of fools. The drive south had proven more complicated than expected. President Rhee had been nimbler than anticipated and was now rumored to be in Taegu. Onward to Taegu, Kim would pursue the craven coward. Only when Rhee was in shackles before him, Kim mused, would victory be achieved. With the humiliation of Rhee, the victory would be all the sweeter.

Kim had selected the main lecture hall at the Confucian academy in Taejon for his command post. He was alone and lonely. There was no approach to planning the next phase which was not fraught with risk. Should he concentrate on capturing Rhee, or, should he attack the weak eastern flank of the American's perimeter? Pondering the choices, he stood studying detailed, thematic maps which had been captured when Task Force Smith had been routed. Kim had to admit that the U.S. military had a particular talent for depicting tactical elements on its maps. Kim did not know, or care, that the maps were the products of the Cartography Section of the OSS, established by none other than Wild Bill Donovan.

"Supreme Commander," said General Kang Kŏn, chief of staff, bowing as he approached.

"You have something to report, Kang?" said Kim.

"Sir, as you directed, the bodies of our fallen generals who were slain by the cowardly sniper have been prepared for return to their families. Full military honors will be accorded to our brave comrades."

"Our brave comrades sacrificed so much, their families must receive generous pensions," said the Leader in a muted voice.

"Most definitely, Supreme Leader. We have announced a sizeable reward to whoever brings the guilty sniper to justice."

Kim grunted his approval.

They were interrupted by a young aide who fell prostrate before the leaders. Face down, he lifted his hand to present a sheaf of papers. Kim raised his hand to throttle this insolence. Kang gasped.

"What is this, you, mangy dog?" thundered Kim, his face crimson with rage.

"A thousand pardons, O Supreme Commander. We bear great news. In the mountains outside of Taejon, we have captured the American General in charge of all U.S. forces in Korea," said the soldier, not daring to raise his eyes.

"Can this be true?" Kim asked his chief-of-staff.

Not seeing where the question was directed, the young man blurted out, "Yes, most exalted leader. The Imperialist rat is in the infirmary with a bloody head and a broken shoulder."

A broad, toothy smile beamed from Kim's face.

"Destiny favors our quest!"

CHAPTER

21

Chasing Ghosts

"When your number's up it's up. That's it.
There's no miracle, no magic wand. That's all."

~ Gomax

While they were waiting outside of Seocheon for their own exfiltration on an aircraft that they would board on the ground, Junior bade Seung goodbye. When their eyes met, they confirmed the bond that had grown between the two young warriors. Each knew that he could entrust his life to the other. As their arms encircled, each experienced a warm melancholy wondering when they would see each other again. It would be a lot sooner than either could imagine.

"Break it up, ladies," grumped Gomax. "Our ride is here."

During the flight back to Tokyo, Junior dozed off, thinking about his life since that day in the Baltimore courtroom when the judge gave him the choice of jail or the Marines. Gomax looked at the resting young man, marveling at his maturation from a soft, awkward rube to a resourceful marine capable of assassinating an enemy at 500 yards. Just as the DI had surpassed his mentor, Junior was close to outpacing Gomax. The gunny conceded that the professional calm that Junior displayed when he took out Jupiter and Pluto was impressive. MacArthur had seen something in the young man that Gomax himself had missed. That's why the old man was a five-star and Gomax was a defrocked gunnery sergeant.

"The old man wants both your asses in his office at 0600 tomorrow morning," barked the sergeant major at Gomax and

Junior who were in the showers soaping off the accumulated filth of their last assignment. "And you, Gomax, sick bay in one hour for that snake bite."

The steam masked their reactions. Gomax flipped the bird at the sergeant major. Junior just grinned at the prospect of a free night to see Sachie. Just like that, the soul-sucking grimness of their assignments was replaced by the joyfulness of his love for his angel.

Shifting back and forth on his stool, Junior stared through the condensation-blurred window of the ramen shop down the block from the Teahouse of the Auspicious Blessing. Like young men have done for eons, he was waiting for Sachie to join him.

"Sorry, short notice," said a breathless Sachie, glancing at her wristwatch.

Tongue-tied, Junior was suddenly incapable of speech. The awkward moment was broken by the appearance of a waitress wielding a pencil and spiral pad. Even though this was her favorite eatery, Sachie scanned the menu board on the wall out of habit.

"*Tori paitan ramen, onegaishimasu,* please," said Sachie, holding up two fingers.

"How was your mission?" asked Sachie.

"Went well," replied Junior, remembering his vow of secrecy to MacArthur.

Sachie looked past Junior toward the kitchen. Junior flushed, then, reached across the table to touch her hand.

"I missed you, Sachie," he blurted out.

She searched his eyes and squeezed his hand in acknowledgement.

The ramen arrived and they ate the noodles and creamy, white broth. The slurping noise made by Sachie amused Junior. She held her hand to her mouth, eyes twinkling. When Junior fumbled with his chopsticks, Sachie gave him a brief primer on their use. He picked up every morsel of the delicious chicken and vegetables.

They strolled five minutes to Yoyogi Park. Sachie pointed to various flowers that bloomed in their full, summer glory and repeated their English and Japanese names for Junior. Like a toddler, he mimicked her with such horrific inaccuracy that they both laughed without restraint. It was as if a cloud drifted away, revealing the sun. Like magic, the feeling of relaxed enjoyment just by being together returned. As the sun dipped toward the horizon, Sachie checked her watch.

"Oh, no, I am late for work," said the girl.

Her smile evaporated and a look of distress shaded her face. She took off for the Teahouse at a rapid pace. Junior double-timed after her. She was crossing the street ahead of him when a bus came between them forcing him to wait. By the time the bus cleared, she had disappeared behind the shiny, red door into the Teahouse. It was as if she had been swallowed by the building. A disappointed Junior returned to his billet.

Finally, on a real mattress, Junior slept with total peace. His eyeballs fluttered from side-to-side beneath his eyelids. His body was still. He envisioned a future home with Sachie standing at the door, holding a baby as cute as a miniature geisha doll. The child's arms stretched toward her Daddy who was walking up the path after work.

A loud crash and cursing startled him awake. Gomax stumbled over a trashcan. The sour stench of booze and vomit contaminated the air. Gomax slipped and fell, landing on his back. He laughed maniacally, then made a weird hissing noise like a bus releasing its brakes. Before Junior could rise to help, Gomax was snoring with a sputtering, rasping baritone. Let him sleep it off, thought Junior.

Shortly after 0500, the sun invaded their barracks, its rays stabbing into the gunny's bloodshot eyes. As a buoyant Junior returned from the bathroom with a towel wrapped around his neck, he nudged Gomax with his foot.

"Rise and shine, you've got less than thirty minutes before your ass is grass and MacArthur is the lawnmower," chided Junior who busied himself dressing.

Gomax groaned, belched and rolled onto all fours. His eyes were unfocussed as he headed toward the latrine. Junior shook his head and shouted, "I'll meet you there."

MacArthur was in his office engrossed in reports when Junior arrived. One of the items on the desk bore the title: *Report of Captain McLane Tilton, commanding United States Marines, Amphibious Landing Boisée Isle, Corea, June 16, 1871.* Junior thought that this was the perfect opportunity to raise the subject.

"Sir, may I have a word on a personal matter, sir?"

With a flick of hand, the general invited the young man to sit. When he looked at the concentration on the general's face, Junior's nerve dissolved.

"Maybe this isn't a good time . . . ," mumbled Junior.

"Nonsense, come in," said MacArthur. "What's on your mind, son?"

"Well, sir. You see, sir," said Junior, fumbling for words. "The fact of the matter is that I am in love."

MacArthur straightened in his chair and said, "This is serious. Tell me about her."

Junior unleashed a torrent of superlatives to describe Sachie. MacArthur narrowed his eyes at the mention of her nationality.

"Junior, stop right there. Drop that thought. You cannot marry a Japanese national while you are stationed in Japan. If you were stateside and she was there, it might be different. But, not here. Unless she swims the Pacific Ocean and meets you in California, the Japanese establishment frowns on that type of fraternization."

Junior tilted his head and furrowed his brows.

"Sir, you mean to say that if an American soldier falls in love and wants to marry a Japanese girl, he can't?"

"That's exactly what I'm saying, Junior."

"But, why, sir?"

"Because it's a bad idea, son."

Junior's lower lip curled and his eyes welled up.

"Sir, that's not fair. That's un-American, Sir," he blurted.

"Son, we have a fragile society here that needs special care to re-build itself. We just cannot have interracial marriages. It's a bad idea. So, get this silly notion out of your head."

The general looked past Junior, relieved to see Gomax standing at the door.

"Come in, gunny. We were just about to start."

MacArthur rose and brought his pointer over to the full-length map of Korea pinned on the wall.

Junior was crestfallen. Avoiding eye contact, he fixed his concentration on the map's topography lines, trying to locate a cliff where he might end it all. Maybe then, the general would understand how much Sachie meant to him. Junior barely heard the briefing. Even when MacArthur heaped high praise on the success of their recent mission in Taejon and Seocheon, Junior was lost in his own world, glum.

"I have convinced the Joint Chiefs of Staff of the soundness of this plan, code-named Operation Chromite. The tactical difficulties inherent in attacking this target will lull the Norks into complacency. In addition, a landing at Incheon will save thousands of lives that would be lost if we have to bust out of Pusan. Bottom line - the amphibious landing at Incheon will take place in exactly six weeks on September 15th; the only time for months when the tides are perfect. The 1st Marines and 7th Infantry will lead the charge. Any questions?" asked the general.

"Good," he said, pausing. "Now, for the real purpose of our meeting . . . Colonel."

At the unmistakable clack of female footsteps on the wooden floor, Junior and Gomax turned. She was wearing a service uniform in crisp white. Her hair was pulled back into a bun and she walked ramrod-straight, with her hat tucked under her arm.

"At-ten-shun," shouted Junior, automatically rising at the entrance of an officer.

"Gentlemen, I believe you already know Colonel Cheung," said the general, with a hint of enjoyment at the surprised looks on the faces of Junior and Gomax.

"Well, I'll be a monkey's uncle," said Gomax, slapping his forehead. Then, he leered, "Why, Colonel, ain't you pretty all gussied up like that."

He must still be drunk, thought Junior.

The colonel ignored the slight, she had been subjected to much worse throughout her career. She took her place at the map, next to MacArthur.

"Gentlemen, and I use the term loosely," she said, shooting a look of disdain at the gunny. "With my help, you have a unique opportunity to conquer Incheon."

Junior and Gomax turned to each other, confused.

"I grew up in Incheon. My father graduated from the Merchant Marine College and was a master mariner. I sat on his knee when he piloted tugboats through the perils of Incheon Harbor. After he was appointed Harbor Master at Incheon, I helped maintain his charts relating to tides, shoals, currents, and mudflats."

She paused to sip some water.

"We moved north when my father was transferred to the port of Wonsan on Korea's east coast. I left my country to go to school in California. I graduated from Stanford and returned home before the beginning of WWII. I fought the Japanese in the Korean military. I have lived through the degradation of Korea by the Communists. That's why I defected."

"Thank you, Colonel," said the general. "Gentlemen, welcome to Operation Chromite. Fighting for time against space is no longer necessary. Now, it's all about speed, secrecy, and surprise. Junior, we need detailed pictures of Incheon harbor and the defensive emplacements on the surrounding islands so that Colonel Cheung can help us finalize the invasion plans."

Junior nodded.

"Gomax, we have intel regarding a possible meeting of high-level Nork leaders in Seoul this week. While Junior is taking pictures, I want you to contact local operatives and if you think you can make progress on Operation Solar Eclipse, go to Seoul and nail a few more of those Commie bastards."

"Yessir," said Gomax, smiling for the first time that day.

"Ain't that the damnest, Junya," said Gomax when they headed toward the Armory. "Sheesh, that bitch is something else."

Junior was silent while they prepared. He studied a map of the target area. The plan was for them to jump into occupied territory and contact local partisans at Bucheon, a city located between Incheon and Seoul. Depending on the latest intel, Junior would head west to take photos of enemy positions and Gomax would head east to Seoul.

At climb-out, poised to jump, the feeling of cold air against his face was exhilarating. Junior always enjoyed the rush of adrenaline that accompanied the blast, the term his black-hatted jumpmaster used to describe jumping out of a perfectly good airplane. Springing from the plane, Junior adopted a horizontal position and was belly-flying downward. During freefall, he was free from all worries. His dilemma over Sachie seemed a million miles away.

As gravity accelerated him toward earth, he contemplated the odd symmetry of the landscape below. It extended to the horizon like the victory quilt his Grandma Pauline had created during the war. The ground below was approaching fast, getting closer. Orienting the fruit-tree orchard they had targeted, he veered toward an adjacent pasture.

Junior yanked the ripcord and felt the bump of a severe upward thrust as the parachute blossomed to full canopy. He pivoted the chute so that the wind was in his face for his parachute landing fall. With head down, feet and knees together, Junior touched down and immediately shifted sideways to distribute the shock. His black hat would have been proud of his perfectly executed PLF.

The fragrance of peaches overwhelmed Junior's senses. Some of the fruit had fallen prematurely and released a cloying, sweet aroma as they fermented on the ground. He quickly removed his pack and unbuckled his harness, freeing him to gather his chute for burial. Looking up, he watched Gomax glide into the pasture about fifty yards away.

Once squared away, they walked to a predetermined place on the outskirts of Sosa-gu, a village equidistant between the capital and the port. They hid in an orchard overlooking the main rail line between Seoul and Incheon. As the sun rose in the sky, they waited, and waited. Junior passed the time snapping pictures of passing trains, and marine traffic on the nearby Han River, noting the type and frequency in his pad. After several hours, they heard a familiar warbling and reconnected with Seung and his companion, Min-jun, the guard from the village of Seocheon.

Based on confirmation from Min-jun that a meeting of top *Inmun Gun* officers in the Blue House in Seoul was scheduled for this week, they decided to separate and rendezvous back in Sosa-gu in three days. Hefting his pack containing his priceless camera to his back, Junior and Seung headed west. With his Springfield secure in its padded case slung over his shoulder, Gomax and Injun headed east to the capital.

*   *   *

The acid that is doubt dripped into Kim's mind. Gone was the euphoria of a few short weeks ago when his invasion plans clicked into place like so many tumblers in a lock, each fitting perfectly and operating smoothly. Then, his comrades in Moscow and Beijing had lauded Kim's bright flame. Now, like smoke rising and twisting from an extinguished candle, whispers of gloom touched his coterie of commanders. Hints of uncertainty in battle status reports had edged into subtle pessimism. To stem this contagion before it became toxic, he summoned his leadership to the Blue House in Seoul.

Kim sensed that the momentum of his attack was stalling. Every day he received reports of the massive build-up at Pusan by that devil MacArthur. At the outset, the *Inmun Gun's* tank corps was unstoppable. The 2.35-inch bazooka rockets employed by Rhee's army bounced off the tanks' armor as if launched by a peashooter. However, the United States had altered the battlefield equation by deploying M20, 3.5-inch bazookas with devastating effect on his T-34s. There were rumors that the Americans were sending heavier Sherman and Patton tanks to the theater. If those rumors were true, his major advantage in armored war machines would be significantly reduced.

It was imperative for Kim to rally his officers. He instructed his chief of staff to make the site of the greatest triumph sparkle with confidence. While Kang prepared for a sumptuous show of success, Kim hunted and scoured through everything for new insight, some good news. Kim seethed. That bastard Rhee continued to elude him. All efforts to corrupt the captured American general had failed. Dean toyed with his captors, always appearing cooperative, but yielding nothing. Maybe it was time for more drastic measures.

"My Supreme Leader, I apologize for interrupting your Greatness, but I have someone you should see," said General

207

Kang Kŏn, in his most obsequious voice. With a weariness that matched his mindset, Kim signaled for Kang to proceed.

The general led a young man into Kim's chamber. Despite the appearance of a simple peasant, the slight uptilt of his chin and a certain stiffness in his posture unmasked him as a soldier. There was a gleam of purpose in his eyes that intrigued Kim. As the visitor approached, a faint scent of peaches preceded him. Heeding Kang's instructions, the young man bowed deeply, entoning, "My Supreme Exalted Leader, I am your humble servant."

"Speak!" barked Kim. Then to Kang, "This better be good."

"Yes, of course, Supreme Leader," sputtered Min-jun. "I am a member of the *bowibu*. The chief of the secret police has assigned me to infiltrate the opposition. I have done that and have traveled on many missions."

"Get to the point," said Kim, glaring at Kang for this waste of time.

"Yes, of course, Supreme Leader," said Min-jun, his voice quavering. With one hand raised palm up, he reached inside his shirt. Before Kang could respond to this provocative act, Min-jun pulled out a flyer and handed it to Kang.

"What is this?" demanded Kang.

"It's a flyer offering a reward for the capture of the cowardly scum who slaughtered our dear generals outside of Taejon. I know the sniper. I have brought him to Seoul."

"Where is he?" shouted Kim, showing renewed interest in Min-jun.

"He is on Bugak Mountain with his sniper rifle," said Min-jun. Kang's jaw dropped open in shock at the proximity of the potential assassin. He rushed to move Kim away from the window.

"Bring him to me!" thundered Kim.

CHAPTER

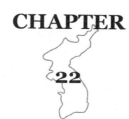

22

Flying Fish Channel

"Once war is forced upon us, there is no alternative than to apply every available means to bring it to a swift end. War's very object is victory - not prolonged indecision."

~ General Douglas MacArthur

Operation Chromite was so important to the effort to defeat North Korea's aggression that the hairs on Junior's arms came to follicle-straining attention when he realized that he might play a small role in such an historic venture. Junior and Gomax had barely cleaned their uniforms from their last mission, code name Operation Solar Eclipse, before they were dispatched to reconnoiter Incheon Harbor behind enemy lines. The urgency of this assignment and the myriad preparations attendant to the mission caused his heartache over Sachie to fade into the background. His love was so strong that he vowed to renew his quest for her when he returned to Tokyo. Junior wanted to write to her before he left, but there was no time, and it was too risky. He had no choice, but to put the mission before his heart, the general before the geisha.

Gomax refused to trust any soldier who lacked Parris Island on their resume. His distrust of Asians was even more virulent. His experiences during WWII, "island-hopping" through the Pacific theater capturing strategic island strongholds held by the Japanese, had left a bad taste in Gomax's mouth toward "the yellow bastards." It motivated him to make Junior promise that he would share no details about their missions to Seung and Min-jun without a compelling need to know. To further compartmentalize their operations, the marines established a system of words and signals to communicate warnings or directions to each other. This safeguard would prove life-saving.

The gravest challenge of the Incheon invasion was the impact of the thirty-foot differential between high- and low-tide. At low tide, the waterways surrounding Incheon turned into impassable mudflats. This meant that during the twelve-hour interval between high tides, the forces on the beachhead would be isolated from direct support until the next high tide. This time period posed the greatest danger.

Naval planners had calculated the optimum date for the invasion was September 15th. Given this time constraint, Intelligence about landing conditions around Incheon and the situation in Seoul necessitated splitting the team in two. Junior and Seung would reconnoiter the entrance to Incheon, while Gomax and Min-jun would go to Seoul to continue Operation Solar Eclipse.

Once Gomax and Injun tramped toward the rising sun, Junior and Seung got to work. Posing as fishermen plying the waters outside Incheon, Junior and Seung spent several days experiencing the often-treacherous currents, shoals and tides influencing the harbor. Drawing on lifelong relationships, Seung had arranged with the skipper of a small, wooden junk for he and Junior to join the boat on its daily runs. The crew of six was so busy tending to the nets and the catch that they ignored the passengers.

The salt air and sunshine were a welcome change for Junior who was used to working in cramped, dirty conditions in the dark. Another benefit of this gig was that they ate what the crew caught, a tasty upgrade from the usual chow. For much of the day, Junior positioned himself at the bow shaded under a tarpaulin and snapped pictures with Maisey as the fishing boat cruised around the coastline. Junior saw firsthand the nearly thirty-foot rise of the tide and the wide expanse of mud, traversed by deep sluices filled with softer and deeper mud, that existed at low tide.

When he wasn't shooting pictures, Junior was below deck, recording his observations in detail.

On their final day, the skipper sailed toward Incheon into Flying Fish Channel, and tacked the junk close to Wolmi-do Island, an island in the mouth of the harbor that was critical to any defense of Incheon. The fortifications on the island sat 350 feet above the water and had a commanding view of the harbor. The arc of a long manmade causeway connected Wolmi-do to the mainland. As they sailed toward the island, Junior squatted in his perch at the bow, snapping pictures of the artillery that bristled from the redoubt like so many porcupine quills.

Suddenly, a North Korean patrol boat sped toward them, klaxons blaring. Staying low, Junior dove into the hold just as the PT boat hove to. He secured his camera behind a false panel and waited.

With his hands raised in submission, the skipper cursed at the North Korean officer who shouted instructions with a bullhorn. The officer gestured for one of his sailors to board the junk and search it. A machine gun-wielding sailor jumped the gap between the vessels and poked his submachine gun under every piece of canvas and behind every cask. Finding nothing, he turned to the officer who bull-horned more orders.

From this brief interchange, Junior surmised that the sailor had been directed to check the hold. Junior had no choice, he would have to submerge himself under the mass of dead and dying fish. As he prepared to hide, he spied his uniform bag hanging on the wall. He reached up with a hand and retrieved the uniform bag. The hook came with it, leaving behind a fresh scar in the wooden batten.

Realizing that there was nothing he could do about the jagged wood Junior stuffed the bag under his body and submerged under the catch. A slight ripple in the mass of fish carcasses was the only evidence of his action. The gill covers of a few of the fish fluttered feebly as they suffocated. Secreted behind a rib-frame, only Junior's nose was above the surface.

The slime and bodily fluids of the catch, combined with the stale bilge water made a nauseating witch's brew. Junior's lungs burned as he limited his breaths. The rolling of the fishing in the waves made the catch slosh enough to cover his nose causing the filthy water to enter his nasal passages. He did not know how long he could resist the gagging reflex. Time was excruciating.

On deck, Seung calculated the distance to his weapon, just in case. The skipper looked to Seung, pleading with his eyes for restraint.

As the sailor approached the hatch, the smell of fish stewing in the heat assaulted his nose. When he gagged, the officer berated him, brandishing his pistol toward the hatch. The sailor took a deep breath and plunged into the foul darkness below. The marine felt for his Bowie knife, just in case.

The *Inmun Gun* sailor covered his nose and mouth with his arm trying to avoid the stench. He squinted as he scanned the hold with his flashlight. If he noticed the raw wood, it did not register as suspicious. He kicked at the pile of fish in a desultory manner, before returning to the opening to gasp for cleaner air. He stayed below deck to avoid the wrath of the officer. When his lungs were about to burst, he clambered up the ladder and signaled all clear to the officer. While waiting for an order to return to the patrol boat, the sailor bent at the waist and gulped air rapidly. Eliciting laughter from his crew, the officer made a show of rebuking the sailor. Then, in uncharacteristic display of mercy, the officer ordered him back on board.

Under the fish blanket, Junior waited for Seung to give him an all-clear signal. Little did he know that the skipper was so spooked by the naval boarding that he forbade Seung from communicating with the American until they had reached a safe drop-off point in a secluded cove several miles away. With every passing minute covered by the odiferous dead and dying fish, Junior's aversion to the silvery creatures grew. By the time Seung came for him, Junior had marinated in the noxious stew for ninety minutes. He vowed to himself that he would never eat fish again.

For the trouble with the patrol boat, the skipper extorted double payment from Seung. Junior stood to the side, alone and ostracized by the crew who recoiled at the malodorous miasma around him. Even the most seasoned sailors gagged if they got to within yards of Junior. Not even stripping naked helped to reduce the stench which seemed to have permeated Junior's body. It was a great relief for all concerned when the fishing vessel was close enough for Junior and Seung to slip over the gunnels and wade to shore not far from the Han River basin. They sank up to their crotches in muck as they slogged through the tidal mudflats. Careful to keep his pack dry, Junior submerged his clothes bag in the surface water in a futile effort to rinse away the stink.

Once ashore, Seung and Junior hiked to a desolate hunting blind that they had previously designated as their rally point. While they waited, Junior scrubbed himself in a nearby stream and donned some native clothes. At the blind, Seung held his thumb and forefinger to his nose, advising him that the stench lingered. Junior returned to the stream for a repeat scrubbing which barely passed muster.

After that, they cleaned and organized their gear for a quick exit. Junior stuffed his equipment into a wicker basket of the type used by farmers who were too poor to own a wagon. Junior adjusted the shoulder straps and filled the basket with enough peaches to cover his pack. He wasn't sure how he was going to carry his rifle while dressed as a peasant. That dilemma would shortly resolve itself.

It was after midnight when a call sign alerted Junior to the presence of someone in the darkness. Junior responded in kind and, as a figure approached, the marine requested the password.

"Salmusa," replied the person. That word rekindled the memory of Gomax's ordeal with the poisonous snake.

Junior stiffened as he watched a solitary figure emerge from the shadows.

"Where's Gomax?" asked Seung.

"We were in the mountain behind the Blue House, when our position was compromised. Gomax decided we had a better chance of survival if we split up. He went north up the mountain and I went west. We agreed to rendezvous here. I thought he would already be here," said Min-jun in Korean. His eyes shifted nervously as Seung relayed his words to the American.

"Good, Injun. We will wait for him," said Junior on hearing Seung's translation.

Min-jun smiled and nodded agreeably. Junior noticed a flicker of relief, or was it something else, that passed across Injun's eyes.

Several hours later, Kim himself led a search party through the woods. It was a welcome diversion from the tedium of reading depressing reports. The smell of the trees and the stealth of the hunt brought back memories of his younger days as a guerrilla fighting the dastardly Japanese. Based on Min-jun's description of Junior's protective behavior toward his equipment and occasional references to pictures, Kim concluded that his target tonight was the Ghost Photographer. Kim was anxious to capture the Ghost Photographer after all these months. In the scheme of things, it might be considered a small victory, but nowadays he would relish any victory.

He had arrayed his men in a circle about a mile in circumference around the hunter's blind. Kim felt a surge of triumph as he signaled the men to advance, gradually reducing their separation. His men pressed forward like silent beaters closing the circular noose on the prey. When the blind was in sight, Kim peered through his binoculars. He blinked in disbelief at the barrel of a rifle being supported by a figure wearing an American uniform. His nemesis was prepared to fight; so be it, thought the Supreme Leader. Kim's heart surged in delight at the prospect of eliminating this thorn in his side.

Kim instructed his leaders that he wanted the imperialist dog caught alive. With his vastly superior numbers, he could easily lay siege on the American. Daylight was approaching. Kim decided to secure his prize at first light.

Junior and Seung retreated toward the river where they hoped to blend in with the local merchants and to board the ferry to the other side of the Han River. In the pitch darkness, it was easy for them to evade the net of Kim's men. They scurried through the underbrush undetected.

Junior was worried for Gomax and thankful for the gunny's foresight in giving Injun the distress password. The young marine wished that he had been there to see the look on his pursuer's face when he discovered the dead body of Min-jun in the stinking marine utilities with the rifle propped in his hands.

The general would be proud of the way he avenged the betrayal of Gomax. Junior chuckled to himself at the likelihood that MacArthur would dock his pay for the cost of the rifle. He would miss his faithful Kára, but took comfort in the fact that he had rendered her inoperable and that she was sacrificed in a good cause.

Of course, Gomax was still missing, and the general hated to lose such a valuable weapon. On the other hand, Junior reasoned, it might make MacArthur stop railing about Junior's failure to pull the trigger when he had Kim in his sights.

"If Kim had been a victim of Operation Solar Eclipse, the war might already be over," said MacArthur when he learned of the chance missed. He said it for show because he secretly relished the chance to display his ingenuity with a plan for a turning movement to get behind the North Korean forces.

215

* * *

His debriefing at headquarters lasted forever. After the tense surveillance operation, the separation from Gomax, and their harrowing escape, all Junior wanted to do was to see Sachie. He realized that she was his source of rejuvenation – his time with her restored his sense of normalcy. The constant threat of death while on a mission made him susceptible to dark thoughts. He had trouble eating and sleeping. Sachie's easy manner and joy in simple pleasures like admiring the summer blooms, helped him unwind.

Junior's heart accelerated as he turned the corner onto the street where the Teahouse of the Auspicious Blessing was located. Something was wrong. The area in front of the building was cordoned off with sawhorse barricades. As he approached it, a military policeman stepped out from the narrow portico to confront him.

"What's your business here, soldier?"

"None of yours," replied Junior, not ready to be deterred.

"I'm sorry, sir, this area is a crime scene and off-limits to all personnel," said the MP.

"Crime scene? What happened here?"

"Several servicemen were murdered here, sir. Here's a wanted flyer, if you have any information," said the policeman.

Junior gaped at the paper. Splashed across the front of the poster was the picture of his beloved. What was Sachie's face doing on a wanted poster? He read down:

WANTED SACHIE MAGIRI

FOR MULTIPLE MURDERS ON SEPTEMBER 1ST

AT THE TEAHOUSE OF THE AUSPICIOUS BLESSING

ALL INFORMATION CONFIDENTIAL

CONTACT U.S. MP POST, HARAJUKU DIST.

Before he could say that there must be some mistake, the door to the adjacent building opened and a woman peered out.

It was Miyumi, the hostess of the Teahouse. Without her makeup Junior did not recognize her at first. Then, with a scrawny finger, she beckoned to him. He walked over to her.

"Junya-san, please come in," she invited.

He removed his shoes and entered a cramped space that was obviously Miyumi's residence. Although spare, it was meticulously appointed with lacquered furniture and fine porcelain figurines of geishas. She gestured for Junior to sit and she scuffled through a beaded divider to a back room. Moments later she returned with a tray carrying tea service. She bowed and served tea. Sitting, she savored the steamy cloud rising from her cup. His mind was a jumble of confusion.

"What I'm about to tell you is most upsetting. As you know, our geishas are in a long tradition of refined, engaging companions. On the first night of September, we had a group of four officers to entertain. We were short-handed, only Sachie and Akiko were available to serve. The men were intoxicated when they arrived. One of them passed around white powder. As the night went on, the girls became more frightened. I should have acted, but I did not."

Junior stared at her, wanting her to continue, while not wanting to hear the horrid details.

"The party became raucous. When Akiko went into the kitchen where I was, two of the men followed her. Sachie was alone with the others. I heard her scream. One held her down while the other pig tore at her kimono. Sachie reached for the ornamental pick that held her hair and stabbed the man who was on top of her in the base of the neck. The pick severed his spinal cord. Before the other man could react, she slashed him on the throat and ripped his jugular vein. Blood spurted everywhere. Sachie's beautiful pancake makeup was speckled with blood."

"My poor darling," muttered Junior.

"The other two men rushed into the salon and bumbled around attempting to revive their friends. Akiko and I helped Sachie escape in the chaos that followed. An ambulance was

217

called and the men were pronounced dead. By the time the police arrived, Sachie was safely away."

"Thank goodness," said Junior.

"The military police were called and the teahouse was declared a crime scene. Even though we told them it was self-defense, they refused to listen, saying that no Jap can get away with killing an American soldier. They began a hunt for Sachie. Fortunately, she is far away," said Miyumi.

Junior knew that Miyumi could not, and would not, tell him where Sachie was. He wanted to know, but did not want to know.

"Tell her I love her and will come for her when this blasted war is over."

Junior's sorrows would soon to be multiplied.

General of the Army Douglas MacArthur, Commander in Chief, Far East, (center) Greets Army Chief of Staff General J. Lawton Collins (left) and Chief of Naval Operations Admiral Forrest P. Sherman, as members of the Joint Chiefs of Staff arrive in Tokyo for conferences concerning Incheon invasion. August 21, 1950.

CHAPTER

23

Operation Chromite

"Now was the time to recognize what the history of the world has taught from the beginning of time: that timidity breeds conflict, and courage often prevents."

~ General Douglas MacArthur

By mid-summer, UN forces had slowed the North Korean invasion and had established the Pusan Perimeter. Kim had gambled on driving the South Korean government and the skeleton American forces off the Peninsula and into the Korean straits within one month. Due to MacArthur's initial strategy of yielding territory to gain time, the possibility of Kim succeeding lessened. Each day, men and war materiel arrived at the Port of Pusan. The opposing forces were now almost equal in number and MacArthur had the weaponry to negate the previous undisputed dominance of the Soviet T-34s. Having failed to achieve a quick victory, the People's Army was exposed and over-extended.

With the situation stabilized, MacArthur's genius went to work. He conceived of a plan to outmaneuver the People's Army by inserting a major fighting force behind Kim's army and severing his supply lines and communications. The plan was to perform an end-run by traveling 150 miles up the west coast of Korea and to capture the port of Incheon and the capital, Seoul which was only twenty-five miles inland. He called it Operation Chromite. Based on an analysis of the tides and the position of the moon, MacArthur chose Friday, September 15th as D-day.

When MacArthur revealed his plan to inflict a devastating blow to the People's Army with an amphibious assault on Incheon, the Joint Chiefs of Staff vehemently opposed Operation Chromite. In August, less than one month before the proposed attack, MacArthur met with all the stakeholders including other Pacific area and Korean War commanders in the sixth-floor conference room at his headquarters in Tokyo. Army General Joseph "Lightning Joe" Collins, Chief-of-Staff, Admiral Forrest Sherman, Chief-of-Naval-Operations, Marine Corps General Lemuel C. Shepard, Jr., and General Idwal Edwards, deputy of Air Force Operations, represented their respective branches.

As Commander Amphibious Group ONE, Rear Admiral James Doyle was responsible for implementing the plan. His staff laid out details of the invasion plans. Doyle's gunnery officer, Lieutenant Commander Arlie Capps started by saying, "We drew up a list of every natural and geographic handicap - and Incheon had 'em all."

There were no beaches at Incheon, only seawalls and piers. A landing force could not establish a beachhead, but, rather, would have to climb the walls or moor at the piers. Once landed, the attackers would be confronted with a city - every building would provide a defensive obstacle.

The natural barriers were even more formidable. The tide ran as high as thirty feet. Thus, there was only a narrow window of a few hours at high tide to perform the operation. When high tide passed, the waterways became impenetrable mudflats over the ensuing twelve hours until the next high tide. A fully equipped soldier would sink up to his waist in mud if he attempted to cross the flats at low tide.

In addition, the only feasible marine access to Incheon was Flying Fish Channel which was narrow and the current flowed at eight knots. The channel was marred by an abundance of rocks and shoals which could disable a landing vessel and block the column of ships behind it. In the words of one Naval officer, "Flying Fish Channel was well-named. A fish almost had to fly to beat the current, and to check his navigation past the mud-banked islands and curves in the channel." Finally, ships traveling on the Channel would be susceptible to sea mines.

After all these red flags had been presented, Admiral Doyle concluded with a tepid, non-endorsement to the effect that an amphibious invasion at Incheon was not impossible.

General Collins echoed the sentiments of Doyle, characterizing Operation Chromite as an "impossibility." He advocated for centering their counter-offensive at the port of Kunsan which was one hundred miles south of Incheon. The Joint Chiefs-of-Staff preferred Kunsan for a breakout invasion. It was a natural target which had none of the detriments of Incheon. On behalf of the marines who would bear the brunt of the impediments posed by a landing at Incheon, General Shepard supported Collins.

When all the arguments against Operation Chromite had been made, MacArthur collected his thoughts. He recalled his father's admonition that "councils of war breed timidity and defeatism." Then, MacArthur launched into a virtuoso performance, shredding each of the arguments against and forcefully promoting the virtues of his plan.

He dismissed Kunsan as the site for an amphibious attack to reverse the momentum of the invaders. He noted that it was too close to the Pusan Perimeter to achieve the desired objectives, specifically relieving the pressure on the Pusan Perimeter and severing the supply lines and communications of the North Korean juggernaut.

"Essentially, establishing a presence at Kunsan simply expands the Perimeter. It does not eliminate the need to breakout from the southern portion of the Peninsula. Gentlemen, we know that a breakout will cost thousands, perhaps, tens of thousands of lives. Nor, will it cut off supplies to the Reds. No, Kunsan does not achieve the objective and is not worth our resources."

MacArthur argued that each impediment at Incheon was actually an advantage. In sum, the North Koreans would conclude that the UN forces would not be so brash to invade at Incheon. Consequently, they would not prepare for it.

"Surprise! We all know the greatest tactical advantage an invading force can have is surprise. This situation is similar to the invasion of Quebec in 1759 by General James Wolfe. The defenders believed that the banks of the St. Lawrence River were so precipitous that no hostile force could scale them. The French focused their defenses to the north of the city. General Wolfe led a small force up the heights from the south and conquered the city, ending the French and Indian War. Gentlemen, our invasion at Incheon will occur on the anniversary of General Wolfe's stunning victory. Surprise is one of our greatest advantages, let's not squander it."

Admiral Sherman shifted uncomfortably in his chair. A knot formed between his eyebrows as he looked at his compadres. MacArthur sensed doubt seeping in and pounced to exploit it as surely as a tiger attacks a wounded gazelle.

"Much has been made about the tortuous waterway leading to the port of Incheon," said MacArthur, boring in on Sherman. "We have acquired expert intelligence about the challenges of navigating Flying Fish Channel. This gives us exceptional power."

Nodding to Colonel Cheung, MacArthur summarized her contribution to the planning. Then, he turned toward Admiral Sherman and said, "My confidence in the Navy is complete, and in fact, I seem to have more confidence in the Navy than the Navy has in itself. (pause) The Navy has never let me down in the past, and it will not let me down this time."

Like an attorney capping a compelling argument, MacArthur concluded, "Make the wrong decision here—the fatal decision of inertia—and we will be done. I can almost hear the ticking of the second hand of destiny. We must act now, or we will die."

Admiral Sherman accepted the challenge and announced his enthusiastic support for Operation Chromite. By force of personality, MacArthur carried the day and Operation Chromite was green-lighted.

A few weeks before the actual invasion of Incheon, Junior again said goodbye to his friend, Seung. Only days earlier, the two men had successfully ferried across the Han River and were exfiltrated to safety. Shortly after their return, Seung was assigned to Naval Commander Eugene F. Clark and an ROK commando group that had the critical mission of reconnoitering Wolmi-do Island and capturing the lighthouse on Palmi-do Island. Once the lighthouse was in friendly hands, it would guide the invasion fleet as it navigated the harbor. Junior was proud that his friend had been chosen for such an important mission. At the same time, he worried for his safety; he did not want to lose another brother-in-arms.

Junior did not have time to reflect on the fates of Gomax and Sachie because he was part of MacArthur's entourage that raced across Japan and boarded the *USS Mount McKinley* en route to the Yellow Sea off the coast of Incheon. The ship plowed through rough seas and high winds as a typhoon ravaged the Sea of Japan. MacArthur's carefully laid invasion plans were suddenly in jeopardy due to the extreme threat presented by violent storm conditions. The general was unfazed. He was so sure of his destiny that the prospect of a typhoon interfering with his plans was inconceivable to him.

Once Junior was on board, he was summoned. An aide to Admiral Doyle escorted the nervous marine to the charthouse, a cramped area not far from the bridge which was filled with navigation charts and electronic equipment. Junior's eyes were adjusting to the dimly lit area when he heard MacArthur's voice. Junior snapped to attention and saluted.

"Easy, Junior, have a seat," said MacArthur indicating a chair next to a small table on which invasion plans were strewn.

"To all hands, I want this charthouse cleared for the next fifteen minutes," boomed the general. Sailors bounded out of the room, relieved to be away from the scrutiny of MacArthur for a few minutes.

"I want to commend you on your Incheon photos. These pictures and your detailed notes have been invaluable to our planning. We're a few days away from the attack and I want you on the bridge with me when the operation starts."

Too green to fathom the honor of being invited to the bridge with this exclusive group, Junior nodded, "Yes, Sir, General."

"Good," said MacArthur. "It's a damn shame that Gomax did not return with you. Our intelligence sources have reported no trace – so, there's hope. He's a resourceful bastard. I wouldn't worry about him."

Junior believed the general.

"Now, about that rifle of yours. You violated the first order of a soldier, secure your weapon at all cost. Do you know what they call a soldier without his rifle?"

When Junior shrugged, MacArthur said, "Dead meat."

The young marine braced himself for the impending hit to his paycheck.

"Until I can find you protection to replace Gomax, I have something for you. Do you know who Audie Murphy is, Junior?"

"No, sir, not really, sir. I think he was a World War II hero, sir."

"That's okay, you were very young when Audie Murphy distinguished himself. He received the most medals for bravery in WWII. A wonderful patriot. Proof that physical size is not everything – it's the size of the heart that matters. Sort of like you," said MacArthur in a kind tone.

224

From beneath the table, the general produced a Thompson sub-machine gun with a sawed-off stock and a shortened barrel. An extended banana clip protruded from between the fore grip and the trigger guard. Junior reckoned that it held 100 rounds.

"This weapon was customized to the personal specifications of Audie Murphy. They chopped it so that he could strap it to his leg. The clip's modified so that it can fire rapid bursts."

Junior stared in amazement. All he could say was, "Wow..." Then, he caught himself and said, "Wow, sir. Thank you, sir."

"I hope to God that you won't need to use it," said the general. "Now, there is one more thing I have to do with you."

"Sir, did I do something wrong, sir?

"No, I have to change your rank."

"General, I'm satisfied. I'm fine with lance corporal," sputtered Junior.

"No, no, I can't have anyone on my staff with that low a rank. I'm going to give you a choice, a battlefield commission. You have a choice, a major, or a chief warrant officer - they're on the same grade level."

Junior paused; his thoughts ran to the recurring news that majors in combat areas had a limited life expectancy and were coming back from the front in green body bags. He said to himself, I don't want to come back in a green bag.

"General, Sir, I'll take chief warrant officer, sir."

Surprise and speed were the keys to success at Incheon. To keep the enemy guessing, the plan included feints up and down the coast to mask the ultimate target, Incheon harbor. Prior to the invasion, UN forces bombed Kunsan and Chinnampo, a port less than fifty miles southwest of P'yŏngyang, at the mouth of the Taedong River, on the west coast, and Samchok on the east coast of the Korean Peninsula. These efforts sowed enough confusion that Kim refused to divert troops to reinforce Incheon even though his Chinese military advisers urged him to do so. Kim believed that he was close to breaking through the Pusan Perimeter and did not want to dilute that effort.

Those charged with the details of the UN amphibious assault had nightmares about Wolmi-do Island. Its location to the northwest of the entrance to Incheon harbor made it the perfect gatekeeper to protect it. In Korean, Wolmi-do means Moon Tip, named for the island's shape hooking around the Incheon basin. The island rose 350 feet above the water, giving it a commanding view of access to Incheon. A causeway connected Wolmi-do to the mainland, allowing reinforcements and re-supply. Adding to its strategic importance - Wolmi-do was situated a few miles south of Kimpo Airfield, the largest airfield in that part of the country.

Prior to the North Korean invasion, Wolmi-do had been a seaside resort for the residents of Incheon. After it fell, the North Koreans rushed to take advantage of Wolmi-do's location which was vital to controlling the port of Incheon. They fortified the island by installing gun emplacements, anti-aircraft batteries, and machine-gun redoubts. The neutralization of Wolmi-do Island by MacArthur's forces was crucial to the success of the amphibious assault.

Intelligence provided by Junior about the placement of enemy artillery batteries on Wolmi-do and Colonel Cheung's knowledge of the hazards of Flying Fish Channel were supplemented by Commander Clark's unit. With accurate information, American and British warships blasted the fortifications on Wolmi-do in the days prior to the invasion. Whenever a Red battery fired at MacArthur's ships, the naval gunners zeroed in on their positions and sent withering return fire. The naval bombardment was supplemented by airstrikes from carrier-based planes. To prevent possible reinforcements from reaching Incheon, the aerial assault included nearby rail lines and roads. These efforts secured the safety of passage into the harbor and opened the way for the marines to attack Wolmi-do.

On that momentous day, the dawn broke as grey and cold as the hulls of the flotilla of the battleships queued along Flying Fish Channel. General Douglas MacArthur and Admiral Douglas Adams were on the bridge of the *USS Mount McKinley* directing the invasion. It was to be one of MacArthur's greatest triumphs, and his last. The general had the rare ability to take aggressive offensive action coupled with a logistical genius to support large-scale military campaigns that could achieve the impossible. During Operation Chromite, 261 naval vessels participated in landing 75,000 marines and infantrymen in a bold stroke to capture Incheon.

Thirty minutes before high tide, the marine assault on Wolmi-do, called Green Beach, commenced with a rocket barrage from the LSMRs which stood for "landing, ship, medium, rocket." This was the first time American naval forces had used LMSRs. They fired over 6400 rockets into Wolmi-do before the marines landed. From Junior's vantage point on the Mount McKinley, each rocket sounded like an express train roaring past.

"There was no moon that night," said Capt. Sears, commander of the Advance Attack Group, "and at first it was as dark as the inside of a cow's belly. As we stood up the channel, we could smell smoke from the burning area ten miles away. There were fires still burning from the previous bombardments."

The first wave landed on Green Beach at 0631, one minute behind schedule. Dust and smoke smelling of a blend of ammonia and rotten eggs filled the air. Ninety-six minutes later, 0807, resistance on Wolmi-do Island was subdued.

Admiral Doyle stood next to General MacArthur on the flat bridge of the *Mount McKinley* when Old Glory was hoisted from the highest point on the island for all to see. MacArthur wore his rumpled campaign hat and a leather bomber jacket. He peered through a pair of field binoculars which bore the scars and scratches of a half a century of searching battlefields for any clue that might tip the scales in his favor. MacArthur fought the fog of war with every fiber of his being. He was unrelenting and resilient once the combatants engaged. He took to heart the lesson of Richard III about for want of a nail... .

"Sir, report from Green Beach. The marines have captured Radio Hill. We now have complete control of Wolmi-do Island, sir," said Lieutenant Commander Arlie Capps, Doyle's gunnery officer.

"Tally?" said General MacArthur.

"One-hundred-and-eight enemy troops dead and one hundred-and-thirty-six captured," said Capps.

"Ours?" MacArthur snapped with disdain for the officer who had reported on the perils of landing at Incheon, almost scuttling Operation Chromite.

The reply from Capps, "Seventeen casualties, sir," was met with a grunt of satisfaction.

While the first phase of Operation Chromite consolidated gains over Wolmi-do Island and unloaded vehicles, ammunition, and supplies, the next phase waited for the tide to rise again. Of particular importance were the M26 Pershing tanks which would rumble down the causeway toward Incheon harbor once the frantic efforts of the engineers made it passable. These tanks would support the next phase – the attacks at Red Beach north of the city and Blue Beach south of the city.

As MacArthur surveyed the terrain around the city, a sense of relief and vindication swept over him. Much like the tidewaters returning down the channels, the general felt the tide of this conflict flowing in his favor. Like a well-designed football play, Wolmi-do, Incheon, Kimpo Air Base, and Seoul would fall under UN control, just as designed in Operation Chromite. He was ebullient. Ever cognizant of the need to prepare for the next phase, MacArthur scoured the deck for Junior. He found the young marine near the bow, staring vacantly at the battle tableau, lost in thought.

"You okay, Junior?" said MacArthur.

Startled, Junior sprang to attention, bug-eyed.

"Yes, general, sir," he spat, snapping off a crisp salute.

"Easy, son. I know that you are concerned about your friends in harm's way. Watching and waiting is like torture. I know. It's what we soldiers do when we are not risking everything," said MacArthur.

Junior nodded, a sullen expression visible on his face. He was angry – angry that Gomax was missing, angry that Seung was somewhere out there in the chaos, and most of all, he was angry that Sachie was a fugitive on the run. Ever the career soldier, MacArthur interpreted the young man's mood as a desire to charge into a hail of bullets for God, country and the U.S. Marines.

"See those LSTs out there?" said MacArthur, steering Junior's gaze to the landing ships lined up for the assault on Incheon. "At the next high tide, those brave soldiers will conquer Red Beach. At 0500 tomorrow, a supporting wave will follow them. You will be on one of those LSTs. Once you land and report to Colonel Murray, I want you to infiltrate enemy lines and head west. Our next stop is Seoul and we need intel on the situation on the ground on the way to Seoul."

Junior tossed and turned that night in his bunk. Brilliant flashes of light, followed by the sounds of naval artillery and explosions shattered the night. It reminded him of the scene memorialized by Francis Scott Key watching the bombardment of Fort McHenry. Only this time the Americans were on offense. Word was that the assaults at Red Beach and Blue Beach had achieved their objectives and Incheon was in American hands.

Unlike the usual grim, introspective atmosphere on a landing craft, the attitude aboard the LST the next morning was almost cheerful. Rumors about the capture of Cemetery Hill and the British Consulate on Observatory Hill coursed through the ranks. The badinage relieved tension. One grizzled veteran bantered that his personal mission was to secure the Asahi Brewery. Laughter erupted when a number of the soldiers volunteered to assist.

When the doors to the LST opened, Junior filed out along with the others. Visibility was poor. Smoke from the previous bombardment and burning buildings, coupled with the rain gave the area a gray-pale green pall. During a briefing with Colonel Murray's aide, Junior learned that they were on high alert for an expected counter attack. He had no details; the only thing he knew was that it would come soon before they could dig in. The aide cleared Junior to pass through marine positions and proceed with his reconnaissance on the way to Seoul.

Staying off the road, Junior entered the hills outside the city. They were not very high, a couple of hundred feet at most. The terrain was studded with large boulders as if they had been sprinkled across the land by giant rock people playing marbles. Junior picked his way through the landscape with his head on a swivel, alert for North Korean troops. He was barely two miles from Red Beach when he caught a whiff of something familiar. His attention was directed toward the aroma of food cooking. Bacon? Was he near a North Korean camp, he wondered? Would they be so careless, or brazen?

He heard voices. It sounded like English. His curiosity peeked, he crept down a hill through the underbrush to find an astonishing sight. He unharnessed his rucksack and hid it in a small fissure in the rocky terrain. He set the trigger on his booby-trap just in case.

Through thick vines, he saw a large, camo-tent. The rear flap was strapped open and Junior was shocked at what he saw. A dozen black soldiers wearing white aprons were tending large aluminum pots bubbling over open flames. Relaxed, they were joking while they worked as if they were at a picnic in Central Park. Just when he thought his shock could get no greater, he heard one voice rise above the rest.

"Arlo?" said Junior as he emerged from his hiding place.

He had not seen his buddy since boot camp. There he was, in the flesh.

"Junior?" said the cook, slack-jawed as the realization sunk in. Junior approached Arlo and the men engaged in an awkward hug, sort of like porcupines mating.

Arlo held Junior at arms-length and stared at the bars on his collar.

"Wow, lookit you," said Arlo. "Hey, guys, this here is my buddy, Junior. We go back to Parris Island. Here I am a cook, and he's a chief warrant officer."

The group hooted and howled.

Amid catcalls and heckles, the staff sergeant who appeared be in charge, stepped forward. "Pipe down. Stop actin' the fool."

"Nice to meet you, Chief. You can call me Lonesome. Can we get you some grits?" said the big man, wiping his hands on his apron extending a meaty paw.

231

Just then, they heard gunfire. From a clearing opposite the mess tent, a marine scout appeared, running as if he was being chased by the devil himself.

"Find cover! The Norks are right on my ass, headed this way! No more than ten minutes out."

Junior reacted quickly. Searching the area, he located the rifles that had been issued to each Marine. He ran to the stack and ordered each of the cooks to take a rifle and a couple of boxes of ammo. A couple of them balked, protesting that they were cooks.

"Listen, soldier, this is no longer a platoon of cooks. It's a marine rifle platoon now. You point that damn thing at anyone not wearing a marine uniform and pull the trigger!"

Turning to the rest of them, he shouted, "Each man, take up a position behind those boulders over there!"

The wait seemed interminable. Junior glanced at the cooks arrayed behind the boulders and wished he had a dozen men like Gomax instead of twelve cooks. A bullet whistled by and thumped into a tree behind him. He looked for Arlo and saw that he still had his white cook's hat on his head. Junior picked up a pebble and tossed it at Arlo who was fixated on the woods in front of him. Wild-eyed to the point of exploding, Arlo turned toward Junior. He mouthed and pantomimed removing his hat. Arlo grabbed his hat and flung it down as if it was on fire.

Junior heard one despairing voice say, "By God, we're gonna see the maker."

He hoped no one else heard it.

A small number of enemy soldiers emerged from the trees. Even though he had not instructed the cooks to hold their fire until the enemy showed in force, Junior was glad that they did – probably because they were too terrified to act. When the vanguard had cleared the forest, one nervous cook fired. Like floodgates bursting after a torrential deluge, the rest of the cooks poured fire into the enemy.

Cries of surprise and anguish filled the area as enemy soldiers fell under the fusillade. Under cover of the fire, Junior scrambled over to Arlo's boulder. His friend was breathing in great gulps, sweat poured from his face, but his rifle had become an extension of his arms and he was firing accurately. The advance group retreated back into the trees. The cooks let out shouts of relief.

"Arlo, can you see Lonesome?"

"He bought the farm when the first Reds cleared the trees."

"Okay," said Junior, as he silently cursed. "Here's what I need you to do. We only have a few minutes before they return in full force and overrun us."

"There's more of them bastards, Junior?"

"Yep, lots more," said Junior, listening to the movement of men running into position around them. His platoon of cooks were arranged in a triangle like bowling pins facing the woods. It might work.

"See how the cooks are set up?"

Arlo nodded.

"Yell to each man by name, his number just like the pins at the alley at Parris Island," said Junior.

"Listen up, men. Jones, you is number one. Richards, two, Walton three . . ."

When each of the men had a number, Junior yelled, "Men, we gotta bug out, but in number order. When I yell your number, you run to the rear. The other numbers, you will fire three rounds into the woods to cover the retreating men. Got it?"

Without waiting for a response, he yelled, "One and two, now. Run!"

KOREA FORGOTTEN SACRIFICE

As Jones and Richards fled to the rear, shots from the other cooks rang out in a ragged staccato.

"Three and four, run! Fire, you bastards."

This time the volley was stronger and more coordinated.

"Five, six, and seven, it's your turn. Run! Fire!"

The volley whipped into the forest as the first men joined in from the rear. When all the men had moved rearward, Junior shouted, "Let's do it again. One and two, run! Fire!"

The ragtag unit executed this withdrawal several times until they were in a less vulnerable position. Junior knew that they had only bought some time. His worst fears came to pass when the mortars started firing. The field of boulders they had hidden behind was blown to smithereens. Chunks of granite and dirt rained down. The area they had vacated was obscured by dense smoke of every shade of black and gray imaginable. What remained of the mess tent raged in flames. The sweet aroma of food was replaced by the acrid stench of cordite and death.

Realizing that they had to keep moving, Junior barked commands for the next withdrawal maneuver. The enemy had advanced quickly along the shore on their left flank. Unencumbered by the obstacles of the forest on the right, the enemy was about to encircle them. Junior and Arlo were the last to withdraw and were easy targets. Arlo twisted and fell when a shot ripped into his side. Junior scrambled over and hoisted him over his shoulder. Junior felt the impact of additional shots hitting his friend. The two men tumbled to safety behind some rocks at a plateau in the hill.

Suddenly, Junior felt a sharp sting in his calf. He lifted his trouser leg to examine the wound. The bullet had hit him in the fleshy part of his leg, leaving a clean, round hole. There was little blood. Scrapping some moss from the rock that sheltered him, Junior stuffed the spongy material into his wound.

Junior turned to Arlo. His face was ashen. His chest erupted in a cough and bloody spittle dribbled down his chin. Unwrapping a sterile dressing, Junior applied pressure to the wound on Arlo's side. His white cook's tunic was soaked red. Junior saw, too, that the right leg of Arlo's trousers was darkening with blood.

"Hang in there, Arlo."

The cook managed a feeble, crooked smile.

In the immediate silence that followed, Junior heard another sound that made his heart leap. He followed the low whistle to a point up the hill behind them. "The cavalry is here to save our asses," he thought. A company of the 5th Marines had arrived. Junior signaled a thumbs up.

When he turned back to Arlo, ready to assure him that help had arrived, his heart sank. The private had lost too much blood. The soldier watched as the youth's vitality waned as if vanishing into a dark vortex. He stared in disbelief as Arlo's expression passed from pain to fear to resignation. Finally, as if switched off, his friend's eyes rolled back in his head. The soldier spun his head around, searching for . . . something . . . anything . . . to reprieve this horrible sentence. There was nothing. Arlo was gone.

"No, no, no," Junior shouted, his voice breaking.

The sound of gunfire startled him back to his precarious reality. He searched the area for the remaining cooks. Each of the men looked to him with terror etched on their faces. Rather than execute another withdrawal maneuver which would give away their position, and allow the Reds to pinpoint their aim on them, Junior shimmied to each man. With his forefinger to his lips, Junior indicated the marine company that was moving in behind them. He signaled for each man to crawl toward the relief force. With smiles that could light up Broadway, each nodded with enthusiasm and followed instructions to safety. With eyes barely able to see through the tears, Junior crawled back to Arlo and dragged his inert body to the marine company.

"Coulda' used you sooner, captain," said Junior when he reached the commanding officer of Charlie Company.

"Chief, you did an amazing job keeping these cooks alive," said Captain Jasper. "We expected to find a bunch of corpses here. Well done . . . ."

His sentence was cut off by a mortar shell that whistled in and exploded about twenty yards in front of them. It was followed by a piercing scream of anguish.

"Medic! Over here, Mims is down. Medic!"

While the mortar methodically raked their position, the Captain ordered his company to reposition and dig in.

"Sergeant, get the radioman over here so that we can call in air support to take out that damn mortar," bellowed Jasper. He scanned the field with his binoculars.

"Dammit. They are setting up a machine gun nest on that hillock," he said to no one in particular. "If they get entrenched there, they will command the road and this valley all the way to the water. These must be the troops from Seoul that we were briefed to expect. Well, they're here and no doubt reinforcements will bring flak-guns. Damn, where's that radio! We gotta get air support before it gets dark."

"Captain, sir," said a sergeant who gulped in breaths. Two months ago, he was an accountant in Cincinnati, now he was at the bloody tip of the spear. "Mims was our radioman. He is KIA and his radio is FUBAR. We are incommunicado."

"Fuck!" hissed Jasper. "Sarge, get a scout back to Colonel Murray. Tell him we're looking at a huge Charlie Foxtrot and need serious assistance ASAP."

Junior watched as the sergeant processed the message. His brow unfurled into a look of shock as he mouthed the words "Charlie Foxtrot means cluster fuck."

Jasper's binoculars scanned the scene over and over, hoping to see something positive or helpful. His focus on the field was shallow, cursory. He was actually scanning his brain for anything from his training that could help in this situation. Jasper was what the veterans called a tweener – one of those unfortunate soldiers who just missed the big war and had to wait for the next one. He had graduated from West Point after WWII and this was his first combat experience. When he received his orders to ship to Korea, he had been elated. This would be his chance to make his bones and move up the ranks. Like an out-of-control bus that screeches to an emergency stop at a precipice, the death of Mims, a nice kid from Colorado, had erased the luster from combat duty. This was real, people died in combat.

"Captain, sir, sorry to interrupt . . ." said Junior.

Jasper looked at Junior as if he was just materialized from outer space.

"Sir, I'm on a special assignment from General MacArthur to gather intel about the counter attack."

"You sure found the right place, Chief," said Jasper.

"Yes, sir, it looks that way. The thing is I have to get back into that valley to retrieve my highly classified equipment," said Junior.

A mortar shell whistled overhead. Jasper looked over the smoldering battlefield and shook his head.

"Not possible."

"I'm afraid I must go. The general will have my head if that equipment gets into enemy hands," said Junior.

"You ain't under my command. If you gotta go, you gotta go."

First Lieutenant Baldomero Lopez, USMC, leads the 3rd Platoon, Company A, 1st Battalion, 5th Marines over the seawall on the northern side of Red Beach, as the second assault wave lands, 15 September 1950, during the Incheon invasion. Courtesy of Naval History & Heritage Command.

Korean War - Battle of Incheon | 1950 | Fight for Seoul | U.S. Invasion of the Korean Peninsula
https://www.youtube.com/watch?v=-65enc17-rA

CHAPTER 24

Machine Gun Madness

"The key is to transcend morality and allow people to utilize their primordial instincts to kill without feeling, without passion, without judgment, because it is judgment that defeats us."

~ Colonel Walter Kurtz, Apocalypse Now

Junior crawled, slithered, and crept back toward where the mess tent had stood. The sun had set behind the hill and the twilight muted the devastation. While the impending darkness was welcome for the concealment it provided, it obscured the dead and body parts that lay haphazardly in his path. One minute, Arlo was joking and jiving and the next he was inanimate, a cadaver. It took all of Junior's resolve to steel himself from the horror. When he finally reached his gear, he was so filled with hatred and anger toward the enemy that he vowed that the bastards would pay with their blood.

Gone was the elation of the command group on the *Mount McKinley* for the taking of Wolmi-do Island, and the successful landing at Incheon. Gone was the fear of harm to Gomax, Seung, and Sachie. That was abstract, a possibility. The death of Arlo was immediate and undeniable. The blood of Arlo on his uniform replaced all of his generalized fear. Holding his friend in his arms as his life-force ebbed away, Junior was driven to an uncontrollable rage. Just then, he heard an enemy machine open fire on the marine company to his rear. He knew what he had to do.

Junior left his gear in its hiding place and moved toward the left flank of the enemy. The waning sunlight illuminated the top of the hill occupied by the enemy. Soon, it, like the valley, would be consumed by darkness. Navigating a wide berth from the machine gun nest, he came upon a deep stream that flowed from the elevation to the rear of the North Korean position. He raised his weapon above his head and plunged into the icy water. His mind flashed to Ribbon Creek where he had nearly succumbed to hypothermia during boot camp at Parris Island. Tears welled in his eyes as he recalled how during that boot camp crisis, Arlo had risked his own life to save him.

Now, on a hill in Korea, he felt the cold permeating his core. No, he shouted to himself, not now, not here. Junior willed himself to the opposite side of the creek and collapsed, shivering. He pounded his body with his arms to bring back his circulation. The sound of the machine gun reverberating through the forest, restored his focus. These bastards had to pay for what they did to Arlo. He slithered like a snake toward the sound. He saw a four-man crew working the gun. Off to the right in a slight depression, he saw a North Korean company solidifying their position. Soldiers scurried around, setting up tents, communication and mess positions, and other logistics.

Junior looked up at the heavens and said, "God, please forgive me for what I'm about to do."

He inched closer to his target. He was about fifteen yards from machine gun nest when he opened fire. Hot lead spewed from the Murphy gun and killed the gunner crew instantly. Junior heard the skin of the gunner sizzle when he draped over the barrel in a death pose. It reminded Junior of the bacon that Arlo had cooked earlier that morning when Junior discovered the mess tent.

The machine gun stopped firing. A vacuum of silence followed.

A North Korean officer reacted, barking orders to check the machine gun. Soldiers sprinted into action and raced up to the emplacement. Time seemed to slow for Junior. He ripped an asbestos glove from the dead ammo handler and put it on his left hand. Grabbing the barrel, he yanked the gun from its tripod. He secured the handle and pulled the trigger. The gun thundered to life, spewing bullets on the soldiers who were charging toward him.

The heat from the gun felt good. Watching the enemy fall and writhe in pain excited him. He freed several ammo belts and carried the weapon of death down toward the enemy camp. He mowed down everyone in his path. Then, backlit against the canvas of the mess tent, he saw the shadows of more men. Junior sprayed hot lead across the mess tent and heard men scream and fall.

He crossed the compound toward the mortar site. The more he strafed the company, the stronger he felt. Junior swept the gun toward an officer who darted behind a tree. A fusillade of bullets nipped after him as he desperately sought a shield. Bullets ripped chunks of bark and wood from the tree. Junior heard the officer groan as bullets tore into his exposed leg. Before falling, the officer leaned around the tree and shot at Junior. The first bullet hit Junior's left shoulder. The officer's last gasp shot struck Junior in the side.

There was a momentary silence when the machine gun stopped. Junior released the machine gun and sank to his knees. A short distance away, at the opposite end of the camp, he heard the mortar crew shouting. He knew that once they reached the clearing and saw the death he had rained on their camp, they would kill him. He had to do something before he passed out. Pineapples; that was it.

He felt for the grenades attached to his vest. With his good hand, he wrenched them free. Pin to teeth, he yanked and threw two grenades in succession. A sharp pain coursed through his right forearm. One of the mortar crew had fired before the first grenade exploded in the mortar pit. The second grenade landed and rolled amidst the startled crew. When it detonated, it left a jigsaw puzzle of body parts scattered throughout the immediate area.

Junior had no idea how much time had elapsed; but he heard American voices far away as though the sounds were being filtered through a cloud of maple syrup.

"Sir, over here. He's still breathing. Corpsman, over here STAT."

Junior felt himself being lifted onto a stretcher. Light from a flashlight blazed into his eyes. A face hovered over him.

"It's that crazy photographer," said Captain Jasper.

Junior blinked.

"Do you think you are superman? Are you the entire Marine Corps?"

"No, sir, just a stupid photographer kid that saw you guys were in trouble and I tried to help you," said Junior, in a barely audible voice.

Jasper shook his head in disbelief.

"Do you realize how many enemy troops you killed?"

Junior gave a drowsy shrug, as the morphine took effect.

"Over 200," said Captain Jasper to an unconscious Junior.

In his report to General MacArthur, Captain Jasper emphasized the number of lives spared by Junior's heroics. One fact from the report which impressed MacArthur the most was the statement that from the time the machine stopped firing on the marines, until the grenades exploded, only seven minutes had passed.

Junior was patched up at the nearest Mobile Army Surgical Hospital and subsequently transported to Tokyo in a diesel-powered submarine. When he opened his eyes in the recovery room after surgery in Tokyo General Hospital, he received a distinguished visitor.

"What in the hell did you do?" barked MacArthur.

"I beg your pardon, general."

"I'm giving you a general order, you will never, ever again involve yourself in any major battle we have over there."

During Junior's convalescence in a hospital in Tokyo, Operation Chromite succeeded in epic fashion. On the heels of the landing at Incheon, UN forces turned their attention to the airfield at Kimpo. It was the largest airport in Korea and MacArthur considered it essential for tactical air support. The North Koreans were so disoriented and demoralized by the reality of 75,000 hostile forces that landed at Incheon that the defense of Kimpo was tepid at best. By September 17th, just two days after the amphibious landing at Incheon, the air base at Kimpo was under American control. MacArthur transferred air support command from Tokyo to Kimpo Air Base and men and materiel flowed into the country.

It took only two weeks after the conquest of Incheon for UN forces to reach Seoul and re-establish control over the capital of the Republic of Korea. Operation Chromite inserted a massive UN presence behind North Korean lines and severed the already-degraded communications and supply lines to Kim's Army. The invaders were stranded in South Korea.

General MacArthur had every reason to crow. Operation Chromite was an unqualified success and he had silenced the naysayers. The general celebrated his master-stroke by displaying another facet of his personality – the genius of publicity. MacArthur ascribed to the old saw attributed to P.T. Barnum, the shameless American showman, that "There is no such thing as bad publicity."

Running a proverbial victory lap, MacArthur announced that the war would be concluded by Christmas 1950. Much like Kim's ill-conceived expectation that the south would fall within a month, MacArthur's belief that resistance in North Korea would crumble within months was wishful thinking. Tragically, the death, casualties and devastation on the Korean Peninsula would continue for another thirty-four months.

Ever cognizant of the impact of psychological victories, the general discovered an opportunity when his troops reasserted control over Seoul.

"General, we have something that I'm sure you will enjoy seeing," said Lieutenant Haig when MacArthur arrived in Seoul. The aide led the general's entourage to a garage on the grounds of the Blue House. Inside was a vehicle covered with a white tarpaulin. With the bravura of a carnival barker, Haig lifted the cover and stood there smiling. In the dimly lit space, Haig leveled his hand and displayed the limousine that Stalin had given to Kim Il Sung.

"For your touring pleasure . . . a shiny, new Stalin-mobile," said the junior officer with a broad smile.

MacArthur beamed. Appreciating the propaganda value of this prize, he chuckled and said, "Get President Rhee over here for a photo opportunity. I would like to present him with this vehicle."

MacArthur hosted a ceremony welcoming President Rhee back to Seoul and the restoration of the government of South Korea. When Kim saw the picture of South Korean President Rhee behind the driver's seat of his ZIS limo, Kim flew into a rage so violent that took his Makarov pistol and blasted his personal Jeep, a Soviet GAZ-67 utility vehicle. The headlights and split-screen windshield were shattered during the tantrum.

After several weeks of convalescence in a Tokyo hospital, Junior was ambulatory. General MacArthur visited him twice. On the first occasion, Junior was so full of painkillers that he was barely conscious. He vaguely recalled the general saying something about how he had always faced enemy fire without fear because like General George Washington, when Providence wanted him to die the bullets would hit their mark; until then, he braved the barrage.

"I guess you are blessed in the same way, Junior."

The next time MacArthur visited, Junior was alert and beginning to walk along the ward, albeit with difficulty.

"The doctors tell me that you are going to have a full recovery. None of the bullets struck bone. You, my lad, need some R&R. . . . rest and relaxation," said MacArthur when Junior gave him a puzzled look.

"Oh, sounds good, sir."

"Here are your orders. Be at the air strip at 0600 tomorrow. Pack your dress uniform," said MacArthur, with a look that said don't ask.

After several days of traveling, Junior was in his dress blues waiting outside the hotel lobby on the morning following his arrival in Washington, DC. He had spent most of the flights from Tokyo sleeping in a jerry-rigged cot on the military transports. It felt good to be on the ground back in the states. When he put his dress uniform on, he was stunned at how loose-fitting it was. As he tightened the belt, the material bunched so much that it made him think of Sachie and how her belt pulled the fabric of her kimono snugly around her waist. A wave of sadness flushed over him. He hoped that she was safe away from the clutches of the authorities. Junior knew that the charges against her would forever bar their chances of life in the states.

His orders were terse – stipulating only that he be outside his hotel in dress uniform at 0900 on Thursday. Where or what he was doing was not specified.

An official government vehicle pulled up and he was instructed to get in. A short ride later, the car pulled across from a series of row houses. Exiting, he stood on the curb facing a green area. Through the trees, he spied the White House, partially obscured by scaffolding.

A voice behind him called, "Hey, Chief, are you Junior?"

"Yes."

"Come this way, sir," said a young marine corporal, beckoning Junior toward a four-story row house adorned with black shutters.

"Welcome to the Blair House, sir. Follow me, please," said the corporal. Junior was confused over why the general would send him to a private residence.

The guard took him to a small room off the main hall where several men waited for him. A tall man in a business suit approached Junior. The man had graying temples and a military air.

245

"Listen carefully. We are going to take you to a private room where my men are stationed. I have CIA men and six marine special operatives there. They are all armed. You will follow directions to the letter. Understood?"

Junior nodded solemnly and thought, "Oh my God, they are going to kill me."

The tall man led Junior to a large wooden door and knocked three times. Junior closed his eyes hoping to avoid his fate. The door opened into a large square office. A short man in a gray suit rose from behind a desk. The soldier blinked twice in disbelief. It was the Commander-in-Chief. As if injected with starch, the young marine stiffened and snapped off his best salute.

"At ease, soldier," said President Truman from behind his desk. "Please have a seat."

"Yessir, Mr. President."

Junior tightened his jaw to keep his mouth from flopping open.

"Ordinarily, I would meet you at the White House, but the termites kicked us out. The place was falling apart. Poor Bess feared for her life every time she used the stairs. So, here we are in the government guest house. My apologies."

The President glanced at the clock on the opposite wall, then down at the desktop which was covered with panels of embossed morocco leather. He fingered a polished, mahogany box.

"Okay, let's get down to business," said President Truman. "You're working for Wild Bill, right? You're that marine that does all that shit that is supposed to be taking pictures for us?"

"Yes, sir. I guess that's me."

"I have a bunch of medals for you. Lord knows that anybody that's done all the shit you've done deserves more than that."

"Mr. President, I don't know what you're even talking about."

Truman stood and walked around the desk to Junior who reflexively stood. The President opened the box and indicated several medals.

"On behalf of a grateful nation, I award you these Purple Heart medals for military merit. This medal was established by General George Washington for those who were wounded in combat. Thank you," said the President, hanging the medals over Junior's head.

Hanging from purple ribbons, the heart-shaped medals were purple, bordered in gold. In the center was a profile of the first President. Junior's own heart pounded as he strained to look at the additions to his uniform.

Truman was not finished. He reached into the box and removed two additional medals. Each hung from a red, white, and blue ribbon and bore a five-pointed gold star with a laurel wreath in the center punctuated by a silver star. He hung them on Junior.

"On behalf of a grateful nation, I award you these two Silver Stars in recognition of gallantry in action. . . ."

"I'm sorry, Mr. President, but I don't understand. What's this for?" said Junior.

"Now, don't you interrupt your President, son. From what I read about your actions in combat, you most certainly deserve these medals. I'm talking about wiping out an entire enemy company by your lonesome. Amazing. I'm talking about going behind enemy lines to secure invaluable intelligence which saved lives. I'm talking Operation Solar Eclipse and about gallantry in action."

The President smiled and withdrew a parchment from the box.

"General MacArthur told me that you were as modest as you are fearless. He told me that you refused to be nominated for the Medal of Honor. Well, let me tell you, these medals are equal to the Medal of Honor and I am giving you a Presidential Citation to show my appreciation for your efforts at Incheon which came at great personal sacrifice. The Citation reads: In September 1950 Chief Warrant Officer Nilberry acted with

247

uncommon valor to single-handedly eradicate an enemy stronghold, killing hundreds of enemy soldiers and destroying a valuable installation. He distinguished himself conspicuously by gallantry and intrepidity at the risk of his life above and beyond the call of duty. Congratulations."

"Mr. President, that's awful flattering. I want to tell you something about these medals. They're not mine. They belong to the men I fought with who didn't make it."

"Chief, what do you think about this war?"

"Mr. President, I'm doing what I was trained to do. I don't think this war is something this country believes. We've lost a lot of men, a generation. How many more do you want us to lose in Korea?"

"Don't you think I carry that burden with me every day? I wake up each morning with a pit in my stomach fearing that we will provoke Russia or China into this fight. That World War III will begin."

"I got news for you Mr. President, they are already in it big time. Make no mistake, I've seen the Russkies and Chinks wearing North Korean uniforms."

"You're a smart-ass SOB, aren't you?"

"No, Mr. President. I just call the game the way I see it."

"I wish I had a hundred of you," said the President in a wistful tone.

The door opened and the tall CIA agent said, "Chief, it's time to go. The President has pressing business."

"Wait a minute," said Truman. Then, he looked at Junior and gave him a Class A salute.

"Semper Fi."

"Semper Fi, Mr. President."

CHAPTER

25

Giocondo in Red China

"Now, this is not the end.

It is not even the beginning of the end.

But it is, perhaps, the end of the beginning."

~Winston Churchill

For Junior the tenor of the war definitely changed after the Incheon invasion. Not only had he achieved a significant promotion to Chief Warrant officer, but he returned to working alone. Unfortunately, there was still no sign of Gomax since the gunnery sergeant went missing on their mission to Seoul before the invasion. The young marine's isolation was increased by Sachie's absence. His relationship with the beautiful geisha had served as a valuable safety valve from the pressures of the danger he faced on every mission. Without her gentleness, Junior was adrift in a world of brutality. These circumstances left Junior angry and prone to reckless violence.

After his meeting with President Truman in Washington, Junior returned to Tokyo. With each passing day, his experience in the Blair House seemed more like a gauzy newsreel with stilted figures enacting a medal ceremony than reality. Once he took off his dress blues, he returned the medals to the mahogany box and forgot about them. He donned his utilities and caught a military transport back to the war.

After the success of the September 15th invasion, MacArthur pressed the advantage provided by the Incheon landing. UN forces captured Kimpo Air Base within days and had retaken

Seoul by the end of the month. The turning movement at Incheon disrupted communications and supplies to the North Korean army. Incheon changed the dynamic of the conflict.

However, contrary to MacArthur's assertion that the war would be over by Christmas, the situation was more like Churchill's assessment after the British defeated the German *Afrika Korps* under Field Marshall Rommel at El Alamein during WWII, that, "Now, this is not the end. It is not even the beginning of the end. But it is, perhaps, the end of the beginning."

It was the middle of October 1950 by the time Junior returned to action. Across from the *Dai-ichi* Life Insurance Company building, the Imperial Gardens were a chromatic celebration of autumn. If Sachie had been there, she would have explained to him that it was *Koyo* time, the autumnal transformation of the leaves from verdant green to ginko gold and maple red. He watched as couples strolled languidly through the paths that were manicured with a precision which was in diametric contrast to his experience. He realized that his young life had been a series of chaotic lurches and wondered where he was destined to careen next. His question was answered within minutes of his return to MacArthur's headquarters.

"Red China!" shouted Major General Donovan.

"Junior, we have to find out if those bastards are serious about entering this conflict," said MacArthur.

"That's right. We have contradictory reports. Some that say that they are already in Korea. There are unverified reports that Chinese forces are using young women carrying babies to ambush UN troops. These accounts are so fantastical that they defy belief. Even the Chinks would not stoop that low. But who knows?" said Wild Bill.

Seeking to keep the discussion from degenerating into rank speculation, MacArthur stated, "We have other reports to the effect that Mao believes that Korea is Stalin's fight and Mao refuses to commit Chinese troops to save Korea. I believe that the Chinese are keeping their powder dry, just waiting for their chance to seize Taiwan. Mao could care less about Korea."

"Douglas, I have a different view. For centuries China has considered Korea vital to its security. Mao has said that the two countries are 'as close as lips and teeth,' which is a variant of the Chinese saying that 'without lips the teeth are cold.' This means that Korea is the lips that protect the Chinese teeth. It's only a matter of time before Mao intervenes in Korea."

Junior watched in awe as the two titans engaged in a robust debate which included reference to maps, photographs, and intelligence reports in an effort to convince the other. Ultimately, both conceded that neither had definitive proof. That was when they turned to Junior.

"We want you to go to China and take pictures of their military installations along the Yalu River at the border. Your flight leaves at 0600 tomorrow. Dismissed," said the general.

Junior snapped off a brisk salute, pivoted, and exited the conference room.

After the success at Incheon and the recapture of Seoul, MacArthur focused his offensive on the opposite coast of the Korean Peninsula. He ordered an invasion of the port city of Wonsan on the east coast. A key objective was control over Kalma Airfield at Wonsan. By October 10th, American-led forces occupied the airfield which was designated K – 25. Within two days, K – 25 was fully operational and the United States Air Force Cargo Combat Command was transporting military supplies to UN forces pushing north.

When Junior landed there, he encountered a frenzied beehive of activity. It took him quite a while to locate his contact. Junior found him bent over a section of the Ornithopter in a far corner of the airfield.

"Whatcha doing?" asked Junior.

"I'm patching a stress tear in this wing, so that I can fly some dumbass photographer around over the Yalu River," said Mako, grinning broadly. He dropped his tools and bear-hugged Junior.

"Mako, we got a lotta ground to cover. When do we start?"

251

"Wheels up in two hours. As soon as that DC2 is fueled and ready to go. You got time to grab a hot meal and a heavy flight suit and gloves. It's gonna be cold where we're headed. Oh, yeah, you're gonna need a pair of goggles," said the affable pilot.

Junior sat behind Mako in the Ornithopter as it bounced down the runway attached by a tow rope to a DC2. The big plane lumbered down the runway until it reached take-off velocity. When the tow line caught, they felt the light plane shudder so violently that they feared it would tear asunder. Once the DC2 leveled off, the pilot followed the coast until they reached a long, narrow valley that led to the border with China. Junior concentrated on the endless mountainous terrain in an effort to avoid thinking about how cold he was.

Hours later, when the Yalu River was in sight, Mako radioed their taxi and synchronized the release of the cable. On release, Mako banked the Ornithopter sharply away to avoid the whiplashing cable as it was winched into the DC2. In the waning daylight, he landed the *Giocondo* in an open field, taxiing her around for a quick take-off if needed. They deplaned and prepared for the next phase of their mission.

The plan was bold and crazy enough to work. Their success hinged on the unique skills of Mako and Junior. Over the next seven days, they would fly along the 500-mile border between China and North Korea to locate and photograph Chinese military forces that might be preparing to enter the war. The seasonal prevailing winds were west-northwest, following the river at an average of 8 – 10 mph. This would enable the plane to use minimal propulsion and glide silently. The *Giocondo* was equipped with the latest infrared-night-fighter technology which would enable Mako to locate and land the plane in open fields under moonlight or early dawn conditions. Stealth, surprise, and superior equipment were the keys to success . . . along with a good dose of luck.

* * *

252

The convoy of trains which transported the North Korean leader pulled into the railyards in the city of *Sinŭiju* in the northern most part of the country. Tucked away in the center of the second string of railroad cars was a forest-green coach, custom made to accommodate the needs of the Supreme Leader. With polished wooden floors, oriental rugs, and architectural paneling of quarter-sawn oak, Kim's suite trumpeted opulence incongruous to wartime. The only flaw in the room was the patina of yellow film on the walls from the incessant cigarette smoking of the Supreme Leader.

Kim Il Sung sat on the camel-colored sofa in his office aboard the armored train car that served as his mobile headquarters. Next to him was an end-table inlaid with mother-of-pearl in the design of Mt. Paektu, the sacred mountain of the revolution, beneath a five-pointed red star. A nearly empty bottle of soju and a crystal whiskey tumbler which he had just drained rested on the tabletop. A sheaf of battle reports littered the sofa next to him.

Kim removed his black-framed eyeglasses and stared, unfocused, at the map of his country hanging on the opposite wall. Last week, there were blue flags and pins concentrated in a corner of the peninsula, surrounded by a multitude of red pins and flags depicting the strong line of his army on the verge of driving his enemy into the sea. Now, the blue markers appeared in the middle of the peninsula, surrounding and enveloping the red markers which were less concentrated and tinged with elements of blue. MacArthur had performed a perfect enveloping maneuver, trapping the DPRK army in the south and threatening annihilation. The dictator poured himself another *soju* and belted it down with a sour look on his puffy face.

He ground his palms into his eye sockets in a futile effort to stop the pounding in his head. His elbows rested on his knees and his hands propped his head. This was not what he envisioned when he dreamed of his return to North Korea after invading the south. Mere weeks ago, he had ridden his Russian limousine into Seoul. From that early triumph, his army had driven the cowardly imposters of the Syngman Rhee government into the sea. Well almost; the imperialist dogs stopped his advance at Pusan. Ultimate victory was within reach when that bastard MacArthur thwarted him by invading at Incheon.

With communications and supply lines to the south severed, Kim's army was in full retreat. He struggled to keep up with the chaos. The latest report was that the UN forces led by the X Corps had landed at Wonsan on the east coast and another prong of enemy forces led by the 8th Army was advancing on his capital of P'yŏngyang on the west coast.

Faced with imminent military collapse of his forces in the south, Kim sent distress telegrams to Comrade Stalin and Chairman Mao imploring them to rescue his army before MacArthur vanquished it altogether. Indicative of his desperate straits, Kim had relocated his seat of government to Sinŭiju in the extreme north of the country. It was located across the Yalu River from the Chinese city of Dandong in case he had to leave the country quickly. While Kim took it for granted that he could escape to China, the last thing Mao wanted was to have the North Korean government in exile inside China, especially with the Americans in hot pursuit. Mao feared a declaration of war by the United States against China.

As Kim replayed the disastrous turn of events in his head, he thought that, perhaps, he should have listened to Mao's advice not to devote all his resources to pressure Pusan but to retreat a bit and draw the enemy out where he could be defeated. Kim could not heed this advice because he was so blinded by his desire to send Rhee's traitorous clique to the grave. Knocking back more *soju*, he lamented how the Americans had turned his plan to conquer the south in a month into a bitter folly. The abrupt reversal of fortunes made him appreciate the truism that every commander knows: victory is claimed by all, but failure belongs to one alone. Kim was about to learn just how true that was.

If only there were some secret time machine or magic wand that could change the situation. In this vein, he took out the single sheet of paper that he had extracted from Dr. Ishii's diary. He implored the page to reveal its secrets and save his dreams from MacArthur's destruction. The paper sat in mute defiance. No one had been able to break the encryption. Not even the painful torture death of numerous Unit 731 personnel had helped. One poor bastard in extreme agony had uttered the word Chosin before he died. That had set off a rabid search of the hydro-electric complex known as the Chosin Reservoir. But months of manhours engaged in meticulous examination of the labyrinth of tunnels and caves had yielded nothing. In the end, he had concluded that it was a fool's errand based on the rantings of a man desperate to stop the pain.

"Speak to me," screamed Kim at the silent paper before he broke down sobbing.

A short while later, Supreme Commander Kim heard indistinct voices outside his office. The door flung open. A short, imperious man entered. He was followed by Kim's executive officer who sputtered warnings that the Commander was not to be disturbed. Kim nonchalantly covered the Ishii paper with a folder and motioned for his XO to desist.

"General Peng, how good it is to see you. Please have a seat," said Kim Il Sung kowtowing to the Chinese military leader. Kim scurried past the general and closed the door.

"Would you like some tea . . . or, perhaps, something stiffer?" asked Kim, with eyes lowered.

"Nothing," said Peng gruffly.

The survivor of several decades of war, Peng was burly, tough and a shrewd commander of men in trying circumstances. He was Mao's most accomplished and trusted military officer. In his early 50s, he was one of Mao's inner circle. Peng served as the commander on the fabled Long March in 1934, the strategic year-long retreat of the Red Army from the Nationalist Chinese Army of Chiang Kai-shek. During that trek for survival, the Red Army traversed more than 5,600 miles over some of the most difficult terrain of western China. It saved Mao's army and solidified his command of the Chinese

Communist revolution which succeeded some fourteen years later.

Now, in the autumn of 1950, Peng convinced Mao that MacArthur's thrust into North Korea was an existential threat to his fragile regime. In his words, it was "a threat to strangle the newborn in the cradle." If the Americans succeeded in conquering North Korea, China would have the hated American Imperialists on his southeastern border – a totally unacceptable situation.

Mao knew that his regime lacked the economic or military might to conduct a direct war with the hated capitalists. The Chairman's best chance to oust the Americans rested on the simple, yet elusive, commitment from Stalin to provide Soviet air power to neutralize the Americans' control of the skies. He placed the achievement of this objective in the capable hands of his Foreign Minister, Zhou Enlai who was already in Moscow on a mission to convince Stalin of the mutual advantages of supporting a Chinese intervention in Korea. Like the switch-back passes on the rugged Korean mountains, Stalin and Mao performed an inscrutable dance over this question. One day the answer was *da*, the next day the answer was *nyet*.

The ever-cagey Stalin sought to mollify Mao by giving the Chinese leader something valuable to him which had little worth to Stalin. In the closing days of WWII, the last Manchu emperor of China was captured by the Red Army as he attempted to escape to Japan. Pu Yi, who had become emperor at the age of two, collaborated with the Japanese until the end of WWII. He was incarcerated for five years in a Soviet prison until Stalin saw an opportunity to gain some favor with Mao by releasing Pu Yi. The disgraced former Chinese emperor provided Mao with sacred seals of the dynasty that Mao used to bolster the legitimacy of the People's Republic. On his return to China, Pu Yi was charged with war crimes and would spend the next ten years of his life in a prison, eventually released when he became "rehabilitated." To Mao, the conviction and eventual conversion of Pu Yi was a valuable propaganda tool.

Tired of waiting for Stalin to commit, Mao concluded that armed conflict with America was inevitable and he decided to send his troops into North Korea regardless of Stalin's air support.

The Chairman's next problem was Kim Il Sung. Mao had little regard for Kim whom he considered a Soviet flunky. Mao turned to Peng to step into the breech. The Chinese dictator warned Peng to be tough with Kim because he was "a number one pain in the butt."

"What's the current military status?" said Peng, in a tone that none of Kim's sycophantic staff would dare use. Kim blinked. Only his alcohol-addled weariness kept him from lashing out at this effrontery.

"Our main problem is transportation. We don't have enough trucks and railway stock. The enemy has destroyed many bridges and railways from the south, leaving the First Army Group in the west trapped between the invaders from Incheon and Walker's forces from Pusan. The Second Army Group in the east is not trapped yet, but is struggling with the same transportation issues," said Kim in a low, discouraged monotone.

Arms crossed with his chin resting on one hand, Peng stood before the map pondering. Kim thought he heard words like disgraceful, travesty, and hopeless muttered by the Chinese commander, however he could not be sure due to his lack of facility with the language. After an interminable wait, Kim blurted,

"Do you have an answer to my telegram requesting military assistance?"

Peng scoffed at the Korean's impudence and continued his geographic scrutiny. Kim frowned and poured himself another drink. After a long minute, Peng pivoted toward Kim.

"Who conceived this amateurish attack?" asked Peng. Kim bristled.

"I did, general. Success was predicated on two circumstances that failed to materialize. First, we were promised by Comrade Pak that 200,000 guerrillas would rise up in the south to support our advance. Nothing close to that happened. Second, we had every reason to believe that the United States would not intervene. Officials high in the American government declared that Korea was not within their zone of concern. That turned out to be mistaken. The current situation is not our fault; we are unlucky," responded Kim.

Peng chided Kim for his extreme naivete. "You are hoping to end this war based on luck. That is not realistic. We have to fight using tactics and techniques that ensure victory. We should fight no battle we are not sure of winning . . ." said Peng. As he droned on with his platitudes, Kim was encouraged by his use of the word "we."

When Peng felt that he had chastised Kim enough, he advised Kim that the Chinese would send volunteers to intervene on behalf of North Korea on one condition.

Kim was so excited and relieved that he shouted, "Well done! Excellent!"

Peng realized that Kim was ignoring the last phrase.

"Of course, the one condition is that I will be commander-in-chief and you will be my adjutant."

It took a second for Kim to process what Peng had said, then, the smile melted from his face like wax on a candle, becoming formless and distorted. Just as he was about to explode in rage, Kim assessed Peng's demeanor and realized that an outburst might drive away Chinese support. Kim applied the first lesson and did not enter a battle that he knew he could not win. Peng smiled in the same way that he did when his *Shih Tzu* learned a new canine trick.

"Good. We should begin preparations for our volunteers to defend a line north of the P'yŏngyang – Wonsan railroad. If the invaders advance above that line, roughly the 39th parallel, we will crush them," said the new commander-in-chief.

Later, when Kim returned to his residence which was known locally as the Central Luxury House, he wept quietly. The realization that the Chinese under General Peng were prepared to concede one half of his country up to the P'yŏngyang – Wonsan line was too painful to bear.

* * *

As soon as they landed in Tokyo, Junior and Mako were whisked to MacArthur's headquarters. They were exhausted and grimy from their weeklong mission in China. MacArthur's top military and intelligence leaders hovered around numerous maps of Korea when the two men entered. MacArthur thrust a mug of coffee into Junior's hand and gestured for him to stand at the head of the conference table.

"Junior, tell us about the situation in China," said MacArthur.

"Yes, Sir. By flying at night, we minimized visual detection. Mako did a great job locating open fields and landing and taking off in less than optimal conditions," said Junior. "Before the mission, I was concerned about the modifications to the camera. But, I've got to say, they worked out great. As you know, the Leica's night photography capabilities are second to none. The tech guys added a copper tubing heating element to keep the parts and film from freezing. Another innovation we used was overlapping exposures to create a sense of depth."

General Willoughby interrupted, "We don't need a lecture on camera technology. We need to know how you reached the conclusion that the Chinks have over 300,000 troops on the border when our sources place that number at 30,000."

"My sources confirm that 30,000 number. Mao wants no part of our Eighth Army. He knows that we will make mincemeat out of them. Furthermore, Stalin has refused to provide air support. Mao won't risk his army to save Kim," said General Almond.

"I think that the generals value the information from spies over pictures that are tinted green, as if that disqualifies them," said Major General Donovan, splaying photos across the conference table as if he were disclosing a winning poker hand.

"Gentlemen, let's focus on what we know, not what we hope," said General MacArthur. "We haven't heard from Commander Hayfisch. Can you explain the discrepancy?"

Mako cleared his throat, hoping to disguise his aversion to scrutiny by brass. He was a pilot first and foremost who loved the freedom of the wild, blue skies. He became a pilot to escape the strictures of the chain of command.

"Well, sir," he began in a voice that was so low that MacArthur cocked his head toward him.

"What? Speak up, son."

"I'm sorry, General. I meant to say that the PVA is used to hiding. They're good at it. They spent decades fighting the Nationalists from the shadows. We took pictures at night when they are most active. I think that they retreated underground during the day to hide their activities. When the spies observed their camps during the day, only skeletal crews were visible," said Mako.

Willoughby scoffed. He picked up several of the photos from the conference table.

"You want us to believe that these mottled rectangles are doors to underground installations?"

Mako nodded.

"And that ten times as many troops are housed underground during the day?"

"Yes, sir, General Willoughby. That's what we saw," said Mako.

"Preposterous," blurted Almond. "Do you realize how much space, sanitary facilities, and storage would be needed to accommodate that many men and their equipment? Impossible! I say that Willoughby's spies are more reliable."

General Willoughby smirked and turned toward MacArthur.

"General, you are the master of logistics. Do you believe that the Chinks are capable of hiding over a quarter of a million soldiers in dirt tunnels along their border?"

MacArthur sighed. He glanced at Donovan to see if he had any rejoinder. Wild Bill knew when logic trumped grainy, green images.

"Sir, the pictures are what they are," said the colonel.

CHAPTER

26

Operation Solar Eclipse – Mourning Venus

*"Water shapes its course according to the ground
over which it flows; the soldier works out his
victory in relation to the foe whom he is facing.
Therefore, just as water retains no constant shape,
so in warfare there are no constant conditions."*

~ Sun Tzu, The Art of War

The mood around the *Dai Ichi* headquarters was decidedly upbeat. The month of October was a banner one for UN forces. On October 7th, the General Assembly of the United Nations adopted a resolution which stated that the UN's goal was "a unified, independent and democratic government" for all of Korea. The Joint Chiefs of Staff instructed MacArthur to proceed with operations leading to "the destruction of the North Korean armed forces." In the wake of the recapture of Seoul and the breakout of General Walker's Eighth Army from the Pusan Perimeter, MacArthur was poised to occupy North Korea's capital of P'yŏngyang and the critical port city of Wonsan on the east coast of the peninsula. The military situation was unfolding perfectly for MacArthur's hidden agenda.

After their last mission across the Yalu River, Junior and Mako enjoyed a celebratory dinner at the *Mizutaki Genkai* where they enjoyed the restaurant's signature dish, the chicken hotpot. The tension of a harrowing week in the hostile regime of Red China evaporated in the steamy, savory ambience of one of Tokyo's premier restaurants.

"What do you make of Almond's claim that there are only 30,000 Chinese troops on the border?" asked Mako as they waited for the matcha ice cream they had ordered.

"He says he has information to support that, so who am I to say different?" replied Junior.

"The man is a raving egomaniac. I think he is going to get a lot of American soldiers killed by underestimating the Chinese. I just pray that your boss stops at the P'yŏngyang – Wonsan line. You don't want to provoke the Chinese Communists," said Mako, tasting the unique frozen dessert. "Wow! This matcha stuff is phenomenal. You have got to try it."

"The color reminds me of marine olive drab," said Junior, who lifted a spoon to his lips. "Hey, this stuff is good – not too sweet and a little bitter."

The next morning Junior was on a plane back to P'yŏngyang where he was ordered to report to the motor pool. As he waited to sign out a vehicle, he re-read his orders. He was to drive north and report to the commanding officer of a Republic of Korea Ranger unit which was conducting reconnaissance for the push north. It seemed odd that MacArthur would assign him to an ROK unit. Oh, well, he thought, MacArthur knows best.

"Here's y'alls Jeep, Chief," said Sergeant Amos Kreller, recently of Mobile, Alabammy as he would say. "She's gassed up an' ready to roll. Where y'all headed?"

"Up towards Unsan," replied Junior tersely.

"That there is about sixty clicks if you stay along the river. Y'all take care now and bring my baby back safely," he said, slapping the hood of the vehicle.

"Will do, Sarge," said Junior as he put the Jeep into gear. Clearing the gate, he was on his own heading deep into enemy territory. He enjoyed the pull of the "Go Devil" engine as he accelerated through the gears. The U.S. Army got it right when they commissioned American car makers to create an entirely new vehicle at the outset of WWII. Before then, the army used horses and larger trucks to travel through war zones. The

Army requested designs for a light reconnaissance and command vehicle. The first vehicle of this type was designed by the Bantam Car Company, a company deemed too small to handle the volume needed. The Army directed Willys and Ford to produce the vehicles based on the Bantam design.

The version manufactured by Ford was officially denominated the Ford GP Government Pygmy, ¼ ton, 4x4 utility vehicle, the initials GP stood for general purpose which quickly evolved into the word Jeep. Equipped with four-wheel drive, it was rugged, relatively compact at eleven feet long by five feet wide. More important, it was easily transportable, capable of being airdropped by motorless gliders. It was the ideal "go anywhere, do anything" vehicle suitable for modern warfare.

The further he drove into the mountains, the colder it became. The late October sun provided little warmth. He hoped that the general was right when he said that the troops would be headed home by Christmas. A wave of nostalgia filled his consciousness. A warm fire, luscious food, holiday cheer . . . nah, that wasn't his family, that was a Charles Dickens fantasy.

Suddenly, the road twisted hard right. When Junior turned into the curve, the Jeep skidded toward the edge. His mind flashed back to that night in Baltimore. Until now, he had not remembered skidding before the crash. Here on this mountain, the memory flooded back. He downshifted and applied even pressure on the gas and hoped that the Jeep would steady before he ran out of road. The Jeep responded like a thoroughbred and negotiated the turn like it was on tracks. Better slow down, he thought. Better yet, time for a urine break. He stopped on the side of the road and took care of business.

Refreshed, he continued along until he came to a checkpoint. He asked for directions to the commanding officer. Various hand signals and pantomimes brought him to a clearing where a pair of guards stood before a tent. They saluted as he approached and lifted the flap. A man with his black hair buzzed in a severe military cut stood studying a map on an easel board with his back toward the entrance. He wore the uniform of an ROK officer. He was evidently in deep thought because he did not budge at the sound of Junior entering.

Junior was about to say, "Reporting for duty . . . ," but, when he recognized the other he warbled a few distinctive notes. The man froze in place.

"Junior! My goodness. How good it is to see you, my friend," said newly minted Captain Lee Seung, with a wide grin.

Junior effected a mock salute, then embraced his comrade-in-arms.

"Lookit you. A real officer, wow," said Junior admiringly.

"You don't look too shabby yourself, Chief," said Seung, drawing out the last word for emphasis.

"Tell me how undercover agent Seung became an ROK officer."

"After our reconnaissance mission of Flying Fish Channel, I hooked up with a couple of ROK commandos and helped them take the lighthouse at Palmi-do Island," said Seung.

"That was you? Getting that lighthouse working was a huge help to the invasion. General MacArthur said that without that lighthouse a ship or two might have run aground and clogged the channel. Great work!" said Junior.

"Later, when we got to Incheon, the ROK officers convinced me to join. They promised me my own recon unit and here I am," he said, opening his arms in an encompassing gesture.

"So, what's going on up here?" asked Junior.

"It's very strange. On the surface, everything is quiet. I just get a strange feeling. At night we hear noises, but it's like ghosts are walking in the woods. The local villagers hear things. Nothing tangible. The roads are empty. Weird," said Seung.

"Let's go ghost hunting tonight. Just you and me," said Junior.

264

Later, after the sun dipped below the horizon, the two men smeared camo grease over their faces and geared up. They did not need camo grease on any other body parts because of the cold. Seung led the way north through the forest. In the murky moonlight, Junior followed the silvery clouds of breath ahead of him. After several uneventful hours, they took a break. While Seung unpacked some cold grub, Junior froze, hand raised.

"Did you hear that?"

Seung shook his head from side-to-side. On a following breeze, the noise returned. From faraway, they heard the low rumble of diesel engine.

"Junior, one of the village elders told me about an old logging trail over the next ridge. Maybe the enemy is using it. Let's head there now."

Junior nodded and followed Seung into the darkness.

Hours later, they hid in a copse of trees overlooking an incredible operation. Hundreds of soldiers were building what looked like a massive branch awning over an entire valley. Other soldiers worked on structures covered by camouflage nets to accommodate thousands of men. Still others moved self-propelled artillery, tanks, and ammunition into caves and other openings in the mountain. Using Maisey's night-vision capabilities, Junior acquired numerous pictures of the operation. It was later determined that these troops were Chinese. In a thinly veiled subterfuge, Mao called these forces the People's Volunteer Army, or PVA. Among the equipment they were deploying were Soviet *Katyusha* multi-barreled rocket launchers mounted on trucks. These rocket launchers would be used with devastating effect in the Chinese offensive which would catch UN forces by surprise in the coming days.

Junior gestured to Seung that they should establish a blind up in the trees overlooking this installation. They spent the remaining hours of darkness creating a hideaway. When dawn approached, the activity below them ceased and they settled into their lair to rest and wait. Junior withdrew the cards from

Operation Solar Eclipse and studied the faces of North Korean leaders until his head nodded and he slept.

Hours later when the sun slipped behind the ridge, the valley below slowly came alive. Although the cramped location and cold were uncomfortable, Junior and Seung realized that they were witnessing one of the most pivotal operations of the conflict. The full-scale engagement of Chinese forces was a game-changing event. The high command of the UN forces had routinely and consistently rejected scenarios involving intervention by the Chinese Communists. MacArthur reasoned that Red China's priority was the "liberation" of Taiwan and that Mao did not have the economic and military strength to inject China into Kim's fight and risk exposing his industrial base in northeast China to American bombing. This miscalculation of China's strategic interests and resolve would result in prolonging the conflict and lead to millions of additional casualties and untold suffering.

The arrival of three armored personnel carriers caught Junior's attention. From the flurry of activity and obsequious gestures by men already on the scene, Junior surmised that important personages had arrived to inspect the progress of the operation. His eyes were drawn to one man in particular who strode confidently, if not arrogantly, ahead of the others who trailed him like puppies fawning for attention. Junior sharpened the focus on his lens and identified one of the generals from the Solar Eclipse deck. It was Venus, also known as General Chekal Danjo, an ethnic Korean who had fought in the Red Army against the Japanese in WWII. For the next several hours, Junior tracked Venus with the night-scope around the encampment like a bloodhound following a unicorn.

When Venus sat outside what appeared to be the mess tent, Junior instructed Seung to take sighting readings. Checking that they were suitably concealed to withstand a furious daylight search, Junior decided to take the shot. He closed his left eye, stabilized his breathing, and centered the crosshairs on Venus's head. Seung whispered the wind speed and direction. Junior pressed the fleshy part of his pointer against the steel of the trigger. He applied a steady squeeze through the trigger arc. The bullet traveled as aimed and struck Venus over the left eye, snapping his head back violently and twisting him around almost completely. The report of the shot echoed off the mountain on the far side of the valley.

Watching through their scopes, Junior and Seung burst into grins that rivaled the morning light. Pandemonium cascaded through the enemy camp as word of the assassination spread. The two friends had to stifle chuckles as they watched a dozen Chinese soldiers pointing in different directions indicating the source of the lethal bullet. Junior fixated on the officer in charge who was trying to organize pursuit. Tapping Seung, Junior nodded for a reading. Seung whispered. Junior sighted and squeezed the trigger. Another bullseye sent the officer sprawling against the mess tent, dead.

Junior surveyed the ensuing confusion and made a precipitous decision to bug out. Seung's eyebrows arched in surprise, but he never hesitated. After placing a time-delay grenade in their lair, Junior and Seung raced out of the tree. With any kind of luck, they would have almost an hour lead before the Chinese troops would have an idea where to search for the snipers.

*　*　*

Many gifted field leaders have a preternatural sense of anticipation and intuition. General Peng Denhuai was no exception. Despite the on-again, off-again commitment from Stalin to provide air support, Peng knew Mao well enough that his commander would ultimately decide that Korea presented a favorable field of action for a confrontation with the United States, regardless of Soviet assistance. The mountainous terrain in the distant Korean Peninsula served to neutralize, if not negate, the advantages of American economic, air, and naval superiority that would apply to a conflict in Taiwan, for example. Peng proceeded with his preparations as if the battle order had already been issued.

"Comrade Kim," said Peng to the North Korean leader, "It is time to reposition your headquarters. We are moving to Kanggye to set up our field operations command center for our counteroffensive."

Kim was dumbstruck. All of his communications and command structure had been relocated to Sinŭiju and had achieved a semblance of normalcy. Plus, his family was comfortably ensconced in the Central Luxury House. Most important, he was a short distance across the Yalu River to safe sanctuary in Communist China and the Yellow Sea. If an emergency evacuation became necessary in the coming weeks, his retinue could travel across the frozen river without having to board a boat.

The erstwhile Supreme Leader had no choice but to comply with the command to move to Kanggye. For the second time, he relocated his "capital," this time to a city which was 135 miles east of Sinŭiju into central North Korea and over thirty miles from China. Although the location was less desirable than Sinŭiju, it did have certain military advantages. Situated at the confluence of four rivers on flatlands nestled among mountains, Kanggye had developed into a strategic transportation hub and staging area. The city was a center for mining and forestry, industries which could prove useful to military operations. It was closer to the reservoirs at Manp'o and Chosin, which Mao considered prime assets to preserve.

A sullen Kim Il Sung arrived in Kanggye only to receive a report which sent him spiraling into darkness. No sooner had the rolling headquarters parked at the siding, then Kim's chief-of-staff ambled up the stairs to the platform at the rear of the railway car. He dreaded his role as the bearer of bad news. He never knew how his boss would react. On many occasions, Kang had witnessed messengers beaten with the riding crop that Kim carried, copycatting General George Patton. On other occasions, Kim would transfer the courier to some remote or dangerous outpost as punishment. General Kang hesitated, composing his thoughts.

"Kang, I heard you slink up the stairs, you might as well enter," came the angry voice of Kim Il Sung.

Kang took a deep breath and forced his shoulders back as he entered the car. Kim's uniform was disheveled and there were seams on his face from having slept with his face against the raised piping on his uniform sleeve. Bleary eyed, Kim glared at his assistant.

"My dear Supreme Leader, I'm sorry to add to your burdens, but I have tragic news," said General Kang Kŏn in a voice that was a combination of timidity and sadness. Exhaling an exaggerated sigh, as if to say, what else could go wrong, Kim nodded.

"We have just received a report that General Chekal Danjo and another officer have been victims of a cowardly sniper attack at the staging area outside of Unsan," said Kang, displaying a limp piece of paper in a defensive gesture.

"No, it can't be," shrieked Kim, slapping at the paper held by Kang. "No, no, no, I just spoke with him yesterday. Say it is not so. Say it . . . please."

Kim covered his face with his hands and moaned. "Not Danjo, not my oldest and best comrade. Not Danjo," he repeated, sinking into his chair, formless, as if his skeleton had turned into rubbery *guksu* noodles.

"They believe that it was the Ghost Photographer because they found no trace of the shooter," said General Kang in almost a whisper.

A look of anguished rage contorted Kim's face. He sprang toward Kang and gripped the lapels of his uniform.

"We must catch that bastard. He killed my *budal chingoo*, best friend! Order the next in command to spare no effort to find that damn Ghost Photographer. Unleash the hounds, fire up the helicopters! Do whatever is necessary, but bring that bastard to me!" he screamed in a voice that was so filled with vengeance that Kang feared for his own life. Before Kang could retreat, Kim demanded that Chekal's remains be brought to Kanggye for proper funeral services.

General Chekal's body was delivered to the ceremonial tent of the *mudang*, or shaman where it was laid on a board and shielded by a special curtain. His uniform was removed and pointed north, while his name was repeated three times. Next, the *mudang* performed the *seup*, or ritual cleaning, The body was washed with perfumed water. Trimmings from nails and hair were placed in small pouches called, *choballang*, for placement in the casket and one for subsequent delivery to the family as a sacred memento. The *mudang* oriented the body toward the south and plugged his ears and nose with cotton. Korean tradition called for putting coins over the eyes; however, in this instance, one eye socket had been completely obliterated. Creating a lattice out of wooden chopsticks, the *mudang* improvised a structure to hold the coin over the missing eye. To sustain the deceased on his journey, the shaman scooped three spoonfuls of rice into Chekal's mouth.

Before the body was laid in the coffin, ashes were sprinkled in the bottom of the coffin. The body, attired in silk burial garb of subdued grey, was wrapped with quilted hemp cloth and placed in the coffin along with a few pieces of everyday clothes of the deceased. The coffin was closed and covered with a silk banner decorated with dragons.

In a separate chamber of the "mourning room," the shaman set up a picture of Danjo from his graduation from the military academy. Led by Kim, mourners filed by to pay their respects. The room was suffused with the fragrance of incense and chrysanthemums. Wearing a dark suit and a white armband, Kim approached the picture, knelt and bowed toward the shrine two-and-a-half times. After a short moment of silence, he rose. He took a bottle of *soju* and poured some into a glass. After kissing the glass, Kim took a sip and, then, poured the spirits into a hole in the coffin.

Red-eyed, Kim exited with his jaw set in angry resolve that he would wreak vengeance on the sniper who slew his *budal chingoo*.

CHAPTER

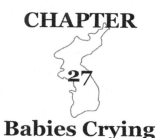

27

Babies Crying

"Take no part in the worthless deeds of evil and darkness; instead, expose them."

~ Ephesians: 5:11

The Sunday, October 15th meeting on Wake Island was the first face-to-face meeting between the leaders since the successful invasion at Incheon and the re-taking of Seoul. As a pretense for the meeting, President Truman bestowed a Distinguished Service Medal on MacArthur. The President lauded MacArthur for his "indomitable will and unshakable faith" and his "shining example of gallantry and tenacity in defense and of audacity in attack."

Once the ceremony was over, Truman and MacArthur retreated to a private conference room where they evaluated whether UN forces should advance into North Korea now that the army of the DPRK had been broken. Truman was concerned that any incursion by UN forces above the 38th parallel would prompt a military response by the Red Chinese.

"Mr. President, October is the most important month of the war," said Douglas MacArthur. "We have them on the run and will be able to end the threat to South Korea once and for all if we crush them in their own territory."

"The Indian Ambassador to China, K.M. Panikkar, has told our ambassador in New Delhi that Mao considers the presence of Imperialist troops in North Korea as an unforgivable provocation. He will never allow American troops to reach the Yalu River. Furthermore, our intelligence agencies report that

Red China has built up its forces in Manchuria and the Red Army is fully capable of engaging UN forces in North Korea," said the President.

"Seriously, Mr. President, are you going to rely on the word of the Indian Ambassador to Beijing? India has refused to send troops to the UN effort. They are obviously sympathetic to the Reds."

"It's not only the Indians who are saying that Red China will intervene. I met with the First Secretary to the British Embassy in Washington. A chap named Harold Philby, he is the liaison to the CIA. Philby's sources confirm that Chairman Mao views armed conflict with the U.S. as inevitable and he would rather it not occur on Chinese soil," said the President.

"The introduction of forces onto the Peninsula by Mao would be sheer madness. If the Chinese tried to get down to P'yŏngyang, there would be the greatest slaughter," said MacArthur. "Mr. President, Uncle Joe Stalin controls the board here. There will be no intervention without Russian support and they don't have the stomach to confront us."

"Just a week after our success at Incheon, the Chinese Foreign Ministry issued a statement clearly reaffirming that it will always stand on the side of the Korean people '. . . and resolutely oppose the criminal acts of American imperialist aggression against Korea and their intrigues for expanding the war.'"

MacArthur shook his head and chuckled. "You know that Mao is a notorious liar and that his regime is wobbly at best. Trust me, Mr. President when we advance north of the 38th parallel, the Red Chinese will not intervene and the war will soon be over."

Seduced by the prospect of an early end to the war, the President acquiesced to MacArthur's judgment. Unfortunately, MacArthur was wrong on both counts.

* * *

272

Meanwhile in the mountains between P'yŏngyang and Unsan, Junior and Seung were running for their lives. They wasted no time putting as much space as possible between themselves and the pursuing enemy soldiers. They had discovered the construction of a secret, hidden military installation in a valley west of Unsan. In addition to capturing the large-scale facility on film, Junior had successfully terminated a high-value target known as Venus in the assassination program Operation Solar Eclipse. Now, they were being hunted by a new, determined enemy, Chinese soldiers of the People's Volunteer Army.

Although the friends had much experience evading enemy troops, this escape from the enemy was about to become more complicated by the use of a different technique. In the distance, they heard the howling of dogs. Clearly, their situation had just gone from bad to worse. Seung did a quick calculation of the progress of the dogs and figured that their lead had just been cut in half. He knew that they probably did not have enough time to make it to a village where they had planned to commandeer a getaway boat. Realizing the change in circumstance, Junior searched for a place to make a stand if necessary. Staring at the dark prospect of a firefight with dozens of professional soldiers, Junior's spirits sank. Then, good fortune intervened.

From a covert vantage point, they could see the pack held by their handlers on long leather leashes as they located the tree which held the sniper-hide. The dogs yelped and whined, straining to continue the hunt. As the handlers surveyed the situation, the tree erupted into a fire ball that consumed the men and their canine hunters. When Kim learned that the Ghost Photographer had eluded him again, he cursed.

With buoyant spirits, Junior and Seung trekked back to the Ranger camp. A courier from MacArthur greeted them. He took Junior's film and handed him orders to proceed north and rendezvous with the 8th Cavalry Division at Unsan. Seung had similar orders to connect with the ROK's 1st Infantry, also at Unsan. As soon as Seung's unit was ready, the two buddies traveled together. It was the last week of October and morale among UN forces was high. The fighting capability of the North Korean Army had been seriously degraded and the objective of destroying Kim's military was clearly within reach.

American forces under General Frank Milburn were preparing a Thanksgiving Offensive in hopes of ending North Korean resistance. A key element of this strategy was to secure the town of Unsan. It was a municipality of strategic importance due to its location as a passageway to the Yalu River. The Samtan River formed the eastern flank of the town. Forested foothills surrounded the town to the north and northeast. The most significant feature to the west was the Nammyon River. Roads to the nearby towns of Myongdang to the southwest and Yonghung-dong to the west were separated by a ridge dubbed "Bugle Hill," and from Unsan to hilly foothills. Much like the hamlet of Gettysburg in the American Civil War, the relatively undistinguished area of Unsan was about to become the pivot point of the war. As the site of the Chinese First Phase Campaign, the Battle of Unsan signaled a tectonic shift of the nature and stakes of the conflict.

"Chief, we have orders for you to go to Bugle Ridge to the southeast and scout that area. Our checkpoints report an unusual amount of refuge traffic and there are rumors of concentrated enemy in that sector. See what you can find out," said Major Dexter, the senior intelligence officer on General Milburn's staff. When he wasn't serving in the military, Warren Dexter was a pharmacist from Boulder, Colorado. His wire-rim glasses and genial manner disguised the fact that during WWII, he had been a covert operative spying on the Third Reich for Wild Bill Donovan. When the Korean conflict erupted, Donovan prevailed on Dexter to re-enlist. Dexter was smart, tough, and perceptive. His first impression of Junior and Seung was favorable; he knew competence and courage when he saw it.

"As for you, Captain Lee, your orders are to find out what's going on to the northeast. Our aerial reconnaissance has encountered dense smoke and we need to know whether it's from forest fires, or whether there is something else going on up there," said the major.

"Yessir," came the simultaneous reply, accompanied by crisp salutes.

As they left, Junior quipped, "Hey Seung, dinner's on me tomorrow."

"You got it," said the affable Korean.

Junior mounted his Jeep and headed toward Bugle Ridge. After a short drive, he reached a checkpoint where a young MP gave him directions.

"It's up through these here woods a few miles. You'll find Bravo Company up there. They are monitoring refuge traffic heading toward Unsan. In the last few days there has been a dramatic increase in civilians crossing over the ridge to get to safety. Ask for Lieutenant Moldovsky when you get up there, Chief. You can park your buggy over here," said the military policeman, saluting and pointing to a makeshift area containing several vehicles.

"Thanks, corporal," replied Junior, returning the salute.

Hefting his gear onto his back, Junior marched toward the ridge. He made good progress through undergrowth and spindly evergreen trees that thinned the higher he went. Early morning clouds increased and a light intermittent rain fell. Junior lengthened his stride, enjoying the physical exertion after so many days sitting in the Jeep and confined in the sniper blind. Breathing the pine-infused air deeply, he lapsed into a memory of his days with Sachie at Mount Fuji. He resolved to find her before he was sent home when this blasted war ended by Christmas . . . at least that was the scuttlebutt.

His attention was drawn to the sound of babies crying, or so he thought. Emerging into a clearing, he saw a company of American soldiers assisting refugees who were climbing down a rocky ridge. At the top of the ridge he saw silhouettes of dozens of people. The clouds parted and a burst of sunlight illuminated a most amazing sight. Several hundred yards away, he saw women descending awkwardly through a notch in the ridge. As they advanced, a scene of primal sensuality emerged. The young women were wearing thin, cotton dresses that clung to their bodies due to the recent rainstorm. One of the noncoms remarked about how revealing and sexy the young women looked. The women carried infants in their left arms and their right arms were concealed behind the babies. The suggestive clothing and the hungry cries of the infants were distracting. Why did every woman hold the baby the same way, he wondered?

Like a flash of lightning, Junior remembered the warning from Major General Donovan about the use of baby-carrying women to engender sympathy before opening fire on unsuspecting Americans.

"Take cover! Take cover!" yelled Junior.

He whipped out his Murphy gun and rained fire on the women. Junior squinted in part to shield his mind from the carnage he was inflicting. When all the women lay dead on the hill, Junior felt the barrel of a .45 caliber service pistol against his temple.

"Who the hell are you? What the fuck just happened?" yelled Lt. Moldovsky.

Junior slowly lowered his machine gun and raised his hands.

"Sir, Chief Warrant Officer Nilberry, assigned to General MacArthur, SCAP HQ, sir. Please lower your pistol and I'll explain, sir."

"Sergeant, handcuff this man," said Moldovsky to a burly noncom at his side. He complied, using extra force, no doubt on account of his disappointment at being deprived the possibility of some extra-curricular fraternization with the barely-clothed women.

The lieutenant ordered a squad of soldiers to inspect the scene at the notch. After an interminable interval, one of the soldiers clambered down the rocks toward the officer.

"Sir, you ain't gonna believe it. Every single one of those bitches had an AK-47 behind the babies. They were going to fill us full of lead. If the Chief wasn't here, we would all be tits up-dead, never to see Jolene again," said the man.

Moldovsky inhaled deeply, considering the shitstorm he was about to experience. He gestured to the sergeant to release Junior.

"Accept my apologies, Chief. There's no way we could have known . . ." mumbled the lieutenant.

"No problem, lieutenant," said Junior as a chill wave surged over him as the adrenaline in his blood stream subsided. "You have any medicinal alcohol, sir? I sure could use a jolt."

A smile of relief swept over Moldovsky.

"I've been saving a bottle of Jack for an occasion like this," said Moldovsky, steering Junior toward his tent.

*   *   *

The first thing Seung did before embarking on his mission to the northeast to investigate the fires was to speak with several refugees from the mountains. Using the local dialect and wearing the traditional black peasant attire, he made them comfortable. When he looked in their eyes, he saw fear and confusion. Many were barely coherent; however, Seung detected a common theme. The character of the enemy forces had changed in ways that led to one conclusion – the actions of the enemy army were decidedly Chinese. None of the people interviewed had first-hand knowledge of the source of the forest fires in their region, but each was adamant that the fires were not natural. Typically, fires of this intensity occurred at the end of a long, hot summer, not this late in the year. More telling, however, were the consistent reports of the persistent stench of burning petroleum and its attendant black smoke. The peasants also recounted hearing strange noises after dark; yet, there was no visual confirmation of enemy presence.

Armed with this knowledge, Seung geared up and was pleased to see that Junior had returned and would be joining him on his march north that evening. Leaving behind the flatlands around Unsan, the topography rose as Junior and Seung entered the mountains. After a night of hiking, they found a hideout in a cave in a ridge overlooking a long, narrow valley characteristic of the region. Cutting through the valley was a shallow, meandering river flanked by a crude dirt road that was little more than a path choked with scrub vegetation.

Before sundown, Seung crept down to the valley floor and, using camouflage techniques learned from Junior, secreted himself in the roadside undergrowth. He chose this location to acquire as much firsthand intelligence as possible. Junior stationed himself on the ridge overlooking the valley. As he later reported, the tragic events of that night began with the raucous squawking of the aviary population in the area. Flocks of woodpeckers, owls, and falcons came flying from the northern reaches of the valley in panic mode as if escaping a natural disaster.

Woodland mammals came after the birds, racing along the banks of the waterway. What followed next was unexpected and horrifying. Rows of skirmishers entered the valley walking quite a distance on the forest-side of the road ahead of a T-34 tank. Perched on the lead tank alongside the turret were soldiers wielding flamethrowers. They sprayed burning petroleum about sixty-five feet ahead of the tank and watched as everything in its path was incinerated. Once the initial wall of flame subsided, the tank advanced and another wall of fire followed. The night time forest was punctuated by retina-blotting bursts of bright yellow, orange, and red flames. It wasn't long before a layer of smoke filled the valley, obscuring aerial discovery of the distinctive road-clearing activity.

Junior could hear the rumble of diesel engines from additional armored behemoths as they waited in the forest. Junior realized that Seung was trapped. His only possible escape was to flee toward the river. Junior descended partway down the valley side in order to cover Seung when he broke toward the water. Hidden in the trees on the slope, Junior tried to locate Seung, but he was too well camouflaged. Suddenly, he saw a figure rise and race toward the river. At that instant, a stream of burning liquid engulfed the running figure.

Helpless, Junior watched in horror as the camo blanket worn by his colleague caught fire. Ablaze, Seung twisted and flailed. Junior heard screams of anguish as Seung tried to reach the water. He crumbled to the ground, a writhing mass of fire.

Junior watched in stunned disbelief. He retreated only when the heat and smoke was impossible to bear. The stench rising from the valley triggered his nightmare experience as a child triggered by the image of his uncle's immolation in Germany. He retched. Tears streaked down his soot-stained cheeks as he ran.

Several days later when Junior finally made it back to the base in P'yŏngyang, he got incoherently drunk.

"Damn, damn, damn!" he exclaimed. On this moonless night, only the distant lights of the waterfront on the Taedong River illuminated the night. His tears were inconsequential to the icy water that flowed past him.

"Mr. Jack, why am I still here? Why didn't I perish like Gomax, Arlo, and Seung and . . . ?"

Too many to recall. Images that were burned in his memory intruded, overwhelming control, refusing to remain suppressed. They surged like floodwaters driven by hurricane winds, crashing against his fragile psyche. He inhaled deeply, trying to calm the shallow breaths that wracked him. Tilting back the familiar black and white label on the bottle of

Tennessee whisky, he gulped the amber liquor with mindless abandon.

"Stop!" his brain screamed.

But the images would not stop. Since he had arrived in Korea, they were unrelenting. Features flashed before him – a forehead misshapen by blunt force, the jagged edge of a dismembered ear, a shattered jawbone that would no longer pivot, a smashed nose - shards of men, the price of battle. Never without blood; sometimes scarlet spurts, other times black-brown seepage clotted with dirt. There was blood everywhere. The eyes were the worst because they most embodied his fallen brothers-in-arms. Eyes stared; some fierce with rage, some vacant, lifeless. Arlo's eyes haunted him the most.

Junior had prepared for battle with fear and fatalism that came from experience. As Gunnery Sergeant Gomax, the tough WWII combat veteran, had taught during training, "When your number is up, there is nothing y'all can do about it. No precautions, no actions, nothing on God's green earth can spare y'all. Till then, all y'all can do is fight like those bastards are trying to rape your momma. Remember, your buddies are counting on y'all and y'all gotta count on them. Do your job and pray it ain't your time."

This credo had served him well in combat so far. Yet, the utter lack of predictability during combat had, on more than one occasion, caused him to shake so violently that he wanted to roll into a ball and hide. Fortunately, these episodes never prevented him from performing his job. Sadly, the numbers of too many of his buddies had come up in the damn frozen mountains of Korea.

Junior sobbed, remembering Arlo's smiling face when they first met. Junior was the tough kid from the projects who was at Parris Island with the admonition from the sentencing judge that 'I do not want to see your face again, or else,' still ringing in his ears. Arlo was the wide-eyed kid from Appalachia who marveled at the plumbing in the barracks.

When a weird fate re-united them in the rugged terrain outside of Incheon, their brief, pleasant encounter had been interrupted by a fierce firefight. Only the Lord knew how he and Arlo had survived the barrage that killed several of the cooks. Then, before they could reach safety, Arlo had been shot in the side and the leg. Junior had held his buddy closely, hugging his neck while exhorting him to stay with him until reinforcements arrived.

"Hang in there, Arlo. The cavalry is here to save our asses."

Arlo gave him a feeble thumbs-up. Shots peppered the boulder they hid behind. When he turned back to the private, ready to assure him, his heart sank. The private had lost too much blood. Junior watched as the youth's vitality waned as if vanishing into a dark vortex. He saw as the private's eyes passed from pain to fear to resignation. Finally, as if switched off, the private's eyes rolled back in his head. The soldier spun his head around, searching for . . . something . . . anything . . . to reprieve this horrible sentence. There was none. Arlo was gone.

"No, no, no," he shouted, his voice breaking.

Junior gulped down more of the liquor that burned his throat and joined the roiling cauldron in his gut. As he stared over the surface of the river, another face floated before him — it was Seung's. Junior recollected how during their first mission in Chongjin, Seung had exhorted him not to kill the policemen. Seung's wisdom and sense of humor at Junior's odiferous predicament while they sailed Flying Fish Channel before the Incheon invasion brought a wry smile. As Seung's face floated before Junior, it was consumed by a burst of flame, his features incinerated. Junior wept.

He opened the briefcase which held his medals. He heard the high-pitched voice of President Truman reading the citation, saying that Junior had "acted with uncommon valor . . . had distinguished himself conspicuously by gallantry and intrepidity at the risk of his life above and beyond the call of duty." With a sense of shame, Junior recalled his numb acceptance of the combat medals from the Commander-in-Chief on behalf of "a grateful Nation."

The wind whipped the surface of the river into a slushy foam. He gulped another swig of whiskey. Tears mixed with the sharp sleet that stung his cheeks. The soldier withdrew one of the medals from the case and swayed as he peered at it. The embossed figure of Minerva, the Roman goddess of war and wisdom stared back. Some called the engraving elegant; others heroic. What an oxymoron – war and wisdom. Minerva was a beguiler, tempting male hubris into committing atrocities.

"You bitch! You fraud! All you do is suck the marrow out of young men."

Fingering the pointed edge of the star, the soldier tried to raise his arm, but a jolt of pain stymied him. His shoulder ached from the round, purple wounds there. After another swig of Mr. Jack, he switched the bottle to his right hand and put the medal into his left. Edging closer to the water, his boots sunk into the mud beneath the eddying water. As he lifted his good arm, he staggered. His damaged leg buckled and he tumbled to his knees in the frigid water. With an instinctive drunken lurch, he stood. More blood flowed. Images of eyes bore down on him.

Light from a distant bridge reflected off the engraved surface of the medal. He gripped the pointed edge so tightly that the skin ruptured. Cold, muddy and wounded, he cursed. With a forceful whip of his arm he flung the medal, muttering, "Drown, you evil bitch. I don't deserve you!"

The metal object whizzed toward the water. It landed with a soft plunk, floated silently with the current until the blue silk ribbon became saturated. Just as mysteriously as the soldier had skirted death on the battlefield, the medal sunk below the surface into oblivion. Junior staggered to his feet and heaved the entire briefcase into the river to be swallowed forever.

* * *

Over the next ten days, Chinese troops under the command of General Peng encircled and slaughtered ROK and American forces in what came to be known as the Battle of Unsan, a resounding victory for the People's Volunteer Army in the First Phase Campaign. It was a devastating blow to the UN forces. It halted and reversed the momentum MacArthur had so brilliantly created in the aftermath of the Incheon invasion. And, it demonstrated to the Chinese military command that they could neutralize American advantages and deliver horrific losses. From a tactical standpoint, the success at Unsan validated the Chinese excellence in the stealth deployment of their troops and equipment. As General Peng stated in his report to Chairman Mao, once his troops were in position, they engaged in three fierce actions – "fierce fire, fierce assault, fierce pursuit."

Kim Il Sung adjusted the pins on his map and for the first time in weeks felt a glimmer of optimism stemming from the success of General Peng. Adjutant Kim fantasized over how he would pulverize the foreign devils into dust which he would mix into concrete to bury their putrid remains. He choked on Peng's next move – withdrawal and the release of prisoners.

Why would the Chinese general refuse to press his advantage and show weakness by returning captured soldiers? Peng would only respond by mentioning the need to rely on Kim. The erstwhile Supreme Leader swallowed his *soju* in a state of confusion.

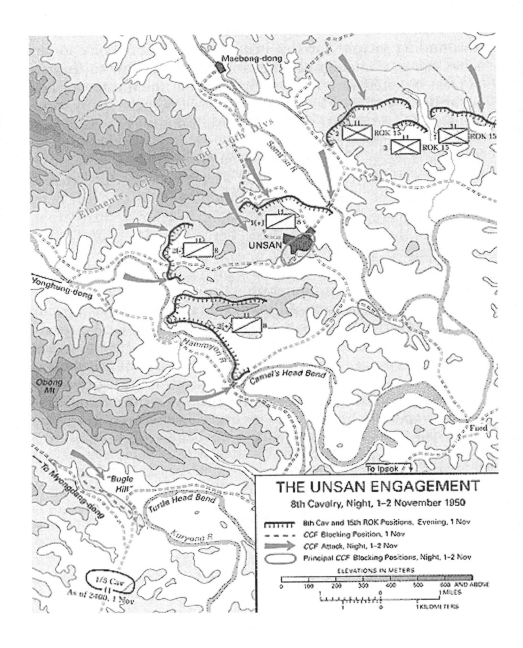

Maebong-dong

ROK 15

2

3 ROK 15

ROK 15

Samun R.

Elements, CCF 115th and 116th Divs

UNSAN

Yonghung-dong

Namnyen R.

Camel's Head Bend

Obong Mt

Ford

To Ipsok

To Myongdang-dong

"Bugle Hill"

Turtle Head Bend

Kuryong R.

1/8 Cav
As of 2400, 1 Nov

THE UNSAN ENGAGEMENT

8th Cavalry, Night, 1–2 November 1950

⊥⊥⊥⊥⊥⊥ 8th Cav and 15th ROK Positions, Evening, 1 Nov

– – – CCF Blocking Position, 1 Nov

➤ CCF Attack, Night, 1–2 Nov

◯ Principal CCF Blocking Positions, Night, 1–2 Nov

ELEVATIONS IN METERS

0   100   200   300   400   500   600 AND ABOVE

1 MILES

1 KILOMETERS

CHAPTER 28

Project Ramona

"I am shameless, impolite and sly. I play tricks, tell lies, use spies and never keep promises. I have an unsatiable desire for power and women, and I am always prepared to defeat my enemies ruthlessly. You can uphold your political correctness and your righteous hatred towards me in your mind, but you are always the loser. I am shameless, but so what?"
~ Mao Zedong

Much like the diminishing daylight as the season changed from autumn to winter, the optimism so prevalent in October in the days and weeks after the Incheon invasion, gave way to stark pessimism in November. MacArthur's exuberant pursuit of North Korean forces north toward the Yalu River produced an over-confidence that led to deadly hell-broth of miscalculations, mistakes, and bad luck. The disastrous defeat of UN forces at Unsan was just a prelude. The Battle of Unsan was pivotal because it demonstrated Chinese military acumen which in turn convinced Joseph Stalin to provide air support to the successful Maoists.

As shocking as the defeat at Unsan was, what happened next confused the American leadership. The Chinese army withdrew back into the mountains. Although the combined intelligence services of the UN nations could not confirm how many Chinese troops were in North Korea, their presence was undeniable. MacArthur received reports that along the front UN prisoners of war were being returned. The SCAP mistakenly deduced that the PVA lacked food and resources to prosecute an extended campaign and were signaling their weakness. Like a patient fly fisherman, General Peng tantalized his quarry with mixed signals.

Not only did MacArthur reach the wrong conclusion about the resolve of the Chinese and Soviet Communists to limit the Imperialist presence in northeast Asia, he failed to outfit his forces with cold weather gear. Maybe MacArthur thought that the conflict would be over before such equipment would be needed. If so, he failed to notify the frigid winds that swept into North Korea from Siberia a month ahead of forecasts.

The tragic result was troops plagued by frostbite and equipment failures; a deadly combination that caused deaths, suffering, and combat inefficiency. It was so cold, that the propellant properties of gunpowder used in artillery shells were compromised. Mechanized equipment routinely stopped working, batteries failed, and rifles jammed. Soldiers learned that their body warmth was invaluable to keeping batteries functioning and keeping frost from disabling the detonators of hand grenades.

The ingenuity of soldiers trying to keep warm knew no bounds. They filled empty artillery shells with gasoline and burned it for warmth. Others scavenged anything that would burn for fuel. The enemy saw this and booby-trapped bundles of rice straw used to protect rice paddies, causing numerous deaths and disfigurements. Finding a tent mate or companion at a sentry outpost frozen to death was not a rare occurrence. To the unbiased observer, MacArthur's miscalculations were inexcusable. Could it be that MacArthur's focus was elsewhere?

To Junior, inactivity was poison. So, it was with great relief that he opened orders for his next mission. MacArthur directed him to go to Chosin Reservoir and rendezvous with a captain who worked for military intelligence. He left immediately after Thanksgiving dinner, even though it meant he would arrive a day before schedule.

With a heavy heart due to the horrific death of his friend Seung, Junior was already numb as he drove into mountains deep in North Korea. His Jeep had little trouble negotiating the snow-covered mountain passes, but he grew tired at the reality that after every mountain was yet another mountain. The trip took longer than expected and the increasing cold which permeated the vehicle like an evil vapor made it difficult to feel his ears, fingers, and toes.

The Chosin Reservoir was in a remote and isolated area approximately fifty miles south of the Yalu River which formed the border between North Korea and Manchuria in northeastern China. The Chosin Reservoir was built by Nichitsu (the Japanese Nitrogenous Fertilizer Company) in the 1930s. A series of dams, underground aqueducts, caves, and tunnels were constructed ostensibly to channel water from the Changjin River to produce electricity downstream at three electrical power stations. The project created a ten-mile long lake nestled in the Jangbaik Mountains.

In later years, military historians would debate the wisdom of the advance by UN forces to the Chosin Reservoir. They already controlled the major population centers of North Korea. The reservoir itself was unimportant; just a large lake created by a dam. Travel from the reservoir to Kanggye, China or the Soviet Union was nearly impossible. The roads were hardly more than ox trails. The three power stations were located twenty-six miles south of the Funchilin Pass on the east face of the mountains. The reservoir was a dead end, in more ways than one.

"Hey, Chief, welcome to balmy Fort Frigid, the frostbite capital of South Hamgyong Province. We are in the middle of a heat wave; the thermometer broke zero this afternoon. But, watch your tootsies tonight – it's going double digits below. Whewee," said Sergeant Harris Newcombe, a black man from the Smoky Mountains of North Carolina. His normal espresso complexion was tinged blue from the cold.

"I'm used to cold, but this here is wicked," said Junior. "Do me a favor, help me set up those smudge pots in my tent so that my chemicals thaw."

When everything was set up, the sergeant pointed toward a tent standing apart at the edge of the camp.

"There's the mess, Chief."

By the time Junior returned, his tent was a toasty 39°. He set up his mobile darkroom with the expectation that he would be able to develop photographs by the following evening. Tomorrow would be a busy day of shooting around the camp – he hoped his shooting would be limited to photographs. Junior busied himself with his camera, jerry-rigging copper tubing around it that he would fill with heated, low-viscosity lubricant. He hoped that this, coupled with the harness strapped to his body would protect Maisey, his Leica camera.

"Excuse me, Chief, would you mind some company?" asked a short, rotund figure. When he unwrapped his scarf, Junior saw that his visitor was a man of the cloth. His wire-rimmed glasses condensed when he entered the warmth of the tent.

"Sure thing, padre. Make yourself at home. I'm just finishing up," said Junior.

"Thank you, my son. Ahhh, this warmth is glorious," he sighed. "My name is Gabriel Cardinal Loyola. I'm here ministering to the troops. I never expected such severe conditions. I thought it was cold back in my hometown north of Boston, but this reminds me of the Book of Job where it is written, 'The waters become hard like stone, and the face of the deep is frozen.'"

This earned the Cardinal a perplexed glance. Junior recalled advice from Gunny Gomax who drilled into them that a true soldier must learn to disregard extreme conditions. To dwell on discomfort made it worse. He reached into his duffel and pulled out a flask.

"This may not be sacramental wine, padre, but I think some good ol' Kentucky bourbon might take away the chill," said Junior, passing the vessel to the Cardinal whose eyes had brightened.

A strong pull on the liquor and a satisfied sigh later, the Cardinal said, "Thank you. You know, the Curia is considering liberalizing the liturgy to make it more accessible to the average person. I may have to recommend to the Pope that we substitute bourbon for wine when we celebrate mass."

This levity was interrupted by Sergeant Newcombe.

"Begging your pardon, Cardinal, we need your attention. Me and the boys from the Grim Reaper Squad have a new victim. The night guard shift found Lance Corporal Moishe Cardoza frozen to death at his post. Can you say some prayers over him?"

Saddened, the Cardinal reached for his satchel and removed a yarmulke, prayer shawl, and Torah. He bundled up and said, "Duty calls. I won't be long."

A short time later, the Cardinal returned, flapping his arms against his torso for warmth. Without a request, Junior proffered the flask to the appreciative cleric.

"Sir, how do you know what to do? How do you know what to say for a Jewish soldier?" asked Junior.

"When I realized that I was called to become a chaplain, I spent time studying with rabbis. I learned The Jewish Prayer for the Dead. It's a prayer called *El Malei Rachamim*, 'God, full of Mercy.'"

"I'm sure that your words are a great comfort to Cardoza and his buddies. We all need to believe that we will be honored in our sacrifice if it happens. Forgotten sacrifice is the shame of a nation," said Junior.

On the following day, Junior took too many pictures of soldiers suffering from frostbite and other deprivations. He became distraught at the pervasive tragedy. Junior managed to maintain his sanity by sharing his distress with Loyola. His conversations with the Cardinal served to give him a different, more mature perspective on his experiences and losses. The portly priest counselled Junior on acceptance of the deaths of many good men, especially, Seung and Arlo. The Cardinal helped to reconcile the brutality and irrationality of war with the nobility of the war's purpose. Junior had never heard the phrase "just war" before. Listening to the Cardinal explain it was comforting.

Once a bond of trust had been established, Junior unburdened his deepest sorrow.

"Your Eminence, I am torn over my feelings for a young Japanese woman and the rules of the military against me marrying her. I cannot stop thinking of her. I want to spend my life with her, but it is wrong. What should I do?"

"It is not uncommon when in a war zone for soldiers to think they love someone who gives them shelter from the storm. Do you love her, my son?" asked the cleric who interrupted Junior. "Don't answer out loud. Search your heart, examine your motives and pray for guidance from the Lord."

*   *   *

"Hey, what the fuck. You're lettin' the cold in," shouted Junior who bolted upright in his cot, reaching for the pistol under his folded poncho that served as his makeshift pillow. In the pre-dawn darkness, all Junior could see was a large arm holding the tent flap open.

"At ease!" barked a man who shined a light into Junior's eyes. With a hand reflexively shielding his eyes, Junior stood. In an effort to stay warm, he had gone to sleep fully-clothed.

"Captain Hijame, here. This is Tech Sergeant Emmet Kitay," said the officer in a clipped accent that Junior was unable to identify. The tent shrank as the two men set themselves down on whatever would support them. Junior sat on the edge of his cot.

"What is so important that you have to wake me up before the dawn's early light, sir?" said Junior, looking from one to the other. Despite the dim light, Hijame's eyes were hidden behind aviator sunglasses. As Junior would learn later, the captain suffered from weakness of the eyes due to excessive handling of radioactive material. He was a slightly built man, taller than Junior. Hijame wore a narrow-trimmed moustache that curled ominously down the sides of his mouth. It gave him a sinister Oriental look. His head swiveled to confirm that they were alone.

"Ramona," said Hijame in a low whisper.

Blank-faced, Junior tried to fathom what was happening.

"Jesus Mary and Joseph, he has no clue," rasped the sergeant. He was a bulky man, with the gravelly voice of a chain smoker.

"OK, OK, keep your shirt on," said Hijame without irony. He inhaled.

"I would have thought the General MacArthur would have already read you in on this. No matter. Here's the Reader's Digest version. Ramona is the code name for our investigation of Japan's atomic bomb program during WWII. We know that they had research and bomb-making facilities in Manchuria and Korea. We are here because recently uncovered information links this Reservoir to uranium enrichment activity. With all this water and hydro-electric power, it provides two of the key requirements. The Japanese built numerous tunnels and underground facilities during the war to conceal their program. This effort was executed by the Imperial Navy weapons program and Unit 731," said Hijame, nodding to the sergeant.

Now, MacArthur's vague orders for him to go to this godforsaken place began to make sense. Junior had begun to feel like MacArthur gave him this assignment just to keep him from dwelling on his lost friends.

"I thought that Unit 731 did biological weapons research," said Junior.

"They did plenty of that, but also supported the Navy's atom bomb program using 731's technical testing capability. They had the scientists the Navy needed. I'm an atomic warfare specialist. My job is to identify any equipment, centrifuges and the like used for an A-bomb program," said the sergeant.

"Your job is to photograph whatever we find," added the captain.

"The Japs left in 1945 when the war ended. If there were facilities in China and Korea wouldn't they have discovered them over the last five years?" asked Junior.

"In the first place, the Chinks were too unsophisticated to know what they found and our intel is that they were so cold and desperate that they burned research papers to boil water for their rice. In Korea, the operations were so well hidden that they probably never found them," said Hijame.

"When do we start?" asked Junior.

"Now, let's move out. The sun will be up soon," said Hijame.

"A lot of good that will do," scoffed Kitay.

Along with several trucks, the captain had commandeered a dozen ROK soldiers to do the heavy lifting and provide firepower if needed. The American contingent was blissfully unaware of the massive presence of Chinese fighters hidden in the surrounding mountains. Wisps of snow fluttered in front of the shafts of pale-yellow light coming from the vehicle's headlights. Kitay ground the gears as he navigated the hairpin turns through the mountains. After driving quite a distance, they turned off the primitive road onto what could only be described as an animal trail. The sounds of the engines laboring through the underbrush were joined by the snapping and cracking of frozen branches as they plowed through the forest. They stopped at a rock wall. From the direction of the daylight that was fighting its way into the sky, Junior surmised that they were on the west side of the reservoir.

Captain Hijame ordered the men to dismount and follow him into the woods. They walked single file for several miles. Junior was torn by hunger and boredom. Knowing that times like these were when ambushes occurred, he fought the urge to relax. He flexed his gloved hands to keep the circulation going in case he needed his trigger finger. Just when it appeared that Hijame was lost, they approached a cave-like opening in the rock wall which was obscured by scrub pines. The captain ordered some of the soldiers to clear a path. They entered a large cave. Flashlights were distributed and the party plunged into the darkness.

The inside of the cave was colder than the forest. With a tinge of wistfulness, Junior wished that Hijame had brought torches instead of flashlights. At least, the fire would have brought some warmth. He hoped that their destination was near. Eventually, they reached two large metal doors.

Using a bolt-cutter, Kitay sliced the rusted chain securing them. Junior noticed a dirty sign on the wall adjacent to the entrance. Although it was almost totally obscured by years of dirt, it appeared to be some sort of hazard sign. Whether it was the yellow-black, internationally recognized sign for radioactivity, he could not tell. He heard a couple of the

Koreans chatter in their native language, now wide-eyed, a change from their prior torpor.

Hijame ordered several of the Korean troops to guard the entrance. Despite the language barrier, Junior thought that Hijame's tone was exceptionally harsh to the point of demeaning. Captain Hijame led the rest of the party into a long tunnel. They walked briskly for quite some time before the captain halted to get his bearings. By the way Hijame navigated through the tunnels and past certain corridors while taking others, Junior sensed that he had been there before.

The men labored in the bone-numbing cold. Their breaths produced silvery white clouds in the artificial light as they trudged ever-downward. The absence of wind, sky or anything to orient the senses, gave rise to a feeling of sensory deprivation. Junior focused on the spotlight leading the way deeper into the mountain. At one point, he thought he could hear the flow of water above them, but the sound was so muted that he thought he must be imagining it. Junior thought to himself that the captain must be part mole on account of the alacrity of his movement in near-darkness.

*   *   *

Clad only in his underwear Kim sat on the edge of his bed thinking about his hatred for the Japanese who had brutalized his country for most of his life. The dictator withdrew the coded piece of paper from his steel lockbox. He sipped *soju* and stared at the enigma with such intensity that he mused it might ignite. His concentration was so total that he did not notice someone looking over his shoulder at the paper. His concubine, a lovely Japanese comfort woman whom Kim had appropriated, looked at the paper. Her lips moved soundlessly as her eyes traversed the symbols.

"That's quite intriguing," she murmured.

"What?" said Kim who flinched at her voice. "You startled me."

She giggled coquettishly as he folded the paper with a furtive gesture.

"No, don't hide it. I was enjoying the puzzle."

"You never saw this," he stammered. "Wait, you recognize these symbols?"

"Yes, every Japanese child is familiar with poetic puzzles."

"Tell me more," said Kim, unfolding the paper and handing it to her.

"This is a many-layered poem that describes a beautiful structure, almost like a maze within a castle. At the end of the trail is a great treasure," said Nari.

"What do you see here?" asked Kim. He listened intently as Nari translated the first series of characters in a sing-song voice. As she interpreted each riddle, Kim became more excited. He had spent years trying to solve this enigma by using mathematical analysis and scientific formulas to no avail.

"Why is this fantasy important?" said Nari.

"This is not a fantasy. Let's just say that this is a treasure map," said Kim.

"Where is the treasure?" asked Nari.

"That's the real question. Even if the maze is solved, where is the starting point? Without that, the solution is useless," said Kim in a tone of exasperation.

"May I see that again?" asked Nari.

With his shoulders slumped, Kim exhaled and handed her the paper. His eyes wore the look of a man who had exhausted every possibility and doubted that a Japanese comfort woman could solve the enigma.

Nari was lost in thought. She scribbled on a pad, then crossed out her scribbles. Kim got bored watching her fiddling and put on his uniform. As he reached the door, Nari shrieked.

"I got it!"

*   *   *

After Junior's group and their escorts had walked several miles underground, the captain stopped. The suddenness of the action caused Junior to skid, dislodging some loose pebbles. Several seconds later he heard them clatter to the ground. Junior felt a rush of air coming toward them. A scratching noise by the captain was followed by the whoosh of an object being thrown.

Suddenly, the tunnel burst into a bright, sparky light that floated downward. When the flare hit the bottom, it illuminated a vast chamber filled with machinery.

"Will you look at that?" said Sergeant Kitay. "I did not know that the Japs had the same high-speed centrifuges as the Krauts. This is unbelievable. These babies are the way to highly enriched uranium."

"We gotta keep moving," said Hijame, pushing ahead to a steep stairway cut into the wall. When he reached the floor of the chamber, Junior stared up and marveled at the similarity of the great chamber to pictures of the great cathedrals of Europe that he had seen in books.

The captain directed Kitay's attention to a row of file cabinets.

"In there."

"Bingo!" exclaimed Kitay. "The blueprints!"

"Pack 'em," said Hijame.

While Kitay stuffed the documents into his backpack, Junior photographed the equipment. The captain strolled around pointing the wand of a Geiger counter at various materials. When he heard a few clicks, he said, "This way."

The path down was cruder and steeper than before and they had to concentrate to avoid stumbling into each other. The terrain leveled and Hijame approached a slab of stone. After some rummaging through some gravel on the ground, he located a lever and yanked. The slab slid to the side revealing a well-chiseled tunnel that led to what appeared to be a laboratory. Junior snapped more pictures and reloaded his camera after securing the exposed film in a sealed, battery-heated, container.

They heard the sounds of gunfire and small explosions in the distance. The gunfire ceased.

Somewhere back in the labyrinth of tunnels, Kim Il Sung led a contingent of armed soldiers through the darkness. They stopped as Kim and a figure bundled in an over-sized parka studied a paper illuminated by a flashlight. Nari bit her lip and peered from the paper to the several dark passages in front of them. Like a moth flitting around a flame, Kim paced around Nari. From beneath the thick quilted jacket, a slim hand emerged and pointed toward a narrow channel in the rock.

"There, we must go through that opening," she said. "We are looking for a massive cavern ahead."

Deeper in the mountain, Hijame, Kitay, and Junior rushed through the dusty facility grabbing any notebooks and papers they could find and stuffing them into duffels.

"We don't have much time. Kitay, set the charges," commanded Hijame.

Junior looked around for an exit from the lab. His chest deflated when he saw only solid walls. He quickly calculated the amount of ammo he was carrying and the best position to cover the entrance. He did not know how many soldiers were chasing them, but he did not like their odds.

"Fuck," exclaimed Kitay. "I only have the blueprints. I handed the pack with the explosives to one of the ROK soldiers who was with us. He's back with the others you ordered to guard our rear."

"We don't have any time. We'll have to make a run for it," said Hijame. Kitay unslung his weapon and positioned himself behind a counter readying for the onslaught. The captain squeezed behind a large cabinet in the corner and started grunting.

"Hold on. I have some C4 in case I have to blow this camera," said Junior.

"Great," said the captain. "Set it up by the trapdoor over here with a tripwire so that they cannot follow us. Kitay, over here. Help me with this."

Putting his right index finger to his lips, Kim raised his hand to halt his group. He cocked his ears, listening. As Nari stared at the sheet, her mind clogged from too much pressure in too short a time. Kim heard the faint sound of voices ahead. He unholstered his pistol and waved his group forward.

As Junior rigged the plastic explosive, Hijame and Kitay slid the cabinet aside to reveal a trapdoor. When Junior finished his booby-trap, he turned to see an empty room. He dashed over to the corner and saw his companions climbing down a rope ladder. What he saw next defied description.

"Come on, Junior, hurry," said Hijame who had reached the ground and was running toward a rowboat at the shore of an underground river.

Junior was halfway down the ladder when he heard excited voices in the lab above him. He had another twenty feet to climb before reaching the ground. Seconds later he saw several faces peering over the edge at him. They were shouting and gesticulating wildly preparing to fire at him.

A tremendous explosion and fireball behind them rocked the crater. A soldier in flames fell toward him knocking Junior off the ladder. He crashed into the rock floor with the burning soldier on top of him. Junior was pinned. He tried to churn his legs but nothing happened. He couldn't move.

Flames from the burning corpse licked at his coat and creeped toward his face. Junior struggled with all his might to no avail. He heard footsteps coming toward him and saw boots. It was Kitay. With a loud scream, he seized the dead man and lifted him off Junior. Kitay grabbed Junior's arm and slung him over his shoulder. His breathe came in gasps as he carried the wounded Junior to the boat where Hijame was waiting.

Kim reached the entrance to the lab with Nari just as the C4 exploded. They flattened against the stone wall just in time to avoid the flames erupting from the aperture. They were showered by rocks and debris released by the explosion.

Once the relief of narrowly escaping obliteration passed, Kim's face exhibited frustration that was beyond description. After years of struggling to solve the enigma of the paper from Ishii's notebook, Kim was on the verge of tears. His jaw clenched and his eyes took on a dimension of disorientation that frightened Nari. She took him by the hand and led him back through the tunnels.

In the days that followed, the shock of recent events incapacitated Kim. His mood darkened when he heard rumors that the notorious, Japanese war criminal Shirō Ishii had been sighted at the secret underground facilities at the Chosin Reservoir, but had escaped capture. Even more disturbing to Kim was the portion of the report which mentioned the capture of an advanced, sophisticated camera and its subsequent destruction. Kim surmised that the Ghost Photographer had once again escaped his clutches. The North Korean leader screamed until his voice degraded to a hoarse croak.

*　　*　　*

As November waned, the situation within the People's Volunteer Army was anything but settled. Peng was weary of shuttling between Shenyang and North Korea for vacillating discussions about whether to intervene. General Peng advocated for prompt, forceful action to repel the Imperialist dogs from China's doorstep. Others urged patience until the Soviets committed equipment and air cover. Still others argued that efforts to reconstruct the economy would be stymied by war.

While leadership courted Soviet air support, General Peng moved several divisions of the PVA across the Yalu River into

North Korea. He reasoned that once open hostilities with UN forces began, any bridges over the Yalu would be targeted by American air power, potentially stranding his army in China. Peng established his headquarters on the northeastern border with China near the capital city of Sinuiju in North Pyongan Province. To avoid hostile air strikes, he sheltered his operations in caves near a gold mining complex.

During a break in one of the interminable discussions, an aide handed Peng a message from General Yang Di that shocked him. He excused himself and headed back to his HQ to deal with the new situation. On the ride back, he re-read the message over and over, fretting over how to communicate the news to the Chairman. Peng knitted his eyebrows, trying to convince himself that the death of another soldier was not a special event. This was not a regular soldier. Peng unfolded the message.

We regret to inform you that at 1000 hours on 25 November, 1950, Secretary Mao Anying was killed by a napalm bomb dropped by hostile forces on a building in Tongchang County, North Pyongan Province.

The general frowned at the news. The eldest son of Chairman Mao (the only sane surviving son) was the victim of a sortie by four U.S. Air Force B-26 Invader attack planes. The Chairman's son had disobeyed orders to stay below ground. The younger Mao and a couple of friends were outside cooking breakfast when the jelled gasoline struck their building and incinerated the occupants. General Peng crumpled the paper and withheld the news for the next two months.

Peng directed his attention on the Second Offensive Campaign. The pieces on the chessboard were aligned in favor of the PVA – UN forces had ventured too far into North Korea and were strung across miles of mountainous terrain connected only by narrow gravel roads that provided fragile logistical support at best. Radio communications among UN forces were virtually impossible, rendering them incapable of cross-support. The Chinese general depended on the hubris of MacArthur and Almond to make their predatory forces oblivious to the fact that they had become prey to over ten clandestine divisions of Chinese soldiers.

In his zeal to reach the Yalu, General Almond, who was in command of X corps, a force of about 30,000 men, committed a fundamental mistake. He divided his forces. He sent the 3,000 members of the Army Regimental Combat Team (RCT-31) to the eastern shore of the lake, and some 25,000 marines to the southern and western sides of the lake occupying three separate locations from the reservoir to a central supply base in Hagaru-ri.

Despite reports of Chinese soldiers in the area, Almond denigrated them as a threat characterizing them as fleeing remnants. Intent on attacking, Almond ordered Army Colonel MacLean to forge ahead, "Don't let a bunch of Chinese laundry-men stop you." On the night of November 27th with the temperature at twenty degrees below zero, Almond's ill-conceived plans would result in one of the most disastrous carnages in American military history. Only the resourceful actions of the marines averted total annihilation.

*   *   *

"Now, we spring the trap," said General Peng to no one in particular. Catching the X Corps in a vulnerable position in the Jangbaik Mountains in unfavorable winter conditions, the battle plan was simple: "Attack at all points, maintain pressure everywhere, but always search for a gap. When a gap was found, flow through it and attempt to segment the defense."

The Chinese Volunteer Army executed its Second Offensive Campaign flawlessly. Ten PVA divisions comprised of 120,000 fighters under the leadership of General Song Shilun, emerged from hidden positions and attacked along a thirty-mile front. With horns blaring and burp guns blasting, the Chinese troops surrounded and overwhelmed the Army RCT and drove the marines back to Haragu-ri in disarray.

Staring at Peng's strategic campaign map, Kim Il Sung watched in awe, at the arrows depicting the precision movement of 120,000 Chinese soldiers. The red arrows encircled the blue mass representing 30,000 UN forces. Over the next few days, the blue pins thinned and moved back toward the coast. Kim relished each report from General Song detailing an American setback as if it were a tasty morsel at a banquet.

For his part, Peng worried about the confidential addendum that surmised that Ishii had stolen top secret atomic bomb research. Although the existence of a cache of Japanese atomic bomb research was known to his superiors, the Chinese had not shared this information with the North Koreans. If Peng had known that Kim possessed General Ishii's diary with the key to the location and contents of the secret nuclear cache, Peng would have been tempted to shoot him dead on sight.

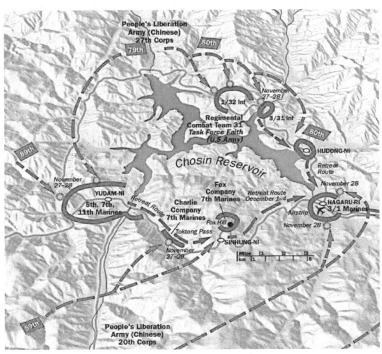

CHAPTER

29

The Big Bugout

"Everything was frozen. The plasma froze and the bottles broke. . . We couldn't change dressings because we had to work with gloves on . . . We couldn't cut a man's clothing off to get at a wound because he would freeze to death."

~ Lt. Commander Chester Lessenden

Between the extent of his injuries and the potential for shock, Junior was in bad shape. Giving the oars to Sergeant Kitay, the captain shifted toward Junior in the boat. Applying his medical knowledge, Hijame administered a shot of morphine and opened his own coat and embraced Junior in an effort to keep him warm. The narrow escape from enemy forces was too close for comfort. He was getting too old for this. Yet, he had to admit that MacArthur's daring plan was worth the reward. They had recovered valuable research data that had been lost for half a decade and feared to be in the hands of his blood enemies.

The take-out point near Hargu-ri was clogged with ice making it impassable. As Kitay prepared for the arduous task of chopping through the frozen tundra, Hijame checked Junior's vital signs.

"We're losing him. His pulse is weakening. We don't have time to chip through the ice," said Hijame.

"You have a better idea?" said Kitay, his voice dripping with sarcasm.

"As a matter of fact, I do. Step away," ordered the captain. He reached down along Junior's body for his Murphy gun. Pulling back the bolt, he opened fire on the ice. Chips and splinters of shattered ice filled the air. Kitay covered his ears to mute the deafening noise in the enclosed space. Minutes later they were above ground again. The racket attracted the attention of a marine patrol and, minutes later, the small party was in a helicopter heading for the coastal city of Hamhung. Junior received medical treatment to stabilize him for the rendezvous with the Supreme Commander.

When they arrived at Yonpo Airfield just outside Hamhung, MacArthur's Constellation was waiting on the tarmac. Although MacArthur visited the war zone frequently to see the situation with his own eyes, the general never spent a night in Korea.

With Junior on a stretcher nearby, MacArthur and Hijame huddled together in the conference section of the plane. Hijame displayed his haul to the general using a professorial tone, explaining the highlights of the material. Drifting in and out of consciousness, Junior heard snippets of conversation. Words and phrases like hydrogen isotope fusion, deuterium oxide, and plutonium floated through his mind without registering. Later, when he was asked about the journey to the hospital in Tokyo, he recalled nothing after he was knocked senseless by the falling soldier.

"Thanks, Shiro," said MacArthur. "This deserves a celebratory drink. Steward, where's that Daignjo sake from the Emperor?"

After Hijame retired to the sleeping compartment for a well-earned rest, MacArthur approved orders for a total evacuation of X Corps and the 8th Army through the port of Hungnam to South Korea. As distasteful as it was to order withdrawal, the general had accomplished one of his top objectives. Having acquired the Imperial Japanese Navy's nuclear research, MacArthur felt that his hand for employing the nuclear option in a war against the Communists was solidified. The general looked forward to his next meeting with the President.

Before taking off for Tokyo, MacArthur radioed his two top generals to report to Tokyo for an emergency meeting the following day. MacArthur knew that Almond, CG of X Corps and Walker, CG of the 8th Army, would be livid at his order to leave their troops while they were surrounded and outnumbered by the PVA. Adding insult to injury, MacArthur insisted that Almond and Walker keep their departures secret, even from their staffs.

*　*　*

At the same time MacArthur was meeting with the top echelon of the American military in Tokyo on November 29th, the troops on the ground faced a desperate, almost hopeless, situation. On the east coast of the Reservoir, RCT-31 was surrounded and overrun over the course of the next four days. The silver lining of this disaster was that it bought time for the Marines on the west coast to evacuate their wounded and much of their equipment via the makeshift airfield at Hargu-ri. UN air power would prove even more decisive over the next few days, especially at the Funchilin Pass.

The retreat was orchestrated under the leadership of Marine General Oliver P. Smith. As he navigated the single-lane gravel road which wound through cliffs and ridges as treacherous and wild as any in Korea, Smith issued one of the most reality-denying statements in the annals of military statements: "Retreat, hell. We're not retreating. We're just advancing in another direction."

The troops on both sides faced every hardship imaginable. Far more devastating than the lack of food, water, and sleep was the cold. Temperatures well below zero were the norm. Poorly equipped to handle the extreme weather, thousands in both armies froze to death, or lost fingers, toes, and ears to frostbite. Somehow, the Marines fought their way back through Hagaru where thousands of casualties were air-lifted out. From there, they battled the Chinese and the elements to the village of Koto-ri where things went from bad to worse. Several miles south of Koto-ri was the Funchilin Pass. Consisting of a ten-mile-long section of road perched on a cliff above a chasm, this was a critical portion of the escape route.

"What have you got on the repairs, captain? We've got a convoy to keep moving" said General Smith, looking up from the reports on his camp desk.

"The PVA knows this is our only way out, sir. They keep blowing the bridge. Yesterday was the third time they dynamited the bridge," said Captain Jameson. "The gap is about thirty feet wide, sir."

"Options?" Smith puffed on his pipe as he listened. Jameson turned to Lt. Col. John Partridge, commanding the 1st Marine Engineer Battalion and in charge of all engineer units at Koto. He wore the triple-crenelated-tower insignia of the engineering corps on his collar.

"General, the good news is that we have the machinery to do the job - we have a couple of bridge-laying six-ton Brockway transporter trucks. The bad news is that we don't have anything to cover that gap."

Smith puffed on his pipe for a minute, then said, "Over the last ten days, we fought our asses off to escape the Chink army. I'll be God-damned if some punk-ass bridge is going to strand us here to perish in this frozen wasteland. We've got to get these 14,000 men across that bridge. Hell, we've got a hundred thousand refugees who are trailing us to escape from the commies. What do you need to get it done?"

"What we need is at least four Treadway bridge sections that we could probably cantilever over that span. Unfortunately, the nearest ones are at least fifty miles away down on the coast. The PVA controls the pass to the south. We can't get the pieces here over land in time. Especially with the blizzard that's heading our way," said Colonel Partridge.

"Alright, let's fly 'em in," said Smith matter-of-factly.

"Sir, each section weighs about two tons – even if we could get 'em in the air, how would we land 'em. They'd be shattered on landing. It can't be done," said Partridge.

It was that last phrase that Smith took as a challenge.

"Get me, General Tunner of the U.S. Air Force's Combat Cargo Command. He said to call if I needed anything," said the General to his aide. After developing a plan with General Tunner, Smith recalled a statement from the legendary Arctic explorer Matthew Henson. "It will work, if God, the wind, leads, ice, snow and all the hells of this damned frozen land are willing."

Twenty-four hours later, just ahead of a nasty blizzard, General Smith watched as C-119 Flying Boxcars dropped eight sections of Treadway bridge. Each section was borne by two-forty-eight-foot diameter G-5 parachutes and floated down near the airfield at Koto-ri. Smith ordered extra sections to cover the eventuality that some might be damaged on landing. Working under artificial lights, the engineers performed a miracle and installed the sections over the span just before the wind chill fell to ninety degrees below zero.

During the forty-eight hours that followed, General Smith evacuated all his men, some 1400 trucks, tanks and artillery, and over 90,000 North Korean refugees across the Funchilin Pass. Marine Corsairs pummeled the high ground south of the pass, neutralizing Chinese opposition. When General Smith's convoy reached the flatlands, the troops experienced a veritable heat wave as the temperatures reached the freezing point. The exodus through Hungnam was code-named Christmas Cargo.

Following the withdrawal of UN forces after the debacle at Chosin Reservoir, General Peng pressed his advantage. The PVA recaptured the capital city of P'yŏngyang by December 5th and would reconquer Seoul soon after the New Year. The situation for UN forces in North Korea continued to deteriorate. On Christmas day, MacArthur's forces would lose General Walton Walker, commanding officer of the 8th Army, in a fatal traffic accident when his command car collided with a truck driven by an ROK soldier. Walker's tragic death was eerily similar to the death of his mentor General George Patton who also died from injuries received when his Jeep was hit by a truck in 1945.

By the end of December 1950, UN forces had retreated some 120 miles, back below the 38th parallel. In Beijing, Mao crooned. In P'yŏngyang, Kim brooded. In Tokyo, MacArthur schemed. In Washington, Truman fumed.

With the Marines – From Chosin to Hungnam
https://www.youtube.com/watch?v=PbSPG1k9tss

Image USAF photo
Funchilin Pass bridge
demolished by PVA –
Battle of Chosin Reservoir

Image courtesy of the
18th   Air Force

C-119 Flying Boxcar
delivering Treadway
bridge section

Image courtesy of the 18th
Air Force

Dual G-5 parachutes with
Treadway bridge section

CHAPTER

30

Wake Island Massacre

"All warfare is based on deception."

~ Sun Tzu

The purga, an intense arctic wind, swept from the Siberian tundra into the Japanese capital on that early-December day. To MacArthur, it brought to mind the frigid conditions experienced by the Continental Army at Valley Forge during the American Revolutionary War. The purga matched his mood as he entered the intensive care unit in Tokyo General Hospital to visit Junior. MacArthur's combat photographer had been seriously injured while on a highly-classified operation at the Chosin Reservoir. The prognosis was grim. Once Junior had been stabilized, the doctors assessed the damage to his spinal cord.

"We're sorry to report that the crushing impact he received was so severe that the nerves have been irreparably damaged and he will never be able to walk again," said an officious-looking physician from behind his surgical mask. When delivering bad news, the doctor used the mask to hide from patients and family. It was particularly effective when dealing with high-ranking officers like General MacArthur.

The hopelessness of the diagnosis drove MacArthur into a rage.

"That cannot be!" thundered MacArthur. "I want to speak to the head of the department."

"I am the head of the department," replied the doctor somewhat timidly.

"Well then, take off that silly mask and tell me about any experimental procedures you can use to get this soldier back on his feet. I need him for important missions."

The head nurse in the room felt embarrassed for the doctor as he fumbled haplessly with the surgical mask. It was dangling comically from his left ear when he replied, "As you know, general, spinal injuries . . ."

"Don't tell me what I know. Tell me something positive that I don't know," snapped MacArthur.

The doctor was cowed into silence.

MacArthur turned to the nurse and growled, "Get me a line to Walter Reed Hospital, Dr. Ransahoff, ASAP."

"Yessir," said the nurse, glad to be excused momentarily from the general's wrath.

Three days later, MacArthur was in the intensive care unit when several nurses wheeled Junior into the recovery room. By dint of his five stars and unbending tenacity, MacArthur had assembled a team of the finest surgeons to operate on Junior's injured spinal cord. Over eighteen hours, the team used microscopic instruments and advanced techniques to, as Junior later quipped, "put Humpty back together again."

The lead surgeon, Dr. Ransahoff, appeared at the door. His face was etched with fatigue and concern as he approached the general.

"Douglas, it's been a long time. The years have been a friend to you," said Dr. Ransahoff, grasping MacArthur's hand and pulling him close.

"Thanks, Gilbert. From what I hear you've had yourself a spectacular career. I truly appreciate your efforts here," said the general.

"My pleasure. These are the kind of challenging cases that give us surgeons the opportunity to embellish the legend. You certainly know how that works, right, Doug," he said, with a wry grin.

Relaxed in the company of an old friend, MacArthur chuckled. The strain of the last seven months vanished momentarily from his face. In the next instant, SCAP, the Supreme Commander of Allied Powers, returned, along with the worry lines, crow's feet, and spider veins.

"Tell me, Gil, give me the skinny, the naked truth on Junior's prognosis," said MacArthur,

"To be perfectly honest, Douglas, it's going to take a miracle for him to recover fully. The trauma involved a tremendous amount of torque and compression. When we examined the spinal cord, it looked like the pieces of an Escher puzzle. Not to worry, we were like a tag team, taking turns putting the nerves back in order," said Gilbert.

"How much time before we have a good idea?" asked MacArthur.

"Total traction for the next month, then, a month of rest, after that rehab – it could take four months," said Ransahoff. "But I assure you that we will monitor his recovery closely. Junior needs round-the-clock care. He's young, strong, and determined. Barring any setbacks, I give him even money."

"Thanks, Gil," said MacArthur with a slight croak in his voice.

After midnight, when the hospital staff had completed their rounds and the ICU had settled in for the night, a slight figure climbed the stairway. Clad in black, the figure crept toward Junior's room with feline stealth. Junior was heavily medicated and in no position to alert the nurses, let alone defend himself. Like a shadow, the figure entered the room and approached the bed. She peered into Junior's face as if to make sure that it was the right person, the one whose face she had seen. Reaching into her clothing, the figure began to

KOREA FORGOTTEN SACRIFICE

withdraw an object when she was grabbed from behind by a strong man.

"What the hell are you doing?" screamed Kitay who emerged from the corner where he had been keeping vigil.

"I friend. I friend for Junya," squealed the diminutive woman who bicycled her legs in the air and tried to wriggle out of the sergeant's grasp.

Kitay dropped her. She gathered herself and reached into her waistband, producing a letter. It was addressed to Junior. Kitay took the letter and placed it in a drawer in the nightstand next to Junior's bed. By the time he turned back around, the woman had backed out of the room and disappeared. Kitay noticed a glint of light on the floor – it was a bracelet that had come off during the tussle. The sergeant could not read the Japanese characters on it, so he tossed it into the drawer with the letter. The name of Sachie's friend, Miyumi, was engraved on the bracelet.

* * *

Due to the heroic efforts of many branches of the U.S. military, UN troops along with most of their equipment and munitions evacuated North Korea from the port of Hungnam. Although not quite as harrowing as the withdrawal of Allied forces at Dunkirk during WWII, the long defensive march from the Chosin Reservoir over seventeen days from November 27th to December 13th averted annihilation and deprived Mao of his most ardent goal. It was the longest withdrawal in the history of the American military.

Although the chairman could not fully appreciate the ramifications of the secrets taken by MacArthur's team from right under the control of his generals, he was livid and scared. Mao knew that MacArthur would now become even more dangerous. Despite the humiliating defeat of the capitalist dogs, or, perhaps, because of it, Mao braced himself for an onslaught of atomic weapons on industrial and military installations in Manchuria, northeastern China.

Mao's recriminations over Peng's failure to annihilate the imperialist aggressors would have verged on hysteria had he known who was present at an emergency meeting convened by MacArthur. In attendance were: Vice Admiral Turner Joy, Commander, Naval Forces Far East; Lieutenant General George Stratemeyer, Commander, Far East Air Force; Major General Doyle Hickey, chief of staff, Far East Command; Major General Charles Willoughby, Far East Command, chief of intelligence; Major General Courtney Whitney, Advisor to MacArthur's staff; Brigadier General Edwin K. Wright, Far East Command; General Almond, Commander, X Corps; and General Walton Walker, Commander, 8th Army.

MacArthur assembled the leadership might of the American Far East Command to advise them of the latest developments which he characterized as a kairotic moment. As MacArthur would explain at the meeting, Kairos was the youngest child of Zeus and was known as the god of opportunity. The word kairotic traced its roots to archery where it denotes "the seizing of, and striking forcefully through an opening." The atheist Mao would have cringed in disgust at MacArthur's characterization.

When MacArthur entered the conference room on the sixth floor of SCAP headquarters, the conversational buzz halted abruptly.

"Easy. This is a no blue falcon meeting. Everything said stays here. We have a kairotic moment before us, gentlemen," said MacArthur.

Over the next several hours, MacArthur briefed them on the intelligence breakthrough achieved due to the materials recovered by Captain Hijame's team at Chosin Reservoir and the implications for putting an end to the scourge of communism.

"In conclusion, I have forwarded the materials on hydrogen isotope fusion and the fabrication of a new nuclear element known as plutonium to the laboratory in Los Alamos, New Mexico with instructions to manufacture weapons for utilization. Preliminary estimates are that we would need between thirty and fifty of these bombs to create a swath of radioactive cobalt across the border between the Chinese border with the Korean Peninsula rendering it an impassable wasteland for generations. I am preparing a request to the Joint Chiefs for field commander's authority to deploy these weapons as needed."

"What about the Russkies?" asked a voice from the rear.

"Uncle Joe will tremble in his boots if he knows what's good for him. The Russian bear will pull its claws in and go into hibernation until the next century when it's safe to come outside again."

*   *   *

During the winter months after the withdrawal from Hungnam in December 1950, the Chinese "volunteers" pushed UN forces out of the north and battled over the waist of Korea, around the 38th parallel. Morale in the 8th Army was abysmal and its fighting capability was significantly degraded. There was a distinct possibility that the entire Peninsula might be lost.

President Truman convened a meeting of the Joint Chiefs of Staff in Washington. The atmosphere in the conference room at the Blair House was as gloomy as the low, gunmetal-gray clouds hung ominously in the March sky in the nation's capital. General Omar Bradley, chairman of the Joint Chiefs, reviewed the cables from the Far East while waiting for the President. Carrying a leather portfolio with his daily materials, the President entered. The room quieted to order.

"Good morning, gentlemen," said the President. "Omar, what news do we have from Korea?"

"We have received a series of requests from SCAP that fall into three categories: first, he wants to "drive forward with all speed and with full utilization" using all forces. Second, he specifically wants authorization to bomb air bases and munitions dumps inside China. Third, he wants the discretion to use tactical nuclear weapons as necessary," said Bradley, the WWII hero known as the Cobra.

There was an audible hush at the mention of nuclear weapons. Truman who had been perusing a document, straightened in his chair and adjusted his eyeglasses. The President glanced expectantly around the conference room. All he saw was negativity in the faces of his advisers.

"What's your opinion, Omar?" asked the President.

"Mr. President, expansion of this conflict into China is the wrong war, at the wrong place, at the wrong time, and with the wrong enemy," said Chairman Bradley.

"Any dissent on that point?" the President asked the group.

Seeing none, he addressed the Joint Chiefs.

"We do not want to see the conflict in Korea extended. We are trying to prevent a world war - not to start one . . . . But you may ask why can't we take other steps to punish the aggressor. Why don't we bomb Manchuria and China itself? Why don't we assist Chinese Nationalist troops to land on the mainland of China? If we were to do these things we would be running a very grave risk of starting a general war . . . . If we were to do these things, we would become entangled in a vast conflict on the continent of Asia and our task would become immeasurably more difficult all over the world. I believe that we must try to limit the war to Korea for these vital reasons: To make sure that the precious lives of our fighting men are not wasted, to see that the security of our country and the free world are not needlessly jeopardized and to prevent a third world war."

The President instructed Bradley to prepare appropriate responses to MacArthur making it abundantly clear that under no circumstances would there be a violation of Chinese sovereign space and that tactical nukes were out of the question. Truman asked Bradley to stay for a private meeting after the Joint Chiefs adjourned.

When the President and General Bradley were alone, Truman sat next to Bradley. The President sighed deeply.

"Omar, that bastard is driving me crazy."

"He has had that effect on many presidents, sir. I guess his pig-headedness contributes to his positives. Don't worry, Mr. President, I'll rein him in," said Bradley, in a tone that lacked assurance.

"I'm afraid he has pushed me over the edge," said Truman, with a sense of determination that the general had not seen before.

"I know that he has bordered on insubordination, sir. But . . ."

"No buts, Omar . . . look," said the President, handing a paper to Bradley.

He studied the paper, then exhaled in disbelief. "Whew, I've seen him pull a lot of crazy stunts, but I did not think he was capable of this."

Standing, Truman grabbed the paper and growled, "That miserable son-of-a-bitch wants to sow a belt of radioactive cobalt from the Sea of Japan to the Yellow Sea. Who the fuck does he think he is?" said the President, his voice rising, in anger.

"That's it! He's gone! Fix the paperwork to relieve MacArthur of his command immediately, Omar."

"With all due respect, Mr. President, it might be better to do it in person," said Bradley.

"Alright, schedule me for Wake Island as soon as possible and order that son-of-a-bitch to be there before I get there. I won't tolerate his shenanigans and wait one second for him," said Truman. Then, half to himself, he chuckled, "Firing that bastard is going to be fun."

*　　*　　*

After a morning of rigorous exercise to rehabilitate his motor skills, Junior was resting on his bed, semi-awake. A knock on the door frame drew his attention. The man standing there looked remarkably different from the last time he had seen him. Substituted for his normally ramrod straight posture were slumped shoulders and a chin-line that drooped noticeably. His face and movements were those of a man much older than the MacArthur of just a few weeks earlier. General MacArthur looked every bit the old soldier destined to fade away. Even his uniform seemed to have a diaphanous quality to it, as if it had been laundered far too many times.

"I'm going to sit over here for a while," he said, pulling up a chair that was new when MacArthur was a cadet rooting for the West Point Equestrian Team. He sat lost in thought for a few minutes.

Junior blinked the fatigue out of his eyes. There was a sadness about MacArthur, that was similar to the look MacArthur had when Junior reported that Gomax was missing in action.

"How are you, son? Are you walking yet?" said MacArthur in a low voice.

"Getting better every day, sir. The therapist tells me that I'm his miracle patient. He brags about me to the doctors with each baby step I take," said Junior, brightly.

"Good, good," said MacArthur absently. "I have something to say and I'm going to take my rank off my shoulders, and I'm going to talk to you friend to friend."

"Okay, general, whatever you say."

"I just came back from a meeting with President Truman on Wake Island. He relieved me of duty, fired me. I don't understand, I've been in this man's army for 57 years. Why

317

did this little bastard say 'Goodbye, go home' and that's it? I don't understand why."

"General, I'm not a very well-educated person. But you forgot one thing that even I know. We only have one commander-in-chief, and that's the President of these United States. God thank the United States of America and the forefathers. They told George Washington there's one commander-in-chief. Not even you, even if you had ten stars, would have the opportunity to be the top dog. The top, top dog is the President of the United States."

He looked at Junior and said, "I guess I'd forgotten that. I'd really forgotten that and I thought after all the years and the rank that I have that I deserved to be that. I guess you're right. I guess it's time for this old soldier to just fade away."

CHAPTER

31

Kites over Waterfalls

Sunlight streaming on Incense Stone
Kindles violet smoke;
Far off I watch the waterfall plunge to the long river,
Flying waters descending straight three thousand feet
'Til I think the Milky Way has tumbled
from the ninth height of Heaven.

~ Li Bo, translated by Burton Watson

On the last day of Junior's rehabilitation, his favorite nurse, Motoko, handed him a bin with his belongings. As Junior packed things into his duffel, a shiny object caught his eye. Perplexed, he lifted a delicate bracelet bearing characters he could not decipher.

"Motoko, there must be a mistake. I don't recognize this bracelet. It's not mine," said Junior.

Turning it over in her hands, her eyebrows knitted. As she examined the characters, Junior continued to pull items from the bin for packing.

"These are Japanese letters. It's a woman's name. Do you know a Miyumi?" she asked.

"Miyumi. Yes. I do," answered Junior, thoughtfully. "She's a friend of . . ."

He was distracted by an envelope pressed against the side of the bin, next to where the bracelet had been. Motoko watched in amazement as this pleasant but generally shy, morose patient turned jubilant. He read and re-read the missive inside the envelope. She could see a plan formulating in his head.

"Thanks for everything, Motoko, you are a sweetheart!" said Junior who shocked her with a kiss on the cheek. He left the ward humming a lilting melody.

Junior's destination was Iriomote, a thinly populated island in the Ryukyu archipelago southwest of the main islands of Japan. The passengers hurried off the ferry at Iriomote Island and joined relatives and friends on the landing. Junior adjusted his duffel onto the wheeled contraption that Dr. Ransahoff had sketched for the mechanic in the motor pool. With a noticeable limp and drag of his right leg, Junior wheeled the luggage down the gangplank. He searched for his guide. Emerging from the shadows of the ferry office, a youngster sprinted toward the American.

"Junya-san? You Junya-san? Yes?" said the boy in an excited voice.

The weary American nodded. The boy wrestled the bag away from Junior who put up only token resistance. The boy played with the wheeled bag, alternately racing and turning it so it tilted to the point of almost capsizing. He laughed with a joy reserved for the young and innocent. The boy led Junior to another, smaller boat that cruised up the Urauchi River to the Gunkan Stone. From there, they trekked to a magical, mystical place - Mayagusuka Falls.

The gentle roar of falling water ahead was the first indication of something special. Above the tree-line a colorful object flitted in the wind. A kite dipped and darted in the breeze, like a welcoming beacon drawing him near. The kite was a traditional hexagon, decorated with the image of a Japanese warrior depicted in vivid primary colors. This was a celebratory kite flown for famous warriors. It was a symbol of gratitude for the benevolence of the Diety for returning the warrior from battle. The person guiding the kite was obscured from his view.

When he cleared the vegetation and looked up, he gasped at the sight of waterfalls so beautiful they almost defied description. At the crest, the river narrowed and flumed through a rocky notch. Granite, layered like a stake of pancakes, formed the rock face of the falls. Water gushed and gurgled over a ledge cascading over a series of terraces that fanned wider as the crystal-clear water tumbled into a talus strewn with boulders. In this sacred place, a sense of peace and well-being flooded over Junior.

As Junior got closer to the kite-flyer, his heart raced. It was Sachie! She smiled shyly, uncertain of Junior's reaction. Junior whooped a cry of elation and rushed toward her as fast as his injured body could move on the wet rocks. Water enveloped and swirled around their legs as they met in the midst of the falls, embracing tightly with so much emotion that they never wanted to separate. Sachie caressed Junior's face and released the kite string. So entranced were the lovers that they were indifferent to the fate of the kite. A gust of wind captured the kite and lifted it upward, ascending to the peak of the falls. It grew smaller and faded away; the wind taking it where warriors go when the battle is done.

THE END

EPILOGUE

For three days in March 1953, the body of Joseph Stalin lay in state in the Hall of Unions. The cause of death for the seventy-four-year old dictator was reported as a stroke due to atherosclerosis and hypertension. On the day of his funeral, tens of thousands of mourners assembled in Trubnaia Square, Moscow. As the grieving crowd pressed to glimpse Uncle Joe's coffin, it degenerated into a monstrous whirlpool that rampaged wildly, crushing and trampling five hundred people. The deadly chaos seemed an appropriate coda to the life of the tyrant who was responsible for the deaths of tens of millions.

Just before noon on March 6th, the funeral cortege carried Stalin to Red Square where his body was to be interred in the mausoleum which held the remains of Vladimir Lenin. After eulogies and a moment of silence, bells of the Kremlin tower chimed the hour to mark the burial of the man whose name meant Man of Steel. The dictator who had ruled his country with a ruthless savagery that transformed his country into a superpower was gone and so was his strangle-hold on world events.

The Soviet dictator once said that, "The death of one man is a tragedy, but the death of thousands is a statistic." Despite the millions of casualties during the Korean War, Joseph Stalin considered the deaths much more than a statistic. He considered the war as an opportunity to debilitate the two biggest threats to his ambitions. In the way that the use of leeches by quack physicians in the Middle Ages weakened their patients, Stalin used Kim and Rhee to bleed and exhaust Red China and the United States.

After the Chinese offensive in late 1950 which drove the UN forces south, the opposing forces were arrayed on either side of the 38th parallel. It was a stalemate, with the adversaries basically back to where they were when the hostilities started. The war should have ended in early 1951. Instead, like drunken brawlers who forgot why they were fighting, the antagonists continued to pummel each other for almost two more years. All attempts to bring rationality to the situation were thwarted until the passing of one man.

Less than 55 days after Stalin's death, the parties agreed to a ceasefire. An armistice agreement ending the conflict was signed at Panmunjom, DPRK on July 27, 1953. Efforts at a lasting peace and reunification are perpetually ongoing.

* * *

After Truman fired MacArthur, the general returned to the United States and testified before the Senate Armed Forces and Foreign Relations Committees on May 3, 1951. MacArthur used the opportunity to criticize President Truman's foreign policy and advocate for a complete military engagement to destroy the threat of international communism. The hearings lasted for seven weeks.

During his command of UN forces, General MacArthur complained that the enemy seemed to anticipate his every move. For the most part, MacArthur's concerns were dismissed as self-serving paranoia. Subsequent events would validate MacArthur's suspicions.

Several weeks after MacArthur's testimony before the U.S. Senate, two men traveled to Southampton, England and boarded the steamship *Faliase* at midnight on May 26th, 1951, for a weekend cruise across the Channel to France. Their destination was St. Malo, a French port in Brittany a reputation as a haven for pirates, vagabonds, and spies. Due to the abundance of weekend trippers, there was no passport checkpoint at St. Malo.

The two men were senior members of the British Foreign Service and MI6, the fabled British intelligence agency. Their names were Guy Burgess and Donald Maclean. They were also spies who were defecting to the Soviet Union. They were members of the Cambridge Five, British agents who had met at college and became career diplomats who compromised British and American intelligence for decades.

The last member of the group to defect was Kim Philby who was stationed at the British Embassy in Washington D.C. during the Korean War and had access to all Pentagon communications shared with MacArthur's *Dai Ichi* headquarters and shared with the British Military. After the Armistice, the field general for the Chinese People's Volunteer Army admitted he would not have committed his forces against MacArthur's if he did not have assurances that the President and Joint Chiefs would prevent retaliation by MacArthur against vital supply and communication lines. So deep and effective was Philby's espionage operation that he continued spying for his communist masters for another decade. Philby absconded for Moscow in 1963. For his betrayal, Kim Philby was rewarded by the Soviets with the Order of Stalin and his picture on a postage stamp.

*   *   *

Prisoners-of-war often suffer grievously and, if they survive, are scarred physically, emotionally, and spiritually. Two POWs of note deserve mention here due to their disparate treatment.

General William F. Dean, the American general captured after the Battle of Taejon, remained a prisoner of war for the duration of the conflict. Notwithstanding having suffered serious injuries and lengthy imprisonment, General Dean remained resolute in refusing to reveal what he knew to his captors. He was released as part of Operation Big Switch after the armistice was signed in 1953. For his heroic service in Korea, General Dean received the Congressional Medal of Honor.

As WWII concluded, Dr. Shiro Ishii, the notorious commander of Unit 731, attempted to avoid capture by faking his own death. He was captured by American forces. General MacArthur granted Ishii and many of his subordinates, immunity in return for their cooperation in providing data and information on biological warfare which in MacArthur's words "could not otherwise be obtained." Dr. Ishii retired to Japan where he ran a medical clinic until his death. Ishii was never prosecuted for the horrors committed by Unit 731 under his command.

*   *   *

The man with deep worry lines around his eyes tugged the young boy along toward the motor stable where his prized possession was. The frigid December wind could not dampen his spirits. His Chinese comrades had driven the imperialist dogs from his capital city and he was reclaiming P'yŏngyang as his seat of government.

The boy stumbled over a chunk of concrete, rubble from the recent conquest of the city. With a yank that pulled the short, nine-year-old off balance, Kim Il Sung exhorted the boy to move faster.

"Jong-il, pay attention! I want you to remember all this destruction. This happens when you are not strong," said the self-anointed Great Leader.

The boy whimpered an affirmation. He would have preferred to be with his mother by the warm hearth, eating *jjinppang*, fluffy steamed buns filled with sweet red bean paste. For now, he was stuck in downtown P'yŏngyang walking with his father. The youngster tightened the bandana covering his nose in a vain effort to keep away the acrid smells of a city that was the site of recent military conquest. Burned-out vehicles, looking like the corpses of prehistoric creatures and buildings with ragged, gaping holes filled his line of sight. The worst part of the scene was the charred bodies littering the streets. Here and there, packs of feral dogs looking gaunt and mangy roamed in search of food. Jong-il pressed closer to his father.

"My son, you must learn to erase this wretched scene from your eyes and replace it with a city of wide boulevards lined with trees and terraced gardens. Look, over there will be public buildings surrounded by reflecting pools and connected by clean, quiet trolleys. All free of course, thanks to *juche*, the spirit of self-reliance and socialism that motivates our people," said Kim. "One day when I am gone this will all be yours."

The father smiled as they reached a garage door. He lifted the door, squinting as his eyes adjusted to the dim light.

"Now, I will show you something truly spectacular. It was a gift to me from the great Soviet leader, Joseph Stalin," said Kim.

"Oh, no," he exclaimed as he walked up to the ZIS limousine. Rather than the shiny, majestic vehicle transported from Moscow, Kim beheld a filthy hulk with a cracked windshield, resting on flat tires. When he tried to open the driver's door, the hinges creaked and the door hung askew like a road sign hanging by one chain from its post. Inside the cab, the seats were stained and slashed. A look of revulsion mixed with sadness fanned across his face.

The dictator clenched his jaw and vowed to create a society obedient to him where outrages like this would be severely punished.

* * *

The old fisherman sat on the front porch of his shanty overlooking the moorings at Sakiyama Bay. His gnarled fingers toyed absently with an olive-green *magatama* that had dangled from his neck since he was a young man. His vision was blurred and he could barely discern the figure of his grandson on the fishing boat. The boy cranked the motor, flashed a smile and waved to his *Ojisan*. The glare off the turquoise water caused the old man to squint. His thoughts drifted to the awkward time when he was a teenager like his grandson and his wife's cousin taught him to navigate the shoals around the island searching for fish.

A photo album balanced on his knees. It was open to an image of the grandfather surrounded by his two sons and four grandsons. By virtue of his clothing and hair style, Junior appeared almost as Asian as his family members.

"Junya-san, come inside and have some tea. I have news for you," said a petite woman with her gray hair bunched in a bun atop her head. Realizing that her husband had not heard her, she stepped onto the porch and touched his shoulder. Gesturing to come inside, she smiled. Her lined face radiated the contentment that comes from decades of marriage tranquility.

The man had trouble rising. His back, stiff from an old war wound, made it difficult to straighten. Junior shuffled toward the kitchen table. Sachie removed gold wire-rimmed glasses from a sleeve pocket in her colorful kimono.

"Kai, your favorite grandson, brought the mail from Uehara this morning. I want to read you a story from the *Military Times*. 'On August 1, 2018, there was a repatriation ceremony at Osan air base in South Korea. After a summit with President Donald J. Trump, Kim Jung Un, the North Korean dictator, released the remains of fifty-five presumed UN war dead as a goodwill gesture. The remains will be flown to Hawaii where they will undergo intensive forensic DNA analysis. In one instance only, the remains were accompanied by a military dog tag. It belonged to Gunnery Sergeant Alvaro Gomax.' Junior, your friend is finally going home for a proper burial."

Junior blinked, releasing a single tear. It ran down his wrinkled cheek until it was absorbed by his gray goatee. A rush of memories from long ago flooded his mind. When Gomax was interred at Arlington cemetery the funeral escort presented a flag to his next of kin and expressed the traditional condolences:

On behalf of the president of the United States,
the United States Marine Corps and a grateful nation,
please accept this flag as a symbol of our appreciation
for your loved one's honorable and faithful service.

Timeline

1882 - the United States recognized the independence and territorial integrity of Korea by entering into a treaty of amity and commerce.

1905 - when the Russo-Japanese War ended, Secretary of War, William Howard Taft, met with Japanese PM Katsura to clarify that the Philippines were within America's zone of influence and that Korea was in Japan's zone of influence.

1910, August 29 - Sunjong, the last monarch of the Chosŏn dynasty of Korea which had ruled for 500 years, relinquished his throne, marking the beginning of Japan's colonial reign over Korea for the next 35 years.

1931 - Japan staged the Mukden incident as a pretext to invade Manchuria and set up puppet government of Manchukuo led by former Chinese Emperor Pu Yi.

November 1943 - at the Cairo Conference the United States, Great Britain and China declared that ". . . in due course Korea shall become free and independent."

February 4 - 11, 1945 - at the Yalta Conference, Winston Churchill, Joseph Stalin, and Franklin D. Roosevelt proposed a trusteeship involving the United States, China, and the Soviet Union, which could last twenty to thirty years.

August 8, 1945 - the Soviet Union declared war on Japan.

August 24, 1945 - the Soviet Red Army entered P'yŏngyang, North Korea.

December 1945 - at the Moscow Conference, United States, Soviet Union, and Great Britain created the Joint Soviet-American Commission charged with establishing a provisional Korean democratic government.

November 1947 - the United Nations General Assembly approved elections to be held throughout Korea to choose a provisional government for the entire country. The Soviet Union opposed.

May 10, 1948 - the people of South Korea elect a national assembly, setting up the government of the Republic of Korea (ROK) four months later. The north refuses to take part.

September 9, 1948 - the Democratic People's Republic of Korea (DPRK) was proclaimed with Kim Il Sung as the Soviet-designated premier.

March 1949 - Kim Il Sung went to Moscow to request a large increase in assistance so that he might pursue reunification of Korea by force. Stalin refused.

June 1949 - with the creation of the Republic of Korea, the United States withdrew 50,000 American occupation troops.

August 29, 1949 - U.S.S.R. detonated its first atomic bomb.

October 1, 1949 - Mao declared victory in the civil war and announced the establishment of the People's Republic of China.

January 1950 - Soviet Union boycotted the UN Security Council over its refusal to replace Chiang Kai-shek's government with Mao's government as China's representative in the United Nations.

January 12, 1950 - at the National Press Club, Secretary of State Dean Acheson defined America's strategic defense perimeter in Asia, excluding Korea.

February 14, 1950 - People's Republic of China and the Soviet Union enter into Sino-Soviet Treaty of Friendship and Alliance by which the Soviets recognized Red China and extended a $300 million loan to help it recover from the ravages of the long civil war.

March 1950 - Kim Il Sung returned to Moscow and argued passionately for permission to unite Korea using Soviet military materiel. Stalin assents.

June 25, 1950 - 135,000 soldiers from communist North Korea crossed the 38th parallel and invaded the Republic of Korea.

June 25, 1950 - UN Security Council denounced North Korea and called for a cessation of hostilities and return to the 38th parallel.

June 26, 1950 - President Truman directed General Douglas MacArthur to evacuate American dependents from Korea and to assist the ROK Army.

June 27, 1950 - UN Security Council passed resolution recommending that assistance to South Korea as needed to "repel the armed attack and to restore international peace and security to the area." President Truman ordered the Seventh Fleet of the U.S. Navy moved into the Straits of Taiwan.

June 30, 1950 - President Truman ordered ground troops into action in defense of the Republic of Korea.

July 5, 1950 - Battle of Osan, 30 miles south of Seoul, U.S. troops defeated.

July 7, 1950 - the UN asked the U.S. to lead the Unified Command to put down the North Korean aggression. President Truman appointed General MacArthur the commander of a forty-eight-nation force.

September 15 - 19, 1950 - MacArthur planned an audacious turning movement and successfully conducted an amphibious invasion at Incheon. Within two weeks, UN forces occupied Kimpo Airfield and recaptured Seoul.

October 10, 1950 UN captured the DPRK port of Wonsan.

October 12-17 1950 - Mao Zedong concluded that American troops on the Yalu River posed an existential threat. Mao ordered Chinese communist volunteer forces into the conflict.

Oct 17 - 19, 1950 - Battle of P'yŏngyang capital of North Korea, occupied by UN forces.

October 19, 1950 - Mao's People's Volunteer Army (PVA) crossed the Yalu River.

October 25 - November 4, 1950 - ROK took control of the strategic town of Unsan, one of the access points to the Yalu.

November 1950 - Soviet air units arrive to oppose UN.

November 27 - December 14, 1950 - Chosin Reservoir Campaign. With superior numbers PVA surprise-attacked UN forces at Chosin Reservoir and UN forces withdrew to Hungnam and evacuated below the 38th parallel.

December 5, 1950 - Chinese PVA retook P'yŏngyang and re-crossed the 38th parallel.

December 9, 1950 - Chinese PVA retook Wonsan.

December 15 - 24, 1950 - Christmas Cargo: UN forces, including 1st Marines and 90,000 North Korean refugees evacuated from Hungnam.

January 4, 1951 - Chinese PVA retook Seoul.

April 11, 1951 - President Harry Truman relieved General Douglas MacArthur of his commands.

June 1951 - with battle lines once again set along the pre-invasion boundary, Soviets propose cease-fire to UN.

May - June, 1951 - Congressional hearings about Korea and MacArthur.

November 27, 1951 - both sides agree the existing battle lines would be the final dividing line between North and South Korea if a truce is reached in 30 days.

April 1952 - truce talks are deadlocked over voluntary repatriation.

October 8, 1952 - truce talks are adjourned.

March 5, 1953 - death of Joseph Stalin.

April 26, 1953 - truce talks are resumed, and the Communists agree to voluntary repatriation.

July 27, 1953 - representatives for the United States, China, and North Korea signed the Military Armistice Agreement at P'anmunjŏm terminating hostilities and establishing a demilitarized zone at the 38th parallel. South Korea refused to sign.

April 5, 1964 - General Douglas MacArthur died.

April 27, 2018 - South Korean president Moon Jae-in and North Korean leader Kim Jong-un commit to enter into an official peace treaty ending the Korean War.

People, Places, and Things

Adams, Ansel (1902 - 1984) prominent American photographer and conservationist. He revolutionized landscape photography, using a clear, hard approach. His black and white images of the American west became iconic.

BAR - Browning Automatic Rifle was used by the U.S. Army as a portable light machine gun during the Korean War. A modified BAR weighed 16.5 lb and was capable of firing between 500 - 650 rounds per minute.

Beijing, China - means northern capital and in 1420 was officially denominated as the primary capital of the Ming Dynasty. It was distinguished from Nanjing which means southern capital.

Beria, Lavrentiy Pavlovich (1899 - 1953) Director of the U.S.S.R.'s atomic bomb project, chief of the Soviet NKVD secret police. He led espionage efforts of Klaus Fuchs and the Rosenbergs to steal American atom bomb secrets. Beria vetted Kim Il Sung and recommended him to Stalin.

candirú - a parasitic, freshwater catfish, native to the Amazon River Basin. According to anecdotal evidence, the tiny fish will follow a urine stream and penetrate the penis of a man urinating in the river. It has barbs that make removal painful. Also known as toothpick fish, pencil fish, or vampire fish.

Donovan, William "Wild Bill," Major General (1883 -1959) lawyer, diplomat, soldier and spy, credited with founding the Office of Strategic Services (OSS) during WWII to gather intelligence for the United States. After the war, the OSS morphed into the Central Intelligence Agency. He was the first

American soldier to receive the highest awards the country has to offer - Medal of Honor, Distinguished Service Cross, Distinguished Service Medal, and the National Security Medal.

Chekal Danjo, Major (1911 - 1950) second-in-command in Kim Il Sung's guerrilla band.

Cheung, May, Colonel (1917 - 1987) defector from North Korea whose assistance in planning the amphibious assault on Incheon was invaluable.

Dean, William, General (1899 - 1981) Medal of Honor recipient who was captured in August, 1950 by the North Koreans after the Battle of Taejon and remained a P.O.W. until the war ended.

doka - forced eradication of Korean culture by Japanese occupiers.

DC2 - aircraft produced by the Douglas Aircraft Company. Due to its capability of flying low and slow, modified versions were utilized by U.S. intelligence to extract packages, often human, using a specialized catch-and-hoist system.

gaijin - Japanese for stranger.

Gomax, Alvaro, Gunnery Sergeant (1908 - 1950) USMC drill instructor. Distinguished combat veteran who often clashed with superiors. Master of camouflage and survival tactics.

Han River - the primary waterway of the capital city of Seoul, S.K. and a strategic link between the Yellow Sea and the central western regions of South Korea.

Hayfisch, A.C., Lieutenant Commander (1923 - 2000) U.S. Navy flyboy, handle Mako.

hunhuzi - local Manchurian warlords, spies, and mercenaries.

Incheon - port located near Seoul, site of surprise amphibious assault by General MacArthur to get behind enemy supply lines and turn tables of war.

Inmun Gun - North Korean's name for the People's Army. See also, KPA.

Ishii, Shirō (1892 - 1959) Surgeon General of the Imperial Japanese Army who directed Unit 731, a biological and chemical warfare unit notorious for its forced and frequently lethal human experimentation during the Second Sino-Japanese War (1937-1945). He often used the alias Captain Togo Hijame.

juche - principle of national sovereignty, pride, and self-sufficiency, as applied means isolationism.

Khabarovsk War Crime Trials (December 25 - 31, 1949) Soviet military tribunal tried many Japanese prisoners for war crimes, including twelve members of Unit 731 for the manufacture and use of biological and chemical weapons in violation of the *Geneva Protocol for the Prohibition of the Use in War of Asphyxiating, Poisonous or other Gases, and of Bacteriological Methods of Warfare.*

Kang Kŏn, General (1918 - 1950) chief of staff of the Korean People's Army who worked with Soviet Generals to devise a battle plan acceptable to Comrade Stalin.

Kim Il Sung (1912 - 1994) anti-Japanese guerrilla who joined Soviet Red Army during WWII. He was installed by Stalin as leader of DPRK and became repressive dictator who led invasion of South Korea.

Kimpo Airport - originally constructed in 1939–1942, Kimpo was captured by UN forces during Incheon invasion.

Korean People's Army - KPA, a.k.a. the *Inmun Gun* to the Koreans.

Lee, Seung, ROK Captain (1934-1950) spy for Syngman Rhee in DPRK who befriended Junior.

Loyola, Gabriel Cardinal (1891 - 1957) an American Roman Catholic cardinal assigned to San Antonio, Texas before becoming the senior chaplain at the U.S. Military Academy at West Point during General Douglas MacArthur's tenure as Superintendent. Chaplain during Korean War.

MacArthur, Douglas, General (1880 - 1964) born into a military family, Douglas MacArthur graduated first in his class from West Point in 1903. During World War I, he was the commanding officer of the famous 42nd 'Rainbow Division' and he was the most decorated officer of WWI, receiving 7 silver stars and the Distinguished Service Medal. He and his father were the first duo to receive the Medal of Honor. During WWII, he led Allied forces in the Pacific and became Supreme Commander of Allied Powers (SCAP) overseeing the reconstruction of Japanese society in the post-war era. He was credited with legal, economic, and constitutional reforms which transformed Japan into a modern constitutional democracy.

Magiri, Sachie (1934 -   ) geisha at the Teahouse of the Auspicious Blessing, Tokyo, Japan.

Mao Anying (1922 - 1950) eldest son of Chairman Mao who died in North Korea during a bombing raid by UN. Anying had two brothers, one pre-deceased him and the other spent much of his adult life in a mental institution.

Mao Zedong (1893 - 1976) commonly known as Chairman Mao, leader of the communist revolution who defeated the nationalist forces of General Chiang Kai-shek and established the People's Republic of China in 1949. He ruled China until his death.

MiG - design initials for Mikoyan, formerly Mikoyan-Gurevich, a Russian design bureau founded in 1938 to design and build fighter aircraft. MiG 15 fighter jets were sent by Soviets to North Korea to counterbalance UN air superiority.

Mukden Incident - an abortive sabotage attempt on September 18, 1931, that Japan used as a pretext to invade Manchuria and install a satellite state under the rule of Pu Yi, the last Chinese emperor. It was called Manchukuo.

Murphy, Audie (1925 - 1971) legendary WWII hero. He was the most highly-decorated American infantryman during the war.

Nilberry, Junior (1933 - 2019) Marine combat photographer assigned to General Douglas MacArthur during the Korean War. Called the Ghost Photographer by the North Koreans for his elusive success in disrupting their operations.

Pak, Hŏn-yŏng (1900 - 1955) leader of Communist Party in South Korea who organized a network of clandestine cells which he promised would support Kim's invasion of the south.

Peng, Denhuai (1898 - 1974) senior military commander under Mao Zedong who participated in the Long March (1934–35). Assumed command of People's Volunteer Army after the collapse of the KPA following the Incheon invasion. He signed the armistice at P'anmunjŏm on July 27, 1953.

Project Ramona - code name for OSS investigation of Japan's atomic bomb program during WWII in Japan, Manchuria, and Korea.

Puller, Lewis Burwell "Chesty," General (1898 - 1971) served with distinction in WWII and Korea. Inspirational commander of the 1st Marine Regiment landing at Blue Beach, Incheon and at the Chosin Reservoir. Namesake of Marine tradition "Good night Chesty, wherever you are."

Pusan - highly strategic port city in the southeastern tip of the Korean Peninsula where North Koreans drove American and South Korean forces in their initial offensive. American forces defended the Pusan Perimeter and gained time for massive UN troop build-up to prevent North Korea from occupying the entire peninsula.

Pu Yi (1906 - 1967) the last Manchu Emperor of China who abdicated and later collaborated with the Japanese during WWII as the Emperor of Manchukuo, the Japanese puppet state established in Manchuria.

Rhee, Syngman (1875 - 1965) elected 1st president of Republic of Korea in UN-sanctioned election in 1948. Educated in the U.S., Rhee opposed ceasefire and refused to sign armistice to end hostilities.

Ridgway, Matthew, General (1895 - 1993) highly-regarded military leader who assumed command of 8th Army when General Walker died. Succeeded MacArthur as head of UN forces.

SCAP - Supreme Commander of Allied Powers.

shakuhachi - a bamboo flute-like instrument played by geishas in Japan.

soju - a clear, distilled, vodka-like drink of Korea.

Stalin, Joseph (1878 - 1953) leader of U.S.S.R. after Lenin from 1920s until his death. Manipulative, Machiavellian ruler of communism worldwide. Greenlighted invasion by North and stalled peace talks. A.k.a. Uncle Joe.

Stormy petrel - a type of seabird known for flying low over the water. One who brings trouble, or whose appearance is a sign of coming trouble. Name given by Junior to the custom aircraft flown by Mako.

Taegu - strategically located city, fifty miles northwest of Pusan, in South Korea which became the communications and transportation center for the 8th Army during the defense of the Pusan Perimeter in the early weeks of the North Korean offensive.

Taiwan – island across the Straits of Taiwan 110 miles from mainland China that became the Republic of China when Chiang Kai-shek and his nationalist forces took refuge from the Communist Chinese in 1949 at the end of the civil war. Previously known as Formosa.

Thompson submachine gun, "Tommy gun" - American-made, .45 caliber weapon capable of firing 500 rpm.

Tokyo War Crimes Tribunal (1946 - 1948) military court convened under auspices of United Nations which tried Japanese military leaders for war crimes and crimes against humanity.

Truman, Harry, President (1884 -1972) VP under FDR during WWII. Ascended to presidency when FDR died in 1945. Established the Truman Doctrine, committing to containing communism wherever it spread. Commander-in-chief during Korean War who clashed with General MacArthur until he relieved him of command in April 1951.

Unit 731 - Japan's biological weapons program which produced lethal bacteria on a mass scale to create epidemics. Led by Surgeon General Dr. Shiro Ishii. The experiments conducted by Unit 731 included the dispersal of plague-infested fleas into enemy territory, and experimentation on human subjects.

Walker, Walton, General (1889 - 1950) commander of 8th Army during the Korean War, led the defense of the Pusan Perimeter. Tragically killed in a traffic accident during the withdrawal of the 8th Army during onslaught of PVA.

Willoughby, Charles, General (1892 - 1972) chief of intelligence for General MacArthur during WWII and the Korean War.

Wolmi-do - Strategically-located island at northwest entrance to Incheon harbor. Wolmi-do means Moon Tip, named for the island's shape hooking around the Incheon basin. The island rose 350 feet above the water, giving it a commanding view of access to Incheon.

Military Jargon

ASAP - as soon as possible.

CG - commanding general.

Charlie Foxtrot - cluster fuck.

DI - drill instructor.

FUBAR - fucked up beyond all recognition.

GNATS - ground network aerial tether system.

KIA - killed in action.

LSMR - landing, ship, medium, rocket.

LST - landing ship, tank.

MIA - missing in action.

MOS - military occupational specialty.

Noncom - non-commissioned officers

Rog - abbreviation for affirmation of order, as in "That's a Rog," short for "Roger that."

Salty - experienced.

Semper Fi - motto of USMC, *semper fidelus* means always faithful.

STAT - immediately, derived from Latin word statum.

Steel pot - metal helmet worn by American soldiers.

Stovepipe - practice of bypassing chain of command, whereby a subordinate reports directly to a superior officer.

Tits-up - dead, lying on back, facing up.

XO - executive officer.

ACKNOWLEDGEMENTS

Before embarking on this project, most of what I knew about the Korean War I learned by watching the TV sitcom M.A.S.H. My interest was piqued when I befriended a veteran of that conflict who was assigned as a combat photographer to General Douglas MacArthur. He provided the inspiration for this novel. He has requested anonymity because even decades later he is tormented by demons.

Although there are numerous scholarly works about that war, General MacArthur, his battle with Truman, Mao, and to a lesser extent Kim Il Sung, the Korean War has been in large measure forgotten. With the continuing difficulties caused by the Kim dynasty and the nuclearization of the Korean Peninsula it is important to appreciate how events of the 20th century created the current situation.

In addition to researching extensively, I was privileged to speak with several veterans who provided their insights. In particular, Harold Davis, Edward Matney, and Joseph Rogers were generous with sharing their experiences. I received excellent help on military matters from John Thomas, Peter Connolly, and Lee Ewing. Of course, my Panera buddies were an invaluable source of inspiration and support. Shaun Cherewich, Dr. Lee Mendez, and Lee Ewing are my writing support group which shares weekly coffee at Panera's. The design and graphics of this work are the product of the talent of Christy Meares.

The major constant in all my efforts is the love and support of my wife Rhonda!

Made in the USA
Columbia, SC
13 January 2020